Dear Reader,

I remember well when I began *Splendid*, my debut novel. It was the summer after I'd graduated college; I'd already read everything by my favorite romance authors and was craving more. I found myself daydreaming as my subway train shuttled back and forth between Cambridge and Boston. What if an American came to London, and what if she met a duke? And what would happen if he thought she was a servant? What would happen when he discovered her true identity? Would he be angry? (Well, *yeah*, of course he would, but he'd kiss her anyway, wouldn't he?)

I stopped going to the movies and watching TV. I even stopped reading! All I could do was sit in front of my computer and bang at the keys until Emma and Alex and all of their meddling relatives came to life, and, of course, fell in love. All I had to work with was a sheer love of storytelling and a determination to one day see my words printed on the pages of a book that would actually be purchased by someone other than my mother.

Splendid is, perhaps, not as polished as what I publish today, but there is something very special interwoven in the words—a sense of joy and exuberance that I think one can only find in debut novels. I loved every minute that I spent writing this book.

I hope that *Splendid* brings you as much joy as it did me. . .

Best wishes,

Julia Q.

Books by
Julia Quinn

IT'S IN HIS KISS
WHEN HE WAS WICKED
LADY WHISTLEDOWN STRIKES BACK
(with Suzanne Enoch, Karen Hawkins and Mia Ryan)
TO SIR PHILLIP, WITH LOVE
THE FURTHER OBSERVATIONS OF LADY WHISTLEDOWN
(with Suzanne Enoch, Karen Hawkins and Mia Ryan)
ROMANCING MR. BRIDGERTON
AN OFFER FROM A GENTLEMAN
THE VISCOUNT WHO LOVED ME
THE DUKE AND I
HOW TO MARRY A MARQUIS
TO CATCH AN HEIRESS
BRIGHTER THAN THE SUN
EVERYTHING AND THE MOON
SPLENDID

Julia Quinn

SPLENDID

AVON BOOKS
An Imprint of HarperCollinsPublishers

For my mother,
who let me drag her to all those bookstores.
And for Paul, even though he insisted that
the title ought to be *Splendid in the Grass*.

AVON BOOKS
An Imprint of HarperCollins*Publishers*
10 East 53rd Street
New York, New York 10022-5299

Copyright © 1995 by Julie Cotler
ISBN: 0-380-78074-7
www.avonromance.com

First Avon Books paperback printing: May 1995

Avon Trademark Reg. U.S. Pat. Off. and in Other Countries, Marca Registrada, Hecho en U.S.A.
HarperCollins® is a trademark of HarperCollins Publishers Inc.

Printed in the U.S.A.

20 19 18

Prologue

Boston, Massachusetts
February 1816

"**Y**ou're sending me away?"

Emma Dunster's violet eyes were wide open with shock and dismay.

"Don't be so dramatic," her father replied. "Of course I'm not sending you away. You're just going to spend a year in London with your cousins."

Emma's mouth fell open. "But . . . why?"

John Dunster shifted uncomfortably in his chair. "I just think that you ought to see a little more of the world, that's all."

"But I've been to London. Twice."

"Yes, well, you're older now." He cleared his throat a few times and sat back.

"But—"

"I don't see why this is such a hardship. Henry and Caroline love you like their own, and you told me yourself that you like Belle and Ned better than any of your friends in Boston."

"But they've been visiting for two months. It's not as if I haven't seen them recently."

John crossed his arms. "You're sailing back with them tomorrow, and that's final. Go to London, Emma. Have some fun."

1

She narrowed her eyes. "Are you trying to marry me off?"

"Of course not! I just think that a change of scenery will do you good."

"I disagree. There are a thousand reasons why I simply cannot leave Boston at the present time."

"Really?"

"Yes. There is this household, for example. Who will manage it while I'm gone?"

John smiled indulgently at his daughter. "Emma, we live in a twelve-room house. It doesn't require much managing. And I'm sure that the little that is necessary can be most ably performed by Mrs. Mullins."

"What about all of my friends? I shall miss them all dreadfully. And Stephen Ramsay will be most disappointed if I leave so suddenly. I think he's on the verge of proposing."

"For God's sake, Emma! You don't care two figs for young Ramsay. You shouldn't raise the poor boy's hopes just because you don't want to go to London."

"But I thought you wanted us to marry. His father is your best friend."

John sighed. "When you were ten I might have entertained thoughts of a future match between the two of you. But it was obvious even then that you would never suit. You would drive him crazy within a week."

"Your concern for your only child is touching," Emma muttered.

"And he would bore you senseless," John finished gently. "I only wish Stephen would realize the fruitlessness of it. It's all the more reason for you to leave town. If you're an ocean away, he might finally look elsewhere for a bride."

"But I really prefer Boston."

"You adore England," John countered, his voice bordering on exasperation. "You couldn't stop talking about how much you loved it last time we went."

Emma swallowed and caught her lower lip nervously between her teeth. "What about the company?" she said softly.

John sighed and sat back. At last, the real reason why Emma didn't want to leave Boston. "Emma, Dunster Shipping will still be here when you get back."

"But there is still so much more for me to know! How am I going to take over eventually if I don't learn all I can now?"

"Emma, you and I both know that there is no one I would rather leave the company to than you. I built Dunster Shipping up from nothing, and Lord knows I want to pass it on to my own flesh and blood. But we have to face facts. Most of our clients will be reluctant to do business with a woman. And the workers aren't going to want to take orders from you. Even if your last name is Dunster."

Emma closed her eyes, knowing it was true and nearly ready to cry over the unfairness of it all.

"I know that there is no one better suited to run Dunster Shipping," her father said gently. "But that doesn't mean that anyone else will agree with me. Much as it angers me, I have to accept the fact that the company will falter with you at the helm. We'd lose all of our contracts."

"For no other reason besides my gender," she said sullenly.

"I'm afraid so."

"I'm going to run this company some day." Emma's violet eyes were clear and deadly serious.

"Good Lord, girl. You don't give up, do you?"

Emma caught her lower lip between her teeth and stood her ground.

John sighed. "Did I ever tell you about the time you had influenza?"

Emma shook her head, confused by the sudden change of subject.

"It was right after the disease took your mother. You were four, I think. Such a tiny little thing." He looked up at his only child, warmth and affection shining in his eyes. "You were very small as a child—you're still small as an adult, but when you were young—oh, you were so, so tiny I didn't think it possible that you'd have the strength to fight the illness."

Emma sat down, deeply moved by her father's choked words.

"But you pulled through," he said suddenly. "And then I realized what saved you. You were simply too stubborn to die."

Emma wasn't able to suppress a tiny smile.

"And I," her father continued, "I was too stubborn to let you." He straightened his shoulders as if banishing the sentimentality of the moment. "In fact, I may be the only person on this earth who is more stubborn than you are, daughter, so you may as well accept your fate."

Emma groaned. It was time to face it—there was no way to avoid going to England. Not that a trip abroad could be considered punishment. She adored her cousins. Belle and Ned were the sister and brother she'd never had. But still, one had to think of the serious things, and Emma didn't want to neglect her self-imposed commitment to Dunster Shipping. She glanced back over at her father. He was sitting behind his desk, arms crossed, looking implacable. Emma sighed, resigning herself to a temporary setback. "Oh, all right." She got up to leave—to pack, she supposed, since she'd be leaving the next day on one of her father's ships. "But I'll be back."

"I'm sure you will. Oh, and Emma?"

She turned around.

"Don't forget to have a little fun while you're there, all right?"

Emma flashed her father her most mischievous smile. "Really, Papa, you don't think I would deny myself a good time in London just because I didn't want to be there?"

"Of course not. How silly of me."

Emma put her hand on the doorknob and opened the door a few inches. "A girl only gets a London season once in her lifetime, I suppose. She might as well enjoy herself, even if she's not the society type."

"Oh marvelous! Then you got her to agree?" John's sister, Caroline, the Countess of Worth, exclaimed, suddenly barging into the room.

"Hasn't anyone ever told you that eavesdropping is impolite?" John asked mildly.

"Nonsense. I was walking down the hall and I heard Emma speaking. She had the door slightly open, you know." She turned to Emma. "Now that we have this settled, however, what is all this I hear about you punching a thief in the nose today?"

"Oh, that," Emma said, pinkening.

"Oh what?" John demanded.

"I saw someone trying to take Ned's wallet. He and Belle were bickering about something or other, like they always do, and he didn't notice that he was being robbed."

"So you punched him? Couldn't you have just screamed?"

"Oh, for goodness sake, Papa. What would *that* have accomplished?"

"Well, then, did you at least throw a good punch?"

Emma bit her lower lip in a sheepish gesture. "Actually, I think I broke his nose."

Caroline groaned audibly. "Emma," she said softly. "You do know that I am very much looking forward to having you in London for the season?"

"I know." Caroline was the closest thing Emma had to a mother. She was always trying to get her to spend more time in England.

"And you know that I love you dearly and would not want to change a thing about you."

"Yes," Emma said hesitatingly.

"Then I hope you won't take offense when I say that proper young ladies really don't go about punching unsavory characters in the nose in London."

"Oh, Aunt Caroline, proper young ladies really don't do that sort of thing in Boston, either."

John chuckled. "Did you by chance get Ned's wallet back?"

Emma tried to throw him a haughty look, but she couldn't stop her lips from turning up at the corners. "Of course."

John beamed. "That's my girl!"

Chapter 1

London, England
April 1816

"**Y**ou realize, of course, that there will be hell to pay if my mother catches us." Arabella Blydon looked over her costume with a skeptical eye. She and Emma had borrowed frocks from their maids—much to their maids' dismay—and were presently creeping down the back stairs of Belle's London house.

"There will be a lot more hell to pay if she catches you swearing," Emma commented wryly.

"I really don't care. If I have to supervise one more flower arrangement for *your* party, I'm going to scream."

"I hardly think a scream would be appropriate when we're meant to be *sneaking* down the stairs."

"Oh, hush," Belle muttered ungraciously, tiptoeing her way down another step.

Emma surveyed her surroundings as she followed her cousin. The back staircase was certainly a change from the one she and Belle usually used in the main hall, which curved gracefully and was cushioned with luxurious carpets from Persia. In contrast, the polished wooden steps of the back stairs were narrow, and the walls were whitewashed and unadorned. The quiet simplicity of the stairwell reminded Emma of her home in Boston, which was not decorated in the opulent London style. The Blydon mansion, located in fashionable Grosvenor Square, had been in their family for over a century and was filled with both priceless heirlooms and exceedingly bad portraits of the Blydons of yesteryear. Emma glanced back up at the plain walls and sighed softy as she fought back a pang of homesickness for her father.

"I cannot believe I'm creeping around my home like a burglar to avoid my mother," Belle grumbled as she reached the bottom of the first flight of stairs and rounded the corner to begin the second. "Frankly, I'd rather curl up in my room with a good book, but she's sure to find me there and make me go over the menu again."

"A fate worse than death," Emma murmured.

Belle looked at her sharply. "I'll have you know that I've gone over that blasted menu with her countless times. If she corners me one more time with questions about salmon mousse or roast duck à l'orange, I really don't think I can be held responsible for my actions."

"Contemplating matricide?"

Belle shot her a wry look but didn't reply as she daintily moved down the stairs. "Watch out for this step, Emma," she whispered, hugging the wall. "It creaks in the middle."

Emma swiftly followed her cousin's advice. "I take it you sneak down these stairs often?"

"I used to. It's quite handy to know how to get around this place without anyone knowing what you're up to. I just usually don't go around dressed like my maid."

"Well, it wouldn't do to wear silks if we're going to help Cook get all the food prepared for tonight."

Belle looked dubious. "Frankly, I don't think she's

going to appreciate our help. She's quite traditional and doesn't really think it's proper for the family to be belowstairs." With that, she flung open the door to the kitchen. "Hello, everyone. We're here to help!"

Everyone looked absolutely horrified.

Emma quickly tried to remedy the situation. "You could use two extra pairs of hands, couldn't you?" She turned to Cook and flashed her a wide smile.

Cook threw up her arms and shrieked, sending clouds of flour billowing through the air. "What in God's name are you two doing down here?"

One of the kitchen maids stopped kneading dough for a moment and ventured a question. "Pardon me, miladies, but why are you dressed like that?"

"I don't think the two of you ought to be in my kitchen," Cook continued, placing her hands on her formidable hips. "You'll get in the way." When neither of the two young ladies showed any inclination of leaving, Cook clenched her teeth and started waving a wooden spoon at them. "In case you hadn't noticed, we have a lot of extra work to do down here. Now off with you before I call the countess."

Belle quaked at the mention of her mother. "Please let us stay, Cook." She was fairly sure that Cook had a proper name, but everyone had called her that for so long that nobody actually remembered what it was. "We promise not to get in the way. We'll be a great help to you, I'm sure. And we'll be quiet, too."

"It just isn't right having you down here. Don't you two have anything better to do than play at being kitchen maids?"

"Not really," Belle answered truthfully.

Emma smiled to herself, silently agreeing with her cousin. She and Belle had gotten into nonstop mischief since they had arrived three weeks earlier. It wasn't that she'd *meant* to get into trouble. It was just that there seemed so little to do in London. Back home she kept busy with her work for Dunster Shipping. But in London, bookkeeping was not deemed an appropriate pastime for women, and it seemed that proper young English ladies had no other duties besides getting fitted for gowns and learning how to dance.

Emma was bored beyond belief.

Not that she was unhappy. As much as she missed her father, she rather liked being a part of a larger family. It was just that she didn't feel useful. She and Belle had started to go to great lengths to entertain themselves. Emma smiled guiltily at their exploits. It had certainly never occurred to them that the stray cat they'd taken in only two weeks earlier might be infested with fleas. There was really no way they could have guessed that the entire first floor of the Blydon mansion would have to be aired out. And Emma hadn't really intended to give the entire household such a good look at her undergarments when she'd shimmied up a tree to save that same cat.

Her relatives really ought to have thanked her. During the week they were getting rid of the fleas, the entire family quit London and had a marvelous holiday in the country, riding, fishing, and staying up all night playing cards. Emma taught her relatives how to play poker, a game she had bribed her neighbor into teaching her back in Boston.

Caroline had shaken her head and sighed that Emma was a bad influence. Before Emma's arrival Belle had only been a bluestocking. Now she was a bluestocking and a hoyden.

"Goodness," Emma had replied. "That's better than being just a hoyden, isn't it?" But she knew she could tease Caroline. Her aunt's love for her was apparent in both her endearments and her scoldings, and they usually acted much more like mother and daughter than aunt and niece. That was why Caroline was so excited about Emma's debut into London society. Even though she knew that Emma ought to return to her father in Boston, she secretly hoped Emma would fall in love with an Englishman and settle down in London. Perhaps then Emma's father, who had been raised in England and lived there until he married an American woman, might also return to London to be near his sister and daughter.

So Caroline had arranged a huge ball to introduce Emma to the *ton*. It was to be held that night, and Emma and Belle had fled belowstairs, not wanting to get trapped into taking care of all the last-minute arrangements for the party. Cook was having none of it, however, telling the young women over and over again that they would only get in her way.

"Please, can't we assist you down here? It's a ghastly scene upstairs," Emma sighed. "Nobody speaks of anything besides this party tonight."

"Well, you'll find that's all we're talking of down here, little missy," Cook replied, wagging her finger. "Your auntie is having four hundred guests tonight, and we've got to cook for the lot of them."

"Which is exactly why you need our help. What would you like us to do first?"

"What I'd like for you to do is get out of my kitchen before your mama finds you down here!" Cook exclaimed. Those two had come down to the kitchen before, but this was the first time they'd been so audacious as to actually dress up in plain clothes and offer to help. "I can't wait until the season gets started so you two scamps have something to do with yourselves."

"Well, it starts tonight," Belle stated, "with Mama's ball to introduce Emma to the *ton*. So maybe you'll get lucky, and we'll have so many suitors that we won't have time to bother you."

"God willing," Cook muttered.

"Now, Cook," Emma put in, "have mercy on us. If you don't let us help out down here, Aunt Caroline will have us arranging flowers again."

"Please," Belle cajoled. "You know how much you love ordering us about."

"Oh, all right," Cook grumbled. It was true. Belle and Emma did cheer up the kitchen staff with their crazy antics. They also lifted Cook's spirits; she just didn't want them knowing it. "I s'pose you two devils will annoy me all morning 'til I give in. Goes against my good judgment, this does. You need to be getting ready abovestairs, not dancing around my kitchen."

"But you adore our charming company, don't you, Cook?" Belle grinned.

"Charming company, my foot," Cook muttered as she hauled a sack of sugar out of the pantry. "You see those mixing bowls out on the counter? I'll want six cups of flour in each. And two cups of sugar. Now be careful with that and stay out of everyone's way."

"Where's the flour?" Emma asked, looking about.

Cook sighed and started to head back to the pantry. "Wait a minute. If you're so eager to have my job, *you* lift those big sacks."

Emma chuckled as she easily carried the sack of flour back over to where Belle was measuring out sugar.

Belle laughed, too. "Thank goodness we escaped

Mama. She'd probably want us to start getting dressed already, and the ball is more than eight hours away."

Emma nodded. In all honesty, she was quite excited about her first London ball. She was eager to put all those fitting sessions and dancing lessons to use. But Aunt Caroline was nothing if not a perfectionist, and she was issuing orders like an army general. After weeks of gowns, flowers, and music selections, neither Emma nor Belle wanted to be found anywhere near the ballroom while Belle's mother was getting everything ready. The kitchen was the last place Caroline would look for them.

Once they started their measuring, Belle turned to Emma, her blue eyes serious. "Are you nervous?"

"About tonight?"

Belle nodded.

"A little. You English can be a little daunting, you know, with all of your rules and etiquette."

Belle smiled sympathetically, pushing a lock of her wavy blond hair out of her eyes. "You'll do fine. You've got self-confidence. It has been my experience that if you act like you know what you're doing, people will believe you."

"Such a sage," Emma said affectionately. "You read too much."

"I know. It will be the death of me. I will never"—Belle rolled her eyes in mock horror—"find a husband when I've got my nose in a book."

"Did your mother say that?"

"Yes, but she means well, you know. She would never make me get married just for the sake of getting married. She let me refuse an offer from the Earl of Stockton last year, and he was considered the season's biggest catch."

"What was wrong with him?"

"He was a bit concerned by the fact that I like to read."

Emma smiled as she scooped some more flour into bowls.

"He told me that reading wasn't appropriate for the female brain," Belle continued. "He said it gave women 'ideas.'"

"Heaven forbid we have ideas."

"I know, I know. He told me not to worry, however, that he was certain he could break me of the habit once we were married."

Emma shot her a sideways glance. "You should have asked him if he thought you'd be able to break him of his pompous attitude."

"I wanted to, but I didn't."

"I would have."

"I know." Belle smiled and looked up at her cousin. "You do have a talent for speaking your mind."

"Is that a compliment?"

Belle pondered the question for a few moments before answering. "I rather think it is. Redheads aren't really in fashion just now, but I predict that you—and your outrageous mouth—will be such a success that by next month I will be informed—by Those Who Inform—that red hair is positively the latest thing and isn't that lucky for my poor cousin who has the misfortune of being American."

"Somehow I doubt that, but it's very kind of you to say so." Emma knew she wasn't as lovely as Belle, but she was satisfied with her looks, having long ago decided that if she couldn't be a beauty, at least she was unusual. Ned had once called her a chameleon, pointing out that her hair seemed to change color with each shake of her head. One glimmer of light set her locks aflame.

And her eyes, normally a clear violet, smoldered and darkened to dangerous black when she was in a temper.

Emma scooped some flour into the last bowl and wiped her hands on her apron. "Cook!" she called out. "What next? We've measured out all the flour and sugar."

"Eggs. I want three in each bowl. And no shells, you hear me? If I find any shells in my cakes, I'll keep them in the kitchen and serve up your heads instead."

"My, my, Cook is fierce this morning," Belle chuckled.

"I heard that, missy! Don't you think I didn't. I'll have none of that. Now, if you're going to be in my kitchen, get to work!"

"Where did you put the eggs, Cook?" Emma rummaged through the box where perishable food was stored. "I don't see them anywhere."

"Well, you can't be looking hard enough, then. I knew you two would have no cooking sense." Cook stomped over to the box and flung it open. Her search, however, proved as fruitless as Emma's. "Well, I'll be. We're out of eggs," Her scowl returned with a vengeance and she bellowed, "Who was the fool that forgot to get eggs from the market?"

Not surprisingly, no one raised her hand.

Cook scanned the room, her gaze finally resting on a young maid who was hunched over a pile of berries. "Mary," she called out. "Are you done washing those yet?"

Mary wiped her wet hands on her apron. "No, ma'am, I've still got pints and pints to go. I've never seen so many berries."

"Susie?"

Susie was up to her elbows in soapy water as she hurriedly washed dishes.

Emma looked around. There were at least a dozen people in the kitchen, and all of them looked terribly busy.

"Well, this is just dandy," Cook grumbled. "Four hundred to cook for, and I've got no eggs. And no spare hands to go fetch more."

"I'll go," Emma volunteered.

Both Belle and Cook looked at her with expressions that were somewhere between shock and horror.

"Are you crazy?" Cook demanded.

"Emma, it simply isn't done," Belle said at the exact same moment.

Emma rolled her eyes. "No, I'm not crazy, and why can't I go to the store? I'm perfectly able to fetch some eggs. Besides, I could use a little fresh air. I've been cooped up inside all morning."

"But someone might see you," Belle protested. "You're covered with flour, for goodness sake!"

"Belle, I haven't met anybody yet. How could I be recognized?"

"But you can't go about in your maid's frock."

"This frock is exactly why I *can* go out," Emma explained patiently. "If I wore one of my morning dresses, everyone would wonder why a gentle lady was out without an escort, not to mention on her way to the market for eggs. No one will look twice at me if I'm dressed as a maid. Although *you* certainly cannot accompany me. You'd be spotted in a second."

Belle sighed. "Mama would kill me."

"So you see . . . if Cook needs all her help in the kitchen, I am the only solution." Emma smiled. She smelled victory.

Belle wasn't convinced. "I don't know, Emma. This is highly irregular, letting you go out by yourself."

Emma let out an exasperated sigh. "Here, I'll pull my hair back tightly just like our maids do." Emma hastily rearranged her hair into a bun. "And I'll spill some more flour on my frock. And maybe smear a little on my cheek."

"That's enough, now," Cook interjected. "We don't need to be wasting any of my good flour."

"Well, Belle?" Emma asked. "What do you think?"

"I don't know. Mama wouldn't like this one bit."

Emma put her face very close to Belle's. "She isn't going to hear about it, is she?"

"Oh, all right." Belle turned to all of the kitchen maids and wagged her finger. "Not one word of this to my mama. Does everyone understand?"

"I don't like this at all," Cook said. "Not at all."

"Well, we haven't much choice, have we?" Emma put in. "Not if you want cakes at the ball. Now why don't you put Belle to work squeezing those lemons, and I promise I'll be back before you even notice I'm gone." And with that, Emma grabbed some coins out of Cook's hands and slipped out the door.

Emma took a deep breath of the crisp spring air when she reached the street. Freedom! It was so nice to escape the confines of her cousins' home every now and then. Dressed as a maid, she could walk along unnoticed. After tonight, she'd never again be able to leave the Blydon mansion unchaperoned.

Emma turned the final corner on the way to the market. She took her time as she ambled down the sidewalk, stopping to glance in every store window. Just as she'd expected, none of the ladies and gentlemen out strolling gave more than a passing glance to the small, red-haired maid covered with flour.

Emma hummed cheerfully as she entered the

bustling market and purchased several dozen eggs. They were a little awkward to carry, but she was careful not to grimace. A kitchen maid would be used to carrying such burdens, and Emma did not want to spoil her disguise. Besides, she was fairly strong, and it was only five short blocks home.

"Thank you very much, sir." She smiled at the grocer, nodding her head.

He returned her grin. "Aye, you new around here? You sound as if you hail from the Colonies."

Emma's eyes widened in surprise. She hadn't expected questions from the grocer. "Why, yes, I did grow up there, but I've been living in London now for many years," she lied.

"Aye, I've always wanted to see America," he pondered.

Emma groaned inwardly. The grocer seemed ready for a long, engaging conversation, and she really needed to get back home before Belle started worrying about her. She started backing out the door, smiling all the way.

"Now you come back sometime, little missy. Who did you say you worked for?"

But Emma had already scurried out the door, pretending that she hadn't heard his question. By the time she was halfway home, she was in high spirits, whistling happily, quite certain that she'd pulled off her charade without a hitch. She walked slowly, eager to prolong her little adventure. Besides, she enjoyed watching all the Londoners go about their daily business. In her maid's costume, no one paid her any mind, and she could stare quite shamelessly as long as she looked away whenever anybody glanced back at her.

Emma craned her neck to watch an adorable

little boy of about five or six years scamper out of an elegant carriage drawn by a pair of matched bays. He clutched a small cocker spaniel puppy, scratching it between its ears. The black and white puppy returned his affection by licking the boy across the face, and he squealed with laughter, prompting his mother to poke her head out of the carriage to check up on him. She was a beautiful woman with dark hair and green eyes that shone with obvious love for her son. "Don't you move from that spot, Charlie," she called to the boy. "I'll be with you in one moment."

The woman turned back toward the interior of the carriage, presumably to speak to someone. The little dark-haired boy rolled his eyes and shifted his weight from foot to foot as he waited for his mother. "Mama," he implored, "hurry up." Emma smiled at his obvious impatience. From what her father had told her, she'd been exactly the same way when she was small.

"Just one minute, scamp. I'll be right down."

But right then, a calico cat streaked across the street. The puppy suddenly let out a loud bark and jumped out of Charlie's arms, chasing the feline into the street.

"Wellington!" Charlie shrieked. The little boy broke into a run, following the dog.

Emma gasped in horror. A hired hack was barreling down the street, and the driver was completely engrossed in conversation with the man sitting next to him, not paying the least bit of attention to the road. Charlie would be trampled underneath the horses' hooves.

Emma screamed. She didn't stop to think as she dropped the eggs and raced into the street. When she was but a few feet away from the boy, she made a headfirst dive through the air. If she had enough momentum, she prayed, she'd knock them both out of the way before they were run over by the hack.

Charlie yelped, not understanding why a strange woman had jumped at him, slamming herself into his side.

Just before Emma hit the ground, she heard more screams.

And then there was only darkness.

Chapter 2

Emma heard voices before she opened her eyes.

"Oh, Alex!" a female voice wailed. "What if that maid hadn't been here? Charlie would have been trampled! I'm a terrible mother. I should have been watching him more closely. I should never have let him get out of the carriage before I did. We should just stay in the country where he won't get into so much trouble."

"Now, Sophie," a masculine voice said firmly. "You are *not* a terrible mother. You must, however, stop your screeching before you terrify this poor girl."

"Oh, yes, of course," Sophie agreed. But in a few moments she was sobbing again. "I cannot believe this has happened. If Charlie had been hurt, I don't know what I would do. I would just die. I would. I would just wither up and die."

The man sighed. "Sophie, please calm yourself. Do you hear me? Charlie is fine. There is barely a scratch on his body. We just have to realize that he's growing up, and we need to keep a closer eye on him."

Emma moaned softly. She knew she should let these people know that she'd regained consciousness, but in all honesty, her eyelids felt so terribly heavy, and her head was pounding uncontrollably.

21

"Is she coming around?" Sophie queried. "Oh, Alex, I shan't know how to thank her. What a brave maid. Perhaps I should hire her. Maybe the people she works for now don't treat her nicely. It would just break my heart if she's mistreated."

Alexander Edward Ridgely, the Duke of Ashbourne, sighed. His sister Sophie had always been something of a chatterbox, but she did seem to prattle on even more than usual when she was nervous or upset.

Just then Charlie spoke up. "What's the matter, Mama? Why are you crying?"

Charlie's voice only served to make Sophie cry even harder. "Oh, my baby," she wailed, clutching the boy to her chest. She took his face between her hands and started covering it with loud kisses.

"Mama! Stop that! You're getting me all wet!" Charlie attempted to wriggle out of his mother's grasp, but she grabbed him closer until he hissed, "Mama, Uncle Alex is going to think I'm a *sissy*!"

Alex chuckled. "Never that, Charlie. Didn't I promise to teach you how to play whist? You know I don't play cards with sissies."

Charlie nodded vigorously as his mother let go of him rather suddenly. "You're teaching my son how to play whist?" she demanded between her loud sniffles. "Really, Alex, he's only six years old!"

"Never too young to learn the way I see it. Right, Charlie?"

Charlie broke into a wide toothless grin.

Sophie sighed loudly, despairing of ever keeping a firm feminine hand on her brother and son. "You two are both scoundrels. Scoundrels, I say."

Alex chuckled. "We are, of course, related."

"I know, I know. More's the pity. But enough about cards. We must attend to this poor girl. Do you think she will be all right?"

Alex picked up Emma's hand and felt for the pulse on her wrist. It was strong and steady. "She'll be fine, I imagine."

"Thank goodness."

"She'll have a hell of a headache tomorrow, though."

"Alex, such language!"

"Sophie, stop trying to play the prig. It doesn't suit you."

Sophie smiled weakly. "No, I suppose it doesn't. But it does seem as if I ought to say something when you curse."

"If you feel you absolutely must say something, why don't you simply curse back?"

Amidst this banter, Emma let out a small moan. "Oh my!" Sophie exclaimed. "She's coming around."

"Who is she, anyway?" Charlie suddenly demanded. "And why did she jump on top of me?"

Sophie's mouth fell open. "I cannot believe you just said that. You, dear boy, were almost run over by a hack. If this nice lady hadn't saved you, you might've been trampled!"

Charlie's little mouth formed a large *o*. "I thought maybe she was just a little crazy."

"What?" Sophie shrieked. "You mean you didn't even see the carriage? You're going to have to learn to be more careful."

Sophie's loud voice made Emma's head pound even harder. She moaned again, wishing that these people would give her just a few minutes of silence.

"Hush, Sophie," Alex admonished. "Your shrieking is obviously bothering her. She needs a bit of quiet before her head stops hurting enough for her to open her eyes."

Emma sighed. Obviously there was at least one person in the carriage with common sense.

"I know, I know. I'm trying. I am. It's just—"

"Look, Soph," Alex interrupted. "Why don't you go to a market and get some eggs to replace the ones she dropped? There's a terrible mess over there. It looks as if nearly all of them are broken."

"You want me to get eggs?" Sophie's brows furrowed together as she contemplated such an improbable act.

"It can't be *that* difficult to purchase eggs, Sophie. I understand that people do it every day. I saw a market a few blocks back. Take my coachman with you. He'll carry them back."

"I don't know if it's proper for you to be alone in this carriage with her."

"Sophie," Alex ground out between his teeth. "She's just a kitchen maid. Nobody is going to demand that I marry her for a few minutes alone in a carriage. For God's sake, *just go and get the blasted eggs!*"

Sophie drew back. She knew better than to push her older brother's temper too far. "Oh, all right." She turned around and daintily stepped out of the carriage.

"Take the boy with you!" Alex called out. "And keep your eye on him this time!"

Sophie stuck her tongue out at him and took Charlie's hand. "Now, Charlie," she scolded. "You must always look both ways before you cross a street. Just watch me." She made a great show of craning her neck in all directions. Charlie laughed loudly and jumped up and down.

Alex smiled and turned back to the maid, who was stretched out along the cushioned seat of his coach. He couldn't believe his eyes when he saw her race across the street and knock Charlie out of the way of the hack. Bravery was not something he was accustomed to seeing in women, yet this mysterious young maid had just displayed a great deal of that quality. He was drawn to her—he had to admit that. And he wasn't sure why. She certainly wasn't his usual type. Well, he didn't really have much of a "type" when it came to women, but if he did, he was fairly sure this little red-haired thing wouldn't be it. But still, he could tell that she wasn't anything like the women with whom he usually consorted. He certainly couldn't imagine the young ladies of the *ton* his mother was constantly throwing his way risking their lives to save Charlie. And the same held true for the more mature women with whom he spent his evenings. He was intrigued by this uncommon female.

And now she was unconscious, having hit her head with a sickening thud when she and Charlie landed on the cobbles. Alex gazed down at her as he brushed a lock of soft auburn hair away from her eyes. She moaned again, and Alex decided he'd never heard such a soft, sweet sound.

Damn it all, what was wrong with him? He knew better than to get romantic over some serving girl. Alex groaned, thoroughly disgusted by the primitive emotions coursing through him. He couldn't deny that the young woman had somehow affected him deeply. His heart had started pounding wildly the moment he'd seen her lying lifeless in the street, and he hadn't calmed down until he'd assured himself that she was not seriously injured. After checking for broken bones, he'd picked her up and carried her gently back to the carriage. She was small and light, fitting perfectly against his large frame.

Sophie, of course, had wailed the entire time. Thank the Lord he'd been able to get his sister to fetch some more eggs. Her sobs were driving him crazy, but more importantly, he wanted to be alone with the maid when she woke up.

Alex kneeled on the floor beside her. "Come on, my sweet," he coaxed, gently pressing his lips against her temple. "It's time to open your eyes. I'm dying to see what color they are."

Emma moaned again as she felt a large hand gently stroke her cheek. The throbbing pain in her head began to subside, and she sighed with relief. Her eyelids slowly fluttered open, and she was momentarily blinded by the bright sunlight that streamed through the carriage windows.

"Aaaah," she groaned, squeezing her eyes shut.

"Does the light bother you?" Alex was on his feet instantly, pulling the drapes over the windows. He returned immediately to her side.

Emma let out a long breath and opened her eyes ever so slightly. Then she opened them even wider. A man was peering intently at her, his tanned face a scant few inches from her own. A thick lock of midnight black hair fell rakishly over his forehead. Emma longed to reach up and see if it felt as soft as it looked. Then he touched her cheek again. "You gave us quite a scare, you know. You've been unconscious for nearly ten minutes."

Emma stared at him blankly, unable to put together a proper sentence. It was that man, she thought; he was far too handsome and far too close.

"Can you speak, love?"

Emma's mouth fell open. "Green" was the only word that emerged.

Just my luck, Alex thought. The most beautiful kitchen maid in all of London lands in my carriage, and she's completely crazy. His eyes narrowed as he looked at her even more intently and asked, "What did you say?"

"Your eyes are green." Her voice came out strangled.

"Yes, I know. They've been that way for decades, actually. Since I was born, I imagine."

Emma squeezed her eyes shut. Good Lord, had she actually just told him that his eyes were green? What an unbelievably stupid thing to say. Of course he would know what color his eyes were. Ladies probably fell all over themselves to compliment his beautiful, captivating green eyes. It was just that he was so close, staring at her so intently, and his gaze was positively mesmerizing. Emma decided she'd blame her momentary idiocy on her pounding headache.

Alex chuckled. "Well, I suppose we should be grateful that your accident has not left you color blind. Now, do you think you can tell me your name?"

"Emm—um—" Emma coughed, covering up her stammer. "Meg. My name is Meg."

"It's nice to meet you, Meg. My name is Alexander Ridgely, but you may just call me Alex. Or, if you like, you could call me Ashbourne, as many of my friends do."

"Why?" The question tumbled out before Emma caught herself. Kitchen maids weren't supposed to ask questions.

"It's my title, actually. I'm the Duke of Ashbourne."

"Oh."

"You've an interesting accent, Meg. Do you come from the Colonies by chance?"

Emma grimaced. There was little she hated more than to hear the English refer to her country as the "Colonies."

"I come from the United States of America," she said pertly, forgetting her disguise yet again.

"We've been independent for several decades now and should not be referred to as *your* colonies."

"I stand corrected. You are absolutely right, my dear, and I must say that I'm glad to see you have gotten some of your spirit back."

"I'm sorry, your grace," she said quietly. "I shouldn't have spoken out like that to you."

"Now, Meg, don't give me that demure act. I can see that you haven't a meek bone in your body. Besides, I should think you could speak to me any way you like after you just saved my nephew's life."

Emma was flabbergasted. She'd completely forgotten about the little boy. "Is he all right?" she asked anxiously.

"He's fine. You really needn't worry about him. It's you I'm concerned about, love."

"I'm fine, really. I—I ought to be getting back now, I think." Good Lord, he was stroking her cheek again, and she absolutely could not keep a sane thought in her head when he touched her. She kept staring at his full lips, wondering what they would feel like against her own. Emma groaned, blushing at her scandalous thoughts.

Alex caught the sound immediately, and his eyes clouded with concern. "Are you sure you're not still feeling faint, love?"

"I don't think you should call me 'love.'"

"Ah, but I think I should."

"It's not at all proper."

"I'm rarely proper, Meg."

Emma barely had time to digest those words when he proceeded to show her just how improper he could be. She gasped as his lips swooped down to capture hers in a soft kiss. It lasted only a fleeting moment, but it was long enough for all the breath to rush from Emma's lungs, leaving her skin hot and tingling. She stared blankly at Alex, suddenly unsure of herself and of the strange feelings that overtook her body.

"That's just a taste of what's yet to come, love," Alex whispered passionately against her mouth. He lifted his head and peered into her eyes. He saw apprehension and confusion in her face and was immediately aghast at his forward behavior. Tearing himself away from her, he sat down on the cushioned bench on the opposite side of the carriage. His breathing was shaky and uneven. He couldn't ever remember being so strongly affected by a single kiss before. And it was such a small, short kiss. His lips had barely touched hers, brushing ever so gently against her mouth. Still, desire raged through his body, and all he wanted to do was—well, he didn't even want to *think* about what he wanted to do because that was certain to make him feel even worse.

He looked up and saw Meg staring at him with wide, innocent eyes. Hell, she'd probably faint if she could read his mind. He had no business getting involved with a girl like that. She looked barely sixteen years old. He cursed fluently under his breath. She probably even went to church on Sunday.

Emma started to sit up, rubbing her temples as a wave of dizziness washed over her. "I think I ought to be getting home," she said, setting her feet on the carriage floor as she reached for the door. Her cousins had told her that the streets of London were perilous, but nobody had warned her about the dangers that lurked inside a nobleman's carriage.

Alex grabbed her wrist before she reached the handle of the door. He gently settled her back onto the seat cushion, easing her into a sitting position.

"You're not going anywhere. You've just hit your head, and you'll probably pass out on the way. I'll take you back in a moment. Besides, my sister went to fetch you some more eggs, and we have to wait here until she returns."

"The eggs," Emma sighed, resting her forehead against her hand. "I'd forgotten. Cook will have my head."

Alex's eyes narrowed imperceptibly. Were Sophie's fears justified? Was Meg being treated badly in her employer's home? He'd not sit back and watch such a delicate girl be exposed to cruelty. He'd hire her himself before he allowed her to return to a painful existence.

Alex groaned as a fresh wave of desire pulsed through his body. Of course he couldn't hire her. She'd end up in his bed within days. Sophie was right. Meg could go work for his sister. She'd be safe there from the likes of him. Good Lord, he was stunned by his own chivalry. It had been a long time since he'd felt any concern for any woman, except, of course, for his mother and sister, both of whom he adored.

It was well known throughout London that Alex was a confirmed bachelor. He knew he'd have to marry at some point, if only to produce an heir, but he saw no reason why he'd have to make such a sacrifice anytime soon. He kept his distance from all of the ladies of the *ton*, preferring the company of courtesans and opera singers. He had little patience for most of London's social elite and trusted women not at all. Still, ladies flocked to his side at the few social events he attended, viewing his aloof manner and hard cynicism as a challenge. Alex rarely had gentle thoughts about any of these women. If a high-born lady flirted with him, he assumed that she was either exceedingly foolish or knew exactly what—or rather, whom—she wanted. He occasionally shared his bed with them, but nothing else.

He looked up. Meg was still sitting upright, staring demurely at her hands folded in her lap.

"You needn't look so afraid, Meg. I won't kiss you again."

Emma gazed up at him, her violet eyes open wide. She didn't say anything. In all truth she doubted her ability to put together a coherent sentence.

"I said you needn't be afraid, Meg," Alex repeated. "Your virtue is safe with me—at least for the next few minutes."

Emma's mouth fell open at his audacity. Then, disgruntled, she clamped her lips shut and looked away.

Alex groaned as he watched her full lips pursing together. Lord, she was gorgeous. Her hair, which had shone bright red in the sunlight, looked to be dark auburn now that he'd covered the windows. And her eyes—first he'd thought they were blue, then violet, but now they looked quite black.

Emma felt like she was about to explode, bristling at the nerve of this arrogant, overbearing man. She took deep breaths, trying to contain the temper that had already made her famous in two households, on two continents. She lost the battle.

"I really don't think that you should be speaking to me in such a scandalous fashion. It is quite unfair of you to take advantage of my weakened condition in such a lewd way, especially when one considers that the *only* reason I'm sitting here with a throbbing lump on my head—not to mention in the company of quite the rudest man I've ever had the bad fortune to meet—is because I was watching your nephew when you and your sister were too careless to look after him properly."

Emma sat back, pleased with her speech, and gave him her fiercest glare.

Alex was stunned by her tirade but careful not to show his surprise. "You've got quite a vocabulary, Meg," he said slowly. "Where did you learn to speak so well?"

"That's none of your business," Emma spat out, trying desperately to come up with a believable story.

"But I'm terribly interested. Surely you could share with me one little tidbit about your past?"

"If you must know, my mother worked as a nurse to three young children. Their parents were very kind and allowed me to share their education." There, that sounded good.

"I see. How generous of them."

Emma sighed and rolled her eyes at his sarcasm.

"Alex!" a shrill voice called out. "I'm back! And we got twelve dozen eggs. I hope that's enough."

Twelve dozen! Emma's heart sank. There was no way she'd be able to balance all those eggs. Now she'd have to let the duke take her back home in the carriage.

The door swung open and Sophie's face appeared. "Oh, you're awake!" she exclaimed, looking at Emma. "I don't know how I'll ever be able to thank you." Sophie grabbed one of Emma's hands and clutched it in her own. "If there is any way I can help you, please let me know. My name is Sophie Leawood, and I'm the Countess of Wilding, and I will be forever in your debt. Here," she said, thrusting a card in Emma's hand, "take this. It's my address, and you can call me day or night if you're ever in need of anything."

Emma could only stare at Sophie as the green-eyed woman paused for breath.

"Oh, my," Sophie continued. "Where are my manners? What is your name?"

"Her name is Meg," Alex answered smoothly. "And she hasn't seen fit to share her surname with us."

Emma fumed. He hadn't even asked for her surname.

"Never you mind, my dear," Sophie rambled. "You don't have to tell us anything if you don't want to—"

Emma looked at Alex triumphantly.

"—as long as you remember that I will be your friend for life and you can count on me for anything."

"Thank you very much, milady," Emma said quietly. "I will remember that, indeed. But I really would like to be getting back. I have been gone a long while, and Cook will be wondering about me."

"Perhaps you could tell us where you work?" Alex inquired.

Emma looked at him blankly.

"You *do* have a job somewhere? You weren't planning to eat all those eggs yourself?"

Oh, blast, she'd forgotten her masquerade again. "Um, I work for the Earl and Countess of Worth."

Alex knew the address and instructed his coachman. Sophie kept up a steady stream of chatter during the short time it took the carriage to reach the Blydon mansion.

Emma nearly ran out of the carriage.

"Wait!" Alex and Sophie called out in unison.

Sophie reached her first. "I must thank you properly. I'll have nightmares for weeks if I don't." She reached up to her ears, quickly took off her diamond and emerald earrings, and thrust them into Emma's hands. "Please take these. It's just a small token, I know, but perhaps they will help you if you're ever in need."

Emma was dumbfounded. She couldn't very well tell this woman that she was the only heir to a giant shipping business, but at the same time, she could see that Sophie desperately needed to give something to Emma to show her thanks.

"God bless you." Sophie kissed Emma on the cheek and climbed back into the coach.

Emma turned to the coachman and took the eggs from him. She smiled at Sophie and headed toward the mansion's side entrance.

"Not so fast, love." Alex suddenly appeared at her side. "I'll carry these in for you."

"No!" Emma said, a little too sharply. "I mean, I'd really rather you didn't. Nobody will mind that I'm late once I explain about Charlie, but they won't like my bringing a strange man into the kitchen."

"Nonsense," Alex said, reaching for the eggs with the supreme assurance of one who expects his orders to be obeyed.

Emma backed away from him. All hell would break loose if he escorted her into the house, and Belle—to whom he'd most likely already been introduced—started calling her by her true name. "Please," she pleaded. "Please just go away. There will be trouble if you don't."

Alex thought he saw true fear in her eyes and wondered again if she was being mistreated. Still, he didn't want her to get into any trouble on his account. "Very well." He bowed curtly. "It has been a pleasure knowing you, my dear Meg."

Emma turned and scurried into the service entrance of the mansion, feeling Alex's hot gaze on her back the whole way. When she finally burst through the door into the kitchen, she felt as if she'd been delivered from purgatory.

"Emma!" everyone cried out in unison.

"Where have you been?" Belle demanded, hands on hips. "We've been worried sick about you."

Emma sighed as she placed the bag of eggs on the counter. "Belle, couldn't we discuss this later?" She glanced pointedly at the servants, whose mouths were visibly agape as they stared at her unashamedly.

"All right, then," Belle agreed. "Let's go upstairs right now."

Emma groaned. She was suddenly exhausted, and her head was pounding once again, and she didn't know what to do about those cursed earrings, and . . .

"Oh my heavens!" Belle shrieked. Emma, her irrepressible and energetic cousin, had fainted dead away.

Chapter 3

Alex stood in front of the Blydon mansion staring at the servants' entrance. He'd seen a look of sheer panic in Meg's eyes before he'd agreed not to accompany her inside. He scowled, worried that she might be punished for returning so late from the market. Although he'd met the Earl and Countess of Worth on several occasions, when it came right down to it, he didn't know much about them. He had no idea what kind of household they ran. Some of the *ton* treated their servants abominably. And although he refused to believe he felt anything other than lust for Meg, he was terrified that she might be turned out or beaten. He had a strong urge to march right into the Blydon kitchen and make sure that Meg was being treated like the heroine she was. Alex sighed, slightly irritated at the extent of his concern. He wasn't at all sure that she'd completely recovered from her fall. All he really wanted to do at that moment was take Meg into his arms, carry her up to her room and tuck her into bed with a nice cold compress on her head. He groaned at the vision he was painting in his mind. If he managed to get her tucked into bed, he doubted that he'd be able to stop himself from climbing in beside her.

"Alex!" Sophie poked her head out of the carriage. "What are you waiting for?"

Alex tore his gaze away from the mansion. "Nothing, Soph, nothing at all. I'm just a little concerned about Meg. Do you suppose she'll be all right? What kind of people are the Earl and Countess of Worth?"

"Oh, they're lovely. I've met them several times at parties."

"So have I, brat, but that doesn't make them paragons of virtue."

Sophie sighed and rolled her eyes. "If you ever spent more than one minute at the parties that Mama and I force you to attend, you'd know that the Blydons are simply wonderful. They're very kind and not at all stuffy, Mama is extremely fond of Lady Worth. I think they have tea together at least once a fortnight. I don't think we have to worry about Meg now that we know she works here. I cannot imagine Lady Worth allowing anyone to be mistreated in her home."

"I hope you're right. We owe Meg a great deal. It's the least we can do to see to her welfare."

"Don't think I don't know it, dear brother. I intend to call on Lady Worth this week to tell her how Meg saved Charlie. I am certain that she will not allow such bravery to go unrewarded."

Alex climbed into the carriage and sat back into its plush seat as the wheels started rolling. "That's a good idea, Sophie."

"I'd go tonight, of course, but I really don't feel up to it."

"What do you mean you'd go tonight?"

"Really, Alex, you must keep track of things. Lady Worth is throwing a huge bash tonight. I'm sure you were invited. You're always invited to everything even though you never go. If you don't start—"

"Spare me the you'll-never-meet-a-nice-marriageable-female-and-produce-an-heir lecture, please. I've heard it before, and I'm not interested."

Sophie shot him an irritated glance. "Well, it's true, and you know as well as I that you cannot remain a bachelor forever. All you do is carouse with your friends, and they're just as roguish as you are."

Alex grinned rakishly. "Really, Soph, it's not as if I'm lacking for female companionship."

"Oooooh!" Sophie spluttered. "You say these things just to annoy me. I know you do. Those women are hardly worth mentioning in my presence."

"Those women, as you so delicately put it, want nothing from me other than a few baubles, which is exactly why I choose to share my bed with them. They, at least, are honest about their materialistic desires."

"There you go again! You know that I hate to hear about your torrid affairs. I swear, Alex, I'm going to box your ears."

"Cease the histrionics, Sophie. We both know that you love to hear about my so-called torrid affairs. You're just too prudish and proper to admit it."

Sophie slumped in defeat as Alex arrogantly lifted one eyebrow. He was absolutely right. She loved hearing about his adventures—amorous or otherwise. She just didn't want to give him the satisfaction of admitting it. Besides, how was she to keep up her crusade to get him married if he knew how fascinating she found his lifestyle? Still, she made one last attempt. "You know you're going to need an heir, Alex."

Alex leaned toward his sister and smiled at her wickedly. "I would imagine that I'll be physically able to sire a son ten or even fifteen years from now. But if you'd like, I'd be happy to give you the name and address of my most recent mistress. I'm sure she can vouch for my virility."

"Mama, what's virility?" Charlie piped up.

"Nothing you need to worry about for many years," Sophie said breezily. And then in hushed tones: "Alex, I swear you've got to watch what you say around him. He absolutely idolizes you. As it is, he's probably going to be telling all our maids about his virility for the next month."

Alex laughed. "All right, brat, I'll watch my speech, if only to protect your maids from falling prey to his lustful desires. Now, will you just be a good girl and tell me about this ball tonight?"

Sophie arched her eyebrows. "Suddenly interested in the social scene, are we?"

"I just want to check up on Meg. I'll go for my usual fifteen minutes and then leave."

"Lady Worth wants to introduce her American niece to society," Sophie explained. "I hear it's to be a grand affair."

"Then why aren't you going?"

"I just don't feel like going out with Oliver away, and," she smiled shyly and patted her stomach, "I'm expecting again."

"Never say it, brat! That's wonderful!" Alex smiled broadly and swept his sister into an affectionate hug. As dead-set as Alex was against marriage and children for himself, he did love spending time with Charlie and was thrilled at the prospect of another nephew or niece. "Ah, here we are," he said as the carriage came to a stop in front of Sophie's home. "Take care now, sister. Don't overexert yourself." He kissed Sophie on the cheek and patted her hand.

Sophie took Alex's hand as he helped her out of the carriage. "Really, Alex, I'm not even showing yet. I hardly think I need to take to my bed."

"Of course, dear, but you should be careful. Riding in the park is definitely out of the question."

Sophie smiled at her brother's concern. "For all your rakish ways, Alex, you really are an exemplary uncle. Just look at how Charlie adores you."

Alex glanced down at the boy. Sure enough, he was tugging on his coat, begging him to come inside and play. Alex tousled his hair. "Another time, scamp. I promise."

"You know, Alex," Sophie began, "I just know you'd make an excellent husband and father, too, if you'd just take the time to look for the right woman."

Alex crossed his arms. "Don't start with me now. I've had enough lecturing for one day. Besides I've got this damned ball to get ready for." With a wave, he climbed back into the carriage, instructing his driver to take him back to his bachelor's residence.

Sophie waved back, standing on her doorstep, holding Charlie's hand. At least he was going to the party tonight. That was a start. With luck, he'd meet someone suitable.

When Emma opened her eyes again, she was lying atop her bed. The pain in her head had diminished appreciably, but a new ache in her hip more than made up for the loss. Belle was curled up with a leather-bound book in a nearby chair.

"Oh, hello," Belle chirped as soon as she noticed that Emma was awake. "You gave us quite a fright." She got up, crossed the short distance to her cousin, and perched on the end of the bed.

Emma scooted up into a reclining position so that she could see Belle a little better. "What happened?"

"You fainted."

"Again?"

"Again!"

"Well, I didn't exactly faint the first time. It was more like a blow to the head."

"What!?"

"Well, not really a blow to the head," Emma hastily amended. "I fell, and then I hit my head."

"Oh my," Belle breathed. "Are you all right?"

"I think so," Emma replied, gingerly rubbing the fast-growing lump above her right ear. "How did I get up here? The last I remember, I was in the kitchen."

"I carried you."

"*You* carried me up four flights of stairs?"

"Well, Cook helped."

"Oh, God." Emma grimaced at the thought of Cook having to lug her up four flights of stairs. "How embarrassing."

"And Mary and Susie," Belle added.

Utterly mortified, Emma sank back into the bed as if trying to disappear among the voluminous quilts.

"Actually, it wasn't very difficult at all," Belle continued, oblivious to Emma's distress. "First we wrapped you in a blanket. Then I grabbed your shoulders, Cook took your feet, and Mary and Susie spaced themselves out between us."

"And I didn't wake up?"

"You did make a few odd noises when we rounded the corner on the second landing, but no, you were most definitely unconscious."

"Odd noises?"

Belle's expression turned sheepish. "Well, actually it might have had something to do with the fact that you crashed into the endpost when we turned the corner."

Emma's eyes opened wide, and her gaze flew

down to the sore spot on her right hip that she'd been rubbing absently.

Belle smiled wanly. "It could very well have been your hip that hit the endpost. I seem to recall we clipped you somewhere in the middle."

Suddenly a dreadful thought entered Emma's mind. "What about your mother?"

"None of us exactly told her what happened," Belle hedged.

"But she must have heard the commotion."

"Yes, well, she did seek me out once we got you up here."

"And?" Emma prodded.

"I told her you swooned."

"Swooned?" Emma's eyes widened in disbelief.

Belle nodded. "From the excitement of your first big ball and all that."

"But that's ridiculous! I never swoon!"

"I know."

"Aunt Caroline knows I never swoon!"

"I know. You're not exactly the swooning type."

"She didn't actually believe you, did she?"

"Not for one second," Belle quipped, tapping her slender fingers on her book. "But Mother can be marvelously tactful sometimes, and so she left it at that. As long as you appear at the ball tonight in good health and spirits, she won't say a word. I'm sure of it."

Emma pulled herself up into a sitting position so that she could examine all her new aches and pains. "What a ridiculous day," she sighed.

"Hmmm?" Belle looked up from her book, which she had started to read again. "Did you say something?"

"Nothing interesting."

"Oh." Belle glanced back at her book.

"What on earth are you reading?"

"*All's Well that Ends Well*. Shakespeare."

Emma felt compelled to defend her education. "I know who wrote it."

"Hmm? Yes, of course you do." Belle smiled absently. "I brought it in to read while waiting for you to wake up."

"Good grief. How long did you think I was going to be unconscious?"

"I had no idea, actually. *I've* never swooned before."

"I didn't swoon," Emma ground out between clenched teeth.

"So you say."

Emma sighed as she looked up at her cousin's mock-innocent expression. "I suppose you want me to tell you what happened."

"Only if you want to." Belle reopened the leather-bound volume and began to read again. "I have all the time in the world, you know," she added, looking back up at Emma. "I've decided to read the complete works of Shakespeare. I'm doing the plays first, then poetry."

"Are you serious?"

"Absolutely. I'm going to do it in alphabetical order."

"Do you realize how long that is going to take?"

"Of course. But I figure that with the way you're going, I'll be spending plenty of time at your bedside."

Emma narrowed her eyes. "What do you mean by that?"

"Who knows how soon you'll be unconscious again?"

"I can assure you I have no such plans for the immediate future."

Belle smiled sweetly. "I imagine you don't. But

if you don't tell me what happened this afternoon, I might just knock you out myself."

Many hours later, Emma sat at her dressing table wincing while Meg, her maid, fussed with her hair. Belle sat beside her, undergoing similar torture.

"I don't think you're telling me everything," Belle admonished.

"I told you," Emma sighed. "I fell down after I knocked the little boy out of the path of the hack. Then I hit my head."

"What about those earrings?"

"The boy's mother gave them to me. She thought I was a maid. I'm planning to call on her tomorrow to give them back. How many times do you need to hear this?"

"I don't know." Belle narrowed her eyes suspiciously. "I still think you're leaving something out."

"I saved the boy. I got the earrings. Period." Emma gave Belle a sharp nod for emphasis.

"Emma, you were gone for an hour! Something must have happened between the boy and the earrings!"

"I was unconscious, that's what happened! What do you think, I was ravished by some mysterious man?" Emma groaned inwardly as she realized how close to the truth that speculation actually was. She felt a little guilty for not telling Belle about her strange experience with the Duke of Ashbourne. They usually told each other everything. But Emma felt strangely possessive of her time with the duke, and she didn't feel like sharing her memory with anyone, not even Belle.

"Well, I think it's absolutely famous that it was the Countess of Wilding who gave you those earrings," Belle chuckled, amusement dancing in her bright blue eyes. "I know Sophie fairly well. She isn't very much older than we are. Mama and her mother are good friends. They'll all just scream when they hear what happened. Although perhaps we shouldn't say anything. I don't think Mama would look favorably upon your going out alone dressed as a maid. Still, the situation is most amusing. I can't believe Sophie gave you jewels to secure your future. Why, with your fortune, you could buy and sell us all."

"Hardly," Emma said dryly, pointedly glancing at the string of pearls draped around Belle's throat. "Besides, she did think I was a maid."

"I know, I know. Still, it's just too funny. I do wish that Sophie were coming tonight. I'd love to see her face when she walked into the ballroom and saw the 'scullery maid' decked out in all her finery."

"Really, Belle, that's positively cruel of you. The countess was very distraught this afternoon. She nearly lost her son."

"*You're* calling *me* cruel? You, the queen of all practical jokesters? The same girl who sent poor Ned a fake love note from Clarissa Trent?"

Emma tried to suppress a mischievous grin. "Really, it needn't have been such a big fuss."

"You're absolutely correct," Belle stated with noticeable sarcasm. "And it wouldn't have been, not if Ned hadn't been hopelessly infatuated with the chit."

Emma looked away innocently. "Well, how was I to know that? I haven't made my debut yet, you know. I'm not privy to the latest gossip."

"He only mentioned her name a hundred times a day."

Emma "humphed" and gave her cousin a supercilious look. "Really, it all worked out for the best. Now we all know what a conniving little you-know-what Clarissa is. When it comes right down to it, I saved your brother from a terrible fate."

"I suppose," Belle conceded, "but Ned was so heartbroken when he professed his love for her, and she flatly stated she was holding out for a duke with lots of money."

"I think he was more upset that she wasn't the paragon he'd imagined her to be than he was because she didn't return his feelings. But enough of that. I've learned my lesson—no more interference in Ned's romantic life. Even if I *am* doing the right thing. So tell me, why isn't Sophie coming tonight?"

"I'm not sure. Probably because her husband is away on business in the West Indies for a few months. I think she misses him. It was a love match, you know." Belle sighed romantically.

"It's probably for the best—even if you do have to miss seeing her shocked face. She'd get the surprise of her life if she saw me tonight. I'm sure it will be easier for everyone if I simply call on her tomorrow morning."

"You're probably right. Do say I can go with you, though. I so want to be there when she sees you."

"Fine, fine, of course you can—Ouch!" Emma hollered as Meg tugged on her hair a little too vigorously.

"Quit your complaining, Miss Emma," Meg scolded. "It takes hard work and a little bit of pain to be beautiful."

"Goodness! If it's going to require that much pain, I really don't need to be beautiful. Just leave my hair down. It's much more comfortable that way."

Meg looked agonized. "I couldn't do that. It's not at all fashionable."

"Oh, all right, do whatever you like with it, Meg.

Just try to keep the discomfort at a minimum."

Belle laughed. "Oh, Emma, I don't know how you're going to make it through an entire season."

"I don't know, either. I can never seem to remember how to be correct."

"Stop shaking your head!" Meg yelled. "Else we'll be here all night, and you'll miss the ball."

"With the way my head hurts, that wouldn't be such a bad thing," Emma muttered.

"Did you say something?" Belle asked absently.

"It was nothing." Emma didn't want Belle to know how large the lump on her head really was. Belle was sure to tell her mother, and Emma knew that her aunt would be worried sick. The evening would be ruined unless she ignored the pain and smiled her way through the party. "Why don't you tell me more about Sophie?" Emma said, just to make conversation.

"Sophie? She's a lovely person. Talks a lot, though."

Emma giggled. "I noticed."

"She and her husband are terribly devoted to one another. I know she just misses him dreadfully."

"Does she have any family?"

Belle arched her brows at Emma's interest.

"I just want to know how many people are going to know about my little escapade," Emma said hastily.

"One mother. One brother."

"Really?" Emma tried to sound casual, but her voice came out breathy and excited.

"Yes, I think he must be about nine-and-twenty now. He's absolutely beautiful, with thick black hair and the greenest eyes you'll ever see."

Emma felt pangs of jealousy but quickly suppressed them. The man was an arrogant, overbearing boor, and she was sure she wasn't interested in him in the least. It didn't mater if his kiss had been the most exciting thing that had happened since she'd arrived in London. "You sound quite interested in him, Belle," she said cautiously.

"The Duke of Ashbourne? You must be joking. He's a handsome rascal, but he is positively dangerous. He never consorts with ladies, only women, if you know what I mean. Actually, I barely know him at all, but"—Belle leaned forward conspiratorially—"I've heard that he's left broken hearts all over England. *And* the Continent."

"He sounds quite interesting."

"Interesting, yes. Suitable, not at all. Mama and Papa would have a fit if I set my cap after him. He's a confirmed bachelor. He won't marry for years. I'd bet my pearls on it. And when he does, it will be to some stupid little chit who can be easily managed and then ignored once she produces an heir."

"Oh." Emma wondered why she suddenly felt so depressed.

"He won't even come tonight. I'm sure of it. He's invited, of course. He gets invited to everything, but he never attends unless his family absolutely forces him to. He's probably got scores of fancy mistresses tucked away all over London. Besides, I'm sure you won't want to meet him. He wears a perpetual frown on his face and would probably bite your head off if you said two words to him."

"Goodness, he's beginning to sound most unpleasant."

"Oh, I wouldn't call him exactly 'unpleasant.' Ned has only praise for him. They belong to the same club, you know. He says that all of his friends look up to him. More likely they want to *be* him." Belle shrugged. "He's sinfully rich, you know, and even more sinfully handsome. I think it's just that he so hates the social whirl—hasn't got the patience to pretend otherwise, so he just scowls at anyone who doesn't interest him. Most of my friends are terrified of him—when they're not plotting out how to get him to the marriage altar."

"He must be quite remarkable to wield such power," Emma commented.

"Oh, yes, it's really quite disgusting how he always gets his way. It seems that everyone panders to him."

"Why?"

"Well, there's his title for one thing; he is a duke, you know. And as I mentioned, he is exceedingly wealthy. But if you saw him for yourself, you'd know what I meant. He positively exudes power. He's quite a specimen."

"Belle!" Emma laughed. "Your mama would swoon if she heard you talk this way."

"Mama swoons about as often as you do."

"Then she's due for a good fainting spell any minute now," Emma joked. But inside, she breathed a sigh of relief at Belle's assurance that Alex wouldn't attend her ball. Her head still ached, and she felt utterly exhausted. There was no way that *she'd* pander to the arrogant duke, but with her injury, she just wasn't up for another round with him.

Chapter 4

"**A**shbourne! This is a surprise. I can't believe I'm seeing your ugly face here."

William Dunford, one of Alex's closest chums since his Oxford days, strode across the Blydon ballroom and slapped the duke affectionately on the back. "What are you doing here? I thought you'd categorically sworn off all such gatherings."

"Believe me, I have no intention of remaining at this little *soirée* for more than another ten minutes." Alex kept his tone light, but underneath his temper was starting to flare. The moment he'd entered the ballroom, a hush had fallen over the crowd. Everyone had been utterly shocked to see the Duke of Ashbourne walk through the door in his elegant evening attire. Nervous mamas forced their daughters to swear they'd steer a wide path around the notorious rake (all the while secretly hoping he'd single their charges out for attention), while everyone who wasn't in some way connected with a marriageable female immediately made his way to Alex, preening at the rich, titled gentleman.

Alex sighed. He had no patience for the insipid chatter of the *ton*. All he really wanted was to find Meg, assure himself of her welfare, and leave. His latest mistress was tucked away in a cozy townhouse, and Alex was looking forward to a long, lazy night with her. An evening with Charisse

50

would surely rid him of this strange obsession with the Blydon's kitchen maid.

Alex almost went weak with relief when he saw Dunford striding across the ballroom toward him. At last, some decent conversation.

Dunford was not quite the rake that Alex was, but he came damn close. Most of the *ton*, however, were more than willing to forgive him his tarnished reputation because he was insufferably charming. Alex had never quite learned to follow his friend's example. His cronies praised him as an eminently affable fellow but had to allow that the Duke of Ashbourne bore little tolerance for most of society. He rarely hid his boredom when he was forced into conversation with anyone he found dull, and he gave the most icy stares to those who caused him displeasure. Rumor had it that more than one young lady had been sent scurrying in terror across a room at one of his scowls.

"Do tell, Ashbourne," Dunford laughed. "Why are you here?"

"Why, indeed," Alex muttered. "I'm beginning to wonder the same thing." He'd arrived at the ball a full hour earlier, and during that time he'd scoured the mansion, surprising many a footman and serving maid and interrupting no less than three clandestine couples. Not a single sign of Meg. In desperation, he'd actually entered the ballroom, figuring that there might be a chance that Meg was tending to the refreshments. But he'd had no luck. The serving girl was nowhere to be found. And although he found the prospect of defeat bitter indeed, he was just about to give up his search. Alex sighed and turned to face his friend, happily turning his back on the ogling crowds.

"Fess up, chap," Dunford prodded.

Alex sighed. "It's a long story. I doubt you'd be interested."

"Nonsense. It's the long stories which are usually the most interesting. Besides, if this 'story' has actually brought you into the ranks of polite society, it must involve a female. And that means, of course, that I'm terribly interested."

Alex turned to his friend and briefly recounted the story of how his nephew had been saved by a brave kitchen maid, omitting the part about the strong attraction he felt for her. "So you see," he concluded, "you needn't get so excited. My tale lacks both romance and lust. I'm afraid that you're going to have to accept that my behavior tonight is completely above reproach."

"How dull."

Alex nodded wearily. "Indeed, and I can't stand this crush. I think I'll suffocate if one more blasted dandy comes up to ask me how I've arranged my cravat."

"You know," Dunford began thoughtfully, "I was just thinking that I might take my leave now as well. Why don't we retire to White's and have a few drinks? A good game of cards might be just the thing after your tiring sixty minutes of the social whirl."

Alex smiled caustically at his friend's sarcasm but agreed immediately to the proposal. "Good idea. I can't wait to get—" He stopped short when he heard the sharply indrawn breath of his friend. "What's wrong?" he asked.

"Good Lord," Dunford breathed. "That coloring . . ."

"For Christ's sake, Dunford, who is it now?"

Dunford paid no mind to his words. "It must be Emma Dunster. How could something so lovely have come from those godforsaken Colonies?"

"They're not our colonies any longer, Dunford,"

Alex muttered, remembering Meg's tirade. "They've been free for several decades and should really be referred to as the United States of America. It's only polite."

Alex's strange speech broke Dunford out of his reverie. He turned to his friend with an odd look on his face. "Since when have you become so sympathetic to our errant Colonies?"

"Since—oh, never mind. Who is this blasted woman who's got you so paralyzed with desire?" Alex still hadn't turned to face the ballroom.

"Look for yourself, Ashbourne. Not a classic beauty, I'll admit, but she doesn't look cold, if you know what I mean. Auburn hair with specks of fire, soft violet eyes . . ."

A singularly unpleasant feeling began to grow in the pit of Alex's stomach when he heard Dunford's description of Miss Emma Dunster. It couldn't be . . . No, he assured himself, a gentle lady wouldn't . . . Alex slowly turned around. There, across the ballroom, stood his brave Meg. Except she was no longer Meg, he corrected himself. She was Emma.

Alex reacted instantly. Every muscle immediately tensed to the point of near-pain, and he couldn't decide whether he was furious over her deception or merely overcome with desire. He watched silently as Emma, unaware of his presence, smiled wearily at one of her suitors and rubbed her head absently. Damn, but what was she thinking, dancing the night away when she probably had a serious head injury? Alex scowled, thinking that he'd like to march across the dance floor, grab her by the shoulders, and shake a little sense into her.

But Lord, she really was lovely. Her petite body was wrapped in a gown of violet satin that bared her creamy shoulders and showed just the slightest swell of her breasts. Young women out for their first season were supposed to wear pale pastels, but Alex was glad that Emma had defied convention and chosen a more daring color. It matched her spirit, and, in a sea of washed-out insipid misses, she was a beacon of fire and vitality. She had left her hair unfashionably loose, having secured the front strands up atop her head with a clasp but letting the bulk of it flow down her back like a sheet of fire.

Her coloring spoke of a wild nature, and Alex well remembered her quick temper. But he could also see vulnerability in her eyes, and she was so achingly small. She looked tired, and Alex was positive that her head was still bothering her. Something about her made him fiercely protective, and he was enraged that she might be endangering her health with too much activity.

Dunford chuckled as he watched myriad emotions pass across Alex's face. "I can see that you agree with my assessment."

Alex broke his gaze away from Emma and turned to face his friend. "Don't touch her," he said slowly. "Don't even think about her." He scowled as he noticed that he was not the only man in the room who'd succumbed to her appeal. The young bucks were practically lined up to gain an introduction to the American girl. He made a mental note to have a word with a few of the more eager ones.

Dunford drew back in surprise. "A little possessive when you haven't even met the chit, don't you think?"

"Oh, I've met the chit," Alex growled. "I just didn't know it."

Dunford's brow furrowed in thought until realization dawned. "I gather you don't want to head to White's just yet?"

Alex smiled rakishly. "This party has suddenly grown quite interesting." With that, he scooted along the perimeter of the ballroom, assiduously avoiding Emma's eye. He finally settled into an alcove directly behind her back. A heavy crimson drape shielded him from the view of the partygoers, but he could still hear every detail of Emma's conversations. Leaning back against the wall, he could just barely see her through a crack between the drape and the wall.

"What the devil are you doing?" Dunford demanded just as soon as he appeared at Alex's side.

"Will you keep your voice down? And get back! Someone might see you." Alex yanked his friend back until they were both hidden behind the drape.

"You've lost your mind," Dunford muttered. "I never thought I'd see the day when the lofty Duke of Ashbourne hid behind curtains to spy on a woman."

"Shut up."

Dunford snickered.

Alex glared at him before turning his attention back to more important matters. "I've got her just where I want her," he said gleefully, rubbing his hands together.

"Really?" Dunford asked sardonically. "I rather thought you wanted her in your bed."

Alex glared at him again.

"And," Dunford continued, "it doesn't seem to me that you're even remotely close to achieving that goal."

Alex raised his eyebrows with supreme self-assurance. "Mark my words, I'll be a hell of a lot closer by the end of the night." He put his eye back to the crack of light, smiled triumphantly and, rather like a lion stalking its prey, trained his gaze on the flame-haired woman not five feet away from him.

Emma kept a polite smile pasted to her face as she went though another round of introductions. Her aunt had already declared the ball—and Emma—a glittering success. Aunt Caroline couldn't believe the number of young men who had begged her and her husband for an introduction to their niece. And Emma had behaved beautifully. She was witty and bright and, thankfully, hadn't done anything *too* outrageous. Caroline knew that her niece found it a trial to be continuously correct.

In actuality, Emma wasn't finding her correct behavior overly burdensome. She was simply too tired to live up to her mischievous reputation even if she had wanted to. It was all she could do to keep up amusing banter with the many people she had met that evening. Even with a pounding headache, Emma refused to give London the misconception that she was a shy, retiring miss. It was her opinion that the *ton* already had far too many of those.

"Emma, dear," her aunt called. "I want you to meet Lord and Lady Humphries."

Emma smiled as she held out her hand to the plump pair. Lord Humphries, who looked to be about thirty-five years older than Emma, bowed courteously and kissed her knuckles. "I'm very pleased to meet both of you," Emma said politely, her American accent apparent.

"Then it's true!" Lord Humphries said triumphantly. "You *are* from the Colonies! Good old Percy over there wagered you were from France. 'With a last name like Dunster?' I said. 'No, she's from good English stock, even if she did defect to the Colonies.' And I was right. I'm going to have to go and collect my wager."

Before Emma could say anything more, he'd waddled away in search of his crony. Emma was somewhat surprised at the amount of attention

being paid to her and more than a little flustered
that people were actually making wagers about her
origins. Ned had told her that the *ton* often made
wagers to amuse themselves, but this was ridiculous. Didn't they have anything more interesting to
do with their time? She turned to Lady Humphries,
who'd been stranded by her husband, and smiled
weakly. "How do you do, Lady Humphries?"

"Very well, thank you," she replied. Lady Humphries had a friendly manner but seemed slightly
daft. "Do tell me," she said, leaning forward conspiratorially. "Is it true that wild bears roam free in
Boston? I understand that the Colonies are overrun
with savages and wild beasts."

Emma could see her aunt roll her eyes and groan
in expectation of another of her niece's lectures
about the many wonderful qualities of the United
States. But Emma just leaned forward, took both of
the older lady's hands in her own, and said—just
as conspiratorially as Lady Humphries—"Actually,
Boston is quite civilized. You'd feel quite at home
there."

"No!" Lady Humphries said, shocked.

"No, really. We even have dressmakers there."

"Really?" Lady Humphries's eyes were wide with
interest.

"Yes, and milliners, too." Emma nodded slowly,
her eyes wide. "Of course they often get destroyed
when the wolves come through town."

"Wolves! You don't say!"

"Yes, and they're so terribly vicious. Why, I lock
myself in my home each year for weeks in fear of
them."

Lady Humphries fanned herself vigorously. "Oh
my. Oh my, I have to go tell all this to Margaret. If
you'll excuse me." Eyes wide with a mix of horror

and delight, she darted away from Emma and disappeared into the crowd.

Emma turned to her aunt and cousin, both of whom were shaking with mirth. "Oh, Emma," Belle laughed, wiping tears out of the corners of her eyes. "You shouldn't have done that."

Emma rolled her eyes and gave a harumph. "Well," she declared. "You've got to let me have a little bit of fun tonight."

"Of course, darling," Caroline replied, shaking her head. "But did you have to have your fun with Lady Humphries? Your little tale will be all over the ballroom in less than ten minutes."

"Oh, pooh. Nobody with any sense will believe it. And frankly, I'm not interested in impressing anybody who hasn't got sense," Emma raised her eyebrows and turned to her relatives, silently daring them to reply.

"She's got a valid point," Belle conceded.

"I must admit, I have always found Lady Humphries rather ridiculous myself," Caroline remarked.

"I don't plan on being impolite," Emma explained. "It's just that I think I'll perish of boredom if I have to engage in conversation with any more of these complete ninnyheads."

"We'll do our best to protect you," Caroline replied, a smile tugging at her lips.

"I knew you would," Emma replied, smiling gaily.

After that moment, one of Ned's friends appeared at Emma's side to claim a dance. Alex scowled at the young man from behind the drape as he watched the pair float across the ballroom floor.

"A little jealous, are we?" Dunford inquired.

" 'We' are not the least bit jealous," Alex replied imperiously. " 'We' have no reason to be jealous.

For God's sake, he's a mere boy," he said, referring to Emma's dance partner.

"You're right, of course. That would make him about three years older than Miss Dunster."

Alex ignored his comment. "Did you hear the way she got rid of Lady Humphries?" he asked admiringly. "She was absolutely right. Even my mother thinks Lady Humphries is a ridiculous old windbag."

Dunford nodded slowly, deep in thought. He hadn't seen his friend act this way about a woman since their university days, before he'd developed a deep suspicion of the fairer sex.

"And her comment about not wanting to meet anyone without any sense," Alex continued. "You must admit that she has spirit. And sense, too."

"And she's coming back this way," Dunford pointed out.

Alex immediately resumed his watch. Emma had finished her dance and was returning to her aunt's side.

"Did you have a nice time, dear?" Caroline asked.

"Oh, yes. John is a lovely dancer," Emma replied. "And he's quite friendly, too. He said he'd teach me how to fence. I've always wanted to learn."

Alex felt a knot of jealousy churn in his stomach.

"I don't know if fencing would be quite the thing, but I'm glad you like him," Caroline remarked. "He'd be quite a catch, you know. His father is an earl of considerable wealth."

The knot grew to about the size of a cannonball.

"I'm sure he is, but I'm really not interested in marriage right now."

Alex breathed a heavy sigh of relief. His interests did not lie in that particular direction, either.

Emma patted Caroline on the arm. "Don't worry, dear aunt, when the time comes, I'm sure I'll find the perfect husband. But he'll have to be an American because I don't plan to give up Dunster Shipping."

"There aren't too many Americans from which to choose here in London," Caroline pointed out.

"Then I'll just have to amuse myself with the company of witty young men like John."

Alex's temper began to flare again, and Dunford wondered if he'd have to restrain his friend from jumping out from behind the curtain, claiming his desire, and making a general spectacle of himself.

Just then Belle returned to chat with Emma and Caroline. Her cheeks were flushed pink from her whirl across the dance floor. "Emma," she said breathily. "You must come with me and meet more of Ned's friends. I know you'll love them. And they're all just dying to meet you," she added with a wink.

"Do you think they could wait a few minutes? I have a bit of a headache," Emma said lightly. In actuality, she felt as if someone had taken a club to her temple. Her dizzying dance with John Millwood had only increased her discomfort.

Emma looked meaningfully at Belle, who had promised not to tell her mother of the afternoon's mishap, and then turned to her aunt. "Aunt Caroline, would it be terribly impolite if I retired to my room for ten or fifteen minutes? My head is pounding from all this excitement, and I know that a few moments of quiet is all I need to ease it."

"Of course, dear. I'll just tell anyone who asks that you've just gone to the washroom to freshen up."

"Thank you," Emma sighed. "I won't be long.

I promise." She scooted out of the ballroom and up a flight of stairs to the private quarters of the mansion.

Alex's eyebrows rose when he overheard Emma's request and a delicious grin spread across his face.

"Oh, no," Dunford admonished, correctly interpreting his friend's expression. "Even you can't get away with that, Ashbourne. It's simply not done. You cannot follow a gentle lady back to her bedroom. You don't even know her."

"Oh, but I do."

Dunford tried another tactic. "If you get caught, you'll ruin her reputation on her first night out. You'll have to marry the chit. There'd be no way around it. It would be the honorable thing."

"No one will see me," Alex stated in a matter-of-fact tone. "If anyone asks for me, tell them I've gone to the washroom. To freshen up." With that, he emerged from his hiding place and followed Emma out of the ballroom, his footsteps carefully silent.

The hallway had been left unlit to discourage the tipsy and amorous from extending the party to all corners of the house, but Emma easily found her room. She lit a solitary candle, preferring the semidarkness for her headache. With an unapologetically loud yawn, she kicked off her shoes and settled down amidst the soft white quilts of her bed. Sighing deeply, she rubbed her temples and decided that she had, indeed, enjoyed herself at her first London party. It was true that she'd met a fair number of stuffy and pompous aristocrats, but she'd also been introduced to many intelligent and interesting men and women. If only she hadn't had this blasted lump on her skull. She knew that she would be having a better time if she were feeling more the thing. She was just so incredibly tired.

Emma let her eyelids flutter shut, groaning softly
as she wondered how on earth she was ever going
to rouse herself to return to the party.

Alex moved swiftly and silently into the room,
mentally blessing the well-oiled hinges of Emma's
door. He paused for a moment, regarding Emma
with a tender gaze. In repose, she was soft and
sweet, without a hint of her sharp tongue and rapi-
er wit. A delicate smile touched her face as she
nestled deeper into her quilts, and Alex thought
that there was nothing in this world he wanted to
do more than to take her into his arms and lull her
to sleep. He stopped and frowned, puzzling at his
chaste thoughts. Frankly, he could not remember
the last time he'd had any tender feelings for a
woman.

Suddenly, Emma stretched out her body with a
feline purr. Alex felt lust take over his mind and
body as her breasts strained against the top of her
bodice.

Emma, eyes still closed, sighed in contentment.

Alex stepped back to the door.

Emma curled back into a ball, thinking that soli-
tude was indeed a wonderful state.

Alex shut the door with a resounding click.

Emma's eyes flew open with horror, and she
gasped at the sight of the black-haired, green-eyed
man whose powerful frame seemed to fill her entire
room.

"Hello, Meg."

Chapter 5

For one blessed second, Emma thought she was hallucinating. There was simply no way this green-eyed devil could have come to be standing in her bedroom. And she *had* bumped her head rather soundly that afternoon. She'd heard that such accidents did strange things to one's mind. Then the Duke of Ashbourne bestowed upon her a devilish smile and seated himself in her easy chair.

That was when Emma knew he must be real. No hallucination of hers would behave so abominably. Her breath caught in her throat and she suddenly felt very sick to her stomach. Dear Lord, her relatives had spent the last month teaching her the ins and outs of London society, but no one had told her what to do if she discovered a gentleman—no, a rogue—in her bedroom. Emma knew she should say something, scream even, but not a sound passed through her lips.

And then Emma suddenly realized that she was still stretched across her bed in a very compromising position. Glancing up, she quickly realized that the duke had also noticed. His hot gaze seemed to burn into her skin, and Emma felt herself pinken with embarrassment. She hastily pulled herself upright, clutching a pillow to her chest, eager to shield herself from Alex's eyes.

"Pity," he remarked sardonically.

Emma's eyes flew to his. She still didn't speak, not quite trusting her voice.

He answered the question he saw in her eyes. "Not many women have breasts as lovely as yours. 'Tis a pity to cover them up."

That only made Emma clutch the pillow even tighter. Alex chuckled at her modesty. "Besides," he continued, "you're not hiding from me anything you haven't just shown to all of London."

Except they weren't sitting in my bedroom, Emma thought angrily.

"Really, Meg, or should I say Emma? You can't convince me you're mute. I saw a fair piece of your temper earlier this afternoon. Surely you must have something to say?"

Emma said the first thing that came into her mind. "I think I'm going to vomit."

That comment took Alex completely off guard, and he half rose out of his chair. Emma feared she might actually laugh at the look of utter panic she saw on his face. "Good Lord," he exclaimed, scanning the room for some kind of receptacle. Not finding one, he looked back to the woman on the bed. "Do you mean it?"

"No. Although your presence *does* unsettle my stomach."

Alex was once again taken aback. The American chit had succeeded in completely flustering him— no mean feat. He ought to throttle her for her impudence, but she looked so damned innocent and appealing sitting on the bed with the pillow clutched to her chest that he could only laugh. "Women have told me that I make them feel a number of things," he drawled, "but nausea was never one of them."

Emma ignored his comment. "What on earth are you doing here?" she finally asked.

"Isn't it obvious?" Alex's green eyes twinkled as he leaned forward. "I came to find you."

"Me?" Emma squeaked, hoping there had been some mistake. "You don't even know me."

"You're right," Alex mused. "But I did meet a kitchen wench this afternoon who looked remarkably like you. Red hair, violet eyes. Do you by chance have an identical twin?" He smiled dangerously. "She was nothing like you in temperament, however. A lusty wench, she was. Could barely keep her hands off of me—and kissed me in the most unspeakable places."

"I did not!" Emma roared. "How dare you even suggest it!"

Alex merely raised a single eyebrow at her outburst. "So you do admit that you were in my coach this afternoon?"

"You know I was. There is no use denying it."

"Indeed," Alex agreed, leaning comfortably back into the chair.

"Make yourself right at home."

Alex paid no attention to her sarcasm. "Thank you. You're very kind. And now," he commanded, "I would like a full explanation of how you came to be wearing servant's clothes and traipsing around London unescorted."

"What?!" Emma shrieked, outraged.

"I'm waiting for your explanation." His voice was deadly patient.

"Well, you're not going to get one, you highhanded louse," she said bitterly.

"You're very lovely when you're angry, Emma."

"Must you always say such outrageous things?"

Alex placed his hands behind his head and leaned back, as if he were pondering her angry question. "Actually, I've always prided myself on being slightly outrageous."

"I'll just bet you have," she muttered.

"What was that?"

Emma decided to try another tactic. "I think you're acting more than slightly outrageous. I may be from the United States, but even I know this is not at all the thing." Emma sighed as she assessed her predicament. "Are you determined to ruin me? I'm trying so hard to make my uncle and aunt proud of me."

Alex felt a twinge of guilt at his behavior when he saw Emma's wistful expression. Her violet eyes glowed softly with unshed tears, and her hair seemed to shimmer like fire beneath the flickering glow of the candle. Tenderness washed over him, and he fought the need to hold her in his arms. He wanted to soothe her, protect her, not ruin her. Hell, he wasn't even sure why he'd come up here in the first place.

But he knew he had to fight this strange tenderness toward the American girl. He'd yet to meet a marriageable young miss who could see beyond his title or his wealth. If he let himself feel anything for Emma, he knew he'd only get hurt. And somehow he instinctively knew that she had the power to wound him more deeply than any other.

And so he steeled his heart and sharpened his tongue. "I'm sure your aunt and uncle are most proud," he said, his voice laden with sarcasm. "You had half the *ton*—the male half, that is—positively *drooling* over you. I'm sure you can expect half a dozen offers before the month is finished. You should be able to catch yourself quite a nice title."

Emma flinched visibly at his verbal assault. "How can you say such cruel things? You don't even know me."

"You're a woman," he said simply.

"What has that got to do with anything?"

Alex noticed that, in her ire, Emma had thrown the pillow aside. Her skin flushed pink with anger, and her chest rose and fell with each deep breath she took. Alex thought she looked delectable but fought to keep his desire in check. "Women," he explained patiently, "spend the first eighteen to twenty-one years of their lives sharpening their social skills. And when they think they're ready, they go out into the world, attend a few parties, bat their eyelashes, smile prettily, and catch a husband. The higher the title and the more money the better. And half the time, the poor fellow doesn't even know what hit him."

Emma was obviously appalled, for her horror showed clearly on her face. "I cannot believe you just said that."

"Insulted?"

"Completely."

"You shouldn't be. It's the way of things. There's nothing you or I can do about it."

Emma suddenly felt her anger dissolve into pity. What on earth had happened to this man that had made him so hard, so cruel? "Haven't you ever loved anyone?" she asked quietly.

Alex looked up sharply at her soft question and was surprised to see true concern in her eyes. "And have you loved so many that you're an expert?" he countered in an equally soft voice.

"Not like *that*," Emma said pointedly. "But I will. Someday, I will. And until then, I have my father, and Uncle Henry and Aunt Caroline, and Belle and Ned. I couldn't ask for a more wonderful family, and I love them all dearly. There's absolutely nothing I wouldn't do for them."

Alex found himself wishing he were included in that privileged group.

"I know you have a family," Emma continued, remembering her encounter with his sister. "Don't you love them?"

"Yes, I do." Alex's expression softened for the first time that evening, and Emma couldn't miss the love in his eyes when he thought of his family. He chuckled. "Maybe you are correct. It seems that there are a few women in the world who are worthy of love. Unfortunately, I seem to be rather closely related to all of them."

"I think you're frightened," Emma said daringly.

"I hope you intend to explain that comment."

"You're scared. It's far easier to shut yourself off from people than to love them. If you keep your heart surrounded by strong walls, no one can get close enough to you to break it. Don't you agree?" Emma looked up into his eyes and was startled by his intent gaze. Cursing herself for a coward, she looked away. "You . . . see . . ." she stammered, fighting to keep the courage she needed to speak to him in such a forward manner. "I can tell that you're not a *bad* person. You obviously care for your family very deeply, so you must be capable of love. You're just afraid to make yourself vulnerable."

Alex was stunned by both her soft lecture and its discomforting accuracy. Her quiet words made him extremely uneasy. Didn't she realize that her tender words could tear through his armor far more effectively than any sword? Suddenly uncomfortable, he decided to change the subject before she had another chance to unsettle him.

"You still haven't told me why you were out and about dressed as a servant this afternoon," he said abruptly.

Emma was startled by the sudden turn in the conversation, and the sharpness of his voice roused her ire once again. "Whyever would I explain my actions to you?"

"Because I insist that you do so."

"What? You must be joking!" Emma spluttered. "You overbearing, arrogant, unscrupulous—"

"Once again" Alex cut in smoothly, "I find myself in admiration of your vast vocabulary."

"There are quite a few more where those came from," Emma said between clenched teeth.

"I don't doubt it for an instant."

"Why, you insufferable, odious—"

"Here we go again."

"—PIG!" Emma clapped her hand to her face as she realized what she just said, and she started to shake silently with laughter. She simply couldn't help herself. Sitting on her soft white quilt in a most unladylike manner, she hugged her bent legs to herself and bowed her head as she laughed. Her body rocked uncontrollably as she tried to contain her mirth. The complete ludicrousness of her situation had suddenly been brought home to her, and though she knew she ought to do something like swoon, she simply could not help but be utterly amused.

Alex regarded Emma's laughter with surprise. That a woman could actually find humor in her compromising position—it was inconceivable! But he soon found that her mirth was infectious. His rich chuckle joined her silent laughter as he watched her pale, delicate shoulders rise and fall with each giggle.

Alex's chuckles proved to be Emma's undoing, and she exploded into loud, throaty laughter. Unable to keep a tight rein on her shaking body any longer, she acted just as she would have done if it had been Belle in the room instead of the Duke of Ashbourne, and she flopped out onto her back, legs hanging over the side of the bed.

Alex watched her with fascination. Spread out on the bed, with her flaming hair fanned out against the pale sheets, she seemed not to notice him. Lost in her laughter, she was primitive and without artifice, completely oblivious to his hungry gaze.

He thought she was magnificent.

How was he ever going to keep his hands off of her?

"Oh my," Emma gasped, finally emerging from her fit of laughter. She fought for breath, trying desperately to contain herself. She placed one hand on her heaving chest as she regained control. "Whatever must you think of me?"

"I think," Alex paused as he crossed the room in quick strides and perched himself at the foot of her bed, "that you are beautiful."

Emma pulled her legs back onto the bed and shrank back against the headboard. His silken voice melted her limbs, and she was terrified by her reaction to him. She had to put as much room as possible between herself and the dangerously handsome man who had snuck into her bedroom. "Beauty is only skin deep," she quipped, trying to relieve the tension that hung in the air.

"Very astute," Alex said with a nod. "Allow me to rephrase myself. I think that you are splendid."

Joy shot through Emma like ten thousand tiny flames, and her body tingled with strange, unfamiliar feelings. All she knew was that Alex's presence affected her in ways she did not understand, and she was frightened.

Alex caught her timid gaze. "My dear Emma," he began.

Emma suddenly felt the need to assert herself and regain some self-confidence, which he had washed

away. She straightened her back with false brava-
do. "I am certainly not your dear Emma," she said
primly.

"Really? Then whose dear Emma are you?"

"What an absurd question."

"Not at all. Because"—he caught her unshod foot
and began to massage it—"if you don't belong to
anyone else yet, I think I might make you mine."

Emma gasped as his hands continued to knead
the muscles in her foot. She had never dreamed
that a touch to her foot could send sensations up to
her stomach, she thought frantically as she pulled
her leg to escape his grasp. Her struggles only
strengthened his resolve and his strong, tanned
hands moved upward under the hem of her skirt
to her calf. Emma unconsciously wet her lips as
delicious spasms of pleasure shot up her leg.

"Feels good, doesn't it?" Alex grinned.

"No, I don't think I like it at all," was her strangled reply.

"Oh?" Alex asked innocently. "Then I'll just have
to try harder." His hands lazily moved upward
until he was touching the soft flesh just above her
knee. "Do you like that?" At her dazed expression,
he continued. "No? Perhaps then a kiss."

Before Emma had any chance to react, he tugged
her feet and pulled her down so she that was lying
on her back. He stretched out beside her, the hard
length of his body pressing into her side. Cupping
her chin with his strong hand, he pulled her face
to his and his lips gently met hers.

"No," Emma whispered weakly. She didn't
understand how this man came to be in her
bedroom or how he came to be lying on her
bed, but most of all, she didn't understand why
her body suddenly felt like it was about to go up
in flames.

"Just one kiss," Alex moaned against her mouth, his voice thick with desire. "If you say no after one kiss, I'll stop. I promise."

Emma didn't say a thing, simply letting her eyelids flutter shut as his tongue traced the outline of her lips. That delicate touch proved to be Emma's undoing, and her body responded shamelessly. She snaked her arms around the back of his neck and pressed her hips instinctively into his. Moaning slightly, she parted her lips, barely conscious of her own movements.

Alex took full advantage of her reaction and pressed his tongue into her mouth immediately, searching its inner depths. "God, you're sweet," he murmured huskily. He plunged back into her mouth, pressing and probing. Emma met this intimate caress with an ardor she had never dreamed she possessed, one hand grasping at the silken fullness of his thick hair, the other roaming over the hard muscles of his back.

Alex groaned as her touch ignited him. His mouth never leaving hers, he moved and covered her body with his own, pressing it hotly into the mattress. Emma moaned passionately at this new intimacy, and the sound increased his ardor. "Who'd have thought such a little thing would be so passionate?" he murmured as his lips softly trailed down her soft, white neck.

Emma shivered with desire. "What are you doing to me?" she asked huskily.

Alex's chuckle came from deep in his throat as his lips returned to hers. "I'm making love to you, my sweet. And you feel like you do—" His hand snaked up to close over her breast, and Emma gasped at the stark heat that poured through the satin of her dress and burned her skin. "—because you want me every bit as much as I want you."

"That's not true," Emma said shakily, but she knew she was lying even as the words tumbled from her mouth.

Alex's lips moved across her face to nibble on her earlobe. "Ah, my dear Emma, have they turned you into a prim English miss already?"

Emma could feel his warm breath in her ear as he spoke, but nothing could have prepared her for the onslaught of desire she felt when his tongue suddenly darted out and began to caress her. "Ahh," she sighed, unable to prevent herself from murmuring her pleasure.

Alex only grinned. "Don't be ashamed of what you're feeling, Emma. Never feel ashamed. It's completely natural. There is nothing bad or evil about it, regardless of what society matrons may say."

"I wasn't exactly told such feelings were bad in and of themselves." Emma's voice shook. "I was just told they were bad unless you were married."

Alex grimaced at the *M* word, and his desire receded slightly. "I wouldn't look to me for marriage, if I were you," he chided her gently.

"I wasn't!" Emma retorted, pulling away from him.

"Good!"

"I would never marry you."

"That's very convenient for you because I don't recall asking you to."

Emma fumed. "I wouldn't marry you if you were the last man on earth!" She paused for a second as she pondered what was clearly an overused cliché. "Well, maybe if you were the last man on earth, but *only* then!"

Alex decided he loved her obvious common sense.

"But seeing as how you're not the last man on earth," Emma continued, "which is more than obvious considering the fact that I've got a whole ballroom full of eligible bachelors just down-stairs—"

Alex's mouth quickly drew together in a grim line.

"—I think you should leave right now."

"I disagree."

"I don't care."

"We seem to be at a standstill here," Alex drawled. "I wonder who will win."

"I haven't any doubt of the outcome," Emma said bravely. "Get out of my room!"

Alex raised his eyebrows at Emma's ire. His seeming indifference only served to inflame her further. "Now!" she exploded.

Alex rose to his feet and straightened his coat. "If there's one thing I've learned," he commented caustically, "it's never to argue with a screaming woman."

Emma immediately pouted. "I wasn't screaming. I never scream."

"Oh?"

"I was merely raising my voice."

"For your sake, I hope you weren't screaming," Alex said, "because the last thing we need is your family rushing in. Especially now that we've clearly established our lack of desire to be married to one another."

"Oh, damn," Emma sighed.

"Such language," Alex chided, and then he realized he sounded just like his sister.

"Oh, do be quiet. The last thing I need is a lecture from you." Emma sprang to her feet and smoothed the violet folds of her dress with her hands. "Do I look presentable?" she asked, her eyes wide with need for reassurance. "I don't want to embarrass my family."

"Quite frankly, you look like you've just been kissed. And rather soundly, too."

Emma groaned as she rushed to her mirror to inspect the damage. Alex was right. Her face was flushed and tendrils of hair had escaped her barrette and floated seductively around her face. "Well, at least it shouldn't be too difficult to fix my hair. Meg tried absolutely forever to get it to conform to the latest styles, but I finally managed to convince her that this was simpler, more comfortable, and more flattering."

"Don't tell me you actually have a maid named Meg."

"Yes, well, it's difficult to be overly creative when one has just gotten oneself whacked in the head." Emma struggled valiantly to contain her thick hair in the barrette.

"Allow me," Alex purred as he moved to stand behind her. Emma was shocked when he picked up her hairbrush and began to stroke her hair softly, sweeping it up atop her head.

"I won't even ask where you learned to dress hair."

"You probably shouldn't."

"You have scores of mistresses, I'm sure."

"*You've* been gossiping about me," he accused.

"Only a little," she admitted.

"How unfair of you. I didn't even know your true name." Alex plucked the barrette from Emma's fingers and deftly secured her hair into place.

"Well, now you do," Emma commented, unable to think of anything more interesting to say.

"So I do," Alex replied, for much the same reason.

The two of them paused, simply watching the other tentatively. Emma finally broke the silence. "But you mustn't act as if you know me. I wouldn't want anyone to suspect anything untoward."

"Of course. Although you can be sure that I will seek out a proper introduction as soon as possible. And then you'll have a fine time avoiding me."

"Not for want of trying, I'm sure." The insulting words tumbled out before Emma could stop them, but Alex only laughed softly.

"You do have a charming wit, my dear Emma." His head quickly swooped down as he placed a quick kiss on Emma's surprised lips. "Now go on and return to your ball. I won't follow you for at least a quarter of an hour."

Emma rushed to the door, opened it, and slipped into the hallway. Pausing briefly, she stuck her head back into her bedroom. "Promise?"

Alex chuckled. "Promise."

Chapter 6

~~~~~~~~~~

Emma breathed a sigh of relief as soon as she closed the bedroom door behind her. Although she'd only met the Duke of Ashbourne that day, she knew instinctively that he was a man of his word and would not cause an irreparable scandal by following her directly back to the ballroom. He would keep his promise and wait at least fifteen minutes before reappearing.

Emma moved silently through the dark hallways of her cousins' home until she emerged at the top of the stairs that led to the brightly lit ballroom. She stopped for a moment to survey the scene. Aunt Caroline had surely outdone herself this time. It was really quite breathtaking. Exotic, brightly colored flowers adorned the refreshment tables that lined the walls of the room. Hundreds of serene off-white candles had also been placed around the perimeter of the ballroom. But the most spectacular part were the guests. Dashing men and elegant women swept effortlessly across the dance floor, whirling to the tunes provided by the orchestra Caroline had hired for the evening. The ladies were especially brilliant, their jewels glittering shamelessly in the candlelight as their bright silks and satins floated through the air. The dancing couples seemed to move in unison, as if choreographed, turning the ballroom into a kaleidoscope of light and color.

As Emma smiled at the gorgeous spectacle, she didn't realize she was something of a sight herself. By pausing at the top of the stairs, she had unwittingly given the entire ballroom a chance to stop and stare at her. And stare they did.

"I'm definitely in love," declared John Millwood, one of Ned's university friends with whom Emma had danced earlier in the evening.

Ned laughed heartily. His blue eyes were just as bright as his sister's although his hair was a dark mahogany brown. "Forget it, John. You could never keep up with her. Besides, I thought you were in love with my sister."

"Right, well, still am, I suppose. You've simply got too many beautiful women under your roof. It just isn't fair."

Ned grimaced. "You'd be changing your tune if you had to deal with all the suitors who are continually banging down the door. I thought it was bad last year when it was just Belle, but it'll be hell now that Emma's here, too."

Just then, two more of their friends came rushing over. "Ned, you simply must introduce us to your cousin," exclaimed the young Lord Linfield. His companion, Nigel Eversley, nodded in agreement.

"I'm afraid you're going to have to petition my mother for that. I've given up trying to keep track of all the people who want introductions to Emma."

"She's stunning, simply stunning," John sighed.

"I don't know how much more of this I can take," Ned groaned.

"'Course we'd all be content if you'd simply agree to put in a few good words about us with your sister," Nigel said eagerly.

"I did that last year," Ned retorted. "It didn't do you any good, if you recall."

"You might try putting in a few excellent words, then," George Linfield suggested.

"You three are simply going to have to accept that the last thing my female relatives are going to do is listen to me," Ned said dryly. "Nothing I say ever sways them one way or another."

"A biddable female, that's what I need," George muttered.

"Don't look for one in my family," Ned chuckled.

"What happened to biddable females? Why can't I find one?" George continued to lament his plight.

"They're all ugly and boring," John decided. "Oh God, here she comes!"

Sure enough, Emma had spotted her cousin and was heading straight toward the group of men. "Hello, Ned," she said softly, a vision in violet satin. "Good evening, John. I so enjoyed our dance earlier." John beamed at her friendly words. Emma then turned to the two men she had not met and smiled at them expectantly, waiting for Ned to introduce them.

Ned quickly did the honors. "Emma, this is Lord George Linfield and Mr. Nigel Eversley. We're all up at Oxford together. George, Nigel, my cousin Miss Emma Dunster."

The two men crashed into each other trying to take her hand. Emma looked vaguely embarrassed and heartily amused.

"Excuse me, Linfield," Nigel said in a deep voice, trying to appear older than his twenty-one years. "I believe I was trying to kiss Miss Dunster's hand."

"Excuse *me*, Eversley, I thought I was taking her hand."

"You must be mistaken."

"Really? I rather think you are mistaken."

"You are highly mistaken if you think I'm mistaken."

"Goodness!" Emma exclaimed. "I do believe Aunt Caroline is calling me. It was so lovely meeting you both." With that, she hastily scurried away, trying to find her aunt.

"Oh, brilliant, Linfield, absolutely brilliant," Nigel said sarcastically. "Now you've gone and done it."

"*I've* gone and done it. If *you* hadn't been falling all over yourself grabbing at her hand . . ."

"If you will excuse me," Ned put in silkily, "I believe my mother is calling me as well." He quickly slipped away and followed Emma, hoping she knew where to find her.

Across the ballroom, Belle was dancing with William Dunford. The two had met the previous year and, after a few weeks of courting during which they realized they were not at all suited to one another romantically, they had quickly become close friends. "I hope your cousin is poor," he laughed, watching Linfield and Eversley fall all over themselves trying to meet Emma.

"Really?" Belle asked, amused. "Why?"

"Your family is going to be beleaguered as it is. If she's got money, every fortune-hunter in England is going to be pounding on your door."

Belle laughed. "Don't tell me you're planning on trying for her."

"Good God, no," Dunford exclaimed with a smile, his brown eyes warming as he remembered Alex's obsession with Emma. "Not that she isn't exceptionally beautiful, of course."

"She has a mind, too," Belle said pointedly.

"Imagine that!" Dunford teased. "Really, Belle, I never doubted for one moment that she was every bit as quick-witted as you are. I just imagine that she'll have her hands full without me."

"Whatever do you mean?"

"Oh, nothing at all, Belle," he said absently, scanning the ballroom for Alex. "Nothing at all. By the way, did I mention you look ravishing in blue?"

Belle smiled wryly. "How unfortunate, then, that I'm wearing green."

Emma, meanwhile, was still trying to find her aunt when Ned caught up with her. "I don't suppose you know where Mother is," Ned said, picking up two glasses of lemonade from a nearby table.

"Not a clue," Emma responded. "But thank you for the lemonade. I'm parched."

"I imagine if we stand here long enough, she'll find us. I think she still has about two hundred people she wants you to meet."

Emma laughed. "No doubt."

"I must apologize about the scene back there, Emma. I didn't think they'd act that absurdly."

"Didn't think who'd act that absurdly?" Belle suddenly appeared at Ned's right, Dunford at her heels.

"I'm afraid I introduced Emma to George Linfield and Nigel Eversley."

"Oh, Ned, you didn't! Poor Emma will be beleaguered by them for months."

"Don't worry, Emma," Ned said reassuringly. "They're really good chaps once you get to know them. They just lose their heads around a beautiful woman."

Emma laughed throatily. "Really, Ned, I think you have just given me a compliment. That may be the first one."

"Nonsense. If you recall, I couldn't stop praising

your right hook after you broke that pickpocket's nose in Boston."

Dunford decided he didn't have to worry about Emma having any trouble with Alex. But he did start to wonder if his friend was going to be able to manage the redheaded American. He turned to Ned and said, "Blydon, I don't believe you've introduced me to your cousin."

"Oh, so sorry, Dunford. Been introducing her all night. It's hard to keep track."

"Emma, this is William Dunford," Belle interjected. "He's a great friend of mine. Dunford, I'm sure you realize that this is my cousin, Miss Emma Dunster."

"I certainly do." Dunford took Emma's hand and graciously lifted it to his lips. "It's a pleasure to finally make your acquaintance. I've heard *so* much about you."

"Really?" Emma asked, intrigued.

"But I hardly told you anything," Belle protested. Dunford smiled enigmatically and was saved from further questioning by Lady Worth's voice.

"Emma, darling," Caroline called. "I want you to meet Lady Summerton." The foursome turned to see Caroline heading toward them with a plump lady wearing a purple gown with a matching turban. Emma thought she looked like a pot of grape jam.

"Don't look now," Belle whispered, "but here comes one of those ninnyheads we warned you about, Emma."

"I'm so happy to meet you," gushed Lady Summerton. "You've made quite an entrance into society. There hasn't been anything like it since Belle made her debut last year." The pudgy woman took a deep breath, turned to Emma's aunt, and continued, "And Caroline, you must be so proud. This is surely the party of the year. Why, the Duke of Ashbourne even made an appearance. I don't think he's been to a ball such as this in over a year. You must simply be thrilled!"

"Yes, yes," Caroline murmured. "I heard he stopped by, but I haven't seen him."

"I doubt he's left yet," Dunford said with a wicked grin. "In fact, I'm certain he plans to stay the entire evening."

"Planning to torture me, no doubt," Emma muttered under her breath.

"Did you say something, my dear?" Caroline inquired.

"No, no, I was just clearing my throat," Emma said hastily, clearing her throat.

"Would you like another glass of lemonade for that?" Dunford's voice was solicitous, but from his expression, Emma suspected he'd heard what she said.

"No, thank you," Emma said, holding up the glass in her hand, "I still have some left." She smiled at Dunford and took a healthy gulp.

"Well," Lady Summerton declared as if no one had spoken since her last monologue. "I'm sure even Ashbourne wouldn't dare leave without greeting his hostess, Caroline. I'm positive he'll be here soon. Absolutely positive."

"So am I," Dunford agreed, watching Emma with a twinkle in his eye. She smiled weakly, acutely uncomfortable.

"Of course," Lady Summerton continued, "I'm not sure if you should allow him near your niece, Caroline." She turned to Emma without pausing for breath. "He has a dreadful reputation. If you value yours, you'll stay away from him."

"I'll certainly try," Emma put in brightly.

"Do you know what I heard?" Lady Summerton asked breathily, to no one in particular.

"I'm sure I can't imagine," Ned replied.

"I heard," Lady Summerton paused for emphasis and leaned forward conspiratorially, "that Ashbourne, er, shall we say, 'said good-bye' to his opera singer and has finally decided to look among respectable ladies. I think he's looking for a wife."

Emma choked on her lemonade.

"Are you all right, dear?" Caroline asked. "Is your headache still bothering you?"

"No, it certainly isn't my head that's bothering me."

Lady Summerton plodded on. "Clarissa Trent is after him. Her mother told me. And do you know what?"

Only Caroline was attentive—and polite—enough to murmur, "What?"

"I think she has a chance of getting him."

"I imagine she'll be disappointed," Dunford predicted.

"Well, she did say she was holding out for a duke," Belle said caustically.

"I would rather not discuss her," Ned declared.

"Emma, are you feeling well?" asked Caroline. "You look a trifle pale."

An awkward silence fell over the small group. Finally, Lady Summerton, never one to enjoy conversational lulls, commented, "Er, I'm sure he'll show up soon, Caroline. So stop your worrying."

Even Caroline, impeccably mannered as she was, could not fail to murmur softly, "I wasn't aware that I was worrying."

"What was that, dear?" Lady Summerton inquired.

"Nothing, nothing at all." Caroline shot Emma a

knowing glance. "I was just clearing my throat."

Emma smiled conspiratorially. "Perhaps we should get you some lemonade, dear aunt."

"I really don't think that will be necessary, dear niece."

"Well, I'm sure he'll show up soon," Lady Summerton declared.

Emma estimated that she'd been back in the ballroom for at least fifteen minutes and decided miserably that Lady Summerton was probably right. She wondered how on earth she would be able to go through the motions of polite conversation with the man who had just nearly ravished her in her bedroom. Cowardice finally emerged as the solution and she smiled weakly. "Actually, Aunt Caroline, I am feeling a little tired. Perhaps a little fresh air would help."

Dunford jumped in immediately, eager to provoke Alex's jealousy by walking with Emma in the gardens. "If you would like to go to the garden, it would be my pleasure to escort you, Miss Dunster."

"It would be very difficult for me to meet the guest of honor if you insist upon monopolizing her time," boomed a deep voice. It was all Emma could do to keep from cringing as everyone turned to face Alex.

"Why, your grace," gushed Lady Summerton, "we were just talking about you."

"Were you?" Alex answered laconically, fixing his deadly stare upon the ridiculous woman.

"Er, yes, we were," Lady Summerton stammered.

Emma was stunned by the sheer presence of the man. His tall, broad frame somehow seemed to dominate the entire ballroom. Indeed, a hush had swept across the crowd as everyone craned their necks to watch the well-known duke. He was, Emma had to admit, definitely worth watching. He exuded raw power that seemed barely contained by his elegant black and white evening clothes. His unruly black hair had refused to conform to any sense of a hairstyle, and one lock fell characteristically over his forehead. But it was definitely his piercing green eyes that made him appear so dangerous. And just then those green eyes were fixed right on Emma. "Miss Dunster, I presume," he said silkily, taking her hand.

"H-How do you do?" Emma managed to say. A firebolt charged through her as he lifted her hand to his mouth. And although Emma had only spent one night out in London society, she knew that his lips had remained overlong on the pale skin of her wrist.

"I do very well, indeed, now that I've met you."

Lady Summerton gasped. Caroline's eyebrows shot up in a rather shocked expression. Dunford chuckled. Ned and Belle openly stared. Emma wondered if she'd blushed to a deep crimson or merely a light rose. "You're very kind," she finally said.

"Well, Ashbourne, that may be the first time I've ever heard you referred to as kind," Dunford said dryly.

"It's so kind—er, gracious—of you to come tonight, your grace," Caroline said.

"Indeed," Belle added, not really having anything to say but feeling nonetheless that something was necessary.

"I trust your sister is well?" Caroline inquired. "We were so upset when she sent her regrets."

"Sophie is very well, thank you. We had a bit of a scare this afternoon, but everything is all right now."

"A scare?" Lady Summerton's eyes grew round with interest. "Whatever do you mean?"

"Her son Charlie was almost run over by a hack. He would have been killed if a young maid hadn't run into the street and pushed him out of the way."

Emma could feel Belle's eyes boring into her. She glanced upward, assiduously avoiding her cousin's gaze.

"Thank goodness he wasn't hurt," Caroline said with obvious feeling. "I trust the maid is all right?"

"Oh, yes," Alex replied with a grin. "She's splendid."

Emma decided that the ceiling was, indeed, highly interesting.

"Is that a waltz I hear?" Alex asked innocently. "Lady Worth, may I have your permission to dance with your niece?"

Emma cut in before Caroline could reply. "I think I've promised this dance to someone else." She was certain she hadn't promised the dance to anyone, but it was the best she could come up with under the circumstances. She looked desperately at Ned for assistance. Her cousin certainly had no desire to antagonize the powerful duke, and he quickly discovered the wonders of the ceiling that had so entranced Emma moments earlier.

Alex fixed his green stare upon her. "Nonsense," he said simply. He turned back to Caroline. "Lady Worth?"

Caroline nodded her assent, and Alex swept Emma into his arms. When they reached the center of the dance floor, he smiled warmly down at her and said, "You are almost as beautiful in the ballroom as you are in the bedroom."

She blushed hotly. "Why must you say such

things? Are you determined to ruin my reputation on my first night out?"

Alex raised his eyebrows at her distress. "I don't mean to boast, but I rather think that as long as I don't drag you out of the room and ravish you in the garden, I'm only enhancing your reputation. I don't go to these things often," he explained. "People are going to want to know why I'm so taken with you."

Emma had to concede his point. "Nevertheless, you don't have to make such a show of embarrassing me."

"I'm sorry," he said simply. Emma glanced up sharply at his grave tone and was stunned by the stark honesty she found in his eyes.

"Thank you," she said quietly. "I accept your apology." She stared into his eyes for a few moments longer and then, uncomfortable under the intimate caress of his gaze, quickly shifted her head and focused on his cravat.

"You might want to smile at me," Alex said. "Or, if you can't manage that, at least look up at me. Everyone is watching us." Emma heeded his words and lifted her face. "Much better. It's painful, you know, having you in my arms and not being able to look into your eyes."

Emma didn't know what to say.

After a few moments, Alex broke the silence. "You can call me Alex, if you like."

Emma regained a little of her spirit. "'Your grace' will do just fine, I'm sure."

"But I would prefer you to use my given name."

"I would really prefer not to."

Alex was glad Emma had a bit of her temper back. She had seemed so forlorn when they began their waltz. "You'll seem awfully silly 'your grace-ing' me when I'll be calling you Emma."

"I haven't given you permission to use my first name," Emma reminded him.

"Really, Emma, I hardly think permission is necessary after what we shared less than an hour ago."

"Must you remind me of that? I would rather forget it."

"Really? I think you're lying to yourself."

"You presume too much, your grace," Emma said with quiet dignity. "You don't know me at all."

"I'd like to." Alex's grin was positively roguish. Emma marveled at how a simple smile could completely transform Alex's face. Just moments before, he had appeared hard and uncompromising, nearly sending Lady Summerton cowering across the room with a single glare. Now, his usual cynicism absent, he was almost boyish, his eyes bathing her in a warm green glow.

Emma felt all her mental capabilities slipping away as he pulled her closer. "I think you're deliberately trying to overwhelm me."

"Am I succeeding?"

Emma stared up at him for several moments before she gravely answered, "Yes."

Alex's arms tightened around her petite body. "Christ, I can't believe you said that to me here," he said, his voice suddenly husky. "You're too damned honest for your own good."

Emma lowered her eyes, unable to understand what had moved her to confess her feelings so starkly. "You think I'm too honest?" she said softly. "Well, I'm not finished yet. We met in a most unconventional manner, which is probably why we feel able to speak to one another so bluntly. I think you're a nice man, but a hard man, and I think you could hurt me without even intending to. I'm only in London for a few short months, and I'd like my stay with my relatives to be as happy as possible. So I am asking you please to stay away from me."

"I don't think I can."

"Please."

Alex was amazed at how a single soft word from Emma's lips could make him feel like such a cad. Nonetheless, he felt that after her soul-bearing speech, she deserved nothing less than complete honesty from him in return. "I don't think you understand how much I want you."

Emma immediately went still. "The waltz is over, your grace."

"So it is."

She extricated herself from his arms. "Good-bye, your grace."

"Until tomorrow, Emma."

"I don't think so." With that, she slipped away from him, deftly darting through the crowds until she reached her aunt.

Alex was still as he watched her move through the ballroom, her bright hair gleaming under the flickering candlelight. Her stark honesty had both unnerved him and intensified his desire for her. He didn't quite understand what he felt for her, and this lack of control over his emotions left him completely irritated with himself. With a quick step, he turned decisively away from the young fops and eager mamas who seemed intent on engaging him in conversation. Thankfully, he quickly located Dunford, who was standing at the edge of the ballroom watching him. "Let's get out of here," he said grimly to his friend. Damn it, she'd simply have to accept that he just couldn't leave her alone.

Chapter 7

"**I** am so glad you decided to let me go with you, Emma," Belle said excitedly.

"I have a feeling I'm going to live to regret it," Emma responded. She and her cousin were sitting in the Blydons well-sprung carriage on their way to return the earrings that Sophie had pressed into Emma's hands the day before.

"Nonsense," Belle said offhandedly. "Besides, you might need me. What if you don't know what to say?"

"I'm sure I'll think of something appropriate."

"What if Sophie doesn't know what to say?"

"Now, that's unlikely." Emma said wryly. She glanced down at the diamond and emerald earrings in her gloved hand. "Too bad," she said with a slight grimace.

"What?"

"These are awfully nice earrings."

The carriage came to a halt in front of Sophie's elegant townhouse. The two young women alighted and quickly ascended the stone steps leading to the front door. Emma gave the door a decisive knock. It was opened within seconds, and Emma was treated to the sight of Sophie's comically thin, excruciatingly imperious butler. It has often been noted that butlers are far more discerning than their employers, and Graves was certainly no exception. No one would enter the Earl and Countess of Wilding's home until he deemed them suitable. He stared down at Emma and Belle, black eyes sharp, and said simply, "Yes?"

Belle offered the man her calling card. "Is Lady Wilding receiving?" she inquired sharply, matching the butler's supercilious stare.

"Perhaps."

Emma nearly laughed as she watched her cousin's jaw clench. Belle plodded on. "Would you please tell her that Lady Arabella Blydon is here to see her?"

Graves's eyebrows rose slightly. "Unless my eyesight fails me, which, incidentally, it never does, there appear to be two people on the doorstep."

Belle's chin rose slightly as she ground out, "This is my cousin, Miss Emma Dunster."

"Of course," Graves said accommodatingly. "Allow me to show you to the yellow parlor." He ushered them into one of Sophie's sitting rooms, his feet moving silently across the Aubusson carpet.

"Good Lord," Belle muttered as soon as the butler was out of earshot. "I'm sure I've been here at least thirty times, and I still get grilled on the doorstep."

"He's obviously very devoted to his employers. You should probably try to hire him yourself," Emma laughed.

"Are you joking? I'd probably have to get references just to get into my own home."

"Belle, darling!" shrilled Sophie, sailing into the room in a lovely bottle green morning dress that complimented her eyes. She seemed not to notice Emma standing quietly in the corner as she rushed to kiss Belle on the cheek. "I'm so sorry I couldn't make it to your fête. I heard it was spectacular."

"Yes, it was," Belle demurred.

"My *brother* even went," Sophie said incredulously. "That's a first. Now where is your lovely cousin I've been hearing so much about?"

"She's right behind you."

Sophie whirled around. "I am so pleased to—oh, my God."

Emma smiled sheepishly. "I imagine you're a little surprised."

Sophie opened her mouth, closed it, and then opened it again to say, "Oh, my God."

"Well, perhaps you're a lot surprised," Emma amended.

"Oh, my God."

Belle moved to Emma's side. "I didn't think it was possible," she whispered, "but Sophie really doesn't know what to say."

"This is where you were supposed to jump in and smooth things over," Emma reminded her.

"*I* certainly don't know what to say." Belle grinned.

Sophie took a step forward. "But—you—yesterday—"

Emma took a deep breath. "I'm afraid I had borrowed my maid's frock yesterday."

"Whatever for?" Sophie was slowly regaining the use of her rather extensive vocal prowess.

"That's actually something of a long story."

"It is?" Belle asked.

Emma gave her cousin a cutting glare. "Well, if it isn't exactly long, it's kind of complicated."

"Oh?" asked Sophie, eyes wide with interest. "Then I definitely want to hear all about it."

"Actually, it isn't even all that complicated," Belle mused.

Emma managed to poke her troublesome cousin in the side as she quickly explained how they were trying to avoid her aunt's preparations for the party. "It was either the kitchens or flower arrangements," she concluded.

"A perfectly dreadful fate," Sophie agreed. "However, I can't imagine what Caroline had to say about your adventure."

"The thing is," Emma said meaningfully, "I can't imagine either." She and Belle turned to Sophie with identical nervous smiles pasted to their faces.

"Ohhhh," Sophie breathed, nodding slowly. "I see. Well, you can certainly be assured of my silence. It's the least I can do after you saved Charlie's life. As I said, I'll be forever in your debt."

Emma quickly produced Sophie's stunning emerald and diamond earrings. "So you see," she explained, "considering my true circumstances, I couldn't possibly accept these earrings. Please take them back. They so suit your green eyes."

Sophie's eyes welled with unshed tears. "But I would so like you to have them. They're only trinkets compared with my son."

"I think Emma would feel uncomfortable," Belle said softly.

Sophie looked back and forth between the cousins, her gaze finally resting on Emma. "I do want to give you something in thanks."

"Your friendship will be more than enough." Emma's voice was quiet and deep with emotion, for she knew that Sophie would prove to be a true and loyal friend despite her rather unnerving brother.

Sophie took both of Emma's hands into her own. "*That* you will have always." And then, as if that wasn't enough, she suddenly let go of Emma's hands and embraced her in a warm hug. "Oh! Where are my manners?" Sophie suddenly exclaimed. "Please sit down," she said, motioning toward the golden-hued sofas. Emma and Belle smiled as they made themselves comfortable. "Now, let's get down to what's really important," Sophie said emphatically. "Gossip. I want to hear everything about last night."

"It was marvelous," Belle exclaimed. "I tell you, if Mama wanted to show the *ton* that she considered Emma as dear as a daughter she surely succeeded. She introduced her to absolutely everyone."

"How exciting for you," Sophie commented.

Emma murmured her agreement.

"But also how wearying," Sophie added more sympathetically.

"Oh yes." Emma nodded.

"And everyone was there, simply everyone," Belle continued. "Except you, of course. As you know, even your brother made an appearance. Everyone was incredibly surprised. People couldn't stop talking about it."

"Yes, I too was a bit surprised—" Sophie began. And then she suddenly remembered that her brother had been with her the day before, and, whipping her head around to face Emma, she exclaimed, "Oh my goodness! Whatever did you say? Whatever did he say?"

"Actually, I think I said something along the lines of 'How do you do?' "

"*After* he kissed her hand for twice as long as is proper," Belle added excitedly. "Once people finally stopped talking about how shocked they were at his appearance, they couldn't stop talking about the way he was pursuing Emma."

"Really, Belle," Emma said in a matter-of-fact tone. "I think he was just poking fun at me. He seemed a little upset that he had been so surprised by my true identity. I imagine he likes to feel that he's in command of every situation."

"That's for certain," Sophie grumbled. "Imagine being related to him."

Emma found *that* prospect rather unsettling. "Anyway, he really wasn't paying me that much attention. I didn't think he did anything untoward."

Belle snorted in a most unladylike manner. "Really, Emma, your face was the same color as your hair when you were dancing with him. You were either extremely embarrassed or extremely angry."

Emma shrugged her shoulders, preferring to let Sophie and Belle draw their own conclusions. "I'm sure that's all over and done with. Pardon me for saying so, Sophie, but if your brother is anything like his reputation—which was described to me in excruciating detail—I don't imagine I'll be running into him at many more events."

"Pity," Sophie said softly, the matchmaker's gleam sparkling in her eyes.

"What was that?"

"Oh, nothing at all. Would you like some tea?" Sophie said quickly, ringing for a maid. She'd been nagging Alex to settle down for years now, and in Emma Dunster she'd found her most promising possibility for success. Emma was strikingly attractive, obviously intelligent, and a genuinely nice person. And most importantly for anyone who was about to get paired up with Alexander Ridgely, Duke of Ashbourne, she was very, very brave. Sophie decided she couldn't have dreamed up a better sister-in-law. Emma's sharp tongue would serve her well, too. Alex needed a woman who wouldn't scurry to do his bidding every time he started acting in his domineering manner, which, Sophie had to admit, was most of the time.

"Please do tell me more about your ball," Sophie continued, eager to prolong the visit now that she'd decided she and Emma would soon be related. A servant brought in tea and biscuits, and Sophie quickly got to the job of serving.

"I did get cornered by Lady Summerton," Emma laughed.

Belle joined in. "Lady Summerton is the only person I know who can corner five people at once."

"What a silly woman," Sophie commented. "I think she means well, but she does prattle on."

Emma and Belle both shot Sophie looks of mock accusation. Sophie's eyes opened wide and then she laughed. "Oh, I know that I go on almost as much as she does, but at least I'm usually *interesting!*" With that all three women dissolved into spasms of laughter.

As their laughter began to die down, their cozy threesome was interrupted by a very loud and very angry male voice. "For Christ's sake, Graves, I swear to God I am going to hang you on that coat rack if you don't let me through."

"Oh dear," Sophie murmured. "I really must scold Graves, but I just haven't the heart. He so loves to interrogate."

"No, I will not give my calling card to a butler who has received me at least five hundred times!" Emma didn't think it was possible, but Alex's voice had actually grown louder.

Sophie looked a little sheepish. "I suppose I ought to go out there, but I do so enjoy it when Alex gets annoyed."

Emma was quick to agree.

"Graves, if you value your life, you will get out of my way immediately!" Alex's voice had suddenly taken on a dangerously low tone.

Emma, Belle, and Sophie winced as they saw Graves practically fly by the doorway of the yellow salon in his eagerness to escape Alex's wrath. When

Alex walked in, he was looking over his shoulder at the fast-disappearing butler and didn't even notice that Sophie had guests. "For God's sake, Soph, I'm your brother. Don't you think you can call off your attack dog?"

"He's a little overprotective now that Oliver is away, you know."

"I'll say." Alex finally turned around and noticed that there were three women in the room. He quickly swept his eyes over them, taking in their comfortable position. As his gaze settled on Emma, she lifted her teacup to her lips and took a sip. "My, my," he drawled, "aren't we the best of friends?"

All three women shot him irritated glances. Alex looked a trifle disgruntled at their collective unfavorable response to his presence.

"Don't be tedious, Alex," Sophie said flatly. "I'm entertaining guests. If you're going to be insulting, you can come back later."

"What a welcome," he grumbled as he flopped down inelegantly into a chair opposite Emma and Belle.

"I stopped by to return your sister's earrings, your grace," Emma said.

"I thought I told you to stop 'your grace-ing' me, Emma." Both Belle and Sophie raised their eyebrows at his bold use of Emma's first name.

"Oh, very well," Emma retorted. "I shan't call you anything, then."

Sophie watched the telltale clench of her brother's jaw and somehow managed to stifle what would have been a rather boisterous laugh. "Tea, Alex?" she said sweetly.

"I don't drink tea," he responded sharply.

"Right, of course. I forgot that men such as you don't drink such a silly beverage as tea."

"I would love another cup," Emma said with a smile.

"I wouldn't mind some more either," Belle added.

Alex wondered when the women of the world had united against him.

"I suppose we'll have to ring for another pot," Sophie decided. "Would you like some coffee, Alex?"

"I'd prefer whiskey."

"Don't you think it's a little early for that?"

Alex looked from his sister to Emma to Belle. All three looked back at him with deceptively serene expressions. "Actually," he commented, "I don't think there has ever been a better time for whiskey."

"As you wish."

Alex rose and walked across the room to the cabinet where his sister stored liquor. He pulled out a bottle of whiskey and poured himself a large glass. "Sophie, I had come to inform you of the true identity of our mysterious 'Meg' but I see that she has already beaten me to the task." He fixed his gaze on Emma. "What, I wonder, can your cousin think of your frolics?"

"Her cousin was a part of her frolics," Belle piped up.

Alex turned to give Belle his fiercest scowl. Emma took advantage of his distraction to surreptitiously examine him. As he leaned lazily against the wall, swirling his whiskey, he seemed unusually large and unbearably masculine in Sophie's delicately decorated parlor. His superbly tailored clothes barely contained the raw power of the man. How, she wondered, could one man simultaneously provoke such desire and antagonism in her? At least she assumed it was desire. She'd certainly never before felt anything like the strange fluttering in her abdomen and the wild beating of her heart. Yet even as his mere presence sent her traitorous body reeling into confused longing, his insolence and domineering attitude enraged her, and she ached to let him know just what she thought of him.

Unfortunately, right then what she thought of him was that he was terribly good-looking. Emma grimaced and decided she'd better keep her eyes on Sophie and Belle. Her cousin was doing her best to ignore Alex's scowl, turning to Sophie and asking, "Are you planning to hide yourself from the *ton* for the duration of your husband's trip to the West Indies or will we see you tonight at the Southburys' ball?"

"I had been contemplating retiring to the country, but I find that I've changed my mind. Town life suddenly promises to be terribly interesting this season. Although I don't imagine I'll be able to go out in another few months." Sophie smiled shyly.

"Oh, Sophie! Are you—?" Belle seemed quite unable to utter the word "pregnant" in the company of a man. Sophie nodded vigorously, her face radiant with joy. "I am so happy for you!" Belle continued. "But how difficult for you with your husband gone."

"Yes, Oliver doesn't even know he's about to become a father again. I wrote him a letter as soon as I knew for certain, but I doubt that he's received it yet."

"If you get lonely here by yourself, you must promise me that you and Charlie will come stay with us. We have plenty of room, and it might be terrible to be all alone when you're expecting."

"In case you had forgotten, Lady Arabella, Sophie does have relatives who care about her," Alex said imperiously. "If she moves in with anyone, she'll move in with me."

Belle gulped. "Perhaps she will long for female companionship," she said bravely.

"I'm sure his grace can provide plenty of female companionship," Emma muttered. Then to her complete mortification, she realized that her unpleasant thought had been spoken aloud.

Alex was inordinately pleased at her obvious jealousy, but nonetheless asked sharply, "Would you care to elucidate that comment, Emma?"

"Um, actually, I think I'd rather not," she said weakly.

Alex took pity on the shame and anguish he saw on Emma's face and decided to let the matter rest. "If Sophie desires female companionship," he declared, "she will move in with my mother."

Sophie was also delighted by Emma's jealous comment, wondering blissfully what color dress she'd get to wear as an attendant at the wedding. She did not, however, want to make Emma feel uncomfortable, so she said brightly, "A visit with Mama would probably be just the thing to lift my spirits during the next few months. I imagine we'll head out to the country. The clean air will do me a world of good, and Charlie loves it so. I swear, he turns into a positive heathen once we get him out of town. He's constantly climbing trees and I'm always fearful for him, but Alex does say I must be careful not to coddle him. However—"

"Sophie," Alex said in an indulgent voice, "you're rambling."

Sophie sighed. "So I am."

"But," Emma put in gamely, "you were exceedingly interesting. I do so like trees."

The three women laughed at the reference to Sophie's earlier remark about Lady Summerton while Alex grumbled about being left out of the joke.

"Oh, Emma," Sophie sighed with a smile, slowly regaining her composure. "I wasn't the least bit interesting, but it was kind of you to lie for me."

"It was no trouble at all, I assure you."

"Perhaps it will also be no trouble for you to tell us all about yourself, Emma," Alex cut in.

"Goodness, that would be tedious. I already know all about her," Belle said archly.

Emma wondered when her cousin had grown so daring. "I wouldn't want to bore my cousin."

"I'm sure she won't mind," Alex ground out.

"By all means," Belle said graciously. "I shall chat with Sophie. You wanted to show me your new harpsichord, didn't you, Sophie?"

"I did? Oh, yes, of course, I did! Here, come with me, it's in the blue salon upstairs." Sophie quickly rose and headed for the door, Belle at her heels. "You two will entertain yourselves, won't you?"

Emma wasn't quite angry enough to wish that looks could kill, but she found herself hoping that they could elicit brief but startling pain.

"We'll be just fine." Alex was positively beaming.

"Well done," Sophie whispered to Belle.

"I thought so," Belle returned.

"Come along," Sophie said loudly. "I can't wait to show it to you." With that, the pair slipped out of the room and headed upstairs.

"You must remind me to thank your cousin," Alex drawled.

"You must remind me to throttle her."

"Really, darling, is it so very difficult to be alone in the same room with me? You didn't mind last night." Alex strode across the parlor and settled himself right next to Emma on the sofa. Emma sighed in exasperation. Was there no situation in which he did not feel completely at ease? Here she was, her insides churning like an Atlantic crossing, and he was sitting next to her smiling as if he hadn't a care in the world. It was his nearness, she decided. Strange things happened to her when he was close. It was time to get him to move.

"Umm," Emma began hesitatingly, all of her decisive thoughts flying out the window. "I don't mean to sound like a complete prig—"

"Then don't sound like one."

"But I really don't think you should be sitting so close to me."

"Oh, Emma," Alex sighed. "Have they got your head full of rules and regulations already?" He pinched a lock of her hair between his fingers, unable to resist its fiery allure.

"Please stop, your grace. Belle and Sophie might return at any moment."

"Those two conspirators obviously intended to leave us alone. And I'm sure they'll let us know when they're coming back. When they start descending the stairs, believe me, we'll hear coughing fits like we've never heard before. I wouldn't even put it past them to work in a scream or two."

Emma bristled with anger. "I hate being manipulated."

"Yes, well, so do I. But I will make an exception when the manipulation leaves me stranded alone with you."

Emma shot him a sharp look. "You're always so self-contained. Doesn't anything frazzle you? Doesn't anything ever make you want to scream?"

Alex laughed loudly. "Love, if I told you what makes me scream, you'd go running right out of this room back to the Colonies."

Emma blushed deeply. Even an innocent such as she understood what he meant. "Must you always twist my words? You're such a trial." She crossed her arms against her chest and twisted her torso so that she was no longer facing him.

"Come now, love. Don't work yourself into a snit. Be honest with yourself. Do you so dislike talking to me?"

"Well, no, not really."

"Do you dislike being with me?"

"Well . . . not exactly."

"So what is our problem?"

"Well," Emma began slowly, turning back to face him, "I'm not really sure."

"Fine!" Alex declared happily, resting his arm along the sofa behind her back. "That settles it. We have no problems."

"That's *exactly* the problem!" Emma decided abruptly.

Alex quirked an eyebrow questioningly.

Emma was not deterred. "*You* decided there are no problems so *voilà*! We have no problems. What if *I* think we have a problem?"

"But you just said we didn't have any problems."

"I said no such thing. I said I wasn't sure what the problem was. And now I know. So that settles it. We have a problem." Emma punctuated this declaration by getting up off the sofa and moving to a nearby chair.

"What problem would this be?"

Emma crossed her arms. "You're far too bossy."

"Oh, really?"

"Really."

"Well, it just so happens that *you* need some bossing. Look what happens to you when you're left to your own devices—I find you unconscious in the street!"

"I cannot believe you have the nerve to say that to me!" Emma fumed, getting up to pace the parlor floor. "I was unconscious in the street because I saved your nephew's life! Would you rather I let him get trampled?"

"Forget that," Alex grumbled, unable to believe his own stupidity. "Bad example."

"And another thing—I don't need bossing," Emma said emphatically, working herself up into a fine rage. "I am perfectly able to take care of myself. What you need is a good swift kick to remind you that you are not God!"

"Emma?"

"Oh, be quiet. I don't want to speak with you anymore. You'll probably just laugh smoothly and dish up another sexual innuendo. Frankly, I don't need that kind of aggravation."

"Emma—"

"What?!" she snapped, whirling around to face him.

"I was just going to remark that I don't think I've ever gotten into such a vehement argument with a woman within twenty-four hours of meeting her." Alex stroked his chin thoughtfully, curious about the depth of their emotional reactions to one another. "Actually, I don't think I've ever gotten into an argument like that with a woman ever."

Emma looked away. "Are you trying to insult me?"

"No," Alex said slowly, as if trying to work out a problem in his head as he spoke. "No, I'm not. Actually, I think I've just complimented you."

Emma looked back at him, her expression reflecting the confusion she felt. He was still rubbing his jaw, and his eyes had narrowed perceptibly. Long

seconds passed, and Emma could see a wide assort-
ment of emotions pass over his face. Every now
and then he would start to say something and then
pause, as if a new solution had just offered itself to
him. "Do you know what I think this means?" he
finally said, his words slow and well thought out.
"I think this means we're going to be friends."

"*What?*"

"It's a novel thought, actually. Friends with a woman."

"Don't overexert yourself."

"No, I mean it. Think about it for a minute, Emma.
We do argue incessantly, but quite frankly, I've
enjoyed myself more in the last twenty-four hours
than I have in years."

Emma merely stared at him, quite unable to think
of a response to such a statement. Alex continued,
"I think I like you, Miss Emma Dunster. Of course,
I *want* you, too. That much must be quite obvious
to you. Lord knows it's painfully obvious to me.
But I really do quite like you. You're a good egg."

"*A good egg?*" Her voice came out strangled.

"And I think that if you think about it, you'll
realize you like me, too. When was the last time
you had so much fun?"

Emma opened her mouth but didn't have an
answer.

Alex smiled knowingly. "You like me. I know
you do."

Emma finally laughed, unable to believe his
nerve yet still admiring him for it. "Yes, I guess
I do."

This time Alex's smile was radiant. "Well, then,
I guess we're friends."

"I guess so." Emma was not quite sure how this
truce had come about, but she decided not to question it. Despite her better judgment, she knew that

Alex was right—she did like him. He was completely outrageous and more than a little domineering, but she just couldn't help enjoying his company, even if they did spend half their time yelling at each other.

Just then they heard Belle and Sophie coming down the stairs toward the parlor. Belle started coughing uncontrollably, and Sophie yelped, "Oh my!" Emma rested her face against one hand and began to laugh.

Alex merely shook his head, a wry grin spreading across his face. "Well, my love," he said, "I imagine my sister has just remembered that she doesn't have a harpsichord."

Chapter 8

During the next few weeks, Emma's life settled into something of a routine, albeit a rather exciting and entertaining one. Overnight, she had become one of the most sought-after members of London society. It was quickly decided (by whomever it is that decides these things) that, while her red hair was regrettable, the rest of her certainly wasn't, and so she was hailed a beauty, despite those fiery locks. Some of the more conservative matrons deemed her a little too bold (especially with "that red hair"), but most of the *ton* decided they rather liked talking with a female who could converse on topics other than ribbons and petticoats. And so Emma and Belle (who had acquired a similar although blonder reputation the previous year) went laughingly from party to party, enjoying their popularity immensely. For Emma, this time was a delightful interlude in a life that would surely take her back to her father in Boston where she, as his only child, would eventually defy current industry standards and take over his shipping business.

The only complication was, of course, the Duke of Ashbourne, who had emerged from his self-imposed exile and taken his place in society with a vengeance. No one had any doubts as to the reason for his sudden reappearance.

"He is positively stalking Emma," Caroline once grumbled.

To which his "prey" had shrewdly replied, "I'm not sure if he likes me or if he just likes to stalk."

Of course that statement was only half true. During the previous few weeks, Emma had seen Alex almost every day, and the friendship between them had developed into a fairly strong one. Emma was certain that Alex truly cared for her as a person and not just as some sort of prize to be won. Still, the friendship was often fraught with sexual tension, and, well, Alex did seem to enjoy stalking.

He was as quick as a lion and enjoyed surprising her. Once Emma had gone to a musicale he had said he did not plan to attend. She had been standing idly next to an open window when she felt a warm hand grab hers. She had jerked away, but the hand held firm, and she had heard a familiar voice whisper, "Don't make a scene."

"Alex?" Her eyes darted about. Surely someone noticed a hand snaking through the window.

But the rest of the partygoers had been involved in their own flirtations and didn't notice Emma's flustered expression. "What are you doing here?" she whispered urgently, keeping a benign smile pasted on her face.

"Come out to the garden," he had ordered.

"Are you crazy?"

"Maybe. Come out to the garden."

Emma, cursing herself fifty times for a fool, had made up a story about a tear her dress and stolen away. Alex was waiting for her in the garden, hidden among the trees.

"What are you doing here?" she repeated as soon as she found him.

He grabbed her hand and yanked her deeper into the shadows. "I figured you missed me," he replied cheekily.

"I most certainly did not!" Emma had tried to pull her arm back, but he wouldn't let go.

"Now, now, of course you did. It's all right to admit it."

Emma had grumbled and muttered something underneath her breath about overbearing aristocrats, but one look at his wicked smile was all it took to force her to admit to herself that she *had* missed him. "Did you miss me?" she countered.

"What do you think?"

She felt herself grow bold. "I think you did."

He had looked at her mouth then, looked at it with such longing and intensity that Emma was sure he was going to kiss her. Her mouth went dry, her lips parted, and she felt herself sway toward him. But all he had done was drop her hand with startling abruptness, flash her a smile, and murmur, "Until tomorrow, love."

In a blink of an eye, he had disappeared.

It was moments like these that had tied Emma's feelings into a tangled knot of confusion. No matter how many nights she laid awake thinking about him, she could not seem to sort out her thoughts about Alex.

On the one hand, his domineering attitude provoked her to no end. He was constantly trying to boss her around, although, Emma thought smugly, he was finding that to be no simple task. On the other hand, he was proving to be quite convenient as his mere presence effectively scared off most of her persistent suitors, which was fortunate since she hadn't wanted any suitors in the first place. She was always in demand at parties, but she had skillfully managed to avoid any awkward proposals of marriage.

To complicate matters, Emma was discovering that Alex was truly an entertaining escort and companion. He constantly challenged her intellect and, although he said the most outrageous things to her, she never tired of his company. She privately vowed, however, that he would never hear such high praise from her lips—his ego certainly did not need any polishing. But what most confused Emma was her physical reaction to the man. The mere sight of him somehow set her entire body quivering with expectation. Expectation for what, she wasn't exactly sure, although she imagined Alex knew. Once, when she was confiding her feelings to Belle (who was already up to *Hamlet* in her grand Shakespearean quest), she said that the only way she could describe her reaction to him was that she experienced a "heightened sense of reality."

"It's corny and trite, I know," Emma had remarked, "but it just seems that I'm so aware of everything when he's near. The scent of the flowers is stronger. My lemonade tastes sweeter, my champagne more potent. And it's so difficult not to look at him, don't you think? It's those green eyes of his; he should have been a cat. And then I get short of breath, and my skin *tingles.*"

Belle was blunt. "I think you're in love."

"Absolutely not!" Emma protested, aghast.

"You might as well accept it," Belle advised, pragmatic as usual. "In this day and age it's a rare thing to find someone you love, and it's even rarer to have enough money to be able to do something about it. Most people have to marry for family considerations, you know."

"Don't be silly. I certainly don't want to marry the man. He'd be absolute hell to live with. Can you imagine? He's insufferable, overbearing, domineering—"

"And he makes you tingle."

"The point is," Emma said, ignoring her cousin,

"that I don't want to get married to an Englishman. And he doesn't want to get married at all."

The Duke of Ashbourne's lack of interest in the matrimonial state, however, did not prevent him in the least from flirting with Emma outrageously and on every possible occasion. To be fair, Emma did her share of flirting, too, although she had to admit she wasn't nearly as skilled at it as he was. It was becoming great sport among the *ton* to watch Alex and Emma spar with each other, and wagers had already begun to appear in the books of all of London's most elite gentlemen's clubs as to whether and when the couple would finally marry.

But if any of the young lords who had made such bets had actually taken the time to ask Emma about the situation, she could easily have informed them that wedding bells were certainly not forthcoming in the foreseeable future. First of all, she didn't want to get married. Second of all, Alex didn't want to get married. But the most telling clue was that Alex hadn't even tried to kiss her once since that first night when he had stolen into her bedroom. *That* was what left Emma most puzzled. She suspected that it was all part of some master plan, for she was fairly certain he still desired her. Every now and then she'd catch him looking at her with a fiery gleam in his eye that made her tremble. At such times his gaze would burn hotly into her, leaving her breathless and dazed. Then after a few moments, he'd look sharply away, and the next time Emma saw his face, his cool, unflappable facade would be back in place.

Their sometimes easygoing, sometimes tense relationship continued quite peacefully in this manner until the night of the Lindworthys' ball.

Emma never suspected that the evening wouldn't

be like every other. She was particularly excited to attend the ball because Ned had just returned from a month-long jaunt to Amsterdam with his university friends, and she had missed his companionship during his absence. The entire Blydon household was a flurry of activity as everyone prepared for the evening.

"Emma Dunster! Did you take my pearl earrings?" Belle suddenly appeared in the doorway of Emma's room, resplendent in a low-cut gown of ice-blue silk.

Emma, who was seated at her dressing table, fussed with her hair and ignored Belle's question as she reached for a crystal vial of perfume. "Your father will kill you when he sees that gown."

Belle tugged at the bodice. "It's no worse than yours."

"Yes, but you'll note that I've got a shawl on." Emma smiled blithely.

"Which you will undoubtedly remove when we arrive at the Lindworthys'?"

"Undoubtedly." Emma dabbed a few drops of the scent on the side of her neck.

"But I don't have a shawl that matches this gown. Do you?"

"Only the one I'm wearing." Emma motioned to the ivory shawl that was draped over her bare shoulders. The pale material glowed against the dark green silk gown she had donned for the evening.

"Hell and damnation!" Belle swore, a little too loudly.

"I heard that!" her mother called from her bedroom down the hall.

Belle groaned. "I swear, she must have six sets of ears, her hearing is so good." •

"I heard that, too!"

Emma laughed. "I'd be quiet now before you're really sorry."

Belle made a face. "About those earrings . . ."

"I don't see why you think I'd take them when I've a perfectly good pair of my own. You probably just misplaced them."

Belle sighed dramatically. "Well, I don't know where—"

"Oh, there you are!" Ned's voice called from down the hallway. He poked his head into Emma's room. "You two look ravishing, as usual." He eyed his sister a little more closely. "Belle, are you sure you should be out in that gown? If I crane my neck just so"—he craned his neck in demonstration—"I can see straight down to your navel."

Belle's mouth dropped in horror. "You cannot!" she screeched, punching her brother in the arm.

"Well, maybe not quite, but almost," Ned grinned. "Besides, Father will never let you out of the house dressed like that."

"Half the women in the *ton* are wearing gowns like this. This is a perfectly acceptable style."

"Maybe to you and me," Ned replied, "but not to Mother and Father."

Belle planted her hands on her hips. "Did you come in here for a reason or were you just hoping to torture me?"

"Actually, I was wondering if you were sure that Clarissa Trent would not be attending the ball tonight."

"It would serve you right if she did show up, you miserable excuse for a brother," Belle snapped. "But you can relax, I'm completely certain she's gone to the country for an extended stay."

"Emma?" Ned wanted to be absolutely certain that the cruel girl who had scorned him earlier in the season would not be present to wound him again.

"As far as I know, she's left London," she replied offhandedly, studying her image in the mirror, trying to decide if she liked the hairstyle Meg had created for her.

"She's probably gone to nurse her wounds," Belle guessed, settling down onto Emma's bed.

"What do you mean?" Ned asked, striding into the room and perching next to his sister.

"I'm afraid Clarissa was a little miffed when she realized that Ashbourne was quite determinedly pursuing Emma," Belle smirked. "Clarissa kept throwing herself at him shamelessly, and I must say that his grace was very polite to her at first. Uncharacteristically polite, if you ask me. I think he was trying to impress Emma with his good manners."

"I doubt it," Emma said dryly.

"Well, what happened?" Ned asked impatiently.

"*This* is the good part." Belle leaned forward and smiled with glee. "About a week ago she absolutely *pressed* herself up against him, and believe me, her gown was far lower-cut than mine."

"And?" Ned urged.

"And Ashbourne simply gave her one of those cold stares he's so famous for and said—"

Emma cut in, lowering her voice in imitation of Alex's, "'Miss Trent, I can see down to your navel.'"

Ned's mouth fell open. "He didn't!"

"No, but I wish he had." Emma laughed uproariously, and Belle exploded into giggles.

"What did he really say?" Ned urged.

"I believe it was: 'Miss Trent, kindly remove yourself from my person.'"

Ned was ecstatic. "And then what happened?"

"For a moment I thought Clarissa was going to faint," Belle said animatedly. "At least a dozen people heard the remark, and she'd been telling everyone that she was out to snag him. Which was ridiculous, of course, because it's obvious to everyone that Ashbourne is only interested in Emma. Anyway, after giving everyone the most murderous glare, she fled the ballroom, and no one has seen her since. My guess is that she'll spend a month or so rusticating before she comes back to try to sink her claws into the Duke of Stanton."

"But he's well over sixty!" Ned exclaimed.

"And thrice widowed," Emma added.

"You know how women like Clarissa are," Belle sighed. "She's got it into her head that she wants a duke. Ashbourne was obviously the top choice since he's still young, but I doubt that Clarissa will be choosy now. She wants a title, and she wants it now. If she doesn't get a duke, mark my words, she'll start on the marquesses and earls. That's when *you* had better watch out, Ned."

"But I'm only a viscount."

"Don't be obtuse. You'll be an earl eventually, and Clarissa knows that."

"Well, you can be sure I'll avoid her assiduously now that I know what she's really like."

"You know, Ned, I think that you owe me a favor," Emma declared. "You'd probably still be pining over her if I hadn't sent you that fake love note."

Ned grimaced at the thought of being in Emma's debt. "Much as I hate to admit it, you're probably right. But don't get it into your head to continue meddling in my affairs."

"Oh, I wouldn't dream of it," Emma said innocently.

Belle and Ned both looked at her dubiously.

"It must be almost time to leave," Emma said, rising.

As if on cue, Caroline swept into the room. She was dressed in a lovely midnight-blue gown that complimented the stunning blue eyes she had passed on to both of her children. Her chestnut hair was swept up atop her head, and she certainly did not look old enough to have mothered two adult children. "We really must be off," she announced. With a quick turn of her head, she scanned the room until her eyes fell on her daughter. "Arabella Blydon!" she exclaimed, horrified. "What on earth are you wearing? I do not recall giving you permission to wear such a low-cut gown."

"Don't you like it?" Belle countered weakly. "I think it's rather flattering."

"*I* told her that one could see right down to her navel," Ned drawled.

"Edward!" Caroline said sharply. Emma whacked him in the shoulder with her reticule, flaying him with a mutinous glare. Caroline gave them only a passing glance before she continued her lecture. "I do not know what you were thinking. That gown will give men the wrong idea."

"Mama, everyone is wearing gowns like this now."

" 'Everyone' does not include my daughter. Where did you get that?"

"Emma and I bought it at Madame Lambert's shop."

Caroline whirled to face her niece. "Emma, you should have known better."

"Actually," Emma said truthfully, "I think Belle looks beautiful."

Caroline's eyes widened and she quickly turned back to her daughter. "You may wear that gown when you are married," she announced.

"Mama!" Belle protested.

"Fine!" Caroline huffed. "We'll ask your father. Henry!"

All three members of the younger generation groaned. "I'm sunk now," Belle mumbled.

"Yes, dear?" Henry Blydon, the Earl of Worth, ambled into the room. His brown hair was liberally streaked with silver, but he still retained the air of elegance and affability that had won Caroline's heart a quarter of a century earlier. He smiled lovingly at his wife. She looked pointedly at their daughter. "Belle," he said simply, "you're naked."

"Oh, fine! I'll change my gown!" Belle flounced out of the room.

"Goodness, that wasn't difficult at all, was it?" Henry smiled at his wife. "I'll be waiting for you downstairs." Caroline rolled her eyes and followed him.

"May I escort you, darling Emma?" Ned laughed, offering her his arm.

"But of course, Edward dearest." The two of them followed the older couple down the stairs. Belle proved to be quite speedy changing her gown, and within fifteen minutes the family was on its way to the Lindworthy mansion.

When they arrived, Belle, who had changed into pink silk, pulled Emma aside. "You had better be far, far away from Mother and Father when you take off that shawl," she advised.

"Don't I know it." Emma waited for Henry and Caroline to get swept up in the crush before she turned to Ned and said with mock imperviousness, "You may take my shawl now, Edward."

Ned responded in kind. "Oh, but you know I'm just dying to be your servant." He deftly took Emma's shawl and handed it to one of the Lindworthys' footmen. "Emma," he asked carefully, "you do realize that your dress is every bit as low-cut as Belle's?"

"Of course. We purchased them at the same time. Can you see down to *my* navel?" she asked daringly.

"I'm afraid to try. Ashbourne could descend from the shadows and wring my neck."

"Don't be silly. Oh, look! There's John Millwood. Let's go say hello." Emma, Ned, and Belle wended their way toward John and were soon lost in the crowd.

Alex arrived soon after and, as usual, mentally cursed himself for once again putting himself through the torture of a large London ball. Such affairs were only tolerable with the knowledge that he would find Emma and hopefully whisk her off and enjoy her company without a hundred other onlookers.

Unfortunately, Emma was *always* surrounded by admirers, and it was getting damned irritating. Every day he swore he'd give up this ridiculous process of seeking Emma out and every day he found himself longing to see her—and smell her and touch her—and sure enough, he donned his midnight black evening attire and headed out to participate in the endless round of parties.

The hard part was his damned foolish decision not to try to even kiss her. After seeing Emma nearly every single evening for the last couple of months, it was growing incredibly difficult to keep his hands off of her. Just when he thought he'd memorized every turn of her lips, she would surprise him with a new kind of smile, and he was immediately overcome with the desire to grab her and kiss her senseless. He'd wake up in the middle of the night knowing he'd been dreaming of her because his body was hard and hot with need.

And no other woman could satisfy this ache. He'd long since stopped visiting his mistress, and she'd politely informed him that she'd found another patron. Alex had only sighed with relief, glad to be rid of the expense.

He had originally decided to keep this physical distance between Emma and himself because he wanted to give her time to learn to trust him. When they finally did make love—and he was certain that they would; he only wondered if Emma realized the inevitability of it—he wanted it to be perfect. He wanted Emma to come to him because she wanted him and him only. He wanted her to come to him because she, too, was waking up in the middle of the night drenched with desire.

He just hoped that happened soon, because he was slowly going insane.

"Ashbourne!"

Alex turned to see Dunford making his way through the crowd. "Hello, Dunford, good to see you tonight. Have you seen Emma?"

"My, we *have* become somewhat single-minded these days."

Alex smiled with uncharacteristic sheepishness. "Sorry."

"Not at all." Dunford waved away Alex's apology.

"But have you seen her?"

"For God's sake, Ashbourne, when are you going to just marry the chit and put yourself out of this misery? Make her your duchess and you can see her twenty-four hours a day."

"Really, Dunford, it's hardly come to that." Alex dismissed the idea of a wedding with a flick of his head. "You know how I feel about marriage."

Dunford raised his eyebrows. "You're going to have to get married at some point, you know, if only to get yourself an heir. Your father would turn over in his grave if the title passed out of the family."

Alex winced. "Well, at least I have Charlie. He may not be a Ridgely, but he's certainly as closely related to my father as any child of mine would be."

"Emma's going to have to get married at some point, too. And it might not be to you."

Alex was stunned by the white hot streak of jealousy that shot through him at the thought of Emma lying in another man's arms. But, determined to maintain his unflappable facade, he only said, "I'll deal with that if it happens."

Dunford only shook his head, convinced that his friend was denying the obvious. If Alex wasn't in love with Emma, he was certainly obsessed with her, and that was a better basis for marriage than one usually found among the *ton*. "I did see Emma a few minutes ago," he said finally. "She was surrounded by men."

Alex growled.

"For God's sake, man, she's always surrounded by men. Get used to it," Dunford laughed. "You should just be thankful that most of them are terrified of you. At least half the crowd disperses at the mere mention of your name."

"Well, *that's* a blessing."

"If I recall, she was over there"—Dunford pointed to the far side of the room—"by the lemonade table."

Alex gave his friend a curt nod but tempered it with a smile. "It has, as always, been a joy, Dunford." He turned on his heel and began to push through the crowd. As he made his way toward the area where he hoped Emma was, he was continually waylaid by men and women eager for an audience with the influential Duke of Ashbourne. Alex quelled a few of them with his famous icy stare, nodded to some, exchanged words with a couple, and merely growled at the unlucky ones who caught him as he was finally finishing his journey.

He was not in a good mood.

That, of course, was when he finally caught sight of Emma. Her flaming hair always made her fairly easy to spot. Sure enough, she and Belle were surrounded by a pack of young men whose only problem in life seemed to be deciding to which cousin they should profess their undying love.

The sight of Emma's admirers did not improve his disposition.

He moved in a little closer. She looked ravishing, but then he'd expected that. She always looked ravishing to him. Her hair was piled atop her head, with wispy tendrils left to frame her delicate face. Her violet eyes sparkled animatedly in the candlelight. She threw back her head and laughed at some joke, giving Alex an unobstructed view of her long, pale throat, her creamy shoulders, and the barest hint of . . . Alex frowned. He could definitely see a little more than the barest hint of her breasts. Not that her dress was indecent, of course. Emma had far too much taste to appear vulgar. But if he could see the ample swell of her bosom, damn it, that meant every other man in the ballroom could see it, too.

Alex's already bad mood deteriorated rapidly.

He pushed his way into the crowd surrounding Emma and Belle. "Hello, Emma," he said sharply.

"Alex!" she exclaimed, her eyes glowing with unfeigned enthusiasm.

He strode to her without acknowledging her companions. "I believe you saved this dance for me," he stated, taking her hand and leading her somewhat forcefully to the dance floor.

"Really, Alex, you've got to stop being so autocratic," Emma scolded good-naturedly.

"Ah, a waltz," Alex commented as the orchestra began to play. "How fortunate." He swept her into his arms, and they began to twirl slowly around the room.

Emma briefly wondered why Alex was in such a strange mood but quickly dismissed such concerns, preferring to savor the delicious warmth she could find only in his arms. One of his hands rested lightly on her hip, but from the heat of it, Emma felt like she'd been branded. His other hand held her own, and Emma was convinced that a thousand tiny lightning bolts were shooting up her arm, straight to her heart. She closed her eyes and unwittingly made a soft, mewling sound from deep in her throat. She was completely and utterly content.

Alex heard the tiny sound and looked down at Emma. Her face was slightly turned up to his, her eyes were closed—she looked as if she'd just been thoroughly made love to. Alex's body reacted instantaneously. Every muscle clenched, and he felt himself growing painfully hard. He groaned.

"Did you say something?" Emma's eyes flew open.

"Nothing I can tell you about in the middle of a crowded ballroom," Alex muttered, beginning to steer her toward the French doors that led to the Lindworthys' garden.

"Ooooh, how intriguing."

"I wish you knew exactly how intriguing," Alex said under his breath.

"What did you say?" Amid the din of the crowded ballroom, Emma hadn't been able to understand his words.

"Nothing," Alex said in a louder voice, but the word came out more sharply than he'd intended.

"Whatever is wrong with you tonight? You're positively surly."

Before Alex could reply, the orchestra finished the waltz, and he and Emma bowed and curtsied to each other reflexively. When they were done with the social niceties, Emma repeated her question to him, this time in a more demanding tone. "Alex! What on earth is the matter?"

"Do you really want to know what's the matter?" Alex said harshly. "Do you?"

Emma nodded weakly, not at all sure that she was taking the wisest course of action.

"For God's sake, Emma, every man in this room is ogling you," he ground out, pulling her toward the French doors.

"Really, Alex, you say that to me every night."

"This time I mean it," he hissed. "You're practically falling out of that dress."

"Alex, you're making a scene," Emma shot back. He stopped dragging her but nevertheless continued out into the garden at a more respectable pace. "I don't see what has you so angry. At least half the women here under the age of thirty are wearing dresses which are far more revealing than mine."

"I don't care about those other women, damn it. I won't have you flaunting your charms for the whole world to see."

"Flaunting my charms? You make me sound like a loose woman. *Don't* insult me," Emma warned, her voice strained.

"Don't push me, Emma. You've led me a merry chase for damn near two months now, and I'm at my wit's end." He pulled her behind a large hedge that shielded them from view of the ballroom.

"Don't try to blame this on me. You're the one who is overly sensitive to my dress style!"

Suddenly, Alex reached out and grabbed her upper arms, pulling her close. "Damn it, Emma, you are mine. It's time you understood that."

She stared at him, dumbfounded. Although his actions during the previous weeks certainly demonstrated his possessive nature, this was the first time he had actually verbalized the sentiment. His green eyes were blazing with anger and desire, but there was something else there, too. Desperation.

Emma was suddenly very uneasy. "Alex, I don't think you know what you're saying."

"Oh, God, I wish I didn't!" Alex suddenly crushed her to him, his strong hands sinking into her fiery hair.

Emma gasped at the sheer force she felt in his body. He held her this way for a few long moments, nose to nose. His breathing was harsh and uneven, as if he were lost amidst some internal struggle. "Oh, Emma," he finally said in a ragged voice, "if you only knew what you do to me." With that, his mouth slowly lowered that last inch to cover hers.

The first touch was unbearably sweet, and Emma could feel his body shiver as he fought to contain his passion. His lips brushed softly over hers as he waited for a response. Emma couldn't help herself, and her arms snaked up to encircle his neck. That was all the encouragement Alex needed, and his hands moved down to her back, pressing her even more tightly against him. "I have waited so long to hold you like this," he murmured against her mouth.

Emma was lost in a sea of newfound passion. "I—I think I like it," she said shyly, entwining her fingers in his thick black hair.

Alex's low growl was a sound of pure masculine

satisfaction. "I knew it would be perfect. I knew you would be this responsive." He kissed these words against her jaw, then trailed his lips down to her throat.

Emma arched her head back, not understanding all of these new feelings yet unwilling to stop them, as she knew she should. "Oh, Alex," she moaned, clutching him tightly.

Alex quickly took advantage of the soft sound that escaped her lips by capturing her open mouth with his once more. His tongue darted in, caressing her deeply. His intimate touch brought such pure pleasure, Emma was amazed that she could still stand. She simply hadn't thought it was possible to feel with such intensity. Even their earlier kiss, illicitly shared in her bedroom, could not remotely compare to this one. That first kiss had been exciting because she hadn't known Alex. But now she did. She knew him well, and the knowledge that it was him holding her close made the intimacy all that much more spectacular. All she knew was that she wanted to get closer to him, much closer. She wanted to touch him in the ways he was touching her. Hesitatingly, she rubbed her tongue against the roof of his mouth. To her delight, Alex's response was immediate. Hoarsely moaning her name, he swiftly pulled her to him so that she was pressed intimately against his aroused manhood.

Emma was startled by the evidence of his rampant desire, and this realization of his urgency broke through her passion-induced haze. She was suddenly aware that she was swiftly heading into a situation she probably could not handle. "Alex?" she questioned softly.

Alex took her question to be another moan of desire. "Oh, yes, Emma, yes," he responded. His lips had traveled to her earlobe, which he was sucking gently, and one of his hands had covered her breast. Everything he was doing felt terribly perfect, and it was all Emma could do to say his name again, this time a little more forcefully.

"What, darling?" he asked, cradling her face in his hands as he prepared to tease her lips with his own again.

"I think it's time to stop," Emma said shakily.

Alex was agonized. He knew that she was right, but his body was throbbing, demanding release. But then again, he couldn't very well make love to her in the middle of the Lindworthys' garden. He released her slowly and turned away, his hands on his hips as he fought to regain control of himself.

"Alex? Are you angry with me?"

He didn't move. "No," he said slowly, his breathing still labored. "Just with myself."

Emma touched his shoulder comfortingly. "Don't blame yourself. I was as much at fault as you were. I could have stopped you at any time."

Alex turned around to face her. "Could you?" His smile was wry, and it didn't reach his eyes. He took another deep breath. "Well, Emma, you do realize that this changes things?"

Emma nodded, thinking that his words were an understatement if she'd ever heard one. She did, however, wonder just exactly *how* things were going to change.

"Perhaps you should sneak around to the washroom before you reenter the ballroom. Your hair is mussed," Alex advised, afraid that he'd once again lose control if he allowed himself to speak of anything other than the most mundane of matters. "I've been here before. If you go around the corner, there is a side entrance that leads to the main hallway. From there, you should be able to find a washroom without trouble."

Emma's hand reflexively flew to her head, and she quickly tried to assess the damage. "All right. If you go back now, I'll go fix my hair and won't show up for another fifteen minutes." Her voice sounded breathy, unnatural. "That should quell the gossip."

"It seems we have made a habit of orchestrating separate returns to ballrooms."

Emma smiled at him weakly before she turned and fled around the corner.

Chapter 9

E mma slunk along the side of the Lindworthys' home, muttering ungraciously to herself all the while.

"Of all the stupid things to do. Letting him drag me out of the ballroom into a deserted garden. I should have known something like this was going to happen."

Emma paused, grudgingly admitting to herself that she'd most definitely enjoyed Alex's kiss.

"All right, so I liked it," she grumbled. "But where does this leave me now? I'm prowling around like a burglar, hoping to find a side door that may or may not even exist. My slippers are getting wet, I've probably torn the hem of my dress on a rosebush, and he doesn't even have the least inclination to marry me."

Emma froze. Dear Lord, what had she just said? Thank goodness she had only been conversing with herself. Emma shivered and pursed her lips.

"Banish that thought, Emma Elizabeth Dunster," she commanded, edging around the corner to the back of the mansion. She didn't really want to marry Alex, did she? It was impossible. She'd always meant to go back to Boston and take over her father's company. When she got married, it would be to some nice American fellow who would be happy to run the company with her.

But what if she never found that nice American fellow? And was he really worth finding when she had a rather amazing British one right here, right now?

Emma sighed as the memory of Alex and their few stolen moments flooded her mind. It was time to be reasonable, she decided. Were there really any good reasons why she should even consider the idea of marrying Alexander Edward Ridgley, the oh-so-lofty Duke of Ashbourne?

Well, for one thing, he was a superb kisser.

Besides that!

All right then, he never talked down to her. So many men of the *ton* talked to women as if they were some lower species whose brains hadn't developed fully. Alex always treated her as if she were every bit as intelligent as he was.

Which she was, Emma silently declared with a nod of her head.

Also, she felt very comfortable in his presence. When they were together, she never felt as if she had to hide her true personality under a sheer layer of artifice and illusion. He seemed to like her just the way she was.

Furthermore, he had a delicious sense of humor which was remarkably similar to her own. He certainly liked to tease her mercilessly, but he was never malicious, and he could take a joke as well as he could deliver one. Life with Alex certainly would not be dull, she could count on that.

And, of course, he was a superb kisser.

Emma groaned as she practically fell through the side door. She was going to have to give this matter a little more thought.

Meanwhile, Alex had slipped back into the ballroom by way of the French doors and was doing his best to mingle graciously with a bunch of people in whom he did not usually have very much interest. But he was eager to appear cool and calm in case anyone had happened to notice his and Emma's rather hasty excursion into the garden.

He had just finished telling Lord Acton, a friend of his from White's, about a stallion he had recently purchased, when he spied Sophie and his mother across the ballroom.

"Excuse me," he said smoothly. "I see that my mother and sister have arrived. I really must go greet them." Alex gave his friend a nod and made his way through the crowd to his family.

Eugenia Ridgely, the dowager Duchess of Ashbourne, was not an imposing figure. Indeed, she couldn't have been an imposing figure if she tried. Her green eyes sparkled warmly, and her lips always seemed to form a vibrant smile. Accompanying this friendly demeanor was a dry sense of humor which had made her one of the most well-loved members of the *ton* for years. She'd been born the daughter of an earl and been exalted to the rank of duchess when she married Alex's and Sophie's father, but she had never developed the snobbery that was so rampant among most of society. Her eyes lit up as she saw her son crossing the ballroom in her direction.

"Hello, Mother," Alex said fondly, leaning down to kiss her on the cheek.

"Ah, Alex," Eugenia said dryly. "What a pleasure it is to attend a function and actually see you in person." She held out her cheek, dutifully waiting for his kiss.

It was easy to see where Alex had gotten his caustic tongue.

"Always a pleasure, Mother."

"I know it is, dear. Now where is that darling girl

who has pulled you out of hiding?" She craned her neck, looking for Emma's familiar red hair.

"Actually, I haven't seen her since I danced with her a half an hour ago."

"*I* saw her go out into the garden," Sophie said pointedly.

Alex shot her a dirty look. "I thought you were planning to retire from society."

Sophie beamed, smoothing her hands along her still-svelte figure. "Four months along, and I'm not showing yet. Isn't that lucky?"

"For you, perhaps. As for myself, I'm breathless in anticipation for the day you balloon to the size of a small heifer."

"You beast!" Sophie stomped on his foot.

Alex smiled wickedly. "Ah, my sweet bovine sister."

"Well, it is a pity that Emma isn't here," Eugenia said, pointedly ignoring her children's squabble. "I do so enjoy her company. When did you say you were going to ask her to marry you, Alex?"

"I didn't."

"Hmmm, I could have sworn you mentioned something to me about it."

"That would have been my evil twin brother," Alex said flatly.

Eugenia chose to ignore his sarcasm. "Really, dear, you are simply an idiot if you let her get away."

"So you've mentioned."

"I'm still your mother, you know."

"Believe me, I know."

"You should listen to me. I know what is best for you."

Alex cracked a smile. "I believe that *you believe* you know what's best for me."

Eugenia scowled. "You are so difficult."

Sophie, who had been uncharacteristically silent, suddenly piped up. "I think you should leave him alone, Mother."

"Thank you," Alex said gratefully.

"After all, I don't think she'd have him even if he asked."

Alex bristled. Of course she'd— He smiled sweetly at his sister. "You're trying to goad me."

"Yes, I guess I am. Sisters are supposed to do that, you know."

"It's not working."

"Really? I rather thought it worked beautifully. Your jaw clenched magnificently when I said she didn't want you."

"Ah, I do so adore my family," Alex sighed.

"Cheer up, dear," the dowager smiled. "We're better than most, you know. Take my word for it."

"I shall," Alex said, leaning down to give her another affectionate peck on the cheek.

"Oh, look!" the dowager suddenly exclaimed, motioning toward the dance floor. "There is your friend Dunford dancing with Belle Blydon. Perhaps you should claim the next dance with her. She's a sweet girl, and I wouldn't want her to get upset if she's left alone for the next dance."

Alex eyed his mother suspiciously. "Lady Arabella rarely lacks admirers."

"Yes, well, er, there's always a first time, and I would so hate to see her feelings hurt."

"You're trying to get rid of me, aren't you, Mother?"

"Yes, I am, and you're making it exceedingly difficult."

Alex sighed as he prepared to claim a dance with Belle. "Pray try not to plot my downfall in my absence."

When Alex was safely out of earshot, Eugenia turned to her daughter and said, "Sophie, we must act decisively."

"I agree completely," Sophie replied. "Except that I'm not exactly sure what kind of decisive move we need to make."

"I've given this matter considerable thought."

"I'm sure you have," Sophie murmured, her lips hinting at a smile.

Eugenia shot her a sharp look but ignored her statement. "I have concluded that what we need is a weekend in the country."

"What are you going to do? Force Alex to accompany you to Westonbirt and torture him until he agrees to ask Emma to marry him?"

"Nonsense. We'll ask the Blydons to join us. And of course we will insist that they bring their darling niece."

"It's brilliant!" Sophie exclaimed.

"And then we'll contrive to leave them alone on every possible occasion."

"Exactly. We'll encourage them to go on picnics together, take rides in the woods—that sort of thing." Sophie paused for a moment, pursing her lips in thought. "Alex will see through it, of course."

"Of course."

"But I don't think it will matter. He's so besotted with her, he'll do anything to get her alone—even if that means going along with your less-than-subtle schemes."

"Maybe he will just take the initiative and compromise her." Eugenia clapped her hands together in glee over that possibility.

"Mother!" Sophie exclaimed. "I cannot believe you said that. I can't believe you even thought it."

Eugenia sighed the sigh of weary mothers. "In my advanced years I find less and less of a need for scruples of any kind. Besides, for all his rakish ways, Alex is a man of honor."

"Yes, of course. He's only nine and twenty. I would imagine *he* still has a few scruples left."

Eugenia's green eyes narrowed. "Are you poking fun at me?"

"Absolutely."

"Hmmph. I hope you're enjoying yourself."

Sophie nodded enthusiastically.

"What I was trying to say," Eugenia continued, "is that if Alex happened to compromise our Miss Dunster in some way—"

"Ravish her, you mean," Sophie interrupted.

"Whatever you want to call it, but if such an event were to happen in the, er, heat of passion— you must agree that he would feel honor-bound to marry her afterward."

"Isn't this a rather drastic way of getting your son married off?" Sophie asked, still unable to believe that she was discussing such delicate matters with her mother. "And what about Emma? She might not be exactly thrilled about getting compromised, you know."

Eugenia looked her daughter straight in the eye. "Do you like Emma?"

"Yes, of course."

"Do you want Alex to marry her?"

"Of course I do. I would love to have Emma as a sister-in-law."

"Can you think of a woman who would make your brother happier?"

"Well, no, not really."

Eugenia shrugged her shoulders. "The end justifies the means, my dear, the end justifies the means."

"I cannot believe what a strategist you've become," Sophie said in a hushed whisper. "And furthermore, you can't even be certain that he'll compromise her!"

Eugenia's expression was smug. "He will certainly try."

"Mother!"

"Well, he will. I'm sure of it. I know a rake when I see one, even if he *is* my own son. Especially if he's my own son." Eugenia turned to Sophie with a knowing smile. "He's a lot like his father, you know."

"Mother!"

Her smile widened as she lost herself in memories. "Alex was born only seven months after our wedding. Your father was quite a lover."

Sophie clapped her hand to her forehead. "Don't say another word, Mother. I really do not want to know anything about the intimate details of my parents' lives." She sighed deeply. "I would really prefer to think of both of you as completely chaste beings."

"If we were completely chaste, my dear"— Eugenia chuckled and unceremoniously poked her finger at her daughter— "*you* would not be around now to talk about it."

Sophie flushed. "All the same, I'd rather not hear about it."

Eugenia patted her daughter comfortingly on her upper arm. "If it makes you feel better, my dear."

"It does, believe me. I simply cannot believe you're telling me this."

Eugenia smiled and shook her head. "Propriety, I'm afraid, has gone the way of scruples." With that, she wandered off into the crowd, in search of Lady Worth.

*   *   *

Belle and Dunford, meanwhile, were having a marvelous time waltzing around the ballroom. The waltz was still a rather new dance, and some considered it scandalous, but Belle and Dunford rather enjoyed it, and not just because it annoyed the more staid members of society. Their love of the dance stemmed mostly from the fact that the waltz allowed a couple to actually carry on a conversation without one or the other having to continuously turn his back. They were taking advantage of this feature, rather heatedly debating an opera they had both recently seen when Dunford abruptly changed the subject.

"He's in love with your cousin, you know."

Belle was widely regarded as one of the most graceful dancers among the *ton*, but this time she didn't just miss a step, she missed three. "He told you that?" she asked, agape.

Dunford gave her a little tug to get her back into the rhythm of the dance. "Well, not in so many words," he admitted, "but I've known Ashbourne for ten years, and believe me, he's never been so silly about a female before."

"I'd hardly call falling in love silly."

"That's not the point and you know it, Arabella dear." Dunford paused for a moment as he smiled innocently at Alex, who had just spotted him from across the ballroom. Turning back to Belle, he added, "The fact is he's absolutely crazy over your cousin, but I fear he's got it so firm in his head that he's not going to marry until he's nearly forty, that he won't do anything about it."

"But why is he so dead-set against marrying now?"

"When Ashbourne first made his appearance into society, he had already inherited his title, and he was also fabulously wealthy."

"And quite handsome."

Dunford smiled wryly. "It was a veritable feeding frenzy. Every unmarried lady—and quite a few of the married ones—set her cap for him."

"I should think he'd find the attention flattering," Belle surmised.

"Quite the opposite, actually. Ashbourne isn't blind, you know. It was excruciatingly apparent that most of the women who were fawning over him were more interested in becoming a wealthy duchess than they were in getting to know Alex himself. The whole experience quite turned him off the social scene. He left to fight on the Peninsula soon after, and I don't think his desire to go was entirely due to patriotic fervor. He doesn't exactly hold most women in the highest regard." Dunford paused and looked Belle straight in the eye. "Even you must admit that most *ton* ladies are really quite ridiculous."

"Of course, but Emma's not like that, and he knows it. I would think he'd be thrilled to find someone like her."

"That would be the sensible thing, wouldn't it?" The music came to a stop, and Dunford took Belle's arm and led her to the edge of the dance floor. "But somewhere along the way, this mistrust of women got translated into a decision to avoid marriage as long as humanly possible, and I imagine he's quite forgotten why he became so dead-set against getting married in the first place."

"If that isn't the stupidest thing I've ever heard!"

Before Dunford could answer, they heard a deep voice chuckle. "I have heard a lot of stupid things in my life, Belle. I'm intensely curious to hear the stupidest."

Belle looked up in horror at Alex, who was standing before her to ask her to dance. "Um," she improvised wildly, "Dunford here seems to think that, um, in operas, um, that people should sing less."

"He does, does he?"

"Yes, he does. He thinks that they should talk more." Belle looked at Alex hopefully. He didn't believe a word she was saying and she knew it. Still, she didn't think he'd heard them discussing him, and for that she was blessedly thankful. Unable to think of anything else to say, she gave Alex what she was sure must be a rather weak smile.

"My mother has ordered me to ask you to dance, Belle," Alex said frankly, grinning and ignoring her obvious distress.

"Goodness," Belle replied, "I had no idea that my popularity had sunk so low that men had to be forced by their mamas to ask me to dance."

"You needn't worry. My mother is simply trying to get rid of me so that she and my sister can arrange my life without my interference."

"Plotting your marriage, I imagine," Dunford surmised.

"No doubt."

"To Emma."

"No doubt."

"You might as well just give in and ask her."

"Don't hold your breath." Alex took Belle's arm and prepared to lead her out onto the dance floor. "After all, I'm not the marrying kind."

"Well," Belle declared sharply, "neither is she!"

Back in the side hallway, Emma had landed on the floor in an undignified tangle. Someone had left the side door open, but no candles had been lit in the hallway. As a result, Emma had not seen the doorway until she was right on top of it. She didn't even try to stifle a groan as she slowly rose to her feet, twisting her neck and limbs to stretch out her aching joints. Absently rubbing her sore backside, she found herself fervently wishing that the Lindworthys had thought to lay down a carpet in the hall.

"You know," she muttered, continuing the conversation she'd begun with herself in the garden, "it's fairly clear that Alexander Ridgely is a danger to your health, and you should endeavor to keep far away from him."

"I heartily agree."

Emma whirled around in shock and found herself facing an elegantly dressed, sandy-haired man in his late twenties. She recognized him immediately as Anthony Woodside, Viscount Benton.

Emma groaned inwardly. She had met Woodside during the first few weeks of the season and had disliked him instantly. He had been dangling after Belle for over a year and would not leave her alone, despite her obvious efforts to put him off. Emma had tried her hardest to avoid him at subsequent affairs, but oftentimes she simply could not escape a polite dance. There was nothing overtly offensive about him; his manners were nothing if not correct, and he was obviously intelligent. Emma's low regard for him was a reaction to far more subtle aspects of his character. The tone of his voice, the way he looked at her, the tilt of his head when he surveyed a ballroom—all of this somehow managed to make Emma feel extremely uneasy in his presence. He was a strange man, outwardly courteous to her but at the same time somewhat disdainful of the fact that she was American and did not possess a title. To top it off, Alex seemed to hold him in extremely low regard.

So Emma naturally was not overjoyed to find him facing her in the Lindworthys' hallway. "Good evening, milord," she said politely, trying to brush over the obvious fact that she was quite alone, far from the party, and had just literally fallen into the hallway from the garden. She prayed that he had not seen her sprawled on the floor, but one look at his sardonic smile told her that she was not so blessed.

"I trust you are not injured from your fall."

Emma was exceedingly annoyed to note that he spoke those words to her bosom. She was acutely uncomfortable and longed to tug her dress up, but she would not give the obnoxious viscount the satisfaction of realizing that he unnerved her. "Thank you for your concern, milord," she said through gritted teeth. "But I assure you that I am perfectly fine. If you'll excuse me, however, I really must be getting back to the party. My family will be missing me." Emma started to leave, but he quickly grabbed her upper arm. His grip was not painful, nor was it cruel, but Woodside held her firmly, making it abundantly clear that he did not intend for her to leave anytime soon.

"My dear Miss Dunster," he said smoothly, his silky voice belying his iron grip on her arm. "I find myself intrigued by your presence in a deserted hallway just now."

Emma said nothing.

Woodside's grip tightened slightly. "No sharp comeback, Miss Dunster? Where is that famous wit of yours?"

"My wit is reserved for my friends," she replied icily.

"And your family?"

Emma blinked, unsure of what to make of that comment.

"I have a feeling, Miss Dunster, that you and I will soon be much closer than mere friends."

He let go of her arm abruptly, and Emma snatched it back. "If you think that I would deign to—"

Woodside let out a sharp laugh at the hot determination of her voice. "Really, Miss Dunster, I would not flatter myself so, were I you. I grant that you are attractive, but you do lack the breeding that I require in a woman."

Emma took a step back, wondering if he was speaking about her or a horse.

"I am a Woodside. We may tumble gaudy-haired Americans, but we certainly do not marry them."

Emma's free hand shot up to slap his face, but he blocked her blow before it connected.

"Now, now, Miss Dunster, it wouldn't do for you to antagonize me. After all, once I am married to your cousin, I can easily forbid her to associate with you."

Emma laughed in his face. "You think Belle will marry you? She can hardly bear to dance with you."

Woodside tighted his hold on her wrists until Emma could not help but wince from the pain. Her distress pleased him, and his pale eyes glittered dangerously in the dim light of the hallway. Emma lifted her chin stubbornly, and he abruptly let her go, causing her to stumble back a few steps.

"You shouldn't waste your time with Ashbourne, my dear. He'd never marry the likes of you." With that, Woodside laughed, executed a smart bow, and disappeared into the darkness.

Emma rubbed her sore wrists, slightly disconcerted by the encounter. She couldn't remain in the hallway all night, however, and so she started quietly opening and closing doors, searching for a washroom. After about five tries, she found one and scooted inside, shutting the heavy door behind her. A candle had been left burning inside a lantern, dimly lighting the small chamber. Emma groaned as she surveyed the damage in a looking glass. She was a complete mess. She quickly decided that she lacked the necessary skill to fix her hairstyle, so she pulled out all of her hairpins and left them on the counter, figuring the Lindworthys could think whatever they pleased when they found the pile the next day. She picked up the emerald-studded clasp that had originally held her topknot in place and used it to secure the front of her hair on the top of her head, allowing a few fiery tendrils to curl softly about her face.

"That ought to do," she breathed. "Hopefully no one will notice that I've changed the style. I wear it like this most of the time anyway."

A quick check of her dress revealed that while a few blades of grass had stuck to her hem, no permanent damage had been done. She plucked off the grass and left the blades on the counter with her hairpins. All the more mystery for the Lindworthys to enjoy the next day, she decided, consoling herself with the idea that she might be making her hosts' lives a little more interesting. She scanned her hem for any more errant blades but finally gave up, figuring that if she missed any, at least her gown was green. It was more important than ever that no one suspect her whereabouts. It would not be so dreadful if it were whispered that she had been alone with Alex. But if anyone realized that she had been alone with Woodside— *that*, she could not bear. She still couldn't believe he actually thought Belle would marry him. That must have been what he meant when he said they would someday be more than friends. Emma shivered with distaste, trying to put Woodside out of her mind.

She put her hand on the doorknob and took a

deep breath to regain her composure. Her slippers were undeniably wet, but there was really very little she could do about that, so she stepped back into the dark hallway, hoping she could navigate her way back without further mishap.

When she returned to the noisy ballroom, she poked her head in, anxiously scanning the faces until her gaze fell upon Belle. Emma had never felt more relieved. A more careful scrutiny, however, revealed that Belle was accompanied by Alex and Dunford, and Emma resigned herself to the fact that she was not going to be able to talk to Belle in private. After about thirty seconds of making bizarre hand gestures and praying that nobody saw her, she finally caught her cousin's eye, and Belle came scurrying over, the two men close at her heels.

"Where have you been?" Belle asked urgently. "I've been looking all over for you."

"I was otherwise occupied," Emma commented dryly, her eyes resting meaningfully on Alex's face. Belle did not miss the silent interchange, and she also turned to Alex, hands on hips.

"Good Lord," Dunford drawled. "I feel extremely fortunate that I am not on the receiving end of so many scowls."

"I wasn't scowling," Emma replied, shooting Dunford a look that came dangerously close to a scowl. "I was merely giving him a pointed look. At any rate, it's all over and done with and not very important."

Alex studied her face, thinking to himself that it was, indeed, very important, and furthermore, it was far from over and done with.

"The point is," Emma said, turning to Belle and directing her comments quietly to her, "that I've changed my mind, and I don't feel like getting into an argument with Uncle Henry and Aunt Caroline about the dress." Not to mention Alex.

"Good idea," Belle agreed.

Emma turned back to the two men. "If the two of you would go fetch my shawl, I'd be most appreciative."

"Don't see why it takes two grown men to get a shawl," Dunford pondered.

"Dunford," Belle said determinedly. "Will you please just go?"

Dunford muttered something about hostile blondes, but he dutifully crossed the ballroom to fetch Emma's shawl. And after a fair amount of subtle hints and downright nagging, Alex was persuaded to join him. They returned just in time, for it was only moments after Emma had wrapped the fabric around her pale shoulders when Lady Worth suddenly appeared, a wide smile brightening her features.

"I have marvelous news," she said, turning to the two young women. "Eugenia has invited us all out to Westonbirt for a short holiday." She tilted her head slightly so that she could address Alex. "Isn't that marvelous?"

"Marvelous," he replied with a tight smile, unable to decide whether he wanted to thank his mother or throttle her.

Caroline turned quickly back to Belle and Emma. "Henry has a headache, and I'm afraid that we are going to have to make our excuses immediately. She looked back up at Alex and Dunford. "I'm terribly sorry, but I'm sure you understand . . ." Before either man could reply, Caroline had whisked her two charges away, and within minutes, the entire Blydon family was ensconced in their carriage.

Chapter 10

S eated in the plush carriage, Emma began to replay the past few minutes in her mind and decided that her aunt was acting a trifle strangely—she had certainly never before witnessed such a hasty excursion from a ballroom. She was afraid, however, that Caroline's odd behavior might be a result of her having seen Emma disappear out into the garden with Alex. Emma wisely decided not to mention anything and sat back, waiting for someone else to make conversation.

Belle soon filled the gap. "I can't believe that the dowager just invited us all out to the country on the spur of the moment. Well, maybe I can believe it," she said, looking pointedly at Emma.

Emma looked pointedly away from Belle.

"I am sure we shall all have a marvelous time," Caroline declared firmly. "Eugenia was particularly hoping to spend some time with the two of you," she added, motioning to her daughter and niece.

"I'm sure she was," Ned drawled, winking at Emma.

It was fairly obvious that everyone understood the real reason for the outing.

"Also, Sophie has been missing her husband dreadfully," Caroline added. "Eugenia and I both thought that she would enjoy some feminine company, especially with her baby coming soon." She turned back to her son, not wanting to give anyone a chance to point out that Sophie's baby was not coming for another five months and that furthermore, her condition had very little to do with Eugenia's motives. "You're invited too, of course. Will you come, Ned?"

"I think I'll pass," Ned replied with a wicked grin. "It's much easier to debauch myself when my parents are gone."

Caroline looked somewhat shocked.

Ned only laughed. "It's hard to establish a rake's reputation in the company of one's mother."

"Really, Ned, if you must indulge yourself in such ways, there will be plenty of time after you finish school and move into your bachelor's lodgings."

"No time like the present."

"What are you going to do while we're gone?" Belle asked eagerly.

He leaned forward with a twinkle in his eye. "Lots and lots of things you shouldn't even think about."

"Really? What—"

"Isn't it a blessing," Caroline cut in loudly, eager to change the course of the conversation, "that we have the opportunity to retire to the country for a short while with the Ridgelys, where, without the censorious eyes of London upon us, we can relax our standards of behavior. Somewhat." The carriage came to a halt in front of the Blydon mansion, and, with the aid of her husband, she disembarked and hurried up the front steps and into the foyer.

Emma lost no time in catching up with her aunt. "Don't think I don't know what you're doing," she said in a loud whisper.

Caroline paused for a moment. "Of course you know what I'm doing." She patted her niece on the cheek. "Just as *I* know what *you're* doing."

Emma's mouth fell open as she stared at her aunt in dismay.

"You were wise, my dear, to put that shawl back on." With that, she swept up the stairs and into her bedroom.

The Blydons and the Ridgelys left for the country the following weekend, and much to Alex's extreme irritation, he was not able to arrange affairs so that he and Emma could have a private coach on the trip to Westonbirt. He couldn't even manage to get them into the same carriage. Much as Eugenia was yearning for some kind of compromising situation (which would hopefully lead to a wedding with all possible haste), she couldn't quite bring herself to do anything that might lead to such an incident taking place in a moving vehicle.

So Alex grumbled—and not terribly good-naturedly—as he climbed into the Blydons' coach alongside Henry, Caroline, and his mother, who had declared that the young people should have a carriage of their own so that they could have some fun without their stodgy elders.

"Young people!" Alex had exclaimed. "For God's sake, Sophie's expecting her second child!" And then he muttered something that Eugenia could not quite understand, although she did think she heard the word "stodgy."

"Well," declared Eugenia, "I daresay we won't all be old. I asked Charlie to ride with us."

At which point the young boy leapt into his uncle's arms, insisting that they practice their card games along the journey.

Emma, whose feelings had been fluctuating between secretly hoping for a carriage alone with Alex and kicking herself for entertaining such a thought, was nonetheless pleased at the prospect of three or four hours of conversation and gossip with Belle and Sophie. They first went through all the young unmarried ladies of the *ton*, animatedly dissecting their characters, and when they were done, they started in on the unmarried men. At that point, they were only a little more than halfway to their destination, so they turned to the spicier topic of married ladies and gentlemen. They had begun discussing the various dowagers when Sophie finally declared that they were nearly at Westonbirt. Emma was more than a little relieved. Quite frankly, she was gossiped out.

Alex had told her that he'd spent most of his childhood years at Westonbirt, the ancestral seat of his family, and Emma was intensely curious about the place where he had grown up. So when the carriage rounded a corner and headed through the front gates of the estate, Emma could not restrain herself from craning her neck to see as much of the landscape as possible. The carriage, however, was not an open one, so she had to resign herself to pressing her face up against the glass windows.

"For goodness sake, Emma, one would think you'd never seen a tree before," Belle commented.

Emma immediately sat back into the plush seat, instantly embarrassed about her overly curious behavior. "Well, I do so like the country, you know, and after three months in London, I certainly feel like I've never seen a tree before."

Sophie laughed softly. "I assure you we have plenty of trees here at Westonbirt. Good climbing ones, too. And there is also a rather picturesque stream which Alex assures me is full of trout, although I don't remember his ever bringing any home to dinner."

Just then the wheels of the carriage ground to a

halt, and a liveried footman rushed out to open the
door. Emma was the last to alight, so she didn't get
a very good view of Westonbirt until she finally
escaped the confines of the carriage. She was not
disappointed. Westonbirt was a stately old mansion that defied the word "huge." Built during the
1500s under the reign of Elizabeth I, its floor plan
was in the form of the letter *E* to honor the queen.
The front of the house, which faced north, was the
stem of the *E*, with three wings jutting out in back.
Row upon row of tall, thin, sparkling clean windows danced across the facade, and Emma guessed
that the building must be at least four or five stories tall. As she stepped closer, she was able to
inspect some of the fine craftsmanship of the mansion. Each window and doorway was bordered by
exquisite stone carvings that bespoke of hours of
painstaking work on the part of long-gone artisans.
Emma was awed by the grace and dignity of the
Ashbourne ancestral home.

"Sophie," she breathed reverently. "I can't believe
you actually grew up here. I feel like a princess just
standing in front of it."

Sophie smiled. "I suppose one gets used to the
things one grows up around. But you must see the
rest. The back courtyards are really quite lovely."

"I had hoped Alex might show her the rest."
Sophie, Emma, and Belle turned around to see
Eugenia walking up to them. Several yards away,
Henry was helping his wife down from their car-
riage, and Alex was being mauled by Charlie.

"Oh, I would love to see more," Emma exclaimed.
"I do so love to get out into the country, and the
weather is truly perfect." Sure enough, the gods
had been smiling on England that day. The sky was
cerulean blue, lightly dotted with fluffy clouds, and
the sun shone warmly on Emma's face.

"Alex!" Eugenia called out. "If you can manage to unwrap Charlie from around your neck, I would like you to show Emma a bit of the area."

Emma turned to Belle as Alex tried to loosen Charlie's viselike grip. "Why don't you join us, Belle?"

"Oh no," Belle answered, a little too quickly. "I really couldn't. I accidentally took two copies of *King Henry IV*, Part II from our library this morning." She held up two volumes, both bound in crimson leather, which she had brought into the carriage in case Sophie and Emma had decided to take naps. "I really need to get a copy of *King Henry IV*, Part I right away, and Sophie has promised me that I may borrow it from the library here. I don't know why we have two copies of the second part at home . . ." Her words trailed off.

"I can't imagine," Emma said, well aware that just about everybody had been planning for this moment.

"I can't very well read Part II before Part I," Belle added. "That would be like reading the last few pages of a novel before you started it."

"Not to mention how disruptive that would be to your alphabetic order," Emma put in, not without a small dose of sarcasm.

"I hadn't even thought of that," Belle exclaimed. "Now it is even more imperative that I get my hands on that play."

"Do not question providence," Alex advised as he took Emma's arm, Charlie loping along behind him. "Why don't you get changed into your riding habit, and I'll give you a tour. We'll do the fields now while the sun is out, and I'll show you 'round the house this evening."

Charlie immediately wedged his way between the couple and started jumping up and down.

"Can I come, too? Please, please may I come?" he chirped.

"Not this time, dear," Sophie hastily interjected. "I think you should check on Cleopatra. Mrs. Goode tells me she's due to have kittens very soon. Perhaps even this weekend."

The possibility of kittens proved to be far more exciting than a ride through the nearby fields with Alex and Emma, and Charlie quickly yelped, "Brilliant!" and tore off toward the kitchens, where the black and gold cat made her home right next to one of the ovens.

Within twenty minutes, Emma had settled into her spacious room in the west wing, changed into a fashionable midnight-blue riding habit, and hurried back to the front of the house, where Alex was already waiting for her. He was standing on the front steps, staring at some far off grassy hill when Emma arrived. She silently studied his finely chiseled profile, thinking that she had never seen him look as handsome as he did right at that moment in his expertly cut bottle-green jacket and buff-colored breeches. Her emotions had been in a jumble since their passionate kiss a few nights earlier, and the mere sight of him staring so resolutely into the distance set them churning anew. Emma sighed softly, wondering if she would ever regain her internal balance around this complex man. At the sound of her sigh, Alex turned abruptly to face her, his expression still so serious that Emma suddenly felt terribly self-conscious. Smiling shyly, she smoothed down the blue skirts of her dress with her hands. She parted her lips to speak but couldn't think of anything to say. For the past few months, she and Alex had settled into a comfortable, friendly relationship, constantly bantering with one another as if they had been friends since childhood. But Alex was right. The kiss in the Lindworthys' garden had altered their friendship, and she felt almost as awkward as she had when they had first met.

"I trust your room is suitable?" Alex inquired suddenly.

Emma quickly looked up into his face. The highly charged silence had been broken, and while she missed the sense of intimacy she'd found in his intense stare, she welcomed the return of her wits. "Of course. Your home is lovely. Although," she said laughingly, "I swear I'll never get used to the size of your foyer. I could fit my entire Boston townhouse in it. It would be a close fit in height, however. I might crush your chandeliers." Emma looked up at the crystal chandeliers that dangled from the ceiling, some forty or fifty feet above her. "However does one clean those?"

Alex smiled as he took her arm. "Very carefully, I imagine." He motioned toward the stables, and the two of them descended the steps and strolled in that direction. "I thought I might show you some of Westonbirt on horseback," Alex said, "because it's really a bit too large to do on foot."

Emma smiled in anticipation. "I haven't ridden in ages," she breathed.

Alex looked down at her with disbelief. "Really, Emma, I see you in Hyde Park all the time on that cozy little white mare of your cousin's."

Emma rolled her eyes. "Goodness, you cannot call *that* riding. One can barely trot in that congested park, much less gallop. Besides, even if I could gallop, people would be talking about my *scandalous* behavior for weeks." Emma made a face. "One would think people would have something more interesting to talk about, wouldn't one?"

Alex narrowed his eyes as he looked down at

her. "Why do I get the feeling we're no longer talking about a hypothetical situation?"

"It's possible that I might have ridden my mare through the park at something that could have been described as 'breakneck' speed," Emma conceded, her face a picture of innocence.

He chuckled. "And people talked about it for weeks?" At her nod, he mused, "I wonder why I didn't hear about it."

This time it was Emma's turn to laugh. "I am afraid no one is brave enough to mention my name in your presence, much less malign me in any way." She broke free of his grasp and skipped toward the stables, lifting her dark skirts up so that she could move quickly. Turning around to face him, she called out, "It's marvelous, really. You'll never find out about all the *shocking* things I do, and so I can enjoy a positively angelic reputation in your eyes!"

Alex increased his stride. "'Angelic' is not quite the word that comes to mind."

"Oh?" She continued walking backwards, glancing behind her every few moments to make sure she didn't trip over a tree root.

"'Hellion' is considerably more appropriate."

"Ah, but 'angelic' is an adjective and 'hellion' is a noun, so you cannot use one in the place of the other."

"God save me from educated females," Alex muttered.

Emma paused for a second, wagging her finger at him. "I heard that, you louse."

"I cannot believe you just called me a louse."

"I'm the only one brave enough to do it."

"I'll say," Alex replied, his expression petulant.

"Besides," Emma said, continuing her backwards move toward the stables, "educated women are far more interesting than uneducated ones."

"So the educated women keep telling me."

Emma stuck out her tongue.

"I'd stop now," Alex advised.

She smiled archly. "Do you think I'm not a worthy adversary?"

"Not at all," he said with utmost composure. "I meant you should stop walking. You're about to fall into a trough."

Emma yelped and jumped forward. Turning quickly around, she saw that Alex had not been joking with her and, indeed, she'd just been saved from a soaking. "That water doesn't look terribly clean," she commented, scrunching up her nose.

"Its odor also appears to be considerably less than pleasant."

"Well," she declared, "I suppose I ought to thank you."

"That would be a delightful change," he said, smiling.

She ignored him. "I imagine I'll have to watch where I'm going from now on."

"Perhaps you'll accept my escort?"

She smiled sunnily. "But of course."

Emma took Alex's arm as they walked the rest of the short distance to the stables. When they arrived they were immediately met by a groom, who led out two horses.

"Mrs. Goode sent over a picnic lunch, yer grace. It's waiting for you over there on the bench." The groom handed the reins to Alex.

"Excellent," Alex replied. "And thank you for getting the horses ready for me on such short notice."

The groom beamed. "It were no trouble at all, yer grace, no trouble at all," he said, shifting his weight from foot to foot.

Alex led the horses out into the open. "Here you

are, love," he said, handing Emma the reins to a spirited chestnut mare.

"Oh, she's gorgeous," Emma sighed, stroking the mare's shiny coat. "What do you call her?"

"Delilah."

"That's encouraging," she muttered. "I suppose yours is called Samson."

"Good God, no," Alex responded. "That could prove to be far too dangerous."

Emma looked at him suspiciously, wondered if he were talking about something other than horses, and then decided against saying anything.

Alex quickly grabbed the picnic lunch that his housekeeper had put into a sack for them, and they mounted their horses and were off.

They started out at a trot, moving fairly slowly since Emma was avidly interested in the scenery. Westonbirt was a fertile land of rolling green hills, liberally dotted with pale pink and white wildflowers. Although a great deal of the estate had been used for agriculture for several centuries, the wide fields that immediately bordered the house had been left unfarmed so that the family could enjoy all of the benefits of the countryside in relative privacy. The section through which they were riding was not heavily wooded, although it did possess several large, sturdy oaks that Emma was convinced would make excellent climbing trees. Smiling contentedly, she took a deep breath of the fresh, country air.

Alex smiled at her audible sigh. "It's different out here, isn't it?" he commented.

"Hmmm?" Emma was too content to formulate a complete sentence.

"The air. It's cleaner. It almost tastes good to breathe."

She nodded. "I feel as if I'm purifying myself

with each breath, washing away the London grime from the inside out. I don't think I had realized how much I'd missed the country until I got here."

"I feel the same way every time I'm able to escape town," Alex agreed with a wry smile. "But then after a few weeks I find I'm bored almost to the state of tears."

"Perhaps," Emma said boldly, "you haven't had the right company."

Alex turned his head to face her, slowing his horse to a halt as he looked at her closely. Emma stopped her horse as well, returning his direct gaze. After a few long moments, Alex finally broke the silence. "Perhaps," he said, so softly Emma could barely hear him. He tore his eyes from her and looked straight ahead, shielding his eyes from the sun. "Do you see that tree ahead?" he asked. "Up on the ridge?"

"The one with the peach-colored blossoms?"

Alex nodded sharply. "Yes. I'll race you to it. And I'll even give you a head start, since you're trapped on that monstrous invention they call a sidesaddle."

Emma didn't say a word. Nor did she wait for Alex to yell "go." She simply took off at breakneck speed. When she arrived at the finish line (or rather, the finish tree), one length ahead of Alex, she was laughing with delight, both at her winning the race and at the glorious feeling of complete abandon. Her hair had almost completely broken free of its topknot, and she reached up to unfasten the rest, unselfconsciously shaking her head to let the fiery locks roll down her back.

Alex fought the urge to let himself become captivated by her seductive movement. "You might have waited for the race to begin," he said with an indulgent smile.

"Yes, but then I probably wouldn't have won."

"The point of a horse race is that the best rider should win."

"The point of *this* horse race," Emma replied, "was that the most quick-witted rider won."

"I can see I'm not going to win this argument."

Emma smiled innocently. "Are we arguing?"

Alex cleared his throat. "I can see I'm not going to win this discussion."

"Can one win a discussion?"

"If one *can*," he said in a resigned tone, "I am certainly not doing so."

"You're very astute."

"*You're* very stubborn."

"My father has been complaining about it for twenty years."

"Then I suggest we break for sustenance," Alex said with a sigh. He dismounted quickly, taking with him the satchel with the picnic lunch that the groom had handed him.

"By the way," Emma said as Alex reached up and slid her out of the saddle. "You never did tell me what the name of your horse was."

"Cicero." Alex flashed her a smile as he spread a brightly colored blanket on the ground.

"Cicero?" Emma looked over at him with disbelief. "I had no idea you were so fond of Latin."

"I hate it." Alex grimaced as he remembered hellish Latin lessons at the hands of his boyhood tutors and then later at Eton and Oxford. He sat on the blanket and started to pull food out of the satchel. "I detest it."

"Then why did you name your horse after a Latin orator?" Emma laughed softly as she lifted her skirts slightly above her ankles, daintily settling onto the blanket across from Alex.

He smiled boyishly and tossed her an apple.

"Don't know, really. Just liked the sound of it."

"Oh. Well, that's as good a reason as any, I suppose. I was never terribly fond of Latin myself. It's not as if you could actually talk to anyone with it—besides a few clergymen, I suppose."

As Emma rolled the apple between her palms, Alex reached into the bag and pulled out a bottle of wine and two elegant glasses that had been wrapped in a piece of flannel to keep them from breaking. When he looked back up, Emma was leaning down away from him, studying a small pink wildflower. He gazed down at her and sighed, thinking that he couldn't imagine a more pleasant way to spend an afternoon than riding aimlessly around Westonbirt with Emma. That disturbed him. He didn't like the fact that his happiness and peace of mind were slowly growing dependent on the bewitching, auburn-haired woman seated across from him. When she had come down the stairs earlier that afternoon, she'd looked so heartbreakingly beautiful he had thought he'd been paralyzed. And he knew that she felt the same attraction. He could see it in her eyes. Emma didn't know how to hide her emotions.

But he had to admit to himself—it wasn't just that he was attracted to Emma. Put simply, he liked her. Her wit was razor-sharp, she was as well educated—if not better—than most of the men he knew, and unlike most of the *ton*, she knew how to make a joke without insulting someone in the process. His friends and family kept telling him that he ought to snatch her up, marry her before someone else did or she went back to Boston.

But he absolutely, positively, did not want to be married.

But then again, he was going to go insane if he didn't make love to her soon.

He looked over at her again. She was still

examining the wildflower, pursing her lips in thought as she turned it over to look at its underside. Was she really worth the price of his freedom? Was anyone?

He ran his fingers through his thick hair. Lately he'd been getting kind of depressed when he didn't see her at least once a day.

Emma suddenly looked up, her violet eyes bright with enthusiasm. "Alex?" she inquired, holding out the blossom she'd been examining.

Alex sighed as he met her gaze. He wondered if she'd mind if he threw her down on the blanket and tore off her clothing.

"Have you ever looked at one of these flowers?" she asked. "I mean *really* looked at it? It's quite fascinating."

She looked heartbreakingly innocent. Even more so than usual. Alex sighed again. She'd probably mind.

Chapter 11

Emma immediately noticed the predatory gleam in Alex's eye and braced herself for his attack.

Well, "braced" was perhaps not the most accurate word, she soon decided, recognizing the telltale fluttering of her stomach and quickening of her breath. With a barely audible sigh, Emma cursed herself for her weakness around this man. She gazed up at the handsome face that had become so achingly familiar to her. Alex's green eyes glowed with the promise of something she didn't quite understand but somehow yearned for all the same. Emma swallowed convulsively and wet her lips, lost in his emerald stare. Nervously, she caught her lower lip between her teeth and lowered her violet eyes. If she was going to be honest with herself—and she was desperately trying to do so, regardless of how difficult that task was proving to be—she really had to admit that the truth of the matter was that she wasn't "bracing" herself for anything. In fact, she was eagerly awaiting Alex's next move.

It was all no matter anyway, because Alex didn't "attack," and it was soon apparent that he had no plans in that direction. When Emma turned away, he did not reach over and touch her chin to raise her eyes back to his. Nor did he make any attempt to pull her into his arms. Rather, he turned back to the forgotten bottle of wine in his right hand and busied himself uncorking it.

Emma pushed an errant strand of fiery hair behind her ear and sighed again, wondering how long she and Alex were going to continue in this state of nearly constant tension. She hadn't the least idea how the situation could be resolved, nor could she guess what the outcome would be, but she felt that *some*body was going to have to do *some*thing, and soon. She looked up at Alex, who was pulling the cork out of the wine bottle with a flourish. "Do you need any help with anything?" she inquired politely, mentally scolding herself for not having the courage to say something bold.

The cork slipped out of the bottle with a loud "pop." Alex looked up at Emma, who was sitting quietly, her dark skirts fanned out over her legs. "Well, I suppose you could unpack the lunch," he replied, picking up the satchel. Their hands touched briefly as he handed her the bag, and Emma felt a sharp tingle travel up her arm. Almost involuntarily, she jerked her arm back, surprised by the intensity of her reaction to such a fleeting touch. She looked quickly back up to his face. Alex tore his gaze from her with just as much speed, but Emma could swear that she saw a shy smile cross his features before he saw to the task of pouring the wine. Good Lord, she must be losing her mind if she thought that Alex would ever entertain anything resembling a shy emotion.

Alex, meanwhile, was wondering how he was going to keep his hands off of her if he let himself look at her for more than a split second. "Tell me about your childhood," he said quickly, eager to focus the conversation on something that could not possibly take a provocative turn.

"My childhood?" Emma took the wine glass he held out to her. "What do you want to know?"

"Anything," Alex replied, lazily leaning back and resting on his elbows.

"I'm twenty years old," she reminded him with a twinkle in her eye. "That's quite a lot of time to cover in one afternoon."

"Then tell me about the worst thing you ever did."

"The *worst* thing?" Emma tried to look affronted but didn't succeed, unable to suppress a few giggles. "Surely you don't think I was a troublesome child?"

"Of course not," Alex said mildly, taking a sip of his wine before placing the glass down on a flat spot of land. A devilish smile crept across his face. "I imagine you were a hellion."

Emma laughed out loud and placed her glass down beside his. "Well, I surely looked like one." She twirled a lock of her hair around her fingers. "If you think my hair is bright now, you should have seen me when I was ten. I looked like a carrot!"

Alex smiled at the thought of a miniature Emma racing around her Boston home.

"And I had so many freckles," Emma continued.

"You still have a few across the bridge of your nose," Alex could not help pointing out, thinking that he'd like to kiss every one of them.

"It is very ungentlemanly of you to notice," Emma laughed, "but I'm afraid I have resigned myself to the fact that I will never be completely free of these wretched spots."

"I find them rather endearing."

Emma glanced away, a little startled by his tender compliment. "Oh. Well, thank you."

"But you still haven't answered my question."

Emma looked back at him, a blank expression on her face.

"About the worst thing you did as a child," Alex reminded her.

"Oh," she said, trying to hedge the question. "Well, it's pretty awful."

"I cannot wait to hear it."

"No, I mean it's *dreadful*."

"You're only succeeding in making me even more curious, love," Alex said, a smile creeping across his tanned features.

"I'm not going to be able to avoid telling you about it, am I?"

"I'm the only one here who knows the way home." Alex's boyish smile told Emma that he knew he had her well and truly trapped.

"Oh, all right," Emma sighed, conceding defeat. "It happened when I was thirteen. You know my father owns a shipping business, don't you?"

Alex nodded his reply.

"Well, I'm his only child, and I really love the sea, and I'm also quite good with figures, you know. Anyway, I've always planned on taking over his business eventually."

"There aren't too many women running large shipping businesses," Alex commented quietly.

"There aren't any as far as I know," Emma continued. "But I didn't—I *don't* care. Sometimes we have to be unconventional to realize our dreams. And who could better run the business than me? I know it better than anyone, save my father, of course." She looked at him defiantly.

"You were thirteen . . ." Alex said with an indulgent look, reminding her to get back to the story at hand.

"Oh, right. Well, I decided my father was taking too long showing me the ropes. I had been to the office in Boston countless times, and he even let me offer my opinions whenever he had to make a big decision. I don't know if he ever heeded my advice," Emma said thoughtfully, "but at least he always let me have my say. I also checked over the books to make sure his clerks weren't making any mistakes."

"You checked the books at age thirteen?" Alex asked incredulously.

"I told you I'm quite good at mathematics," she said defensively. "I know most men find it difficult to believe that a woman might have a good head for numbers, but I do. I found quite a few mistakes. I even caught one clerk who was cheating my father."

"Have no fear, darling," Alex chuckled. "I've learned not to be surprised by any of your hidden talents."

"Then I decided that it was time I learned about life on the ships. My father always says that you cannot succeed in running a shipping business if you don't know anything about life at sea."

He groaned. "I'm not sure I want to hear what comes next."

"In that case I won't finish the story," Emma said hopefully.

"I was kidding," he said dangerously, raising one brow as his emerald eyes bore into hers.

"To make a long story short," Emma wisely continued, "I stowed away on one of our ships."

Alex felt irrational anger welling up inside of him. "Are you insane?" he burst out. "Do you know what could have happened to you? Sailors can be quite unscrupulous. Especially when they haven't seen a female in months," he added darkly.

"Really, Alex, I was only thirteen."

"Your age probably wouldn't have mattered to most of them."

Emma nervously scrunched some of the dark blue material of her riding habit between her fingers, a little uncomfortable with the intensity of Alex's reaction. "I assure you, Alex, I've been through all this with my father countless times. I don't need another scolding from you. I shouldn't have even told you about it."

Alex sighed, well aware that he had overreacted. He leaned forward, gently disengaged Emma's hand from her skirts, and raised it to his lips in an act of contrition. "I'm sorry, darling," he said, his voice soft. "It just makes me sick to think that you might have inadvertently put yourself in a dangerous position, even if it was seven years ago."

Emma's heart soared at the tender tone of his voice and the knowledge that he was so concerned for her. "You needn't worry," she assured him quickly. "Everything worked out in the end, and I was not quite so muleheaded as the story might lead you to believe."

Alex continued to stroke her hand with his thumb. "Oh?"

"I didn't just stow away on any old ship," Emma said, trying to ignore the warm sensation emanating from her hand. "One of our captains is a very close friend. He's like an uncle to me. I would never have stowed away on any ship other than Captain Cartwright's. I knew that he was setting sail at eight in the morning, so I snuck out of my house the night before—"

"What?" Alex demanded, his grip on her hand tightening. "You wandered around Boston alone in the middle of the night? You little fool!"

"Oh, hush. It wasn't the middle of the night. It just seemed that way to me because I was too nervous to sleep. It was probably closer to five in the morning. The sun had already started to rise. Besides," she said accusingly, "you promised not to scold me anymore."

"I did no such thing."

"Well, you should have," Emma countered defiantly, tugging her hand from his and reaching for her wine glass.

"All right," Alex agreed, rolling over onto his side and propping his head up on one elbow. "I promise not to interrupt you."

"Good," Emma returned, taking a sip of her wine.

"But I will not promise to refrain from yelling at you when you're through."

Emma shot him a peevish look.

"Nor will I promise not to make *you* promise not to undertake such a ridiculous scheme in the future."

"Please credit me with a little sense." Emma rolled her eyes. "I would hardly creep onto a ship now."

"Yes, but God only knows what else you'd do," Alex muttered.

"May I finish?"

"Please do."

"Well, I snuck out of my house early in the morning, and it wasn't terribly easy because my bedroom is on the second floor."

Alex groaned.

"It was fortunate that I am such a good tree climber," Emma continued. "I had to jump from my window and grab hold of the branch from the oak tree outside my house, wiggle to the trunk, and then ease down to the ground." She looked up at Alex to see if he was about to interrupt her yet again. He made a great show of not saying anything.

"Once I got to the ground," Emma continued, "it wasn't very difficult to make my way to the docks and then onto the ship."

"Didn't your father notice your absence?" Alex inquired.

"Oh, I had all that worked out," Emma said offhandedly. "He always leaves for his office very early in the morning. He never made a habit of looking in on me before he left. He was afraid he would wake me up. I'm a very light sleeper," she explained, her violet eyes earnest.

Alex smiled, thinking that he'd like to have firsthand knowledge of that fact. "What about the servants?" he asked. "Surely one of them would notice you were gone."

"We really don't live in as grand a manner as you do here," Emma said with a light smile. "My father and I don't employ a fleet of servants. Mary, our housemaid, usually came to wake me at half past seven—"

"A barbaric hour," Alex murmured.

Emma pursed her lips and gave him a look of mild reproach. "We also don't keep your crazy town hours in Boston."

"How provincial," he said dryly, just to goad her.

It almost worked. She started to wag her finger at him, then stopped in mid-wag, her hand still suspended in the air. "On second thought," she said slowly, narrowing her eyes, "I am not going to deign to discuss this matter with you."

"I'm crushed," Alex replied, reaching up and snatching her hand. With one swift tug, he pulled her down next to him. Emma squealed as she landed alongside his strong frame, her legs caught in the tangle of her skirts.

"Alex!" she yelped, trying to pull her legs free of the cumbersome material. "What are you doing?"

Alex let go of Emma's hand and reached up to stroke the delicate line of her jaw with his knuckles. "I just wanted to get close enough to smell you."

"What?" she croaked.

"Everybody has their own special scent, you know," he explained softly, his thumb trailing across her full lips. "Yours is particularly sweet."

Emma cleared her throat nervously. "Don't you want to hear the rest of the story?" she said hoarsely. She scrambled up into a sitting position although Alex was not inclined to let her move away from him.

"Of course." His hand moved to her earlobe, which he caught gently between his thumb and forefinger.

"Umm, where was I?" Emma blinked a few times in rapid succession as she realized that Alex had succeeded in turning her into a complete peagoose.

"You were explaining why your housemaid didn't notice you were gone," he reminded her, wondering if her fluttering eyelashes were as soft as they looked.

"Oh," Emma said with gulp. "Well, she *did* notice I was gone, of course, at half past seven when she came in to wake me, but I knew that by the time someone could reach my father and he could make it to the docks, we'd be well out to sea."

"So what happened?" Alex prodded, his fingers leaving her earlobe and moving down to stroke her neck.

Emma looked up into his eyes and was mesmerized by the raw passion she saw there. "What happened when?" she asked blankly, every thought flying out of her head.

Alex chuckled, pleased at her reaction to his caress. "What happened when your father realized you were gone?"

Emma wet her lips and swiftly lowered her eyes and fixed her gaze on his chin, which she figured would be considerably less disconcerting than looking directly into his emerald stare. "Well," she said slowly, trying to regain her composure. "There was nothing he *could* do, really. We were already gone. The trouble started when I finally revealed myself to Captain Cartwright at sunset that evening. I thought he was going to explode."

"What did he do?"

"He locked me in his cabin and turned the ship around."

"A sensible man," Alex commented. "I ought to send him a note of gratitude."

"He didn't give me any food."

"Good," Alex said flatly. "You didn't deserve any."

"I was really quite hungry," Emma said earnestly, trying to ignore the heat on the nape of her neck where Alex's hand rested. "I hadn't eaten for nearly twenty-four hours when he locked me up, and it was another eight or nine hours before we got back home."

"He should have horsewhipped you."

"My father took care of that," Emma replied with a grimace. "My backside was about as red as my hair for the next week."

Alex fought long and hard to resist the temptation to ease his hand down her back and squeeze the part of her body she was discussing. He glanced surreptitiously over at Emma to ascertain whether or not she had any idea of his thoughts. She was gazing over her right shoulder, her eyes fixed on some point along the horizon, her lips curved into a reminiscent smile. Suddenly, as if she felt the weight of his eyes on her, she turned, her bright hair catching a breeze and flying around her face. The delicate smile remained on her features, but Alex saw wariness creep into her eyes. He sighed. She wasn't stupid.

Hell, he supposed that was why he liked her so much.

Emma took advantage of Alex's brief reverie to scoot back across the blanket to her original position, using hunger as an excuse. "I'm famished!" she declared. "I wonder what Mrs. Goode packed for us." She began to rummage through their picnic lunch.

"Not one of Cleopatra's new kittens, I hope," Alex remarked.

Emma made a face. "You're impossible," she decided, pulling out a plate of roasted chicken. She sighed. "I wish she hadn't packed chicken."

"Why not?" Alex asked moving to a sitting position as he reached for a drumstick. "Don't you like it?" He took a vicious bite and smiled rakishly at her.

Emma's face revealed an expression of concern. "It's just so difficult to eat in a ladylike manner."

"So don't act like a lady. I won't tell anyone."

Emma looked hesitant. "I don't know. Aunt Caroline has labored so hard to reform me. I would hate to ruin all her good work with one picnic."

"For God's sake, Emma. Use your fingers and enjoy yourself."

"Really? You won't go back to the assembled multitudes and report that I was not behaving like a proper English lady?"

"Emma, have I ever given you any indication that I wanted you to be a proper English lady?"

"Oh, all right," she capitulated, plucking the other drumstick from the pile and daintily tearing a small piece off. It was all Alex could do not to laugh as she popped the minuscule morsel in her mouth. "It's your turn now, you know," she said with a lift of her eyebrows.

Alex did her one better, arching only his right brow in an expression of supreme confidence.

"I hate people who can do that," she muttered under her breath.

"Hmmm?"

"Nothing." Emma took another tiny bite of chicken. "It's just that it's your turn to tell me the worst thing *you* did as a child."

"Would you believe I was a model child?"

"No," Emma replied bluntly.

"Then would you believe that I was so awful that I would be hard-pressed to settle on one single incident?"

"It's a bit more likely."

"Why don't we strike a deal?" Alex offered, leaning forward and resting his forearms on his knees. "How would you like the story that has the most potential to embarrass me as a grown man?"

"Now *that* is intriguing," Emma said enthusiastically, completely forgetting her resolve to behave properly as she bit into the chicken and tore off a fair-sized piece.

"I was about two or three," Alex began.

"Just wait one moment," Emma interrupted. "Are you trying to tell me that your most embarrassing moment occurred when you were two? That is quite the most ridiculous thing I've ever heard. People shouldn't even be *allowed* to feel embarrassment over what they did as babies."

"Are you going to allow me to finish my story?" Alex inquired with a cheeky tilt of his head.

"Certainly," she replied, magnanimously waving her chicken leg in the air.

"I was about two or three."

"You said that," Emma reminded him, her mouth full.

Alex shot her an annoyed look and continued. "My mother's sister had given me a stuffed dog for Christmas. I wouldn't let it out of my sight."

"What did you name him?"

His expression was sheepish. "Goggie." He looked over at Emma, who was valiantly trying to stifle a laugh. She quickly pasted a wide smile onto her face. "Anyway," Alex continued, "I played with Goggie so much that his stuffing eventually fell out, and I was heartbroken. Or at least my mother tells me I was heartbroken," he quickly added. "I don't remember any of this."

Emma conjured a vision of a small, black-haired, green-eyed boy crying over the demise of his favorite toy and decided that the image was altogether too adorable to think about without the risk of falling in love on the spot. "So what happened?" she asked, giving her head a slight shake to banish the dangerous thought.

"My mother took pity on me and restuffed the dog using her old stockings. And we would have all lived happily ever after except"—Alex said with a lopsided smile—"I continued to abuse the poor animal and it fell apart again, and this time my mother couldn't mend it."

"And?" Emma prodded.

"And this is the part where the story gets embarrassing."

"Oh, good."

"Apparently, I couldn't bear to part with Goggie even when his death was quite irrevocable, and so since I couldn't drag the dog around with me anymore, I decided that the stuffing would do just as well." Alex paused for a moment, casually running his hand through his windswept hair. "You will recall," he said lazily, "that my mother every kindly restuffed the dog with stockings. So for the next few months I wandered the halls of Westonbirt dragging ladies' stockings with me everywhere I went."

Emma laughed merrily. "I don't think that's embarrassing. I think it's adorable."

Alex leveled his eyes on her with a look of mock severity. "You do realize I have a reputation to maintain?"

"Oh, believe me, I am well acquainted with your reputation," Emma replied, her eyes bright with amusement.

Alex leaned forward and tried to appear grave. "I am trusting you with my darkest secret. How do you think it would look if it became known that the Duke of Ashbourne spent his formative years in ladies' stockings?"

"Now, now. You weren't *in* ladies' stockings; you were enamored *of* ladies' stockings. And now that I think about it," Emma paused for a moment, a saucy grin creeping across her face, "it makes perfect sense. You're certainly rather interested in ladies' stockings now."

"What do you mean by that?"

"Really, Alex," Emma teased. "You do have a reputation with the ladies, you know."

"One I'm fast losing due to you," he muttered.

Not hearing him, Emma sailed right on. "No less than two dozen women have warned me about you."

"I wish someone had warned me about *you*," he sighed.

"What?" Emma asked, startled.

Alex leaned forward, his green eyes serious. "I think I'm going to kiss you now."

"You—you are?" Emma stammered, feeling all of her self-confidence and composure drain right out of her.

Alex gazed over at her. Her bright hair had been tossed around by the wind and now framed her face with charming disarray. Her violet eyes were open wide and glowed luminously as they watched his approach. She wet her lips nervously, completely unaware of her own seductive powers.

"Emma," he said hoarsely. "I think I have to kiss you. Do you understand that?"

Emma nodded uncertainly, barely aware of his words as her entire body seemed to catch on fire, ignited by the pulsating heat that rose from his powerful frame.

Alex's eyes finally settled on her lush mouth, and his last rational thought was that nothing short of a natural disaster could prevent his kissing her now. And ever so slowly, he touched his lips to hers.

Chapter 12

Mesmerized, Emma could not tear her eyes off of Alex's face as his mouth descended to rest on hers. The touch was fleeting, his lips lightly brushing hers. She felt paralyzed, barely able to breathe.

Alex lifted his head to look at her. Her eyes still open wide, she gazed up at him as if she'd never seen him before. "Emma?" he questioned, touching his fingers to her chin.

Emma continued to stare at him as he scanned her face with his brilliant green eyes. She fought the urge to reach up and brush a lock of tousled hair from his forehead. He was looking at her so tenderly, she thought that all she really wanted to do was burrow in the warmth of his arms and melt in his embrace. She knew he didn't love her, didn't intend to marry her. But she also knew that he did care for her and that he wanted her very much. And God help her, she wanted him just as badly. She had spent months trying to convince herself that there was nothing special about the strange, new feelings she felt whenever he was near. Alex had said he had to kiss her. It was finally time to be honest with herself. She needed to kiss him, too.

Alex could tell the moment her hesitation gave way to desire. Her eyes softened, and her tongue darted out to wet her lips. But before he could resume the kiss, she stopped him, placing her hand on his cheek and murmuring his name in a husky voice.

Alex turned his head slowly to kiss the palm of her hand. "What, my love?"

Emma's voice was hoarse with emotion. "Will you promise me you'll stop when we should stop?"

Alex looked at her intently, wondering if she understood what she was asking of him.

"I—I don't have very much experience with this sort of thing, Alex." Emma swallowed, trying to work up the courage to continue her request. "I do want to kiss you. I think I want it more than I've ever wanted anything in my life. But I may not know when we should stop, or how I should stop you. I am asking you to give your word as a gentleman to stop us before we do anything—irrevocable."

Alex knew at that moment that she was his. He knew that he could make love to her right there on that very blanket, and she would do nothing to stop him. But he also knew that her mind did not want what her body so obviously desired. Alex looked down at her shining face and realized that there was no way he could live with himself if he took advantage of her trust. "I give you my word," he said softly.

"Oh, Alex," she moaned, her arms stealing around his neck as he bent down over her once again.

"If you only knew how long I've been waiting for this," he murmured, his lips trailing hot kisses across her face and then down the side of her neck.

"I—I think I know *exactly* how long," Emma returned shakily, her voice tremulous under the onslaught of his desire. As he slowly lowered her down onto her back, she sank her fingers into his thick hair, desperately pulling him closer to her.

Something deep inside her seemed to know that this was the right man, and she just couldn't seem to overcome the urge to get as close to him as possible. Unthinkingly, she pressed her body up to his, molding herself against his powerful frame.

To Alex, her innocent movement was like a torch igniting the spark that had been burning steadily inside him for months. "Oh God, Emma," he groaned. "Do you have any idea what you're doing?" He looked down at her. Her dark eyes were burning with newly discovered desire and also—trust. As he lost himself in those violet pools, Alex groaned again. "I can see you do not."

Emma did not understand his cryptic comment. "Is—is something wrong?" she queried, worried that her lack of experience had caused her to do something that displeased him.

Alex leaned down and placed twin kisses on her eyelids. "Believe me, love, nothing is wrong." He chuckled as he saw relief flood her expression. It warmed him to his very core that she was so concerned about pleasing him. "You seem to have a natural affinity for this sort of thing." Privately, Alex was wondering how on earth he'd be able to force himself to stop as he promised Emma, but he did not voice that thought, fearful of breaking the sensual spell that had been cast over their secluded picnic.

Emma flushed with pleasure over his compliment. "I just want to—ohh!" she gasped aloud as Alex's hand stole across her midriff and came to rest on her full breast. The heat of his touch was so searing she was surprised it hadn't burned right through the fabric of her riding habit. Her eyes flew open and her lips parted in surprise at his bold caress.

Alex's smile was one of pure masculine satisfaction. "You like that, don't you, love?" As he felt her nipple harden into a tight little bud through the material of her dress, he squeezed the mound of flesh he held in his hand and watched Emma shiver with desire. He silently cursed the row of tiny buttons marching down the back of her dress that made it next to impossible to pull the fabric down off of her shoulders. With a ragged sigh, he resigned himself to the fact that he would not be able to gaze down upon the full breast and dusky nipple that were proving to be so intoxicating. This setback, however, was probably all for the best considering the vow he had made just moments earlier.

"Oh, Alex," Emma moaned softly. "This is all so very strange." She let out another gasp as she felt his hand creep under the folds of her skirts and caress her firm, sleek calves. Spasms of pleasure shot up her legs to the very center of her being and she sighed with abandon. "And so very nice."

Alex's hand stroked steadily upward until it reached the sensitive spot where the tops of her stockings met pale, soft flesh, and Emma nearly flew off the blanket from the sheer energy that seemed to pour forth from his fingertips. And then, although she could not quite believe it was happening, he moved further still.

"Alex?" she asked breathily. "What—what? Are you sure? I don't know."

Alex silenced her with a soft kiss. "Shh, darling. I promise you that I will not"—he smiled wryly at his melodramatic words—"ravish you right here on the blanket. When we make love, it will be perfect, with no hesitations or misunderstandings between us." He continued to drop gentle kisses across her face to ease her fears as he slipped his hand beneath her undergarments and began to tease the soft thatch of hair that protected her womanhood.

Emma's breath caught in her throat, and she tensed up against him, twenty years of proper upbringing flooding her mind and telling her that she ought not to be in such a situation. She pressed a hand against his chest, feebly trying to push him away. "Wait, Alex, I'm not sure . . ."

"Not sure of what, love?"

Her voice quavered with apprehension. "Of you, of this, of *anything*."

"You're not sure of me?" he asked, trying to tease her fears away. "Are you telling me you'd rather be here with someone else?"

"No!" she burst out. "It's not that, it's . . ."

"It's what?"

"I don't know!" Her mind was screaming that she ought to get up and walk away, but she could not deny the thrilling sensations that poured forth from his every touch. And even as her internal struggle raged, she felt herself relax against him, her body begging for what so frightened her mind.

"Don't worry, love," Alex murmured, relieved by her acquiescence. "I will keep the vow I made to you this afternoon." He took a deep breath, laboring hard to keep his own desire in check. His need for her was painfully apparent, his hard manhood swollen and straining against his breeches. "I just want—I *need* to be inside you somehow. I can't explain it. I just need to feel you right now."

With that he slipped one finger inside her. She was hot and wet, just as he knew she'd be, but so very small and tight. He felt a surge of pride as he realized that he was the first man ever to touch her in so intimate a manner. He felt himself throb with need for her, his manhood begging to trade places with his wandering fingers.

Delicious waves of pleasure shot through Emma's body, and she began to feel herself tensing in expectation of something she didn't understand but somehow knew had to happen. "Alex!" she cried out. "Help me, please. I can't bear any more."

"Oh, yes you can, love." As Alex's finger continued to stroke her intimately, his thumb found the sensitive nub of flesh that was hidden beneath her soft curls.

"Oh, my God! Alex!!" Emma screamed his name in complete abandon. Every little wisp of desire that had been curling through her body moved to one tender spot in her abdomen, and she started to tense convulsively until her world simply burst apart, and she lay limp and exhausted on the soft flannel blanket.

Alex gently slid his finger out and laid his body down alongside hers, propping himself up on his elbow. "Shhh," he murmured comfortingly, trying to ease her back down from her climax. As he stroked her hair, he gazed out over the countryside and began to will his body to calm down, for he knew that he would not be enjoying the same kind of release Emma had. Still, there had been an undeniable sense of satisfaction in pleasuring Emma. And although Alex had always been an extremely considerate and giving lover, this was the first time his own need had become completely secondary to someone else's.

"Oh my," Emma sighed, just as soon as she regained her powers of speech.

"Oh my, indeed," Alex chuckled, running his forefinger along the elegant line of her jaw. "How do you feel?"

"I feel—oh, I don't know how I feel." Emma closed her eyes for a moment, utterly relaxed. A light smile touched her lips, and she reopened her eyes and fixed her gaze on the man before her. "You know more about this than I do. How do I feel?"

Alex laughed aloud. "You feel splendid, my sweet. Absolutely splendid."

"Yes, I suppose I do," she sighed, curling up against him. "Although I wasn't too . . . vigorous?"

He bit back a smile. "No, darling, you weren't too vigorous. You were just perfect."

"Thank you so much for saying that," she said, burying her face in his side. "I wasn't at all sure what to do, you know." She wanted to look up at him, wanted to see the expression in his eyes, but a faint flush of embarrassment crept over her.

"Have no fear. I plan to give you plenty of practice."

"What?" Emma sat up quickly, suddenly extremely eager to smooth her skirts. Alex's words had somehow triggered the return of reality. "Alex, you know we can't be doing this all the time."

"Why not?"

"We just can't. There are too many people who would be hurt. Too many people who expect better of me."

"I can't think of anything I'd like better from you."

"You are being deliberately obtuse. I just—" Emma's face suddenly drained of color. "I can't believe what I just did," she said, her eyes wide with shock over her scandalous behavior. A stolen kiss was one thing, but this—dear Lord, she had let, no begged, Alex to touch her in a most intimate fashion.

Alex groaned as he watched doubt and self-recrimination pour over Emma's face. His body throbbed painfully, and quite frankly he did not have the energy to deal with her sudden attack of feminine sensibilities.

I don't blame *you*," Emma said quickly. "I blame myself. I lost control of myself."

Nothing she could have said would have made him feel worse. She was such a little innocent; she had no idea what kind of sensual pressure he had used on her. How like his brave darling to try to assume the responsibility for their lovemaking. But despite the guilt that was beginning to invade his mind, Alex wasn't feeling particularly charitable. His body was still begging for release, straining his nerves.

"Emma," he said suddenly, his voice even and controlled. "I'm only going to say this once. Do not regret what happened this afternoon. It was beautiful and natural, and you were everything I ever dreamed you would be. If you continue to berate yourself you're only going to make yourself sick. And if you feel that we should never again share our souls as we did today, well, you're just going to have to accept that I will probably put up quite a fight."

They rode home in silence. Emma felt as if her every emotion had been torn asunder. On the one hand, she could not help blissfully replaying the torrid lovemaking she had experienced just moments earlier. On the other hand, she wanted to flog herself once she got home.

Life, she decided, was getting rather confusing.

Alex was not inclined to make conversation, either. His body felt like it was about to snap, and it didn't help that Emma's scent seemed to be everywhere—in his clothes, on his hands, simply floating through the air. He had known from the beginning that he would not find satisfaction, but he had felt that the thrill of pleasuring Emma would be enough. And it had been—until she had begun to doubt herself, cheapening the experience with her shame.

He was going to have to make some major decisions in his life, he decided—and soon. He wasn't sure how much more of this he could take.

By the time the couple finally arrived back at Westonbirt, Emma was in a complete state of confusion. As they entered the cavernous foyer, she mumbled something incoherent to Alex and raced up the long, curving staircase with speed she had never dreamed she possessed.

Alex was left with a fleeting vision of midnight-blue muslin and flaming hair flying away from him. He sighed wearily. He almost wished he could just tell himself that he'd handled her badly. At least then he could try to undo his mistakes. But the fact was that Emma's anguish stemmed from her own feelings of guilt and was probably something that she was going to have to work out on her own. With a frustrated groan, Alex raked his hand through his hair, turned on his heel and strode off to his suite, thinking that he ought to have his valet prepare a chilling bath.

When Emma reached her room, she was still moving with such haste that she practically flew through the doorway, flinging herself onto her bed with complete abandon. Which was why, she later supposed, she had been so surprised when she realized that Belle was lying there, curled up peacefully with a volume of Shakespeare.

"Hell and damnation, Belle," Emma snapped, rubbing her shoulder where it had connected with her cousin's hip. "Couldn't you possibly read in your own room?"

Belle looked at her with innocent blue eyes. "The light is better in here."

"For God's sake, Belle. Try to be a little more creative with your excuses. Your room is directly next to mine, and it faces the same direction."

"Would you believe your bed is more comfortable than mine?"

Emma looked ready to explode.

"All right, all right," Belle said hastily, quickly scooting off the bed. "I admit it. I wanted to hear about your ride with Ashbourne."

"Well, it was fine. Are you satisfied?"

"No," Belle replied vehemently. "This is Belle, remember? You're supposed to tell me everything."

Something about Belle's wheedling tone struck an emotional chord in Emma, and she felt a hot tear spill down her cheek. "I'm not sure I want to talk right now."

Belle took one look at Emma's stricken expression, dropped her book, and then, with her characteristic presence of mind, thought to quickly slam the bedroom door shut. "Oh my God, Emma. What happened? Did he—? Did you—?"

Emma sniffled and wiped away a tear.

"*Did he ravish you?*"

"I hate that word," Emma bit out. "Have I ever told you that I hate that word?"

"Did he?"

"No, he didn't. What kind of a woman do you think I am?"

"A woman in love, I suppose. I hear men can be awfully persuasive when you're in love."

"Well, I'm not in love," Emma returned defiantly.

"Aren't you?"

I don't know, Emma's mind cried out. She didn't say anything.

"I can see that you are at least thinking about it," Belle continued. "That's a start, I suppose. I don't really have to tell you how happy we would all be if the two of you did decide to get married."

"Believe me, I've sensed your feelings."

"Well, you can't really blame us. We do so love having you here in England. Especially me," Belle said gravely. "It's hard when your best friend is an ocean away."

Belle's last remark sent Emma over the edge, and she exploded into tears, hiccuping loudly as she soaked the pillowcase.

"Oh dear." Belle quickly moved back to the bed and began to stroke her cousin's hair from her face. Emma wasn't the crying sort of female, so Belle knew that something serious had occurred. "I'm sorry," she crooned. "I didn't mean to put any pressure on you. We all know that it has to be your decision in the end."

Emma didn't respond, but the tears continued to squeeze out of her eyes. She laid on her side, taking deep breaths as her tears rolled over her nose and dripped onto the pillow.

"You might feel better if you talk about it," Belle commented. "Why don't you come over to the dressing table, and I'll comb out your hair. It looks as if the wind whipped a few tangles into it."

Emma rose and moved slowly across the room, ungraciously rubbing her nose with the back of her hand. She plopped herself down in the plush chair that accompanied the dressing table and surveyed her reflection in the mirror. She looked awful. Her eyes were bloodshot and puffy, her nose was red, and her hair was strewn every which way. She took a deep breath to regain her equilibrium and silently marveled at the society women who even knew how to *cry* with style. A single tear or two, a delicate sniffle—nothing like the heart-wrenching sobs that racked Emma, leaving her feeling like a wrung-out, pathetic mess.

She turned to Belle with another loud sniffle. "Do you know something? I used to be someone else."

"Whatever do you mean?" Belle picked up a comb.

"I mean—and correct me if I'm wrong—I used to have something of a reputation as an exceptional female. I don't mean to boast, but I did."

Belle nodded, trying to hide a smile.

"I didn't simper," Emma continued with a little more enthusiasm. "Or make stupid conversation. I had a quick wit. People used to comment on it." She looked up to Belle for reassurance.

Belle continued her sympathetic nods but was obviously finding it more difficult to contain her smile. She began to pull the comb gently through Emma's hair.

"And I had confidence in myself, too."

"Don't you now?"

Emma sighed, slumping in the chair. "I don't know. I used to feel decisive about my actions. Now I never know what to do. I'm constantly confused, and when I do finally make a decision about something, I regret it later."

"Do you think that all this confusion might have something to do with Ashbourne?"

"Of course it has something to do with Alex! It has everything to do with him. He's turned my entire life upside down."

"But you aren't in love with him," Belle stated quietly.

Emma clamped her mouth shut.

Belle tried a different tactic. "How do you feel when you're with him?"

"It's completely crazy. One moment we're joking like old friends, and the next I've got a lump in my throat the size of an extremely large egg, and I feel like I'm an awkward twelve-year-old."

"You don't know what to say?" Belle guessed.

"It's not that I don't know what to say. I feel as if I've forgotten how to speak!"

"Hmmm." Belle continued to work the tangles out of her cousin's hair. "It sounds quite fascinating. I've never felt that way around a man before." She paused thoughtfully. "Although I am looking forward to rereading *Romeo and Juliet* when I finally get to the *R*'s."

Emma grimaced. "Please recall that they met with a rather unfortunate demise. I'd rather you didn't draw comparisons."

"Oh. Sorry."

It may have been Emma's overexerted emotions, but she didn't think Belle sounded terribly contrite.

"There we go," Belle said matter-of-factly. "All done with the left side." She began combing the back of Emma's hair. "Why don't you tell me about this afternoon? Something must have happened to have put you in such a state."

Despite herself, Emma felt her cheeks grow warm. "Oh, nothing really. We just went for a ride. The countryside here is lovely."

Belle pulled the comb through Emma's hair with a vicious yank.

"Ow!" Emma howled. "What are you doing? I'll be bald by the time you're through."

"You were saying something about this afternoon?" Belle prodded in a sweet voice.

"Give me that comb!" Emma snapped. Belle lodged the offending weapon in her bright hair and gave it a little tug, symbolizing the torture that was yet to come. "Oh, all right," Emma gave in. "We stopped for a picnic."

"And?"

"And we had a perfectly marvelous time. We traded stories about when we were children."

"And?"

"And he kissed me! Are you satisfied?"

"He must have done more than kiss you," Belle surmised. "You've kissed Alex before, and you never started crying like this."

"Well, maybe he did a little more than kiss me." Emma really wished she weren't sitting right in front of a mirror, where she was forced to watch her skin color slowly redden until it matched her hair.

"But he didn't ravish you?" Belle looked almost upset.

"Belle, are you *disappointed* that I made it through the afternoon with my virtue intact?"

"No, of course not," Belle replied quickly. "Although I must admit, I'm a bit curious about 'the act' and all that, and I cannot get Mother to tell me anything about it."

"Well, you won't get any more details from me. I'm just as innocent as you are."

"Not *quite* as innocent, I imagine. I may be naive, but even I know that there is quite a bit between a kiss and 'the act'."

To say that words failed Emma would be a gross understatement.

"Isn't there?" Belle persisted.

"Uh, well, yes," Emma spluttered. "Yes, there is."

Belle plodded on. "Would it be fair to say that you did something somewhere between kissing and 'the act'?"

"Would you stop calling it 'the act'?!" Emma burst out. "You make it sound so sordid."

"Would you rather I call it something else?"

"I'd *rather* you didn't call it anything." Emma's eyes narrowed dangerously. "This is getting extremely personal."

Belle would not be deterred. "Did you?"

"You do realize that you have no shame?"

"None whatsoever," Belle said blithely, giving the comb an impertinent tug.

Emma winced, groaned, and barely suppressed the urge to curse. "Oh, all right," she huffed. At this rate, Belle would have all of her hair pulled out by supper. "Yes," she groaned. "Yes, yes, yes! Are you satisfied?"

Belle stopped combing immediately and sank down into the chair opposite Emma. "Oh my," she breathed.

"Could you possibly stop staring at me as if I've suddenly been ruined?"

Belle blinked. "What? Oh, I'm sorry. It's just that—oh my."

"For heaven's sake, Belle. I wish you wouldn't go on and on about this. It's a trivial matter." *Oh, really?* she asked herself. *Then why were you sobbing your heart out a few minutes ago?* Emma quickly stifled her inner voice. Maybe she had overreacted a little. After all, it wasn't as if she had gotten herself (perish the word) ravished. And, she admitted with a rueful smile, it wasn't as if she hadn't enjoyed herself.

Belle was also weighing the matter carefully in her ever-pragmatic mind. This was big news, indeed. She had privately decided that a wedding between her cousin and the Duke of Ashbourne was imminent. A slight indiscretion before the actual nuptials could be easily overlooked. Still, that didn't mean that Belle wasn't intensely curious about the incident. "Just tell me one thing, Emma," she implored. "What was it like?"

"Oh, Belle," Emma sighed, giving up all attempts at offended maidenly virtue. "It was splendid."

Chapter 13

For all of Emma's determination to put her feminine embarrassment behind her, she still turned into a stammering fool the minute she laid eyes on Alex again.

The evening had started out innocently enough. After Belle had managed to pry all of the details about the picnic she could get out of Emma, the pair had decided to dress for the evening meal. Belle, however, was considerably more interested in choosing Emma's attire than her own, insisting that she wear a deep violet gown that set off her unusual eyes.

"It's the same color you wore when you made your debut," Belle explained. "And Alex was *so* taken with you."

"I doubt he'll remember the color of my gown," was all that Emma replied. Nevertheless, she allowed herself to be talked into the violet silk, hoping that the bold color might bolster her courage. Belle settled on a gown of pale peach silk, which complimented her soft pink and white complexion. When they were done dressing, Emma sacrificed herself on the altar of the hairstylist, and she allowed Meg to fuss with her tresses without the slightest complaint. After Belle's less-than-tender ministrations, Meg seemed a veritable goddess.

As Emma sat there, watching in the mirror as Meg pulled the hairbrush through her bright locks, she had ample time to consider her situation.

Did she love Alex? Belle seemed to think so. But how could she love him when that meant abandoning her lifelong dream of running Dunster Shipping? Part of Emma wanted to throw caution into the wind and grab whatever happiness she could find with Alex. But she knew that if she let herself love him a little, she wouldn't be able to stop herself from loving him wholeheartedly, with every pore of her being. And she was terrified at the prospect of losing herself completely in that love.

As she had told Belle not even a half an hour earlier, she *changed* around him. One tender gaze from him seemed to banish all rational thought, and she had to struggle just to stammer incoherent phrases. If she married Alex, she could certainly forget about ever speaking in complete sentences.

Which brought her to another sensitive point. He might not even ask her to marry him. Alex had a formidable stubborn streak, and Emma couldn't imagine him caving in to familial pressure and asking for her hand unless he was good and ready. And what if he did ask her? Would she say yes? Emma caught her lower lip between her teeth as she pondered her situation. Maybe. Probably. She let out a deep sigh. Definitely. How could she help herself? Dunster Shipping would have to survive without her because she didn't think she could survive without Alex.

But marriage to him was not a guarantee of happiness. Few marriages among the *ton* were based upon love, and Emma knew that a love match had never been one of Alex's highest goals. It was highly possible that he might reach a decision to ask her to marry him based solely on affection and lust. She could well imagine him sitting in his study with his feet propped up on his desk, considering his situation and deciding to marry her just because nothing better was likely to come along.

What would her life be like if she were married to a man who didn't love her? Would it be enough just to be near him or would she lose a little bit of her soul day by day until she was nothing more than a brittle shell? But God help her, she didn't know if she had any alternative because she was beginning to realize that the possibility of happiness apart from Alex was very slim, indeed. She supposed that any small piece of him would be better than nothing because it was true—she loved him. She loved him desperately and she was terrified that she might not be able to find a way to make him love her back.

Suddenly, facing him at dinner seemed a most frightening prospect.

She was fairly successful finding excuses to remain upstairs. There was a loose thread on her gown that needed mending, and she was convinced that she had developed new freckles while she had been out of doors. Meg was immediately dispatched to borrow a little powder from Aunt Caroline. She had just about managed to develop a blistering headache when Belle finally lost all patience and physically pushed her through the door and down the stairs.

By the time Emma and Bell arrived, Alex was already in the drawing room, leaning against a windowsill and absently swirling a glass of whiskey. As Emma walked through the doorway, he gave her a quizzical look, scanning her features intently. Emma did her best to appear blasé, but she had a sinking feeling that she failed miserably. "Good evening, your grace," she blurted out suddenly, painfully aware that she sounded like a bleating sheep. She wasn't sure, but she thought she heard her cousin emit a small groan.

Alex nodded his greeting to Belle, who had strategically positioned herself on a sofa that offered an excellent view of the entire room. After Belle smiled back at him sunnily, he focused his attention on Emma. "I trust you had a pleasant afternoon following our return," he said politely.

"It was very nice, thank you," Emma replied automatically, holding onto the back of a pale yellow chair with a death grip.

Belle watched the exchange with unconcealed interest, her head bobbing shamelessly back and forth between Emma and Alex.

"I feel as if I'm on the stage," Emma muttered under her breath.

"What was that?" Alex inquired cordially.

"Did you say something?" Belle asked at the very same time.

Emma smiled weakly and shook her head. The tension in the room was really quite thick enough to eat.

"I believe I'll have another whiskey," Alex said.

"I have a feeling you might need it," Belle put in with an innocent smile.

"Impertinent chit." Alex smoothly crossed the room and poured himself a drink. As he made his way back to his spot at the windowsill, he brushed very closely by Emma, murmuring in her ear, "Do try not to ruin the furniture, my dear. That's one of my mother's favorite chairs."

Emma immediately let go of the chair and practically flew over an end table in her haste to seat herself next to Belle. When she looked up again, Alex was smiling widely.

Emma, on the other hand, was not smiling at all.

Thankfully, Sophie chose that moment to sail into the room. "Hello, everybody," she said merrily, glancing quickly around the room. "I see that Mother hasn't arrived yet. Hmmm, what a surprise. I would have thought she'd be most anxious to inquire about your ride this afternoon."

"I would have thought so, too," Alex said dryly.

Sophie had no response for that so she scooted across the room and seated herself in the pale yellow chair that Emma had so recently been trying to mangle. Emma slouched a little, slightly deflated by Alex's caustic comment.

"Cleopatra had her kittens," Sophie announced with a smile. "Charlie was thrilled. He's been talking of nothing else all evening. Unfortunately, now he insists upon asking me all sorts of, well, *sensitive* questions, which I do not feel at all prepared to discuss with a six-year-old boy." She sighed sadly. "I do wish Oliver would return home soon."

"I am certain Alex will be able to aid you in the sensitive question department," Emma said peevishly, regretting her words the moment they flew out of her mouth.

Belle made a strange sound that was half laugh and half snort and then started to cough. Emma fought a strong urge to whack her soundly on the back.

Alex continued to lean against the windowsill, his expression inscrutable, and Emma wanted to curse him for looking so devastatingly handsome without even trying. He appeared to be quite fascinated with his perfectly manicured fingernails.

The truth, however, was that he was deathly afraid he'd burst out laughing if he allowed himself to look at Emma. She would never forgive him for that, he knew. There was something so comically adorable about her as she sat there on the couch, absolutely seething. He sensed that there was nothing that irritated her more than watching him appear in complete control of himself while her emotions were churning. He wasn't cruel; he just preferred to see her spitting mad than forlorn and guilt-ridden as she had been that afternoon. He brushed an invisible piece of lint off of his waistcoat and stole a quick glance at Emma. He wasn't sure, but he thought he saw her take a deep breath and exhale it slowly.

He couldn't resist.

"I trust your stay at Westonbirt has been pleasurable thus far, Emma." He was surely going to spend a year in hell for that comment, but it was worth it.

"Just fine," she bit out, refusing to look at him.

"Only just fine?" he said, his face a perfect mask of solicitousness. "We have not been doing our jobs properly then. What else can we do to entertain you?"

"I am certain there is nothing *you* can do," she said pointedly.

Belle's mouth was hanging open.

"Now, that cannot be true," Alex returned. "I shall simply have to try harder. Why don't we go for another ride tomorrow afternoon? There is much I haven't shown you."

He thought Belle was going to fall off the sofa.

"That won't be necessary, your grace," Emma said stiffly.

"But—"

"I said it won't be necessary!" she burst out. Then, realizing that everyone was looking at her most oddly, she added, "I have a bit of a sniffle." She sniffed a bit to demonstrate but of course sounded perfectly clear. Smiling weakly, she folded her hands in her lap and resolved to say nothing else.

Sophie leapt into the silence. "Er, Belle," she said awkwardly. "Why don't you take one of the kittens back with you? I have no idea what we'll do with the lot of them."

"I doubt that my mother will agree," Belle replied. "The last cat was an unmitigated disaster. It had a bit of a flea problem, you see."

"I don't think our kittens have been alive long enough to have gotten fleas," Sophie mused.

"Nonetheless, I imagine my mother will feel quite strongly about it."

"What will I feel quite strongly about?" Caroline asked loudly from the doorway.

"Sophie is trying to convince us to take home one of Cleopatra's kittens," Belle explained.

"Heavens, no!" Caroline replied emphatically. "You may have one out in the country but never again in London." She entered the room, nodding her hello to Alex and then took a seat near Emma, Belle, and Sophie. Henry, who had followed her downstairs, took one look at the collection of women in the corner and headed straight over to Alex.

"Whiskey?" Alex inquired, holding up his glass.

"Don't mind if I do," Henry replied affably, raising a hand to stop Alex from getting up. He quickly crossed the room, poured himself a drink, and returned to Alex's side. "I have a feeling we'll need these this evening," he remarked.

"Strangely enough, that's *exactly* what your daughter said not five minutes earlier."

"How was your ride this afternoon, my dear?" Caroline asked Emma, loudly enough for all to hear.

"It was very nice, thank you."

Alex thought her reply was very weak, indeed. "I had a brilliant time," he boomed.

"I am sure you did," Emma said, mostly to herself, trying to forget it had been she who had cried out in pleasure that afternoon, not Alex.

"Did you say something, my dear?" Caroline asked solicitously.

"No, no I didn't. I was just—er—clearing my throat."

"You seem to do that quite often." Alex couldn't resist Emma's obvious distress, so he crossed the room and took the seat next to Caroline. Henry followed in his wake. "Or at least you do while in my presence."

Emma glared at Alex so ferociously that Sophie could not help murmuring a soft, "Oh my!"

Alex sipped his whiskey serenely, appearing completely unaffected by Emma's ire.

Which, of course, only served to make her even more irate.

At that point, Alex cracked a smile.

"Well!" Caroline declared, only to break the silence. Much to her dismay, however, everybody immediately stared at her and then she had to say something more. "Do tell us more about your afternoon, Emma dear." It seemed to be a popular topic.

"Well, actually—," Emma started, her irritation beginning to get the better of her.

Belle's foot slammed into her shin. Emma gulped with pain, smiled weakly, and replied, "It was lovely, thank you."

Silence fell again, and this time nobody, not even Caroline, was brave enough to break it.

Emma stared down at her lap, her fingers idly plucking at her skirts. She could feel Alex's eyes resting on her, and much as she tried, she could not summon the courage to meet his gaze. As she sat in stony silence, she had to admit that it was herself with whom she was angry, not Alex.

She knew that she was intensely attracted to Alex. But to admit that fact to the gentleman in question somehow seemed to go against every tenet of her upbringing, and it was difficult to turn her back on the set of morals that her father and her aunt and uncle had instilled in her. She was in a fine mess now, wanting him so badly and knowing that she shouldn't allow herself to have him. She could justify her desire by the fact that she loved him, but she somehow had to find the willpower to stop herself from acting on that desire.

It would all be different if he loved her even just a tiny bit as much as she loved him.

Or, Emma thought despondently, if he merely proposed. Marriage to Alex without mutual love was preferable to not having him at all. She looked over at him. He had gone back to examining his fingernails and did not look even remotely like a man who was about to ask a woman to marry him. Emma swallowed and sank back further into the sofa.

"Goodness! It sounds as if we've had a funeral in here. Have you all lost your powers of speech?" Eugenia stood in the doorway of the drawing room, clad in an elegant gown of green silk.

"Actually, Mother, I think everyone is somewhat afraid to open his—or *her*—mouth." Alex smiled widely at his mother as he rose to give her an affectionate kiss on the cheek.

Eugenia looked at her son accusingly. "You haven't been brutalizing our guests, have you?"

"Only me," Emma chirped bravely, causing her aunt to shoot her a remonstrating look.

Alex chuckled, delighted at Emma's barb. "Perhaps I could escort you to supper, Miss Dunster," he said graciously, walking over to her and extending his arm.

"Of course," Emma murmured. What else could she do with such an avid group of onlookers? Smiling prettily at her audience, she rose and tried to take a step toward the door, but Alex's iron grip held her firmly in place.

"I believe we'll bring up the rear," he stated, a little too obviously.

"If none of you mind," Emma hastened to add, feeling her cheeks pinken.

"Oh no, we don't mind *at all*," Eugenia exclaimed, practically hauling her daughter out of the room.

Within seconds the room had been vacated.

"Don't you ever do that to me again!" Emma burst out, wrenching herself from his grasp.

"Do what?" he asked innocently.

"I trust your stay has been pleasurable, Emma," she mimicked, imitating his tone perfectly.

"Oh, come now, Emma. You cannot begrudge me a bit of fun."

"Not at my expense. I was mortified."

"Don't be so angry, love. You know I was only teasing you."

"I know no such thing. It seemed to me that you were merely having a bit of revenge because you didn't get what you wanted this afternoon."

Unable to bear the broken look in her eyes, Alex took her by the shoulders and pulled her against him. "Oh, darling, I'm sorry," he murmured. "I never meant to make you feel that way. Believe me, I got exactly what I wanted this afternoon."

"But—"

"Hush." He placed his forefinger on her lips. "All I wanted was to make you happy, and it seems all I've managed is to make you sad. I was teasing you just now because if I can't have happy, then angry at least is better than sad."

"Well, I'd prefer you didn't resort to such tactics again," she mumbled into his chest.

Alex dropped a kiss on her forehead. "I promise. Now then . . ." He searched for a new topic. "Have you ever seen a room empty out so quickly? It seems that I was not the only one desirous of a private meeting between the two of us. I'd be willing to wager that my mother made it to the dining room in under ten seconds."

"I've certainly never seen my aunt move so quickly before," Emma returned with a wobbly smile. "And I thought Uncle Henry was going to take Belle by her hair."

"Funny, but I'd have thought him above this."

"You must be joking. Aunt Caroline can be quite formidable when she's in a temper. He wouldn't want to provoke her. He's much too fond of his peaceful existence. Besides, everyone is most anxious to see me settled. Not," Emma said quickly, "that we—I have any plans to settle down soon. I have a business to run back in Boston, you know." She felt a sinking feeling in her stomach even as she spoke the words. Hadn't she just decided that Alex was far more important to her than Dunster Shipping? "You shouldn't allow yourself to feel pressured, you know."

Alex looked down at her with a strange expression on his face.

"Although I imagine one would find it difficult to pressure you into anything," Emma continued, looking slightly forlorn.

Alex smiled wryly, wondering how much pressure would actually be required at this point to get him to settle down. "Are you feeling better?" he asked simply.

Emma kept her eyes downcast. "I made quite a spectacle of myself, didn't I?"

"To which spectacle are you referring?"

She blushed at his obvious reference to her passionate behavior. "Actually, I was referring to my rather acute embarrassment after the fact." She paused, forcing herself to look into his eyes. "I think I overreacted," she said softly. "I'm sorry. I hope I didn't upset you."

She looked up at him, her violet eyes wide with trust. At that moment, something inside Alex melted. He couldn't believe that she was apologizing to *him* for her embarrassment over their lovemaking earlier that afternoon. Proper young ladies were taught that any kind of premarital intimacy was akin to eternal damnation, and now that Alex no longer felt as if his body were about to explode, he was really quite impressed that Emma hadn't taken to her bed for a week.

"It's quite natural to feel confused by a new experience," he said, feeling that he ought to say something to comfort her.

"Thank you for being so understanding," Emma said, a faint smile touching her features. "Although I do think it would be wise if we restrained ourselves for the time being." At Alex's raised eyebrow, she explained, "I really cannot describe how awful I felt this afternoon."

"Guilt?"

"That, and confusion, too." Emma turned away and idly examined a small clock that sat on an end table. She was proud of herself for being so honest with Alex, but all the same, such plain speaking was somewhat disconcerting.

"I wish you wouldn't feel that way."

"I wish I wouldn't, too," Emma replied, still directing her words to the clock. "But I'm afraid that I can't control my emotions very well, and I would rather avoid the state of turmoil I was in earlier today."

"Emma?" And then when she didn't respond, Alex said it louder. "Emma?"

Emma turned around quickly, her bright hair settling about her face in soft waves.

Alex touched his fingers to her chin, tilting her face upward so that he could peer into the soft violet depths of her eyes. "I'm still going to try to kiss you, you know."

"I know."

He leaned in closer. "On every possible occasion."

"I know."

His lips were nearly touching hers. "I'm going to try right now."

Emma sighed, caught in the sensual web of his voice. "I know."

"Are you going to stop me?" he murmured against her mouth.

"No." Emma's soft reply was lost as Alex's mouth slanted over hers. Heat poured from his lips, and Emma simply closed her eyes, losing herself in the warmth of the moment.

Alex was painfully aware that he and Emma had precious few moments together. He really would not put it past his mother to come barging into the parlor, declare Emma ravished at the sight of one kiss, and demand that he marry her on the spot. With a groan, he tore himself away from her and took a deep breath.

"This is going to be a long weekend," he muttered, still holding her chin in his hand.

"Yes, I know," Emma said in a very strange voice.

A light smile touched Alex's face as he looked over at Emma. She seemed to be caught in a daze, and her eyes were fixed on a point slightly to the left of Alex's elbow.

"I would love to know what is going through your mind right now," Alex said softly, brushing a wisp of hair off of Emma's forehead.

Emma shook her head slightly as she tried to refocus her eyes. "What?" She blinked a few times. "Do you promise not to laugh?"

"I promise nothing of the kind."

Emma blinked a few more times at that unexpected reply, and then she gazed up at his face. He was smiling at her in a rather indulgent fashion, and his green eyes glowed with the warm promise of love. "Well, I suppose I might tell you anyway," she said softly. "I was thinking that . . . well, that is I was wondering . . ."

"Yes?"

"Actually, I was wondering how on earth I managed to remain standing when you kissed me just now." An embarrassed smile crossed Emma's features, and she looked downward, where her foot was tracing half circles in the carpet. "I felt as if I were melting."

Alex felt something unfamiliar flicker inside him, and there was no way he could deny the comforting warmth that suddenly suffused his body. He leaned over and briefly brushed his lips against hers. "You cannot imagine how happy I am to hear you say that."

Emma was still running her slippered foot along the carpet, absurdly pleased at his words and unable to keep a wide smile off her face. "Perhaps you could take my arm and escort me to dinner?"

"I think that could be arranged."

When Emma and Alex arrived in the dining room, their families were already seated around the long oak table. Because their party only numbered seven, Eugenia, preferring good conversation to formality, had seated everyone toward the head of the table, leaving the other end empty.

"I took the liberty of sitting at the head of the table," Eugenia announced. "I know that propriety dictates that you sit here, Alex, but we *are* an informal group, and I must admit, it prickles my pride to give up my seat to my son."

Alex raised an eyebrow as he held out a chair for Emma, shooting his mother a look that said that he did not believe a word that flew out of her mouth.

"Besides, I rather thought that you and Emma would want to sit next to each other."

"As usual, you are very astute, Mother."

Eugenia's smile didn't waver one bit. She turned to Emma, summarily dismissing her son. "Did you have a nice time this afternoon, my dear? Caroline tells me that you love to ride."

Emma smiled indulgently as she sat down between Belle and the empty seat that was reserved for Alex. Eugenia was the third person that evening to ask that question. The fourth, if she counted Belle, who had been a bit more direct. "I had a lovely time, thank you. Alex was a most gracious escort."

Belle started to cough. Emma shot her a withering glare and gave her a swift kick under the table.

"Really?" Eugenia breathed, enthralled by the scene taking place down the table. "Just how 'gracious' was he?"

This time it was Sophie who did the kicking, and her foot connected soundly with her mother's shin.

"I was extremely gracious, Mother," Alex said in a tone that put an end to the entire subject.

Just then Caroline let out a little yelp as Henry kicked her in the shin. "Henry!" she demanded in hushed tones. "What on earth was that for?"

"Actually, darling," he murmured, gazing warmly into her eyes. "I was feeling left out."

Chapter 14

The next morning Emma found that love had another symptom: she couldn't eat. Or rather, she couldn't eat in front of Alex. She didn't seem to have any trouble at all when he wasn't in the room.

When she arrived downstairs for breakfast, Sophie, Eugenia, and Belle were already eating. Emma was famished, and she sat down, ready to devour what looked like a scrumptious omelet.

Then Alex arrived.

Emma's stomach began to flutter as fast as a hummingbird's wings. She couldn't manage to get down a bite.

"Is the omelet not to your liking?" Eugenia asked.

"I'm not very hungry," Emma replied quickly. "But it's delicious, thank you."

Alex, who had strategically positioned himself right next to her, leaned over and whispered, "I can't imagine how you would know since you haven't tried a bite."

She smiled wanly and put a forkful in her mouth. It tasted like sawdust. She looked over at Eugenia. "Perhaps just some tea."

By lunchtime Emma thought she might perish from hunger. Alex had had to take care of some estate business, so she and Belle had spent the morning exploring the house. When they arrived in the informal dining room, her heart sank when she realized that he wasn't there.

Her stomach, however, rejoiced.

She quickly downed a plate of roast turkey and potatoes, fearful that he would arrive any minute. After she had finished a generous helping of peas and asparagus, she thought to ask Eugenia about his whereabouts.

"Well, I was hoping he'd join us," his mother replied. "But he had to go out to the northwest corner of the estate to inspect the damage from last week's rainstorm."

"Is it very far?" Emma asked. Perhaps she could join him.

"Over an hour's ride, I should think."

"I see." She hadn't realized that Alex's landholdings were quite that vast. "Well, in that case I'll just have some of those lovely meringues."

Emma decided with a sigh that it was most likely all for the best that he'd been called away. If he had spent every minute by her side (which she had a feeling was his original intention), she'd probably have wasted away by the time she got back to London.

But she couldn't deny the fact that, despite the disturbance Alex caused her, she longed for his company every minute he was gone. She went for a ride through the countryside, but she didn't enjoy herself because Alex wasn't there to race her to the apple tree she came across a couple of miles east of Westonbirt. And then he wasn't around to tease her when she deftly climbed the tree or to compliment her aim when she launched one of the apples into the air, pegged a weak branch, and sent five more apples tumbling down. She gave the fruit to Charlie when she returned, and he was so happy about the prospect of fresh apple tarts that he felt compelled to race up and down the stairs six times. His exuberance was infectious, but it just didn't lift her spirits like one of Alex's smiles. Emma doubted that anything could.

On the other hand, it was fortunate that she ate one of the apples while she was perched high in the tree because she certainly didn't eat anything that night at dinner.

She didn't see Alex the next morning, either. Henry had an important meeting with his solicitor that afternoon which he declared he could not miss, and so the entire family left fairly early in the morning. Alex, tired from his treks the previous day and unaware of the Blydons' plans for such an early departure, slept quite late and missed Emma altogether.

Emma only sighed at his absence and helped herself to a hearty breakfast.

Eugenia and Sophie had already made plans to remain at Westonbirt until midweek, and Alex had decided that he couldn't very well leave with all of the storm damage to attend to, so Emma and her family had a carriage to themselves for the return trip. The moment they were on their way, Belle opened her Shakespeare, Henry pulled out some business papers, and Caroline went to sleep. Emma stared out the window, resigning herself to a ride devoid of intelligent conversation.

She wasn't disappointed.

When they arrived back at the townhouse in London, Emma breathed a sigh of relief, swore she'd bring a book on the next long trip, and dashed up the stairs to her room. The entire weekend had been emotionally draining, between her intimate encounter with Alex, her great realization that she loved him, and her inability to see him after that.

The bumpy ride back to London hadn't helped. It hadn't occurred to her how tired she really was until she fell onto her bed and realized that she wasn't going to get up for at least another week.

Or until someone knocked on her door ten seconds later.

"Hello, Emma." Ned opened the door and poked his head into the room before she had a chance to answer. "Did you have a good weekend?" At her weary nod he continued. "Excellent. You look quite refreshed."

Emma, who was lying on her stomach with her right cheek pressed into the bed and her arm twisted over her head at a somewhat unnatural angle, raised her eyes skeptically and realized that he wasn't being the least bit sarcastic; he appeared quite distracted, and she doubted he'd actually taken a good look at her.

"Did you have a good weekend?" she inquired. "I imagine you enjoyed your brief period of freedom."

Ned shuffled into the room, shut the door, and leaned against Emma's desk. "Let's just say I had an *interesting* weekend."

"Oh dear."

"Why don't you tell me about your weekend first?"

Emma shrugged, pushing herself up into a sitting position, her back supported by the mountain of pillows that leaned against the headboard of her bed. "It was exactly what you would imagine."

"A bunch of people trying to get you married?"

Including me. "Exactly. But I still managed to have a good time. It's nice to get out of the city. It's so congested here."

"Good, good." Ned started rocking back and forth on his heels, and Emma got the impression that he wasn't paying any attention to what she was saying.

"Is something wrong, Ned?"

He took a deep breath. "Well, you could say that." He walked over to the window and looked out, turned around and faced her, crossed his arms, uncrossed them, and started pacing.

"You should get more exercise," Emma quipped.

Ned might have heard her, but he certainly wasn't listening. "Nothing is *seriously* wrong. I mean, it's nothing that can't be fixed if I put my mind to it. Of course my mind isn't worth a lot of money, you know."

Emma raised her eyebrows. "Not in the physical sense, no."

"It isn't as if anyone died or anything like that." Ned shoved his hands in his pockets and muttered, "At least not yet."

Emma hoped she'd heard him wrong.

"The thing is, Emma, I need your advice. And maybe your help. You're one of the smartest people I know. Belle, now, she's smart, too. Can't beat her when it comes to literature and how many languages does she speak? Three? I think she can read a few others, too. Not much of a head for math, but she's sharp, my sister is. But she's too damned practical. Just last month she—" Ned stopped, drew back his shoulders sharply and looked at Emma with a stricken expression. "Oh God, Emma. I can't even remember my original sentence. I know I didn't come in here to discuss my sister. What was I saying?" He collapsed into a chair.

Emma bit her lip. Ned's head was hanging over the back of her chair. The situation looked grim, indeed. "Um, I believe it was something about wanting my advice."

"Oh, right." Ned grimaced. "I've gotten myself into a bit of a mess."

"Really?"

"I was playing cards."

Emma groaned and closed her eyes.

"Now, hold on a second, Emma," Ned protested. "I don't need a lecture on the vices of cards."

"I wasn't going to give you one. It's just when the statement 'I was playing cards' is prefaced by 'I've gotten myself into a bit of a mess,' it usually means that someone owes someone else a great deal of money."

Ned didn't say anything; he just sat there looking pained.

"How much?" Emma thought quickly, mentally adding up her savings. She hadn't spent very much of her allowance recently. She might be able to bail out her cousin.

"Er—a certain sum." Ned got up and looked out the window again.

"Just how certain is this sum?"

"Extremely certain," he replied cryptically.

"Just how much are we talking about?!" Emma exploded.

"Ten thousand pounds."

"What?" she shrieked, leaping off her bed. "Are you crazy? Are you out of your mind?" She began to pace, waving her arms wildly in the air. "What were you thinking?"

"I don't know," Ned moaned.

"Oh, I forgot, you're out of your mind. How can I expect you to *think*?"

"You're not exactly being supportive in my time of crisis."

"Supportive? Supportive!" Emma shot him a withering glare. "Support is not what you need right now. At least not the emotional kind. I don't believe this." She sank back down on the bed. "I just don't believe this. What on earth are we going to do?"

Ned breathed a sigh of relief at her use of the word "we."

"What happened?"

"I was playing with a group of friends at White's. Anthony Woodside joined us."

Emma shivered with distaste. She hadn't seen Viscount Benton since their strange encounter at the Lindworthy's ball, but she certainly had no desire to do so. Their strained conversation had left her extremely uneasy and slightly insulted. She hadn't told Alex about the incident; there hadn't seemed to be any need to upset him over it. But still, Emma could not shake the feeling that Woodside had evil plans—plans that involved her family. Now it seemed that her premonitions had come true.

"It seemed impolite not to ask him to join us," Ned went on. "It was supposed to be a friendly game. Very casual. We'd all had a few drinks."

"All except Woodside, I imagine."

Ned groaned, slapping his hand at the wall in a nervous gesture. "You're probably right. The next thing I knew, the stakes were spiraling out of control, and I couldn't back down."

"And you were suddenly ten thousand pounds poorer."

"Oh God, Emma, what am I going to do?"

"I don't know," she said frankly.

"The thing is, Emma, he was cheating. I saw him cheating." Ned raked his hand through his hair, and it almost killed her to see his tortured expression.

"Why didn't you *say* something? How could you just sit there and let him fleece you out of all your money?"

"Oh, Emma," Ned sighed, sinking into a chair and letting his head fall into his hands. "I may be a gentleman of honor, but I'm not stupid. Woodside is one of the best shots in England. I'd have been insane to say something that would provoke him into calling me out."

"Are you certain he'd call you out?"

Ned gave her a look that told her he was more than certain.

"And you'd have to accept? You couldn't just turn your back on him and walk away?"

"Emma, it's a matter of honor. I couldn't show my face anywhere if I were to accuse someone of cheating and then not face the consequences."

"I find this gentlemen's honor business overrated, indeed. Call me practical, but I do think that one's life is preferable to one's honor. At least as pertains to card games."

"I agree, but there is nothing I can do about it. The fact is I owe Woodside ten thousand pounds."

"How long have you got to come up with the money?"

"Normally I'd have to get it to him right away, but because it's a large amount he told me I could have a fortnight."

"As long as that?" Emma said sarcastically.

"I think he gave me the extra time because he likes to feel he has power over me."

"You're probably right."

Ned swallowed convulsively, his hands clutching the arm of the chair. "He said he would forget about the entire matter if I could arrange a tryst between him and Belle."

Emma felt a white-hot flame of rage consume her. "I'm going to kill him! Of all the sickening notions," she spat out, striding to her desk and throwing open the drawers. "Do you have a gun?" she asked wildly, rummaging through her belongings and tossing papers onto the floor. "All I've got is this letter opener." Suddenly an awful thought entered her head and she turned to Ned, her face ashen. "You didn't—you didn't agree?"

"For God's sake, Emma," Ned blazed. "What kind of man do you think I am?"

"I'm sorry, Ned. I know you wouldn't—I'm just so upset."

"I'm not about to trade my sister's innocence for a gambling debt," he added defensively.

"I know." Emma sighed, tapping her finger against her pathetic little dagger. "It's sharp."

"You're not going anywhere with that letter opener. You wouldn't be able to do much damage with it, anyway."

She tossed the knife back onto her desk and sank down onto the edge of her bed. "I never told anyone about this, but I had a run-in with Woodside last week."

"You did? What happened?"

"It was all very strange. He made all sorts of insults about my being American and lacking a title."

"Son of a bitch," Ned swore, clenching his fists.

"That wasn't it, though. He told me he was going to marry Belle."

"What?"

"I swear to God." Emma nodded for emphasis. "And I think he really believed it."

"What did you say?"

"I laughed at him. I probably shouldn't have done so, but the thought of Belle with that bastard was ludicrous beyond words."

"We're going to have to watch out for him, Emma. His obsession with Belle is bad enough, but now you've insulted him, and he'll be out for revenge."

Emma shot him a disbelieving look. "What could he do? Besides collecting your ten thousand pounds, that is."

Ned groaned. "Where on earth am I going to come up with it, Emma?"

"If we can cancel this debt, Woodside won't have anything with which to pressure Belle. We're going to have to come up with a plan."

"I know."

"What about your parents?"

Ned leaned his head against one of his hands, his expression anguished. "Oh, Emma. I don't want to ask them for the money. I feel so ashamed of myself as it is—I don't want them ashamed of me, too. Besides, Father's funds are all tied up. He recently made a big investment in a plantation in Ceylon. I don't think he could come up with that amount of cash so quickly."

Emma chewed on her lower lip, uncertain as to what to say.

"I got myself into this mess. I ought to get myself out."

"With a little help from your cousin."

Ned smiled at Emma wearily. "With a little help from my cousin," he repeated.

"It's probably for the best that Uncle Henry and Aunt Caroline can't help," Emma said. "They would be sick about it."

"I know, I know." Ned sighed and stood up decisively, walking over to the window and gazing out over the busy street.

"It's just too bad that this didn't happen six months from now," Emma said thoughtfully.

Ned turned around sharply, his eyes narrowing. "What happens six months from now?"

"My twenty-first birthday. My mother's family left me some money—I don't know if I ever mentioned it to you. It's been earning interest for quite some time, and I imagine there is enough to cover your debt. But it's in a trust, and I can't touch it

until my twenty-first birthday. Or unless I—"
Emma's voice caught in her throat.

"Unless you what?"

"Marry," she said softly.

"I don't suppose Ashbourne proposed this weekend," Ned said, only half joking.

"No," Emma said sadly.

"It's no matter, anyway. It'd take months to get
the money over from America."

"Actually, it's here in London. My mother was
born in America, but my grandparents emigrated
from England. My grandfather never quite trusted
Colonial banks and kept the bulk of his funds over
here. I guess my mother and father never saw any
reason to move it over even though the States were
independent."

"Well, it's useless even to think about it. No
banker would release the money to you early."

"Unless I married," Emma said softly, her heart
beginning to beat a little more rapidly.

Ned looked at her quizzically. "What are you
saying, Emma?"

"How difficult is it to get a special license?"

"Not very difficult, I imagine, if one knows the
right people."

"I would guess that Alex knows all the right
people," Emma commented, wetting her lips.
"Wouldn't you?"

"You just told me that Ashbourne didn't propose
to you this weekend."

"That's true," Emma agreed, clasping her hands
together. "But that doesn't mean *I* can't propose
to *him*."

Ned's eyes registered disbelief. "I, er, suppose
you could," he said slowly. "I've never heard of
that actually happening, but I don't suppose that
means it cannot be done."

"You think I'm a fool," Emma said flatly.

"No, no, no, of course I don't," he replied quickly. "Ashbourne is a fool if he refuses. Which he won't. I'm sure of it. It's just that he might be a litte surprised."

"A lot surprised."

"A hell of a lot surprised," Ned said, nodding his head.

Emma groaned. "Oh, God. I'm blushing just thinking about it."

Ned drummed his fingers against the wall as he considered the scheme. "But are you sure this would work, Emma? How on earth could you propose to him, have him accept, get married, and get your money—all in a fortnight?"

Her face fell. "I couldn't, I suppose. But I should think the bank would release my money once they knew I was engaged to the Duke of Ashbourne. Alex is a powerful man, you know."

"I know."

"I'm sure an announcement in the *Times* would do the trick. It's almost as good as being married. A gentleman would never throw over a lady once their engagement was in the paper. And the bankers would never dream that anyone would jilt a duke."

"But what if they refuse to release the money early? Bankers can be quite rigid about rules and all that."

"Then I'll have to have a hasty wedding. I don't think Alex would mind." She bunched up bits of her quilt in her hand, her eyes focused on her fingers a she spoke to her cousin. "I hope I have the courage," she said softly.

Ned immediately moved to her side and put his arm around her shoulder. "Emma," he said quietly, giving her a slight squeeze. "You don't have to do this for me. I can solve this problem somehow. I'll go to a moneylender if I have to. I'll be miserable for a few months, a year maybe. But marriage lasts a lifetime. I can't ask you to sacrifice your happiness like that."

"But maybe," Emma whispered, "just maybe I wouldn't be sacrificing my happiness." She looked intently up at her cousin, her violet eyes bright with emotion. "Do you understand? Maybe it's the only chance I've got for happiness."

"But Emma, are you sure you can do it? If Alex hasn't asked you to marry him, what makes you think he's going to accept your offer?"

"I don't know," Emma sighed. "I guess I'll just have to make him accept me, won't I?

Meanwhile back at Westonbirt, Alex lay soaking in a hot, steaming bath. He felt as if he'd ridden to hell and back during the past few days, and every muscle ached from overuse. He was thoroughly irritated with the godforsaken storm that had flooded half his estate, knocked down six trees, and monopolized his attention all day Saturday. Regretfully, the only time he'd been able to see Emma was at breakfast and dinner, and she had spent most of that time picking at her food and avoiding making eye contact.

She was nervous, that was all. He could understand that.

But what he couldn't understand was why he was nervous, too. Oh, he supposed he did a better job at covering it up than Emma did, but he was nearly ten years older than she was and had certainly had far more experience with the opposite sex. It stood to reason that he would be a little bit more self-contained. But even though he managed to act fairly normally, he couldn't deny the heady sense of anticipation he felt whenever she entered the room. Nor could he ignore how utterly disappointed he felt when he got up that morning and discovered that she had already left.

Alex groaned and sank back a little deeper into the tub. He was going to have to figure out exactly what it was he felt for Emma. And then once he did that, he was going to have to figure out what he wanted to do about it.

Marriage?

The notion was beginning to seem more and more appealing. He'd always planned to put off marriage until his late thirties. Then he could do what everyone expected him to do and marry some girl without a personality and promptly ignore her. Well, not so promptly. There was that matter of getting an heir. But once he got that taken care of, he could forget about her existence. He didn't need a wife getting in his way.

But the fact of the matter was—he *wanted* Emma in his way. He went out of his way to get her in his way. The idea of Emma as his wife dispelled all of his earlier notions of marriage. He felt warm inside at the thought of waking up next to her in the morning, of not having to sneak around just to get a moment alone with her. It didn't seem to make very much sense to wait around for a wife he could successfully ignore when he could have one he didn't want to ignore.

And, of course, there was that matter of getting an heir. The process didn't seem tedious anymore if it involved Emma. And for the first time, he found himself looking into the future and trying to picture those heirs his mother kept reminding him about. A little boy with carroty hair. No, a little girl with carroty hair—that was what he wanted. A tiny little girl with carroty hair and big violet eyes who would hurl herself into his arms and scream, "Papa!" when he walked into the room.

And after that, he'd tuck her into bed, grab her mother, tuck *her* into bed, and get down to the business of creating a little boy with carroty hair and big violet eyes.

Christ, it sounded like he'd already made his decision.

Was he crazy? Was he ready to throw over nearly a decade of plans for a tiny red-haired American chit?

Alex groaned again and hauled himself out of the tub, water running down his lean body in thin rivulets. He grabbed the towel that his valet had left neatly folded on a chair near the bathtub, quickly dried himself off, and padded over to his closet and took out a robe. Wrapping it around him, he flopped down on his bed.

He was fairly certain that Emma would accept him if he asked her to marry him. He knew she missed her father and had always intended to go back to America, but he could be flexible. There was no reason they couldn't go visit Boston every other year or so. In fact, the rest of her family was here in London, and he knew they wanted her to stay. He didn't really want a wife who married him because of familial pressure, but he figured he shouldn't look a gift horse in the mouth. There would be plenty of time to convince Emma that she loved him.

Alex sat up like a bolt. Did he want Emma to love him? That might be a little bit more than he could take. If someone loved you—someone decent and kind, that is—you had a responsibility not to trample all over her heart. And while he had no intention of hurting Emma, he knew that he could injure her just by not loving her back.

Of course, maybe he did love her back.

But then again, maybe she didn't love him in the first place. She hadn't actually said as much. He couldn't very well love someone back if she didn't love him first.

He could, however, love her first.

And that meant that he was going to have to convince her to love him back.

But the question was moot anyway because he hadn't yet decided to love her.

Or had he?

Alex bounded off the bed and began pacing to and fro across his room. Had he decided to love her? He didn't know. And furthermore, did a man actually *decide* to love a woman, or did it just sort of grow on you until one day you hop out of a bathtub and realize that you've loved her for ages, for so long that you're not even sure when it all started and that you're really just fighting the inevitable because it's become a habit to thwart your mother and your sister.

Oh God, he loved Emma. Now what was he going to do? Oh, fine, he could ask her to marry him, and she'd probably say yes, but he didn't think that was going to be good enough. He didn't want her to marry him just because she liked him; he wanted her to marry him because she loved him, loved him so much that she couldn't bear the thought of life without him because he was slowly beginning to realize that that was how he felt about her.

Maybe he should test the waters a little before he actually proposed—try to get an idea of what she really felt for him. There was no huge rush to ask her. Now that he had committed himself to this marriage idea, he was eager to get her legally bound to him for life, but he supposed a few days wouldn't make much of a difference. After all, if it became apparent that she wasn't going to return his feelings, he might not want to propose.

Who was he kidding? Of course he'd propose. Napoleon himself couldn't stop him.

But there really wasn't much harm in waiting just a little while—if only for his peace of mind. After all, it wasn't as if she was going away anytime soon. And no one else was going to ask in the meantime. Alex was fairly certain he'd made sure of that. Few men were brave enough to ask her to dance twice in one evening, much less to ask her to marry them. Alex had staked a claim. And it was getting time to claim that claim.

Friday would do nicely. There was some function he was supposed to attend on Wednesday. He couldn't remember where, but his secretary would have it written down back in London, and Emma would certainly be present. He could talk to her then, probe a little and try to guess her feelings. On Thursday his mother was having a small dinner party. He'd have a good chance of getting her alone then. His mother certainly did her best to give him every opportunity of doing so. On Friday morning he'd pick out an engagement ring from the family jewels and then head over to the Blydon mansion, propose, and be done with it.

Except that he really wouldn't be done with anything. Alex smiled peacefully. He would be beginning everything.

Chapter 15

Oh Lord, what was she thinking?

Tuesday afternoon saw Emma standing on the steps in front of Alex's bachelor's lodgings, an elegant townhouse located only five blocks away from the Blydon home in Grosvenor Square. It wasn't very large; Alex didn't like to entertain, and Emma supposed he planned to move into the family mansion when he married.

Which she hoped would be rather soon.

She lifted her hand up to the large brass knocker and then quickly whirled around. "Would you just go away?" she hissed. Ned was loitering about six feet away from the bottom of the steps.

He shrugged his shoulders. "Someone has to walk you home."

"Alex can walk me home."

"What if he says no?"

"Ned Blydon, that is a perfectly cruel thing to say," Emma blurted out, her heart dropping into her stomach. "He's not going to say no," she muttered. "I think."

"What?"

"Go!"

Ned started walking away backwards. "I'm going. I'm going."

Emma watched Ned disappear around the corner before turning back to the brass knocker that was looming large in front of her forehead. Taking a deep breath, she picked up the knocker and let it fall with a resounding thud. The noise was overly loud to her already frazzled senses, and she jumped nervously backwards, catching her heel on the edge of the step. With a small yelp, she flailed her arms, trying to catch her balance until she desperately grabbed hold of the railing, pitching herself forward at a bizarre angle.

And that was her position when the butler opened the door and looked down at her in an extremely quizzical manner.

"Oh, hello," Emma chirped, smiling weakly as she straightened herself as quickly as she could. "Is his grace receiving?"

The butler did not reply immediately, preferring to look her up and down in silent judgment. She was Quality, that was sure, but it was unheard of for a wellborn lady to call unescorted at an unmarried gentleman's home. He was wavering over the wisdom of allowing her to enter when Emma suddenly looked up at him with those huge violet eyes, and he was lost. Closing his eyes momentarily, he went against his better judgment and said, "Won't you come in?" He ushered her into a small parlor just off the main hall. "I'll see if his grace is available."

The butler trudged up the stairs until he located Alex in his study on the second floor.

"What is it, Smithers?" Alex asked absently, barely looking up from the papers he was studying.

"There is an unescorted young lady to see you, your grace."

Alex laid the papers down on his desk, gave his butler a sharp look, and then replied, "I do not know any young ladies who would call on me at home without an escort." He picked up his papers again and leafed through them briskly.

"As you wish, your grace." Smithers started to back out of the room but stopped just short of closing the door. "Are you certain, your grace?"

Alex put down the papers again and looked at his butler with an irritated expression. "Am I certain of what, Smithers?"

"Are you certain that you do not know this particular young lady? She seemed quite, er, earnest, your grace."

Alex decided to humor his butler. "What did she look like, Smithers?"

"She is quite petite, and her hair is a rather bright color."

"What?!" Alex burst out, standing up so sharply he banged his knee on his desk.

The crinkles around the butler's eyes softened slightly. "And she has the biggest violet eyes I have seen since Mrs. Smithers passed on seven years ago."

"Good Lord, Smithers, why didn't you say so!" Alex dashed out of the room and nearly hurtled himself down the stairs.

Smithers followed at a somewhat more sedate pace. "I wasn't aware you were interested in the color of my late wife's eyes," he said softly, smiling wider than he had in seven years.

"Emma!" Alex exclaimed as he bounded into the room. "What on earth are you doing here? Is something wrong? Does your family know you're here?"

Emma licked her lips nervously before answering. "No, no they don't. Except for Ned. He walked me over."

"Your cousin allowed you to come here unescorted? Is he insane?"

"No, although he thinks I am," Emma admitted, her voice a little mournful. Alex didn't look over-joyed to see her. She stood up hastily. "I can leave if this isn't a good time."

"No!" Alex exclaimed loudly as he crossed the room and shut the door. "Please stay. I'm just rather surprised to see you here."

"I know this is highly irregular," Emma began, not having any idea how to broach the subject of marriage. "But I wanted to speak to you private-ly, and you know how difficult it is to get a few moments alone in London."

Alex raised an eyebrow. He knew.

"Ned told me that you returned yesterday after-noon. He said he saw you last night at White's."

Alex wondered if Ned had also told her that he had spent the better part of an hour grilling him about Emma.

Emma stood up suddenly, too anxious to sit down. She began to pace, nervously catching her lower lip between her teeth.

"You do that a lot," Alex pointed out with an indulgent smile.

She whirled around. "What?"

"Nibble on your lower lip. I find it rather endear-ing."

"Oh. Well, thank you."

Alex crossed the room and caught her upper arms in his hands. "Emma," he said in a low voice, looking very deeply into her eyes. "Please tell me what is wrong. You're obviously very upset about something."

Her breath caught in her throat as she stared up into Alex's intense green eyes. With her head tipped back in a vulnerable position, she felt as if he could see into the very depths of her soul. She swallowed convulsively, fighting the urge to press her body against his and simply melt into his arms. She could feel the heat emanating from his body and desperately longed to become a part of that warmth.

Alex could see her violet eyes begin to smolder with desire, and it took every ounce of willpower he possessed not to lean down and capture her lips with his own. He had no idea how to try to make her feel better, but he was fairly certain that what she didn't need was another intimate encounter with him.

Emma didn't know how long she remained in that position before she remembered to breathe, but she finally exhaled and said, "I need to talk to you about something, and I cannot think clearly when you are standing so close to me."

Alex took that as a good sign. "Of course," he said solicitously, releasing her arms and motioning to the sofa where she had been seated just moments earlier. Scratching his chin thoughtfully, he began to consider his situation. He'd been planning to propose to Emma on Friday, but this might be as good a time as any. She must have some tender feelings for him or she never would have dared to come by herself to his townhouse. And after all, he'd have more opportunity here to kiss her senseless after she said yes (which he was praying she would) than he would at her cousins' home, where he'd been planning on proposing. He'd just wait until she told him whatever it was that was bothering her so much, and then he'd ask her. It would be a great moment.

Emma scurried over to the sofa and sat down, perching herself on the edge. "Alex?" she said, leaning forward. "I have to ask you something, and I'm afraid you'll say no."

Alex sat down in a chair adjacent to the sofa. He leaned forward, too, so that his face was not so very far from hers. "You'll never know unless you ask."

"I'm even more afraid you'll say yes," she muttered.

Alex was intrigued, but he didn't say anything.

Emma took a deep breath, swallowed, and squared her shoulders. She'd known this wasn't going to be easy, but she had never dreamed how terrified she would feel as she was trying to get the words out. "Alex," she said suddenly, her voice coming out overly loud. Swallowing again, she willed herself to talk a little more softly. "Alex," she repeated. "I need—that is, I want—No, no." She looked up at him, her eyes wide and luminous. "This is very difficult for me."

"I can see that," Alex said consolingly. He thought she was going to shred the handkerchief she held in her hands.

"Alex, I would like to request your hand in marriage." The words tumbled out very quickly, and Emma suddenly exhaled, not even aware that she'd been holding her breath.

Alex blinked, but other than his eyelids, he did not move a muscle.

Emma looked at him anxiously. "Alex?"

"Did you just ask me to marry you?"

She started to twist the folds of her dark green skirt in her hand, not quite brave enough to look him in the eye. "Yes."

"I thought that's what you said." Alex suddenly sat back, rather stunned. He'd just managed to convince himself that it was time to ask Emma to marry him, and she'd beaten him to the punch. A small voice in the back of his head was telling him that this was a good thing, that if she had actually asked him to marry her, it probably meant that she'd say yes to him when he finally got around to asking her the same question. But an even larger voice in the front of his head was saying that this was all wrong, that she had somehow denied him something he wanted very badly. Damn it, he'd been looking forward to proposing. He'd been rehearsing nonstop for two days. He couldn't get to sleep at night because he couldn't stop himself from playing out various scenarios in his mind. He had even given serious thought to getting down on one knee. Instead he was slouched in a chair that wasn't quite big enough for him while Emma was perched so precariously on the edge of his sofa that he was afraid she'd fall off.

"Emma, are you sure you know what you're doing?" he finally said.

She deflated. That wasn't a very positive response.

"What I mean is," Alex continued, "usually it's the man who asks the woman to marry him."

"I just couldn't wait until you got around to asking me," Emma said, somewhat sheepishly. "*If* you got around to asking me."

"You wouldn't have had to wait very long," Alex muttered under his breath.

Emma obviously didn't hear him because she looked no less anxious than she had earlier. "The problem is that I need to marry you rather quickly, I'm afraid."

Alex thought that was an extremely cryptic comment indeed, since they hadn't performed the act that usually required a woman to marry a man rather quickly.

"This is very uncommon," he said, shaking his head.

"I realize that," she improvised, "but you've often told me I'm an uncommon female."

"I haven't actually heard of a woman proposing to a man," Alex said, measuring his words carefully. "I don't think it's exactly *illegal*, but it just isn't done."

Emma rolled her eyes. She was beginning to understand what was going on here. She had bruised Alex's considerable male pride. Normally she would be enjoying this, but her entire life's happiness was at stake. He was sitting over there, feeling sorry for himself because she'd stolen from him some kind of inherent male right, and he hadn't even given one thought to how much courage it must have taken her to come to his home unescorted and ask him to marry her. This wasn't exactly something she'd been brought up to do. "Methods of proposing marriage" definitely had not been squeezed in between Latin and piano lessons when she was growing up. Nevertheless, she decided that one of them was going to have to be the mature one in this scenario, and it might as well be her.

"Really, Alex," she said with a sweet smile. "You should feel flattered. It's a rare man who has a woman so besotted with him that she defies convention and asks him to marry her."

Alex blinked. "I was going to ask you on Friday," he said in a slightly petulant tone. "I had even rehearsed what I was going to say."

"You were?" Emma exclaimed joyfully. "You did? Oh, Alex, I'm so happy!" Unable to contain herself, she bounded up off of the sofa and knelt in front of Alex, taking both of his hands in hers.

He looked down at her, his expression still a little bit childish. "I was rather excited about proposing. I've never done it before, you know. And now I don't get to."

Emma beamed, giving his hands a squeeze. "You still can. I promise I'll say yes."

Alex sighed and then suddenly looked very seriously into her eyes. "I'm not acting very gracious, am I?"

"No," she admitted, "but I really don't care. I'm just so happy that you want to marry me."

"I haven't said yes yet, you know."

Emma scowled.

"But I will, I suppose, if given the proper encouragement."

"And what would *that* be, your grace?"

Alex looked heavenward in mock innocence. "Oh, I don't know. A kiss would do rather well to start with."

Emma leaned forward, propping her hands on the arms of his chair. "You're going to have to cooperate," she murmured, feeling extraordinarily daring now that he had accepted her proposal.

Alex leaned down, his hands covering hers. "By all means."

He stopped suddenly, his mouth achingly close to hers. "Oh, Alex," Emma sighed, lifting her lips that last half an inch. Ever so gently, she brushed her mouth against his, marveling in the thought that this was the very first kiss she'd initiated and thinking that it must be the sweetest of all for that very reason.

"I'm so very glad I thought to close the door," Alex said, smiling as he nuzzled her neck. "Although . . ." His words trailed off as he reluctantly turned his head away from Emma and twisted his neck until he was facing the parlor door. "Smithers!" he yelled abruptly. "Get your ear away from that door! You've heard everything you wanted to hear! Now be gone with you!"

"Right away, sir," was the muffled reply.

Emma could not help but laugh as she heard footsteps disappear down the hall and up the stairs.

"He's been trying to get me to settle down for years," Alex explained. "Now where were we?"

She smiled seductively. "I think we were about to move over to the sofa."

Alex groaned. He hoped Emma had no plans for a long engagement. He rose from his chair, pulled her to her feet and then off her feet, only to set her down on the sofa. "Oh, darling," he murmured as he sat beside her. "I've missed you so much."

"You just saw me three days ago."

"That doesn't mean I didn't miss you."

"I missed you, too," Emma said shyly. "When I wasn't working myself into a frenzy of nerves about coming here today."

"I'm most happy you did." Alex brushed his lips against hers again, this time deepening the kiss with his tongue, running it along the smooth line of her teeth. When she let out a soft sigh, he took advantage of the moment, pressing in further, drinking her in, tasting her sweetness.

"I'm so glad marriage lasts a lifetime," Emma said softly against his lips. "Because I don't think I'll ever get enough of your kisses." She drew slightly away from him, placing her hand on his cheek. "You make me feel so beautiful."

"You *are* beautiful."

"It is very kind of you to say so, but red hair is hopelessly out of fashion, and besides, it would be impossible for anyone to look as lovely as I feel right this moment."

Alex gazed tenderly down at her face. Her clear, fine skin was flushed rosy pink with desire, and her eyes were wide and sparkling, framed by the longest lashes he'd ever seen. And her lips, oh Lord, they had never looked quite so pink before, nor so full. "Then you must feel very lovely, Emma. Because I've never seen anything in my life as exquisite as you are right now."

Emma felt a warm glow take over her body. "Oh, Alex, please kiss me again."

"Gladly, my love." Placing his hands on her cheeks, he pulled her face to his. Emma offered no resistance at all, and his tongue immediately dipped into her mouth, stroking her soft flesh. Emma shyly followed suit, curiously exploring him in the same manner.

Alex thought that her hesitant caresses would be the death of him, he was so eager for more. He pulled her to him passionately, pressing her body intimately against his own, his hands roving uncontrollably.

Emma moaned with pleasure, barely able to believe the shivering tremors of joy that shot through her body. And then just when she thought she could take no more, Alex placed his hand on her breast, squeezing it ever so slightly. It felt like a fire had burned right through the fabric of her dress, searing her skin, branding her as his future wife. She was slowly losing control; all she could think about was getting as close to him as possible, touching him everywhere.

Just as Emma hovered at the brink of losing herself completely, Alex pulled himself away reluctantly, very reluctantly. "Darling," he said, summoning chivalry he'd never dreamed existed, "I'm going to stop now, before we get to the point when I cannot. Do you understand?"

She nodded tremulously.

"I want our wedding night to be perfect. At that moment, you will belong to me in every way."

"And you will belong to me," Emma said softly.

He dropped a gentle kiss on her lips. "Yes, I will. It will be the most beautiful moment of our lives, I promise you that, and I don't want to spoil it in any way. Now, if you don't mind, I think I would like to put my arms around you and hold you for a few moments before I'm forced to send you back home."

Emma nodded again, unable to find words to express the emotions coursing through her. She had never dreamed it was possible for a woman to feel as utterly full of joy as she did right then. Dimly she realized that he hadn't yet said that he loved her, but then, neither had she, and that didn't diminish her feelings for him in any way. Besides, she could sense his love, feel it, almost touch it. Over the past few months she had come to know Alex quite well. He couldn't hold her like this if he didn't love her at least a little bit. And in time, she knew he would say the words. Perhaps she'd even work up the courage to tell him first. How difficult could that be? She'd already asked him to marry her. Nothing could be scarier than that, and she had come through it just fine. But she'd have to put off talk of love. For now, she was content just to rest in his arms. She'd found a home there.

After a few minutes, Alex knew that he was going to have to take Emma home. She had said that Ned had escorted her to his front door—Alex didn't even want to guess what Emma had done to convince her cousin to bring her here. Nonetheless, he knew that Ned would come for her if she remained overlong, and if that happened, the entire Blydon family might get involved. All hell would break loose. Everyone would be appeased, of course, once informed of their impending nuptials, but Alex thought that it would not be a rather auspicious beginning to their lives together.

And so, with great regret, Alex nudged Emma's shoulder. "Wake up, my love. I'm afraid I'm going to have to take you home."

"I wish you didn't have to."

"Believe me, love, I wish I didn't have to either, but the last thing we want is your entire family descending on us."

Emma yawned and slowly extricated herself from Alex's arms. "I despise reality."

Alex chuckled. "How does next week sound?"

"How does next week sound for what?"

"Our marriage, you ninnyhead."

"*Next week*? Are you mad?"

"Obviously."

"Alex, there is no way I can plan a wedding by next week." Then Emma remembered that the entire point of her proposing to him was that she needed to marry right away.

But Alex had already given in. "Two weeks, then."

"All right," she said slowly. "Aunt Caroline is going to have a fit of the vapors. She'll want a lavish affair, I'm sure."

"Do you want a lavish affair?"

Emma smiled up into his eyes. "I really don't care," she sighed. All she really wanted was Alex. Although, now that she thought about it, she'd always dreamed of a beautiful gown, of gliding down an aisle to meet her future. "A week from Saturday," she said quickly, hoping that she could find a dressmaker willing to work under such time constraints.

"Very well. I'm going to hold you to that date."

Emma giggled slightly. "Please do."

Alex was still wondering about her rather odd comment about having to marry him quickly. Whatever the matter, it must be something urgent for her to defy all convention and propose marriage. "Emma," he said, touching her chin lightly. "I have one question for you."

"Yes?"

"What on earth prompted you to ask me to marry you?"

"What *prompted* me? Well, it's all rather silly, actually, and I could just kill Ned over it, although I have to say it all worked out very well in the end. I really couldn't be happier." Emma looked up at Alex and gave him a sheepish grin. "I needed money, actually, and I can't use my—" She stopped abruptly, horrified by the change that had just come over Alex. His entire body seemed frozen, tensed for a fight, and his face was a granite mask, hard and unyielding. Emma stumbled back a step, almost feeling as if she'd been pushed back by his frown. "Alex?" she said hesitatingly. "Is something wrong?"

Alex felt a white hot rage consume him, and he felt unable even to speak. Fury pounded through his mind, blotting out all reason. *I needed money I needed money I needed money*. Emma's words echoed unyieldingly in his head, and the walls around his heart that she had so recently broken down began to reform. How could he have been such a fool? He thought he'd finally found a woman who seemed to care for him, not for the material comforts and prestige that came along with his name. And he had actually believed himself to be in love with her. What an idiot. In the end, she'd proved to be just like all the others. He couldn't believe she'd actually come out and admitted to him that all she wanted was money. That, he supposed, was a point in her favor. At least she hadn't been devious like all the rest.

Alex stared coldly at her, his eyes two chips of emerald ice. "Get out," he said harshly, practically spitting the words at her.

Emma felt all the blood drain from her face, and for a moment she thought she might faint. "What?" she gasped, unable to believe she'd heard him correctly.

"You heard me. I want you gone."

"But what about—?" She could barely get the words out.

"You may consider any agreement we have reached here today to be null and void." His voice was icy, and he grabbed her arm, propelling her to the door.

Emma felt hot tears welling up in her eyes, and she fought to keep them from rolling down her cheeks as Alex pushed her through the room. "Alex, please," she pleaded as she stumbled out of the parlor and into the main hall. "What is wrong? What happened? Please tell me. Please!"

Alex whipped her around to face him and looked her hard in the eye. "You greedy little bitch."

Emma felt as if she'd been hit. "Oh my God," she whispered, no longer able to control the tears that flowed freely from her eyes.

"Wait outside," he said, roughly, putting her out on the front step. "I'll get a carriage to bring you home." He turned on his heel and stepped back inside. Then suddenly, he turned around. "Don't ever come back."

As Emma stood on the steps, she wondered if she had died. Wiping some of the tears off her cheeks, she took great big gulps of air, trying to regain her equilibrium. She had to get out of there. The last thing she wanted was to return home in his carriage. Pulling her shawl over her head to hide her bright hair, she hurried down the steps and along the street.

Chapter 16

The lonely walk home gave Emma ample time to scrutinize her ill-fated conversation with Alex. It didn't take her long to figure out exactly what had happened. Belle had told her about Alex's first foray into polite society, and Emma knew that he was still pursued relentlessly for his title and his wealth. She also knew that he detested the women who wanted him for these reasons.

Emma realized that when Alex had asked her what prompted her to propose to him, she'd answered the question all wrong. Practically the first word out of her mouth had been "money." But, she thought angrily, he had asked what *prompted* her to ask him, not *why* she wanted to marry him. If he had inquired about that, she probably would have gulped down her pride and told him that she loved him, praying that he'd respond in a similar fashion.

But just because she understood why Alex had reacted as he did didn't mean that she forgave him for the injustice. He never should have jumped to such a vicious conclusion about her. She thought that they had built a more solid relationship than that. She had believed that Alex was her friend, not just another one of her admirers. And as her friend, he ought to have trusted her enough at least to ask her what she meant when she said that she needed money. If he had cared about her, he would have realized that there had to be more to her story than simple greed. He would have given her the chance to explain the sticky situation in which Ned had placed her.

Emma took a deep breath, trying to hold back the tears that threatened to spill down her cheeks. If Alex didn't trust her as a friend, she didn't see how he was going to trust her as a wife. And that probably meant he didn't really love her.

Emma hurried along as she turned the final corner that led to the block where she lived. She had no doubt that Alex would eventually come to his senses and figure out what had happened. He had a stubborn streak that almost matched hers, but he would realize that his image of Emma as a money-grubbing social climber just didn't ring true in light of their two months of solid friendship. He might even apologize. But Emma didn't think she'd be able to forgive him for not trusting her. They could have been very happy together. They could have had a marvelous marriage. Well, she thought spitefully, he had ruined his chances for happiness.

Unfortunately, he had also ruined hers.

Which was why, when Emma finally scurried up the steps and slipped through the front door of the Blydon household, it was all she could do to blink back her tears and race up the stairs to her bedroom before they exploded like a flood. She locked her door with a quick twist of her wrist and threw herself down on her bed, thoroughly soaking her pillowcase within minutes.

She cried with great, big, wrenching sobs that shook her entire body and wrung out her soul. She was oblivious to the noise she was making, nor did she notice the tentative taps that first Ned, then Belle, then finally Caroline made on her door. A piece of her heart had been ripped out that afternoon, and Emma was mourning its loss. Never again would she trust her judgment when it came to men. And the most agonizing part of it was, she knew that she still loved him. Alex had, in a way, betrayed her, and still she loved him. She didn't think she'd ever learn how to stop loving him.

And she hurt so much. Her father had told her that time healed all wounds, but she wondered if there were enough years left in her lifetime to ease the hard, throbbing ache in her heart. Alex had wounded her, and he had wounded her deeply.

But as Emma's tears slowly subsided, another emotion came to join the sorrow, hurt, and pain that racked her body. Anger. Pure, unadulterated anger. How dare he treat her so callously? If Alex couldn't trust her, the woman he supposedly wanted to spend his life with, he must be colder, meaner, more cynical than the *ton* had ever supposed. For all she cared, he could live out his life all alone with his hard little heart.

She was furious.

And so, when Emma finally unlocked her door, and Ned came tumbling into her room, her eyes were still red-rimmed and bloodshot but she wasn't crying. She was seething.

"What on earth happened?" Ned burst out, quickly closing the door behind him. "Are you all right?" He took her by the shoulders, scanning her features intently. "Did he hurt you?"

Emma looked away. Ned's concern for her well-being diffused most of the explosive anger that possessed her. "Not physically, if that's what you mean."

"He said no, didn't he?" Ned surmised. "What

an idiot. Any fool could tell he was in love with you."

"I guess he's the biggest fool of all, then," Emma tried to joke. "Because he surely didn't know it himself." She crossed the room and gazed bleakly out the window for a minute before finally turning back to her cousin. "I'm really sorry, Ned. I know how desperately you needed the money. I don't think I'm going to be able to get it now." Emma let out a harsh little laugh. "Unless *you* marry me, of course."

Ned stared at her in amazement.

"Although I don't think we'd suit," she continued wryly. "Frankly I think I'd laugh if you tried to kiss me. I don't think it's going to work. I'm so sorry."

"For God's sake, Emma!" Ned exploded. "I don't care about the money. I'm not a pauper. I'll find a way to get it." He strode over to her and pulled her into a brotherly embrace. "I'm concerned about you. That bastard hurt you, didn't he?"

Emma nodded, feeling slightly better now that Ned was holding her. A hug worked wonders for the broken heart. "Actually, the only thing that is keeping me from crying right now is that I'm so furious with him. And," she added sheepishly, "I've cried so many tears I think I've dehydrated myself."

"Would you like a glass of water?"

"Actually, I think I would."

"Wait a moment. I'll fetch a maid." Ned led Emma to her bed where she dutifully sat down and then crossed the room and opened the door.

Belle tumbled in.

"Oh, for Christ's sake, Belle," Ned burst out. "Were you eavesdropping?"

Belle picked herself up off the floor with as much dignity as she could muster, which wasn't much, considering that she'd landed on her belly. "What do you expect?" she demanded in an exasperated voice. "The two of you have been creeping around the house for the past two days, obviously conspiring to carry out some sort of nefarious plot, and neither of you has had the decency to include me." She snorted at Emma and Ned, planting her hands resolutely on her hips. "Did it not occur to either of you that I might like to know what was going on? I'm not stupid, you know. I might have been able to help." She sniffed disdainfully. "Or at least had fun trying."

Emma stared at her blankly throughout the tirade. "There wasn't any nefarious plot," she finally replied.

"And it wasn't any of your business, anyway," Ned said, somewhat peevishly.

"Rubbish," Belle retorted. "If it were only *your* business, it wouldn't be any of my business. And if it were only *Emma's* business, it wouldn't be any of my business. But if it is *both* of your businesses, then it's obviously *my* business, too."

"Your leaps of logic are astounding," Ned commented dryly.

"I've quite forgotten what it is we were talking about," Emma added.

"And then!" Belle said dramatically, working herself into a fine little snit. "And then, I came home from the park today only to find that my only cousin is crying her eyes out behind a locked door, and when I tried to go to comfort her, my darling brother stopped me and said, 'Leave her alone. You don't even know what she's upset about. Do be gone.'"

Emma turned to Ned, eyebrows raised curiously. "Did you really say 'Do be gone'? That's a perfectly horrid thing to say."

"Well, I might have," Ned said defensively. "If

you recall, it sounded as if you were dying in here. I was quite worried."

Emma stood up, turned to Belle, and took her hands. "I'm sorry if you felt left out, Belle. That certainly wasn't our intention. It was just that Ned had a problem, I had a solution, and everything happened so fast that we forgot to include you."

"And I'm sorry I made such a scene," Belle replied sheepishly. "But now you really ought to tell me what is going on."

"About which?" Emma asked. "The problem or the solution?"

"Either. Both."

"Well, to sum things up, I asked Alex to marry me."

Belle sank onto the bed, nearly pulling Emma along with her. "Whaaat?"

"And the bastard refused," Ned put in savagely.

"He what? He didn't."

"He did," Emma said with a morose little nod.

"Why?" Belle asked incredulously.

"Actually, that's a bit personal." Emma fidgeted slightly and then quickly added, "And I haven't told Ned a thing about it."

"But why? Couldn't you wait for him to propose? That's how it's usually done, you know. I'm certain he would have gotten around to it sooner or later."

"I didn't really have much time."

"What on earth do you mean? You're not exactly a spinster, Emma."

"That's where I come in," Ned interjected. "Emma was sacrificing herself on the altar of marriage for my sake, I'm afraid."

Belle drew back, looking at Emma with a skeptical glance. "You'd do that for Ned?"

"Anyway," Ned continued loudly, pointedly ignoring his sister's jibe. "I've gotten myself into a bit of a mess. A gambling debt."

"How much?" Belle asked bluntly.

"Ten thousand pounds."

"What?!" Belle shrieked.

"My reaction precisely," Emma murmured.

"Are you crazy?"

"Look, I've already been through all this with Emma," Ned sighed. "Suffice it to say that Woodside was cheating."

"Oh no, not Viscount Benton," Belle groaned. "The man's a swine."

"He's worse than you think," Emma added. "He offered to trade the debt in for you."

"For me? Oh no, you don't mean . . ."

"Actually I think he wants to marry you. And he probably thought that compromising you would be the only way to get you to agree."

Belle shuddered. "I suddenly feel extremely dirty. I think I would like a bath."

"I have a bit of money that my mother's family left to me," Emma explained. "I thought I would give it to Ned so that he shouldn't have to tell your parents about it, but I'm not allowed to touch any of the funds until I marry."

"Oh my," Belle breathed. "What on earth are we going to do?"

"I don't think I have any choice," Ned said. "I'll have to see a moneylender."

"Unless . . ." Emma said thoughtfully, her words trailing off.

"Unless what?" Ned asked sharply. "The last time you said 'unless,' you decided to propose to Ashbourne, and all that got you was a broken heart."

The mention of Emma's shattered emotions nearly sent a tear rolling down her cheek, but she quickly blinked it back.

"You idiot," Belle hissed, kicking her brother in the shin.

"I'm sorry, Emma," he apologized immediately. "I should never have said that. I really didn't mean it the way it sounded."

"It's all right," Emma said in a small voice, glancing over her shoulder so she wouldn't have to look at her cousins while she regained her composure. "While I was talking to the two of you, everything was so, well, normal. I'd almost forgotten to be sad. You just reminded me, that's all."

"I'm sorry," Ned repeated.

"Don't be. I'm sure I'll remember to be sad a hundred times before I fall asleep tonight. And I'm sure I'll remember to be angry a hundred more times. But perhaps, just for now, the two of you can try to help me forget."

"Right!" Belle said quickly, skipping back to their previous conversation. "You said 'unless.' I think you were devising some sort of plan."

Emma stared off out the window for a few more moments before finally replying. "Oh yes. Right. Here is what I think we should do."

Belle and Ned leaned forward expectantly.

"I think we should steal Ned's voucher."

"What?" her cousins asked in disbelieving unison.

"If Woodside hasn't got the voucher, he can't very well try to collect the debt. And there is no way he can convince anyone that Ned hasn't paid up if he doesn't have the voucher to prove it. It's a beautiful plan."

"It might work," Ned said thoughtfully. "When do you want to do it?"

"We'd better start right away. We haven't got

long, and we don't know how many times we'll have to try before we find it."

"How on earth are you going to make sure that he's not home when you steal it?" Belle asked. "I don't think he goes out every night. And I certainly don't know enough about his habits to predict when he would leave if he actually did go out."

Emma looked her cousin straight in the eye. "That," she said decisively, "is where you come in."

Belle recoiled visibly. "I don't like the sound of that."

"Oh, for goodness sake, Belle. I am not asking you to prostitute yourself. All you have to do is send Woodside a flirtatious little note that you are eager to see him at the . . ." Emma bit her lip and looked upward as she mentally scanned her engagement calendar. "At Lady Mottram's ball tomorrow night. We already know that he is thoroughly infatuated with you. I haven't a doubt that he'll race to meet you there. All you have to do is contrive to keep him entertained for a couple of hours while we slip in and grab the voucher."

"And how do you propose I do that? He's probably going to think that Ned has decided to sacrifice my virginity for ten thousand pounds."

"All the better," Emma said with a nod. "He definitely won't leave the ball before you do, then."

"Just don't let him drag you out into the garden," Ned advised.

"Or a balcony," Emma added. "Balconies are often poorly lit. I've heard that quite a bit goes on out there."

"What should I say when people inquire after the two of you?" Belle asked. "They will, you know. I don't think I've gone to a ball alone all season."

"You won't be alone," Emma replied. "I'm sure your mother and father will attend."

"Well, *that* is comforting, I must say." Sarcasm dripped from Belle's every word. "Don't you think they will be just a little bit curious about my spending so much time with a man I utterly despise?"

"Belle, you are an intelligent woman," Ned stated matter-of-factly. "I am certain you will think of something."

"No one will question Ned's absence," Emma put in. "He's a man, you know, and they are allowed to go about as they wish. And as for me, well, just say that I'm feeling a bit ill. My falling out with Alex will probably be the latest *on-dit* by then, and everyone will expect me to be thoroughly heartbroken."

"This is going to be the most horrid, repulsive, disgusting task that I have ever undertaken," Belle sighed, looking as if she had just drunk a glass of sour milk.

"But you'll do it?" Emma asked hopefully.

"Of course."

Tuesday night Alex spent with a bottle of whiskey.

At some point during his drunken stupor, he began to marvel at Emma's wondrous acting talent. She'd have to be very good to fool him for a solid two months. He'd been so certain that he'd known her, really known her, the way he did Dunford, and Sophie, and his mother. She had become such an integral part of his life that he often could predict what she was going to say before she said it. And yet she consistently surprised him. Who would have guessed that such a keen mathematical mind was hidden beneath her bright tresses? Or that she was just about the fastest tree-climber in the British Isles? (This he hadn't seen firsthand, but Belle and Ned had both sworn it was true.)

Surely a woman who could climb a tree, bait a fishhook with a worm (yes, he'd heard all about that, too), and perform long division with the greatest of ease couldn't be the greedy little bitch he'd called her earlier that afternoon.

But when he'd asked her why she wanted to marry him, she'd come right out and said it: money.

But then again, no woman who is dangling after a fortune actually admits to the man in question that all she wants is his money.

She had, however, said she needed money. That much was irrefutable.

But then there was the needling little fact that Emma had quite a bit of money of her own. Alex was familiar with her father's company; it was quite profitable. In all truth, she didn't really need his fortune. If he hadn't been so furious with her that afternoon, he might have remembered that fact.

Something didn't make sense, but Alex was a little too drunk to figure out what.

He fell asleep in his study.

Wednesday morning he nursed a horrific hangover.

He hauled himself up the stairs and collapsed onto his bed, where, amidst the throbbing of his temples and his dangerously queasy stomach, he began to wonder if perhaps some sort of misunderstanding had taken place. It certainly made more sense that Emma's actions over a two-month period ought to carry more weight than a flippant comment made on the spur of the moment.

If that were true, then he'd just made a paramount ass of himself.

But on the other hand, Emma's comment about

needing money validated all of the opinions he'd held about women for nearly ten years. Surely a decade took precedence over two months.

Alex let out an agonized groan. His head was still far too bleary to make such weighty decisions, and truth be told, he was afraid he wasn't going to like himself very much when he finally did reach a conclusion about what had happened the previous afternoon.

Cursing himself for a coward, he drifted back to sleep. It was easier than thinking about her.

When he finally woke up, a few hours after midday, it was not due to his valet's careful prodding, nor to the bright sunlight that streamed through his window. Rather, he was brutally awakened by Dunford, who had artfully wheedled his way past Smithers and plowed right through Alex's valet, who subsequently removed his offended sensibilities to the kitchens where he was nursing a strong cup of tea.

"Wake up, Ashbourne!" he yelled, shaking Alex by the shoulders. "For the love of God, man, I don't think we've got much time to spare."

Alex reluctantly opened his eyes. Christ, it felt as if someone had applied sealing wax to his eyelids. "What are you doing in my bedroom?"

Dunford recoiled from the noxious aroma of stale alcohol on Alex's breath. "Good Lord, Ashbourne, you reek. What did you do last night? Imbibe a winery?"

"I don't recall inviting you into my bedroom," Alex said in an irritated voice.

Dunford wrinkled his nose. "The stench pouring forth from your general direction is really quite amazing."

"In fact, I don't recall *ever* inviting you into my bedroom."

"Don't flatter yourself. There are many other bedrooms I would prefer to occupy. However, we are in dire straits. Desperate measures were necessary."

Alex shot his friend an annoyed glance as he laboriously rose from his bed and crossed over to his washstand, where a bowl of water had been left out the previous night. He splashed his face, blinking a few times as the frigid water started to restore circulation to his brain. "Dunford, what are you talking about?"

"Something is going on over at the Blydon household. Something very strange. I think we need to intercede."

Alex closed his eyes for a moment. "I'm afraid you'll have to proceed on your own. I don't think I'm welcome any longer in the Blydon household."

Dunford raised his eyebrows.

"Emma and I had an argument," Alex said simply.

"I see."

Alex doubted that he did. "It may have been just a misunderstanding," he muttered. "In which case I may be the greatest fool who ever lived."

Dunford declined to comment.

Alex looked at his friend intently. They had known each other for years, and he valued Dunford's judgment. "What is your opinion of Emma? You've spent a fair amount of time with her since she arrived. What do you really think of her?"

"I think you're an idiot if you don't marry her."

"Do you think she'd marry for money?"

"For God's sake, Ashbourne, she's got a fortune of her own. She doesn't need to marry for money."

Alex felt a knot begin to unfold within him as the cold cynicism he'd carried around for years began to crumble. "But do you think she's greedy?" he asked, almost desperately. "Some women never have enough to satisfy them."

Dunford stared Alex in the eye, his warm gaze never wavering. "Do you think she's greedy, Ashbourne? Or are you afraid to take a chance?"

Alex slumped into a chair, his face a portrait of abject despair. "I don't know anything anymore," he said wearily, resting his forehead in one of his hands.

Dunford moved to the window, where he looked out over the busy London streets. He sighed softly, aware of his friend's confusion yet sensing that he needed to keep the last shreds of his pride intact. So Dunford kept his gaze fixed on a tall oak tree across the street as he said, "I've known you for at least a decade, Ashbourne, and in that time I have rarely presumed to offer you advice. But I'm going to do it now." He paused for a moment, trying to collect the words in his head. "You've spent the last ten years resigned to the fate of a marriage that, if not unhappy, would at least be unsatisfying. And then you met Emma, and suddenly the possibility of a happy marriage arose, but you've grown so distrustful of women that all you can do is look for reasons why Emma won't make you a good wife. And I think it's because you know that if you take a chance on Emma, and you aren't happy, it will be far, far more painful than any marriage of convenience you might have imagined."

Alex closed his eyes, unused to such scrutiny of his emotions.

"But there is one thing you forgot," Dunford continued softly. "If you take a chance on Emma, and you *are* happy, you'll be happier than you've ever dreamed possible. And I have a feeling she's worth the risk."

Alex swallowed as he rose out of the chair and went to stand by Dunford at the window. "It isn't easy listening to a dissection of one's soul," he said gravely. "But I thank you."

A ghost of a smile touched Dunford's lips.

"I don't think she'll see me though," Alex said grimly. "I've really botched things up. The damage may be irreparable."

Dunford tilted his head to one side. "Nonsense. Nothing is irreparable. Besides, she may not have a choice."

Alex quirked one eyebrow.

"I think she and Belle have gotten themselves into some sort of a scrape," Dunford explained. "That's why I came over."

"What's wrong?" Alex asked quickly, a sense of panic rising within him.

"I'm not certain. I dropped by the Blydons' to see Belle this morning and while I was waiting for her to come down, I overheard her instruct a footman to deliver a letter to Viscount Benton with all possible haste."

"Woodside!" Alex exclaimed. "Why on earth would she want to contact that bastard?"

"I have no idea. As a matter of fact, I'm quite certain that she thoroughly detests the man. He's been leering at her for over a year. More than once she's begged me to help her escape him. Why do you think I end up dancing with her so often?"

Alex caught the tip of his thumb between his teeth as he tried to make sense of Belle's behavior. "Something is wrong," he said grimly.

"I know. It gets worse. Just as Belle was about to enter the parlor where I was waiting, Emma came rushing down. I don't think she saw me at first because she grabbed Belle by the arm and urgently whispered, 'Did you send it? Did you make sure that Malloy knows to tell him it's most urgent? It's not going to work if he doesn't meet you at Lady Mottram's.'"

"What happened next?"

"That's when Emma noticed my presence. She turned quite pink and started stammering. I don't think I have ever seen her at such a loss before. The next thing I knew, she had run up the stairs."

"Did you question Belle about it?"

"I tried to, but she gave me some ridiculous story about a prank the two of them were playing on Ned. I imagine she was hoping that I hadn't heard her giving the footman the note for Woodside."

"We're going to have to do something," Alex said decisively. "Woodside has no scruples. Whatever they're doing, they're in over their heads."

"We can't stop them, however, if we don't even know what's going on."

Alex planted his hands on his hips. "We'll just have to confront them tonight."

"Right," Dunford agreed with a sharp nod.

"At Lady Mottram's."

Chapter 17

"**H**ow do I look?"

Emma jumped in front of Ned, her lithe form clad completely in black. She was wearing a pair of dark breeches that had belonged to him when he was fourteen. Ned only stared.

"Can I pass for a boy?" Emma persisted. "I'll pin my hair up underneath a cap, of course."

Ned gulped. "Uh, Emma, the thing is, well, no. You don't look like a boy at all."

"No?" Emma sighed. "Darn. And I was so happy to find a pair of breeches that fit, too. They're a little big in the waist." She pulled the waistband away from her body to demonstrate. "But anything smaller would have been too snug in the hips. Breeches just aren't cut to fit a woman's body."

"There might be a good reason for that," Ned murmured, observing the indecent way the breeches hugged her feminine frame. "It's a good thing I'm your cousin," he remarked. "I wouldn't want anyone else to see you like this."

"Don't be such a stickler. Frankly, I find these breeches exceedingly comfortable. It's a wonder that women around the world haven't revolted yet. If you want to know why so many women swoon all the time, you ought to try lacing yourself into a corset."

"Also, Emma, you need to, uh, that is . . ." Ned's

words trailed off, and when Emma looked into his face, he looked almost pained.

"I need to what?"

"You might want to, uh, well, bind your . . ." He waved his hand in the general direction of her breasts. He and Emma usually spoke quite frankly, but he just couldn't bring himself to discuss her intimate body parts.

"I see," Emma said slowly. "Hmmm, maybe you're right. If you'll wait just one moment . . ." She dashed out of the room, returning about five minutes later. Her chest looked much the same. "Sorry," she said sheepishly. "It was too uncomfortable. I'll have to wear a baggy coat."

Ned thought it best to refrain from any more discussion on the subject and held out one of his old coats. "We need to get going," he said. "Try this on. I don't think it'll drag on the floor."

It didn't, but it came perilously close. Emma surveyed her costume. "I look like a waif going to a funeral."

The pair of conspirators slipped out into the hallway and made their way to the back staircase. "Be careful on the third step," Emma whispered. "It creaks. You need to hug the wall."

Ned sent her a wry glance. "Do you sneak down these stairs very often?"

Emma flushed as she remembered the day she and Belle crept down the back stairs dressed as maids. The day she met Alex. "Belle told me about it," she mumbled.

Following Belle's advice, they moved soundlessly down the back stairs, tiptoed through the deserted kitchens, and slipped out the side door into the velvet darkness of the night.

*   *   *

Lady Mottram's party was already well underway when Alex and Dunford, both impeccably dressed in austere black evening clothes, strode through the ballroom doors.

"Do you see them?" Alex asked in a clipped voice, using his height to scan over the heads of the guests.

"No," Dunford replied, craning his neck.

"Emma's not here," Alex stated.

"What do you mean? She's got to be here."

"She isn't. I can spot her hair a mile away."

"Wait!" Dunford suddenly exclaimed. "I see Belle."

Alex followed Dunford's line of vision until he, too, located Belle's blond head. She was surrounded by her usual throng of admirers. "Woodside is hanging all over her."

Dunford furrowed his brow. "And she isn't doing anything to discourage him. Follow me." He moved decisively through the milling crowd, Alex right at his heels.

"Belle!" Dunford exclaimed jovially when he reached her. "You're looking even lovelier than usual." He leaned down and kissed her hand. Belle regarded him with the utmost suspicion. "And Viscount Benton!" He slapped the man on the back. "It's been an age. I've been meaning to ask you about that waistcoat you're wearing. Been admiring it for some time. Where did you have it made?"

With Woodside's attention satisfactorily engaged, Alex focused his energies on Belle. "Lady Arabella," he said curtly, dismissing the rest of the young bucks with a quelling stare. "I need to speak with you in private."

"I have nothing to say to you," Belle replied with a lift of her chin.

Alex turned to Dunford and Woodside. "Would

you mind if I stole Lady Arabella away from you for just one moment? I promise to return her immediately." He winked at Woodside. "I know how fond she is of you, and I wouldn't want to deprive you of her company for too long." With that, he smiled dangerously at Belle, grabbed her wrist, and practically yanked her out onto the balcony. "Where is your cousin?"

"She's not pining away after you at home if that's what you're worried about." Belle gulped, instantly aware that she had told Alex too much.

He caught her guilty look immediately. "Where is she? Is she in danger? Lord only knows what kind of scrape she'll get herself into without someone to watch over her." Alex had no rational basis for the gut-wrenching fear that coursed through him, but somehow he knew that Emma was involved in something dangerous. He also knew that there was no way he could stand back and watch her be hurt in any way.

"She's perfectly able to take care of herself without your assistance. Besides, I wasn't aware that she was any concern of yours any longer."

"Do not toy with me, my lady," Alex warned. "Where is Emma?"

"Look here, your grace," Belle returned in a scathing voice. "You have behaved abominably. I don't know what you said to her, but it must have been dreadful because she won't even speak about it. She walks around the house with the most morose expression I have ever seen, and every now and then she just starts to cry. I hope you're satisfied!" she spat out. "It's all we can do to keep her mind occupied so that she doesn't have to think about the swine who was courting her! Luckily we've got—" She broke off suddenly.

"Luckily what?" Alex demanded. "What are you doing tonight that is keeping her occupied?"

"Did I say 'swine?' " Belle asked offhandedly, tipping her head and tapping her finger against her chin. "I meant 'vermin'!" she hissed. "Now leave me—and Emma—alone!" She snatched her arm away from him and flounced back into the ballroom, heading straight to Woodside and Dunford.

"I am so sorry for Ashbourne's rude behavior," she said prettily, smiling up into Woodside's pale blue eyes. "He was questioning me about my cousin. He's been dangling after her, you know."

Woodside leveled a shrewd look at Belle. "I was under the impression that she reciprocated his feelings."

"Not anymore. In fact, that is why she stayed home tonight. She's still a little upset about the entire affair. But I don't want to talk about Emma tonight. I'd like to learn a bit more about you, my lord. Ned has told me so much about you."

A lecherous gleam sparkled in Woodside's eye as he convinced himself that Ned had chosen to offer his sister in exchange for the ten thousand pounds. "I'm sure he has," he murmured.

Dunford stifled a groan as he spotted Alex striding angrily toward them. "Woodside, you wouldn't mind if I borrowed Lady Arabella for a waltz, would you? I know that Ashbourne just stole her away, but I really must talk to her, too."

"I don't want to dance, Dunford," Belle bit out.

"I think you do," he said in a silky tone, pulling her out toward the dance floor.

Woodside let out an irritated sigh as he watched his prey once again being led away from him. He was just about to go off in search of a drink when Alex appeared at his right shoulder.

"Sorry about that," Alex said with a tight smile. "I'm sure you were looking forward to spending the evening with Lady Arabella. She's very lovely."

Woodside eyed Alex suspiciously. "What's he got to say to her that is so damned important?"

Alex swallowed his distaste for the man and smiled amiably. "Actually, Woodside, it's my fault. You're aware I've been courting Lady Arabella's cousin?"

A conspiratorial smile crossed Woodside's face. He had never believed that the powerful Duke of Ashbourne would actually marry an untitled nobody from the colonies, and so he didn't feel the need to speak of Emma with respect. "The American chit, eh? She looks like a treat, but I wouldn't have thought a man like you would be interested in a colonial."

Alex fought the urge to tear out the man's tongue. "We've had a bit of an argument, you see, and she won't speak to me."

"Send flowers," Woodside said condescendingly. "Or jewelry if you don't think her family will consider it too bold. That always works." He removed an imaginary piece of lint from his sleeve. "Women are easily managed."

Alex wondered how much extra effort would be required to remove the man's lungs along with his tongue. "I've drafted Dunford to plead my case with Belle since I obviously didn't succeed out on the balcony. He's trying to convince her that she ought to convince Emma that she ought to speak with me so that we can resolve our differences."

Woodside nodded. "A wise approach. And if it works, it'll be damned cheaper than a bracelet."

Alex smiled over clenched teeth. "All the more reason the two of us should pray that he's meeting with success."

He wasn't.

Dunford tried just about every tactic imaginable to get Belle to reveal Emma's whereabouts, but she remained implacable. Finally, he decided that blackmail was his only recourse. Clearing his throat a few times, he looked down into Belle's blue eyes, smiled wickedly, and said, "Belle, if you do not tell me this instant where your cousin is, I swear I will cause such a scene it will take you years to live it down."

Belle looked up at him scornfully. "We're in the middle of a crowded ballroom, Dunford. What on earth could you do?"

"I'll kiss you."

"Oh, please," Belle said dismissively.

"I'll use my tongue," he said very slowly and with great meaning.

Belle gasped at his daring. "You wouldn't. You're not even attracted to me. You've told me that before. On several occasions."

"Doesn't matter."

"You'd ruin me."

"At the moment, Belle, I don't care."

Belle took one look into his deadly serious brown eyes and knew that she'd misjudged Dunford. There was an iron will underneath his easygoing facade, and he had just bested her. "I don't have any choice, do I?"

"None."

Belle sighed, feeling utterly sick with despair, yet wondering if maybe, just maybe Dunford and Ashbourne would be able to help Emma and Ned in their scheme.

"I haven't got all night, Belle."

"All right," she relented. "She and Ned are sneaking into Woodside's home. Ned owes him a gambling debt. They're stealing the voucher."

"What? Of all the damned fool things to do!"

"It's a great deal of money," Belle said flatly.

"Your brother ought to learn to pay his gambling debts like a gentleman. Or at least not to wager more than he can afford."

"Woodside was cheating. It's only fair."

Dunford shook his head. "And I suppose your part in all this is to keep the unsuspecting Woodside entertained while your relatives rifle through his belongings."

Belle nodded and then curtsied as the waltz came to an end.

Dunford took her arm and slowly led her back to Alex and Woodside. "Be careful how you go about your task, my dear," he murmured in her ear. "I have a feeling that you and the viscount have different ideas of what constitutes 'entertainment.' Ah, Woodside, here you are," he said brightly, placing Belle's hand on the other gentleman's arm. "I'm returning Lady Arabella into your care. She couldn't stop talking about you."

Woodside nodded slowly at Belle, a sinister smile crossing his lips.

"I'm afraid that Ashbourne and I must now take our leave," Dunford continued. "I trust the two of you will have a pleasant evening."

"I'm sure we will," Woodside said in a low voice. "I was hoping to show Lady Arabella around the gardens. Lady Mottram's are among the best in London."

Belle grimaced and then quickly covered it up with a cough. "Actually, I'm afraid I might be catching a cold. I don't think I ought to go out in the damp night air."

Dunford nodded at the two of them and then propelled Alex toward the door. "She told me everything," he whispered. "I'll fill you in when we get to the carriage."

* * *

"Stop here."

The hired hack that Ned and Emma had engaged for their trip to Woodside's townhouse ground to a halt a block away from their final destination. They didn't need the clip-clop of the horses' hooves alerting any lightly sleeping servants that guests were arriving. Ned paid the driver, and Emma kept her mouth shut, not wanting her feminine voice to ruin her disguise.

They crept lightly down the street until they reached Woodside's residence. He leased a modest townhouse, a fact for which Emma was exceedingly grateful. A large mansion would take far too long to search and would probably contain a fleet of ever-watchful servants. Woodside's relatively small home was unlikely to be well-staffed.

"I think we should go around to the side," Ned whispered. "We'll see if he left any of the windows cracked open. It's a fairly warm night."

Emma gave a quick nod and followed her cousin into the narrow alley that ran alongside the building. They were in luck. Woodside had left the rearmost window partially open, presumably to let some fresh air into a room that otherwise received little ventilation.

"It's a little high," Ned said with a grimace.

"You'll just have to boost me up."

"How will I get in?"

"I guess you won't," Emma replied with a nervous smile. "Unless you can find a foothold in the masonry."

"I don't like this."

Emma didn't particularly like going in by herself, either, but she knew that her cousin would never let her do it if he realized how apprehensive she was. "You'll have to give me a signal if you see someone coming."

"How about a cough?" At Emma's nod, he cupped his hands for her foot and held firm as she drew herself up to the window's level.

"It looks like his study!" she whispered excitedly, slowly pushing the window up higher. "And the door is closed, so I probably won't have to worry about servants coming in."

"I'm going to push up now," Ned said. "Try to get one of your legs up on the ledge. Once you do that you should be able to get inside easily."

As Ned propelled her upward, Emma gritted her teeth and used all of her upper-body strength to push against the ledge as she lifted her leg up and swung it through the open window. After that, it was easy to scoot the rest of her body into Woodside's study, and she dropped herself lightly onto the carpet, mentally blessing her soundless soft-soled shoes. "It's about time my tree-climbing experience served some useful purpose," she said softly.

A tiny gleam of moonlight filtered into the room through the open window, but even after Emma's eyes adjusted to the darkness, she found that she could not see well enough to conduct her search. Reaching into her coat pocket, she pulled out a candle and lit it. With the added light, she scanned the room, her gaze finally falling on the crack underneath the door leading to the hall. Any servant passing by could easily see her candlelight glowing through the crack. Emma quickly shrugged off her coat and stuffed it against the bottom of the door.

"All right," she whispered to herself. "If I were a cheating lowlife, trying to swindle a nice young man out of his money, where would I put his I.O.U.?" The desk seemed the most logical place to start. After all, Woodside certainly wasn't expecting his home to be broken into by Ned and Emma, so he probably wouldn't have gone to great lengths to hide the voucher. Emma pulled open the first drawer. Some quills, writing paper, but nothing that resembled the note that Ned had described to her. Emma moved on to the next drawer. Once again, no luck. She gave the third drawer a tug, but it was locked.

Emma's heart began beating quickly as she rushed to the window. "Ned?" she whispered.

"What?"

"One of the desk drawers is locked."

"Try a hairpin. Many of those old desks don't have very good locks."

"Very well." Emma scurried back over to the desk, where she removed her cap and pulled a pin from her hair. Catching her lower lip between her teeth, she let out a little sigh and thrust the pin into the lock. Nothing. She twisted it around a few times. Still nothing. Finally she glared at the offending drawer and muttered, "You stupid little lock. I have no idea what I'm doing and you know it."

The lock turned. Emma smiled widely. "Well now, that wasn't so difficult." She rifled through the contents of the drawers. There were a few legal papers, something that looked like a lease to the house, and even some money, but no voucher. Emma quickly put the papers back in order and shut the drawer, making sure that it locked as it closed.

She ran back to the window. "It wasn't there," she called down.

"Keep looking!"

With a sigh, Emma turned her attention to a bookshelf that was built into the wall by the door. She supposed that Woodside might have slipped the note into one of the books. Thank goodness this wasn't a full-fledged library. Emma judged there to be only about thirty or forty books. It wouldn't take too long to go through them.

Emma climbed onto a little footstool and started on the top shelf, which seemed to contain the complete works of Shakespeare. Hmmm, she thought with a mischievous smile, perhaps Belle really did have something in common with Woodside.

Alex's carriage pulled up in front of Dunford's townhouse after careening through the London streets at a breakneck pace. Woodside lived only three short blocks from Dunford, so the two men had elected to leave the carriage there, where it wouldn't arouse any suspicion.

"I am going to throttle her," Alex ground out, his long legs carrying him quickly across the street.

Dunford took one look at his friend's furious expression and decided that Alex might actually be serious.

Within minutes they were in front of Woodside's townhouse. "I don't see any signs of forced entry," Alex whispered, scanning the facade of the building.

"I think there's an alley to the side," Dunford returned. "Come on."

The two men strode to the corner of the building and stopped short, peering quietly around the corner. A male figure was standing toward the back of the building, anxiously looking up at a window. "Have you found it yet?" they heard him call out softly.

Alex and Dunford pulled back. "Our dear friend Lord Edward," Dunford mocked.

"Who I am going to throttle just as soon as I'm done with Emma," Alex muttered menacingly.

"Wait here," Dunford said quickly. He moved like lightning, and before Alex realized what was happening, Dunford had his hand clamped tightly over Ned's mouth. Alex quickly went to join them.

"Is Emma inside?" he demanded.

Ned nodded his head, his blue eyes wide with surprise and a healthy dose of fear.

"What on earth possessed you to wait here while she went inside?"

Dunford didn't release his hold over his mouth, so Ned couldn't answer, a circumstance for which he was exceedingly grateful since he hadn't the slightest idea what to say. He had been wondering the very same thing for the past ten minutes, feeling like a fool while Emma was prowling around in the house.

Alex continued his interrogation. "She's looking for the voucher, isn't she? How on earth do you expect her to find a slip of paper in there?"

Once again, Dunford didn't let go of Ned's mouth, so the young man did the only thing he could do to get himself released. He licked Dunford's hand.

Dunford jumped back, thoroughly disgusted. He started to wipe his hand on his coat, then thought better of it and wiped it on Ned's coat.

"I couldn't very well answer his questions with your hand over my mouth," Ned explained tightly.

"Well?" Alex demanded.

"I don't know. I suppose we were just hoping we would get lucky. This was all her idea."

"I'm sure it was." Alex had no doubts that Emma had cooked up this little scheme. He'd have to keep a tighter rein on her once they were married. "You shouldn't have gone along with it, however."

Ned gave him a condescending look. "Have you ever tried to stop her when she's got her mind set on something? She would have come over here alone if I hadn't accompanied her."

"I'm going in," Alex declared.

"I don't think that's such a good idea," Ned said hesitatingly.

Alex leveled an icy stare at the younger man. "Your judgment so far has not proved impeccable."

Ned gulped and stepped back.

"Dunford, will you give me a leg up?"

Meanwhile, back in Woodside's study, Emma had finished her inspection of the bookcase and was just about ready to give up on the study altogether. It looked as if she would have to venture out into the rest of the house, after all. She was not terribly excited about the prospect.

She was just about to lean out the window and give Ned an update when she suddenly remembered the hairpin she'd left on the desk. She certainly did not want to leave any incriminating evidence lying about. Although she supposed it didn't really matter. Once Woodside realized that the voucher was gone, he would know who had taken it. He wasn't stupid. After all, he had managed to swindle Ned out of ten thousand pounds. Emma supposed one had to have some degree of intelligence to cheat with such proficiency.

All the same, Emma didn't want to leave anything that Woodside might be able to take to the authorities, so she went back over to the desk and reached for the hairpin.

That was when she saw the snuff box.

It was sitting atop the desk, highly ornamental, as if it had been imported from Asia. "Oh, please God, please God, please God," Emma chanted, forgetting completely about the hairpin. She shut her eyes in prayer as she lifted the lid. Taking a deep breath, she opened her eyes. A small piece of paper folded several times over lay inside. Barely able to breathe, she unfolded the note.

I, Edward William Blydon, Viscount Burwick, pledge to pay Lord Anthony Woodside, Viscount Benton, the sum of ten thousand pounds.

Below that, Emma saw Ned's familiar signature. It was in that moment of supreme relief that Emma realized just how quickly her heart was beating. "Thank you, Lord," she breathed, placing the lid back on the snuff box and setting it back into place.

"Ned!" she called softly. "I foun—" She whirled around just in time to see Alex vault through the open window, landing on the carpet with pantherlike grace. "You!" she choked, stepping back in shock.

Alex's mouth settled into a grim line. "You, my dear lady, have some explaining to do."

Chapter 18

Emma's mouth fell open.

"However," Alex continued mildly, "I don't think this is the most appropriate place. Did you get that blasted voucher?"

"Actually," she replied archly, "I did." She waved the note in his face.

"In that case, I hope you'll excuse me as I throw you out the window." Alex yanked on Emma's arm and pulled her across the room.

"Wait!" Emma exclaimed. "My coat! I left it tucked against the crack under the door. And I've also got to get my candle." She scurried across the room, picked up her coat, and quickly wrapped herself in it. "Some prowler you are," she muttered.

Alex viciously grabbed the taper off of the desk and blew out the flame, but not before he shot a murderous glare in Emma's direction.

"I'm going, I'm going," she said quickly, scurrying toward the window.

She obviously wasn't going fast enough, because he picked her up and dropped her out the window himself, where she landed in Dunford's waiting arms.

"You're here, too?" she asked weakly.

"If I were you, I'd be grateful for my presence. Ashbourne is nearly ready to explode."

Emma didn't doubt it. She twisted around to face Ned. "What is going on? Why are they here?"

Her cousin only shrugged.

"You can put her down now, Dunford." Alex vaulted down from the window. "Your candle," he said, handing the taper to Emma, who immediately shoved it in her pocket. "Let's get out of here."

"Shouldn't we close the window back up?" Emma suggested.

With great patience, Alex turned back to the window. "Dunford, would you give me a leg up?"

Dunford cupped his hands together to form a step, and Alex reached up and shut the window.

"Actually," Emma said, just when Alex hit the ground again, "it wasn't closed all the way. It was open about three inches."

Alex took a deep breath. Emma gulped as she saw a muscle start to twitch in his cheek. He held steady, however, turning back to his friend. "Dunford?"

Dunford cupped his hands again and hoisted Alex up. Alex pushed the window up a few inches. "Is this all right?" he asked in quite the most dangerously solicitous tone Emma had ever heard.

Emma was still furious with him. "It was a little higher," she said peevishly.

Alex moved the window up another inch.

"A little lower."

He tugged it down. "How about now?"

"Maybe a little—ouch!" She rubbed her ribs where Ned had urgently jabbed her. "That will be fine, I'm sure," she said finally, giving her cousin a hard stare. "Oh, I got your voucher!" she exclaimed, handing it over to Ned. "I almost forgot to tell you. This is it, isn't it?"

Ned unfolded the note, breathing a sigh of relief as he read it. "I cannot thank you enough, Emma."

"Oh, it was nothing, Ned. Actually, I had a lot of fun."

"I, on the other hand, had no fun whatsoever," Alex said very slowly, barely able to contain the rage that threatened to explode all over Emma. He had been so worried about her. Frantic. It had been eight long hours between the time that Dunford had told him that Emma and Belle were up to some strange scheme and when he finally went to Lady Mottram's to confront her. Eight long hours of pacing, of raking his hands through his hair, of wondering what on earth she was up to and if she were in any danger. It had been an agonizing afternoon of nearly dying of guilt over the way he had treated her the night before. And then when he found out that she was planning to break into Woodside's townhouse, he'd wanted to put his fist through a wall. Eight hours of frantic energy and sheer terror on an empty, hung-over stomach did bad things to a man, and Emma's declaration that she was having fun was definitely not soothing his temper.

Emma instinctively stepped back when she saw the dark look on Alex's face.

"May we leave now, or must I throw you over my shoulder?" Alex asked with chilling calmness.

Emma gulped down a nervous laugh, realizing wisely that a giggle would be horrendously inappropriate—and most probably dangerous to her well-being. "That—that won't be necessary," she stammered.

Alex turned his icy glare to Ned. "I trust you can make your own way home."

Ned nodded. "But what about Emma? She'll need an escort."

Alex snaked his arm through hers and pulled her tightly against his side. "I will see her home. Your cousin and I have a few matters to discuss."

"We really could have that discussion tomorrow," Emma put in hastily, trying to extricate herself from Alex's grasp.

He held firm. "No, I don't think we could." He nodded at Ned and started striding down the street so quickly that Emma nearly had to run to keep up with him. Dunford followed at a respectable distance.

"Is it necessary to *drag* me?" Emma gasped, her feet flying down the street.

"If you're wise, you will keep your mouth shut for the next few minutes."

"Well, my legs aren't as long as yours," she muttered ungraciously. "I can't move that fast."

Alex stopped short. Emma, having worked up quite a bit of momentum, crashed into him. "What now?" she snapped.

"I can still put you over my shoulder," he warned darkly.

She shot him a scathing glare. "Don't even try it, you grimy little rodent."

Alex exhaled slowly, clenching and unclenching his fist, desperately trying not to lose hold of the tension that rocked his body. "Come along," he said savagely, once again pulling her down the street.

"Where are we going, anyway? In case you hadn't noticed, I live in the opposite direction."

"We are going to Dunford's house. It's only a few blocks away. We can get a carriage from there."

"Good. Because I expect you to return me home immediately," Emma sniffed. "Your behavior tonight has been deplorable."

Once again, Alex halted in his tracks. Once again, Emma slammed into his side. "Are you *trying* to infuriate me?" he hissed.

Emma stuck her nose in the air. "I really don't care about your feelings, *your grace.*"

Alex nearly cringed at the obsequious way she referred to his title. He pointed his index finger at her as if he were about to launch into a tirade. His face contorted as his jaw clenched, and he fought for words. Finally, he dropped his shaking finger. He still had enough dignity not to shake her senseless in the middle of a public street. Not to mention with Dunford loitering six feet in the background. "Let's get moving," he said tersely, continuing toward Dunford's home.

A few minutes later Alex came to a stop in front of Dunford's neat little townhouse. Emma tore her hand from his grasp and crossed her arms defiantly, glaring daggers at him all the while.

Dunford arrived about fifteen seconds later, took one look at the fuming couple, and said, "I'll go call for my carriage." He took the front steps two at a time. When he reached the top, he turned around and said, "Er, why don't the two of you wait in my hall? Some of the parties will be getting out around now, and I'm sure you don't want anyone to see you standing in the street. Especially in your, er, costume, Emma."

Emma marched right up the steps. "I certainly don't want to get caught up in some scandal which will trap me into marriage with that monster."

Alex didn't say anything; he just marched up the steps right behind her. When they were both safely inside Dunford's front hall, Emma stole a glance at him. The muscle in his cheek was still twitching, and the tension in his jaw and neck was visible.

He was definitely angry. Maybe even as angry as she was. But she didn't understand why he even cared. He had made his disdainful feelings for her abundantly clear the previous afternoon, and his appearance in Woodside's study, presumably to save her from some perilous fate, was really quite puzzling.

"The carriage is ready," Dunford said quietly as he walked back into the hall a few minutes later, his hands clasped behind his back.

Alex grabbed Emma again by her arm. Before he left, he turned back to Dunford and said, "I thank you for all your assistance."

"You'll stop by tomorrow?"

"I may not be through with her by tomorrow." Before Emma had time to question him about that ominous statement, he pulled her through the door and down the front steps. After unceremoniously dumping her in the carriage, Alex strode to the driver, gave him instructions, and then climbed in beside her.

Emma crossed her arms mutinously and then sank back into the corner of the cushioned seat. He'd not get another word out of her, she silently declared. She couldn't imagine why he thought he had the right to prance into her business, take over her life, and then treat her like an annoying piece of baggage. She let out a furious breath of air and then clamped her lips together, determinedly looking out the window. After a minute or two, however, she found she could not contain her rage any longer, and she burst out, "You high-handed louse! I cannot believe the way you have acted this evening."

"A rodent, a monster, *and* a louse all in one evening," Alex mocked. "This must be one of my good days."

"I'll say." Emma went back to glaring out the window. "What on earth!" she shrieked suddenly, whirling around to face Alex. "We just passed my home. Where are we going?"

"We are going to my home."

"Just another example of your blasted arrogance!" Emma blazed. "What right do you have to steal me from my home!"

"If you recall, I didn't steal you from your home. I stole you from Woodside's home, and believe me, you're far better off in my clutches than you are in his."

"I demand that you turn this carriage around this instant and take me home."

"I really don't see how you have any say in the matter, Emma."

She drew back. "Are you threatening me?"

Alex leaned forward so that his nose was very nearly touching hers. "Yes."

As if on cue, the carriage ground to a halt. Alex quickly disembarked, and when Emma wouldn't budge off of the seat cushion, he leaned back in, hauled her out, and flipped her over his shoulder. "We won't be needing you any longer!" he called out to the coachman. With Emma kicking and grunting (she had just enough presence of mind to realize that screaming would result in scores of onlookers, a huge scandal, and then most probably a despicable marriage), Alex trudged up the steps and into the hall, kicking the door shut with a vicious slam.

"Will you put me down?" Emma finally demanded.

"Not just yet," Alex ground out, ascending another flight of stairs.

"Where are you taking me?" she asked angrily, trying to twist her head around so that she could figure out where she was.

"Somewhere where we can talk."

"Where we can talk or where you can lecture me?"

"You are trying my patience, my lady."

"Really?" Emma asked scathingly. "I had hoped that I had already tried it."

Alex strode through a doorway and kicked the door shut, finally dumping Emma down upon a large four-poster bed. She immediately made a mad dash for the door, but Alex ably blocked her, redeposited her on the bed, crossed the room, and locked the door with a resounding click.

"Why you—"

Alex tossed the key out the window.

"Are you crazy?" Emma ran to the window, judging the distance to the ground.

"You'll never make it without injury," Alex said. "You, my dear, are my captive audience, and believe me, I have a few things to say to you."

"Good!" Emma retorted. "I have a few things to say to you, too."

"Emma," he said with dangerous softness. "You ought to be scared right now."

"Fine," she declared, crossing her arms. "Talk away."

Alex took careful stock of her features. She didn't look the least bit repentant, but he was so furious with her, he started his tirade anyway. "First of all—" he thundered.

"Do you mind if I take off my coat?" Emma interrupted sarcastically. "It does seem that I'm to be your guest for some time."

"By all means."

Emma unbuttoned her coat, shrugged it off, and laid it on a nearby chair.

"What on earth are you wearing?" Alex yelled.

Emma looked down at her breeches. "For goodness sake, Alex. I can't very well go prowling around in an evening gown."

Alex's eyes slid down her trim figure, every curve of which was indecently hugged by her breeches. His muscles tightened, and his anger was further inflamed by his body's mutinous response to her. "You have just given me another matter about which to yell at you," he snapped. "I cannot believe your cousin let you out of the house dressed like that."

"Oh, really," Emma scoffed. "You didn't say anything in Woodside's study. I didn't have my coat on then," she reminded him.

"I didn't notice," Alex bit out. "It was dark."

She shrugged. "Get on with your lecture, will you? I've had a long day."

Alex took a deep breath. He was convinced she was deliberately trying to provoke him. He could grant her that. She had every right to be furious with him over his behavior the day before. But that didn't excuse her blatant disregard for her own welfare this evening. "Do you have any idea what kind of danger you placed yourself in tonight?" he finally asked, trying to keep his tone even.

"We had a very good plan," Emma returned. "Which obviously worked."

"Oh, really? Do tell me about this plan of yours. What were you planning to do if Woodside came home and surprised you while you were burgling his study?"

"Belle is keeping him busy at Lady Mottram's. She promised us that she wouldn't let him leave before midnight."

"And what if she failed?" Alex demanded. "Your cousin is hardly strong enough to restrain a grown man."

"Oh, use your head," Emma snapped. "Woodside has been drooling over her for a year. He would never leave a party while she was flirting with him."

"But you couldn't be sure of that. He might have taken ill and had to leave."

"It's called a calculated risk, your grace. We take them every day of our lives."

"Damn it, Emma!" Alex exploded, raking his hand through his hair. "Of all the harebrained, damned fool things to do! If Woodside had caught you he could have thrown you in prison! Or worse!" he added meaningfully.

"I had to take the chance. Ned was in trouble and he needed help. I don't abandon the people I love," she said sharply.

Something in Alex snapped at that moment, and he took her by the shoulders, shaking her and clutching her as if he were holding on for dear life. "Do you have any idea how worried I was about you? Do you?"

Emma gulped, closing her eyes tightly as she tried to quell the tears that had been rolling nonstop down her cheeks for nearly a day. She had to compose herself. She couldn't let him see her cry.

Alex stopped shaking her, but he didn't release his hold, and Emma found his touch oddly comforting. The very heat of him seemed to pour through her shirt, and a small part of Emma longed to throw herself against him and wrap herself in his strong arms. But a larger part of her still stung from his brutal temper the day before. His lack of trust in her had wounded her to the core. "I wasn't aware that you cared, your grace," she answered very quietly.

"Well, I do!" he said savagely, turning away from her and banging his hands down on his writing table. "I care too damned much. I nearly went insane today, knowing that you were involved in some ridiculous scheme and not being able to stop you."

"How did you know?" Emma asked, perching herself on the edge of the bed.

"Dunford overheard you and Belle talking earlier this afternoon," Alex said flatly. "He heard you say something about how imperative it was that Belle meet Woodside tonight at Lady Mottram's. Considering Woodside's character, we were both frantic."

"I would have thought you'd have been content to leave me to the wolves."

"I made a mistake yesterday," Alex said hoarsely, still facing away from her. "I'm sorry."

Emma's eyes widened with shock over his admission. He was a proud man, and she couldn't imagine that apologies came easily to him. As he stood leaning against the table, every line of his body spoke of raw tension and pain. This wasn't easy for him, she knew that. And he was probably racked with guilt over his behavior. Her heart went out to him—she couldn't stop it if she tried, she loved him so much. But none of her tender feelings could erase her pain. "I accept your apology," she said with quiet dignity.

Alex whirled around, hope and doubt colliding in his eyes.

"But that doesn't mean I'll be able to forget," Emma added sadly. "We're not going to be able to go back to the way we were."

"Emma, if you needed money for Ned, you could have asked me for it."

"What was I supposed to do, Alex? Walk up to you and ask you for a loan of ten thousand pounds?"

"I would have given it to you."

"I'm sure you would have, but I wouldn't have felt comfortable with it, and I don't think Ned would have, either. Besides, it seemed silly when I have more than enough money of my own. I've got an inheritance right here in London. It's in trust until I reach my twenty-first birthday." She swallowed nervously, glancing away and studying a medieval tapestry that hung on the wall. "Or until I marry."

"I see."

"I didn't ask you to marry me just for money," Emma burst out passionately, still unable to turn around and face his emerald gaze. "I think it's what gave me the idea to ask you, but it's not why I did it. It was an excuse, I suppose. I wanted you so badly, and I felt trapped. A man can pick and choose who he wants to marry and when, but women have to sit at home and wait for an offer. I was afraid you'd never get around to asking."

Alex sighed. If she'd only waited three more days, this entire mess would have been averted.

"The money was just an excuse," Emma continued forlornly. "I guess I thought that if I had an urgent enough reason, then I could defy tradition and ask you instead of waiting. I don't think I would have had the courage to propose if I hadn't needed to get the money for Ned."

Alex moved to the bed and sat beside her, taking one of her hands and holding it between his own. "Can you understand why I reacted as I did?" he asked, stroking her palm with his thumb. "All my adult life I've been chased by greedy women eager for a title. When you said you needed money—I don't know what happened. I just snapped."

"I just don't understand how you could have thought that of me." Emma raised her stricken eyes to his. *"Don't you know me?"*

Alex looked away, unable to think of any words that might express the remorse he was feeling.

The silence grew interminable, until finally Emma said. "You should have trusted me."

"I know. I'm sorry."

"I can understand your jumping to the wrong conclusion," she said, her voice breaking slightly. "But you didn't even stop to think. You just treated me like a common harlot and threw me out of your house. You didn't even ask for an explanation."

Alex couldn't meet her eyes.

Emma wiped away a tear that threatened to spill down her face. "I would have thought that you knew me well enough to realize that I'm not a 'greedy little bitch.'"

He flinched as she tossed back the cruel words he had blurted out in anger. "I know I was wrong, Emma. Believe me, it didn't take me very long to realize that I had misunderstood you."

"I don't know. I feel very uncomfortable knowing that you don't trust me."

"But I do. I do now."

Emma smiled sadly. "You say you do. I'm sure you believe you do. But I'm not certain that you wouldn't jump to the very same conclusion all over again. You spent ten years hating women. It isn't easy to undo a decade of such strong emotion."

"I don't hate women, Emma."

"Hate, mistrust. It amounts to the same thing."

"I admit that I did not hold most women in the highest regard," Alex said, tightening his hold on her hand. "I didn't know any outside of my family whom I could respect. But you changed that. You shattered every preconception I held about women."

Emma wet her lips as she relived the ugly scene in Alex's parlor. "Obviously I didn't."

"For God's sake, Emma, give me a chance!" he suddenly burst out, jumping to his feet. "You're right! I made an ass of myself yesterday because I didn't trust my instincts. I knew you were everything I wanted in a woman, but I was afraid to admit it. Are you satisfied?" He strode across the room, taking deep breaths of air. Hands on hips, he stared at the very same tapestry that had captured Emma's gaze a few minutes earlier. He didn't turn to look at her when he finally said, "But now you're doing the exact same thing to me. You don't trust me enough to believe that I learned something from yesterday's debacle."

"Oh, Alex," Emma moaned, placing her face in her hands. "I'm so confused. I think I've been confused since the moment I met you."

"You've been confused?" Alex said, turning around as his lips twisted into a wry smile. "You've turned my entire life upside down. Do you know how many damned balls I've been to in the last two months?"

At her blank stare he continued, "More than I've been to in the last ten years! I don't like *ton* parties. I hate *ton* parties. But I went to all of them—gladly—just to be near you."

Emma blinked up at him through watery eyes. "I wish I knew what to do," she said sadly. "Could—could you just—" She bit her lip, fumbling for words. "Could you just hold me? Just for a little while?"

Alex's head rose at her request, and his heart began to beat rapidly. He walked across the room, sat down next to her, and wrapped his arms around her, his lips settling on the tender skin just next to her ear.

Emma closed her eyes, lost in the comfort and solace she found in his arms. When she found her voice, it was very small and quite uneven. "I think that if you keep holding me, maybe I can forget how much I'm hurting."

Alex tightened his hold. "I'm so sorry, Emma," he murmured. "So very sorry."

Emma nodded, finally allowing the tears she'd been holding back all evening to trickle down her cheeks. "I know. And I'm sorry that I worried you so much tonight. I'm not sorry I did what I did," she added with a sniffle and a sheepish smile. "But I am sorry that I worried you."

Alex crushed her to him. "Oh God, Emma," he said hoarsely. "Please don't ever put me through something like that again."

"I won't. I'll try not to."

Alex drew back so that he could see her face. "I've made you cry," he whispered, touching her cheek. "I'm so sorry."

Within the warm haven of Alex's arms, Emma let loose all the tears which had been brimming up within her for the past two days and which she had valiantly fought to conceal from the concerned eyes of her relatives. As each tear fell, it seemed to her that a weight had been lifted from her soul, and she slowly felt the tension leave her body. At some point her tears trickled to a halt, and Alex laid her sleepy body down upon his massive bed. With a contented smile on his face, he slipped off her shoes, pulled the covers up, tucked them under her chin, and kissed her goodnight.

Chapter 19

$\sim\infty\sim$

A few hours later, Emma's eyelids fluttered open, and she groggily took in her surroundings. She took a deep breath and let out a catlike yawn, blinking a few times as her eyes adjusted to the darkness. A faint smell of musk hung in the air, and she sniffed a few times, unused to such a scent in her bedroom. Taking another breath of the heady aroma, she yawned again, squeezing her eyes shut as she twisted her body around, turning onto her side. With a soft sigh, she opened her eyes again. And then she opened them wider, finding herself mere inches away from Alex's face.

That was when she realized that the heavy weight across her hips was Alex's leg. She sucked in her breath, startled by the intimacy.

"Oh my," she breathed, holding herself very still, lest she wake the man sleeping next to her. She hadn't any experience with this sort of situation. If she moved, she'd probably wake him up. On the other hand, her heart was beating so rapidly she knew that there was no way she'd be able to fall back asleep.

It seemed to her that she probably ought to scream. Or faint. That, she imagined, was what a well-brought-up lady was supposed to do in such a situation. But then again, a well-brought-up lady wasn't supposed to *be* in such a situation. Anyway,

she didn't really see how screaming would solve
anything. And swooning seemed a rather stupid
endeavor; one couldn't really *do* anything while
unconscious, and once she awoke, she'd be in the
same place in which she'd started. Besides, Emma
thought wryly, she really wasn't much good at
fainting without a sufficient blow to the head.

There would be a scandal, she supposed, unless
Alex and her family behaved with the utmost dis-
cretion. Actually, there was a very good chance
that Uncle Henry and Aunt Caroline hadn't yet
noticed her absence. When they left for Lady
Mottram's ball, Emma had let them think that
she was retiring early with a headache. They
had been very worried about her because she
had seemed so depressed and tired for the past
couple of days. They told Emma to get some rest,
and she was sure they wouldn't bother her when
they returned. Ned would know, of course. And
Belle, too, who would almost certainly ferret out
the information from her brother the minute she
got back home.

She'd be all right as long as she made it home
before sunrise, when the servants started going
about their daily chores. Her cousins had probably
left the front door open for her. She smiled wryly.
Belle and Ned were probably waiting for her in the
front parlor, taking turns keeping watch through
the window so they could let her in. They wouldn't
want to miss whatever story Emma offered to
explain her lengthy absence.

Emma twisted her head and squinted at the clock
that sat on Alex's nightstand. It was quarter to four
in the morning. Henry, Caroline, and Belle had
probably returned from Lady Mottram's sometime
in the last couple of hours. She still had plenty of
time. It didn't really matter if she left now or in a

half an hour. Whatever damage she had incurred was already done.

Having duly justified her silence, Emma was content to lie in the big bed, studying Alex's face. He looked very boyish while he slept. His dark lashes were sinfully long as they rested against his cheeks, and Emma found herself wishing, not for the first time, that she had lashes like that to frame her own eyes. His hair was rumpled by sleep, and his lips were slightly parted as he breathed steadily.

Alex had thrown a bare arm over the blankets, and Emma could see the very top of his chest. She had never before seen him without a shirt, and she flexed her hand, longing to place it on his chest just to see what it felt like. Her eyes followed his skin to where it disappeared under the covers. He had definitely taken his shirt off, but what about his breeches? Emma gasped. Dear Lord, he wasn't *naked*?

The leg that lay across her hips suddenly felt very strange. Emma caught her lower lip between her teeth as she tried to figure out a way to wriggle out from under him without waking him up. Alex made a sleepy sound as he shifted his weight. He rolled toward her, and Emma found herself even more firmly pinned underneath his leg. There seemed to be only one way to determine the state of his undress. Taking a deep breath, she slipped her hand beneath the covers and slid it down until she reached the soft springy hair on his knee. Emma quickly pulled her hand away. He definitely wasn't wearing breeches.

If he wasn't wearing a shirt, and he wasn't wearing breeches, there was only one other place he could have remained clothed so as to protect her modesty. Emma swallowed. She certainly wasn't going to slide her hand under the covers and touch him *there*. She wasn't even entirely sure what to expect.

She tried a different tactic. Very slowly and very carefully, she lifted up the covers, taking great care not to disturb Alex. Once the blanket was higher than her eyes, she peered in, but she couldn't make anything out amidst all the shadows. Summoning all her courage, she dipped her head beneath the cover, still holding it far enough up to let in the slight glimmer of moonlight that bathed the room. It was still too dark to see anything. Emma grimaced and resigned herself to defeat. If she moved her head any further under the covers, she might crash into something, and she certainly didn't want that. She slowly unfolded herself, returning her head to its original position on the pillow beside Alex.

His eyes were open.

Emma caught her breath and looked closer. His eyes were definitely open, and even in the darkness of the room, she could see humor lurking in those green depths.

"I did not remove my undergarments, if that's what you were trying to discern," he said, and Emma swore she could hear a smile in his voice. "I'm not a complete cad," he continued.

"Thank you," she said sincerely.

"You fell asleep, and I didn't have the heart to wake you up. You're quite adorable when you're sleeping."

"So are you," she could not help saying.

"Thank you," he said, just as sincerely. "How long have you been awake?"

"Not long."

"You were warm enough?"

"Oh, yes," Emma said mildly, marveling at the

absurdity of her situation. Here she was, lying next to a man in bed, in *his* bed, at nearly four in the morning, and they were conversing as politely as if they were in a drawing room. She sighed, letting her gaze float across the ceiling. "We'll have to be very careful when you take me home," she finally said. "If we're very quiet, we won't wake anyone up, and we'll be able to avoid a scandal."

"Don't worry about it," Alex said offhandedly. "I'll take care of everything."

Emma rolled onto her back. Alex made no attempt to move his leg, and it settled into the crook between her leg and hip. "It's very cozy in here," he remarked. "I'm not used to sharing this bed with anyone."

"Oh, really, Alex," Emma scoffed. "You've had scores of mistresses. It's common knowledge."

Alex grinned widely. "Jealous, are we? Now that's a good sign."

"I'm not jealous."

"As it happens, I haven't had *scores* of mistresses. Even I'm not man enough for that. I admit that I haven't lived the life of a monk, but I haven't kept a mistress for quite some time now."

Emma turned her face to his, her eyes questioning.

"It's been at least two months now, I imagine."

That was just about as long as they had known each other. Emma was absurdly pleased.

"And," he continued, "I certainly never brought any of them here. You, my darling, are the first to grace my bed."

"You make it sound as if we have done something that we haven't."

Alex declined to comment; he just took her arm and pulled her to him. "You're too far away," he murmured.

Emma gasped as she was pressed up against the hard length of his body. Cocooned under the bedcovers, his skin had grown very warm, and the heat was melting through her clothes. "Maybe," she allowed. "But now I think I'm a bit too close."

"Nonsense," Alex sighed, sinking his hands into her thick hair. "You smell lovely."

"Rose-scented soap," she said shakily.

"I think I love rose-scented soap." He pressed his lips against the tip of her nose. "I also think you have far too many clothes on."

"Now *that* I know is not true."

"Will you hush?" Alex moved his lips to her face and kissed her eyes shut. Emma felt her resolve begin to melt, and she realized that she wanted to be seduced every bit as much as he wanted to seduce her. As he continued to rain light kisses across her face, she tried to rationalize her position. She knew what she was doing was wrong. Or at least everyone told her it was wrong. But something inside her told her that this was very right, that she belonged here with Alex, lying in his arms. It was as if all the warmth in the world had accumulated inside of him and was now shining out of his emerald eyes onto her. And was she really such a sinner for loving him so much? Emma didn't think so. She deserved this one moment of bliss. Her decision made, she took a deep breath and tilted her face up to his, parting her lips slightly when his mouth settled on hers.

Alex sensed the change in her instantly, and the desire that he'd been almost afraid to feel rocked through his body once he realized that she wasn't going to reject him. "Oh God, Emma. I want you so much," he moaned. "I've wanted you for so long." As he began to unbutton the man's shirt she was still wearing, he realized that his fingers were shaking, and he smiled sheepishly, feeling very much like a green boy. As each button slipped out of its hole, Alex got the feeling that he was unwrapping a delicate treasure. His breath caught in his throat, and he realized that he had never before felt this kind of nervous, exhilarating anticipation. Finally, the last button popped free, and he parted the shirt, revealing a silky chemise that bared more than it hid.

He placed his strong hands on her midriff and slowly pushed the chemise upward, the silky material rubbing sensually against Emma's glistening skin. She shivered, unable and unwilling to contain her response to the strange and beautiful feeling of Alex's hands through the thin silk of her chemise. Dear Lord, how she wanted him, wanted this. Her entire body felt aflame, burning up with weeks of unfulfilled need.

Alex paused when the bottom of the chemise was settled just below her breasts. He raised his eyes to hers, offering her one last chance to stop him, but all he saw in those violet pools was desire and trust. "Sit up for a moment," he said huskily. Emma did so, and he pulled the chemise up over her head, sucking in his breath as her full breasts were finally revealed to him. "You are so beautiful," he murmured, gazing upon her with reverence. "So beautiful."

Emma flushed under his intense gaze, her skin tingling in anticipation. When his hand settled around her breast, she gasped, barely able to comprehend the sensations that shot down to her abdomen. And then he squeezed, and she knew she was lost. "Oh Alex," she moaned, awash in pleasure. "Kiss me. Please kiss me."

Alex's chuckle came from deep in his throat. "As

you wish, my darling." He leaned down and captured her rosy nipple between lips, sucking gently as his hand continued to massage her other breast.

Emma nearly screamed. "Oh my God!" she burst out. "That wasn't what I meant."

"Mmm, I know, but it's very nice, isn't it?"

Emma couldn't deny that it was, so she sank her hands into his thick hair, pulling him tightly against her. If she held him close enough, she decided wildly, he could never stop all these delicious things he was doing to her.

Alex smiled as his lips trailed a path down her stomach, pausing to run his tongue around the edge of her belly-button. "I think we need to do something about these damned breeches." He undid the buttons and slowly lowered them down her legs. "Not that you don't look darling in breeches, of course, but don't think I'm going to let you out of the house dressed like that again." With a quick tug, Emma's breeches joined her shirt and chemise on the floor, and Alex slid up the length of her so that his nose was touching hers. "I don't think anyone else needs to know just how sweetly rounded your bottom is." As if to prove his point, he cupped her backside with his hands and gave it a squeeze, pulling her tightly against him.

"Oh my," Emma breathed. She was now completely nude except for her unmentionables, and he felt so hot and hard against her. Timidly, she stroked the warm skin of his back, eager to explore him but unsure of what to do. "Do—do you like this?" she asked.

"Good Lord, Emma," Alex said hoarsely. "The mere sight of you makes me want you. You have no idea what your touch does."

Emma blushed but did not stop stroking his back, and when Alex moved to take off her last piece of clothing, she made no attempts to stop him. "You're going to have to take off yours, too," she said, unable to believe her own daring. "I may be new at this, but even I know it won't work with your undergarments on."

Alex laughed out loud at that and almost blurted out how much he loved her. But he held back, not quite ready to declare his feelings before she did. Instead, he quickly rectified the problem at hand, sliding his undergarments off and covering her body with his.

Emma's heart started beating wildly as Alex's lips descended on hers. His hands seemed to be everywhere, stroking, probing, and squeezing, yet still she wanted more. Finally, his hand settled over her womanhood, and she felt herself buck up off the bed at the pleasure of his touch. Though he had caressed her there once before, and she knew what to expect, somehow everything seemed much more intimate now that they were in bed, his bare skin pressed up against her own. Suddenly she felt his forefinger enter her, and every muscle in her body tensed.

"Shhh," he murmured. "I just want to make sure that you are ready for me. I'm bigger than my finger, and I don't want to hurt you."

Emma relaxed slightly, and Alex continued his sensual movements, caressing her most private nub of flesh with his thumb. As pleasure shot through her, Emma could feel herself growing wet with desire and she groaned, her hips instinctively writhing beneath him.

Alex labored to keep his breathing even and steady. It was taking all of his control not to plunge into her right away and lose himself in her softness. But he was determined to make this first experience perfect for her. He knew that his would be an empty pleasure if Emma did not also find her climax. Somewhere along the way, her happiness had become vastly more important to him than his own.

Emma felt her body arch as hot sensations streaked through her. "Alex, please," she begged. "Please. I need you."

Emma's stark declaration proved to be Alex's undoing, and he quickly positioned himself to enter her. "Are you ready?" he asked hoarsely. At her feverish nod, he pressed forward. Lord, but she was tight. "Shh," he said, more to soothe himself than her. "I'm going to take it slowly. I want to give you a chance to get used to me." With a groan that was half pleasure and half frustration, he pulled out a tiny bit and then pushed forward again, ever so slowly.

Emma was convinced at that moment that she was going to die. There was simply no way her body could take any more of the pressure that was building up inside of her. "Please," she moaned, tossing her head from side to side. "I want—I need—" She shuddered. "Oh God, I don't know what I want!"

"Shh, darling, I do. But you're not quite ready for it yet. You're so small. I'm afraid I might hurt you." Alex thought that there could be no greater aphrodisiac than the sight of Emma writhing in his bed, utterly consumed by passion. But still, he kept his own desire in check, forcing himself to take it slowly. And then, just when he was convinced he could restrain himself no longer, he reached her maidenhead.

"Emma?" he said, his voice rough with passion. But she was so lost in her own haze that she didn't hear him. "Darling?" he asked, a bit more loudly. She looked up at him, her eyes barely able to focus on his face. "Darling, this may hurt you a little, but I promise you it will only be this one time."

"What do you mean?"

Alex grimaced as he propped himself up on his elbows. Dear Lord, had no one explained this to her? "It's because you're a virgin. I have to break your maidenhead. It might hurt, but I promise that it will go away, and it won't pain you next time."

Emma gazed at his face. He looked so concerned for her, his eyebrows furrowed and his eyes a softer green than she had ever seen them. "I trust you, Alex," she said softly, reaching up to put her arms around him.

Every last shred of self-control that Alex possessed snapped at that very moment and he surged forward. Emma let out a soft cry at the rending of her maidenhead but found that the pain was quite minimal and was soon replaced by the luxurious pleasure of Alex's insistent lovemaking. With every stroke, she felt an urgent warmth shoot through her body until suddenly it all became too much, and her entire body tensed and almost froze. She couldn't move, she couldn't breathe, and then finally her entire world exploded, and she collapsed, purely and utterly spent.

A spasm of white-hot need shook Alex's body as he felt her muscles clench around his manhood. The primitive rhythm of his body grew fast and frenzied, and then he plunged forward one last time, erupting with ecstasy as he poured himself into her.

Emma heard him cry out at the moment of his release, felt him collapse atop her, and as she drifted down from her own climax, she thought that she had never before felt so completely content. "I feel good," she sighed.

Alex chuckled as he rolled off of her. "So do I, my love, so do I."

"If I had known I was going to feel this good, I might not have kicked you out of my bedroom the day we met."

Alex cupped her face in his hands. "It wouldn't have been this beautiful, my darling, because we hadn't come to care for each other yet."

Emma snuggled closer to him at his tender words. Surely now he would tell her he loved her. But he didn't. She sighed. She was too happy to worry about it just yet. He couldn't have made love to her like he just had without loving her a little, could he?

They remained in that position for several minutes, Emma burrowed against Alex as he absently toyed with her hair. Finally, she tilted her face up and asked the dreaded question. "What time is it?"

Alex glanced over the top of Emma's head to the clock that sat on his nightstand. "It's nearly half past four."

"I'll have to go home," Emma said regretfully. Dear Lord, she hated to think about reality, but she was going to have to get home sooner or later. Preferably sooner. "The servants will be up and about any time now, and I don't want them to see me coming in. Their gossip rivals that of the *ton*, you know. If one housemaid sees me, it will be all over town by tonight."

"Who cares?"

Emma twisted around quickly to look at him, shock and remonstration mixing in her eyes. "What do you mean, 'who cares?' I would rather not see my reputation dragged through the gutter, thank you very much."

Alex gave her a rather perplexed look. "What's

this about a gutter? We'll be married by next week. In a fortnight, all the furor over a hasty marriage will have died down, and the only thing anybody will be calling us is 'romantic.'"

An irrational knot of indignation began to blaze within Emma at his high-handedness. It was just like him to declare that they were getting married next week without even bothering to consult her. "Was that supposed to be a proposal of marriage?" she asked tightly.

Alex stared at her, dumbstruck. "We *are* going to get married, aren't we?"

"I certainly don't know. No one asked my opinion."

"For God's sake, Emma. We have to get married now."

"I don't have to do anything I don't want to, your grace," Emma declared, scooting across the bed and clamping the quilt down under her arms.

"Emma, *you* asked *me* to marry you just two days ago."

"And if you recall," she sniffed, "you refused."

"Hell and damnation, woman, are we going to go through that again?"

Emma didn't say anything.

"Wonderful," Alex muttered. "This is just what I need. A female in a snit."

"Do not speak to me that way!"

Alex's eyes flashed with arrogance. "I was not speaking to you, my dear, I was speaking about you. And if you weren't acting like such a damned fool, I'd be kissing you, instead."

Emma jumped out of bed at his insult, taking the quilt along with her. "I don't have to stay here and listen to you defame me!" she exploded, tripping over the coverlet as she tried to pick her clothing up off the floor. Each piece had been flung aside passionately, so she had to cross the room several times to gather it all, painfully aware of how foolish she must look as she desperately tried to keep her body covered with the heavy quilt.

Alex tried a different tactic. "Emma," he said softly, "after all we've shared, don't you want to get married? I'll go insane if I can't hold you in my arms every night."

"You are despicable!" Emma stormed, her cheeks pink with fury. "I cannot believe the nerve of you! How dare you try to seduce me into marrying you!"

"Well, it seemed to be working," Alex said with a lopsided grin.

"Aaaargh! I could—I could—Oooooh!" Emma's anger had reached proportions where her vocabulary retrieval was not quite what it should be.

"Kill me? I wouldn't if I were you. It'd make a terrible mess."

Alex's unflappable demeanor sent Emma's rage spiraling out of control. She picked up a vase and raised it over her head, getting ready to launch it at him.

"Please," he choked. "Not the Ming vase."

Emma lowered her arms, inspected the artifact with a discerning eye, and then placed it back down on the table. She picked up a snuff box. "How about this?"

Alex grimaced. "Well, if you really must . . ."

The snuff box missed his ear by a hair's breadth.

"Destroying my belongings isn't going to solve anything," Alex said, bounding off the bed, completely unconcerned with his nakedness. "You *will* marry me."

"Has it ever occurred to you to ask for something rather than demand it?" she burst out furiously, trying to pull up her undergarments without dropping the coverlet. Her anger only grew when Alex's lips quirked with amusement at her predicament. "Oh, I beg your forgiveness, your grace," she said, her voice dripping with ice cold sarcasm. "I forgot. A duke doesn't have to ask for anything. He doesn't have to earn anything. He can have whatever he wants. It's his due." Emma whipped her head around as she said the last words, and she was stunned by the seething expression on Alex's face. Horrified, she took a step backwards, still clutching nervously to the blanket which shielded her from his furious gaze.

"Emma," he said very tightly, "will you marry me?"

"No!" She could barely believe she had said it, but the word actually came out rather forcefully.

"That is it!" Alex exploded. He crossed the room in swift, angry strides and snatched the coverlet away from Emma. She desperately tried to cover herself but soon found that that wasn't really necessary, for Alex seemed intent on shoving her into her clothes. "I have had enough of your petty tantrums," he bit out, pulling the chemise over her head. "If you wanted to prove to me that you are not a shrinking miss who can be ordered about, you can rest assured. You have done so. Now stop acting like a child and accept the inevitable. You *will* marry me, and you will do it with a smile on your face."

Emma flashed him a sickeningly sweet grin. "Is that good enough, your grace? We wouldn't want it to get out that the great duke of Ashbourne had to force a woman to marry him." She regretted the words the minute they flew out of her mouth, instantly aware that she had gone too far. Alex's face was a mask of barely concealed rage, and his grip on her upper arms tightened until Emma was

sure she would be bruised. "I'm sorry," she said in
a strangled voice, unable to look him in the eye.

Disgusted, Alex let go of her and crossed the
room to the chair on which he had left his evening
clothes a few hours earlier before crawling into
bed next to Emma. With sharp, savage movements
he dressed himself, and all Emma could do was
stare, awed into silence by his rigid control of his
temper.

When Alex finished dressing, he tossed Emma her
overcoat and crossed the room to the door, giving
it a vicious yank. It didn't budge, and Alex swore
viciously as he remembered that he had locked it
the night before.

"The key," Emma whispered in horror. "You
threw it out the window."

He ignored her as he strode into his dressing
room and disappeared. Within seconds the door
to the room opened from the outside. Alex's broad
shoulders nearly filled the entire doorway. "Let's
go," he said tersely.

Emma wisely chose not to rage at him about
his letting her think they'd been trapped in the
room the previous evening, and she lost no time
in following his bidding, half afraid of his obvious,
although tightly leashed, fury, half figuring that
she wanted to go home anyway, so wasn't she
getting what she wanted? She scrambled down the
stairs and waited in the front hall while Alex woke
up one of his footmen and asked that a carriage be
made ready. "It will take a few minutes," he said
when he returned, silently daring her to protest
the delay. "I'm afraid my household isn't used to
activity at this time in the morning."

Emma gulped and nodded, keeping her gaze
fixed on the floor. She was starting to feel a
little ashamed of her tantrum. It was probably

very natural for Alex to assume that they would get married now that they had slept together. But nothing seemed to provoke her ire like his high-handed manner, and something within her had snapped when he simply announced their forth-coming nuptials. Now, as she looked hesitantly at his still-furious visage, she quickly realized that for all her outspokenness, she wasn't brave enough to venture a word.

Ten minutes later she was hustled into a carriage, and with dismay she noticed that the first streaks of dawn were beginning to light the sky. The servants at the Blydon household would already have begun their morning chores. They would notice her uncon-ventional arrival and tell their friends who worked in other households, who in turn would tell their employers. Emma sighed wearily. There would be no avoiding a scandal.

It wasn't a long ride home, but by the time the carriage pulled up in front of the Blydon mansion the sun had risen, and London was beginning to wake up. Alex quickly jumped down, practically dragging Emma along with him.

"There is no need to be so rough, your grace," Emma said indignantly as she stumbled up the steps behind him.

Alex whirled around and took her chin in his hand, holding her face up so that she could not avoid looking him straight in the eye. "My name is Alex," he said sharply. "Since we will be married this weekend, I would appreciate it if you would remember that."

"This weekend?" Emma said weakly.

Alex didn't answer; he just started banging furi-ously on the door.

"For God's sake, Alex! I have a key!" Emma grabbed at his arms, trying to stop the noise. She pulled the key from her pocket and let them in. "Now will you go?" she pleaded. "I can see myself up to my bedroom."

Alex flashed her a wicked smile. "Henry!" he bellowed. "Caroline!"

"What are you doing?" Emma hissed. "Are you determined to ruin me?"

"I am determined to marry you."

"What is going on here?"

Emma looked up. Henry and Caroline were scurrying down the curved staircase, looking at the couple in the hall with expressions of confusion and shock.

Alex planted his hands on his hips. "I have thoroughly compromised your niece," he declared. "Will you please insist that she marry me?"

Caroline didn't bat an eyelash. "This," she announced, "is most peculiar."

Chapter 20

Emma bit her lip and did her best to stand up straight. Her knees were knocking, her pulse was racing, and her mind was screaming out with self-recrimination. She closed her eyes in anguish. This time she had really done it.

Her uncle Henry looked as if he might explode. "Get up to your room *this instant*," he snapped, poking his finger in Emma's direction. Her eyes widened, and she fled up the stairs, not daring even one backward glance.

From her position next to Ned on the first-floor landing, Belle gasped as Emma flew by. She had never, ever seen her father this angry.

"And you," Henry bit out, turning his wrath toward Alex and completely ignoring the younger man's higher rank, "into my study. I'll deal with you just as soon as I speak with my wife."

Alex nodded curtly and exited the hall.

"And to my two obedient children," Henry called out without turning. "I suggest you both go to your rooms as well and meditate on why you did not see fit to inform your mother and me of your cousin's whereabouts last night."

Belle and Ned left with alacrity.

When Henry was finally alone with his wife (even the servants had wisely quit the scene), he turned to her and sighed. "Well, my dear?"

Caroline smiled wearily, hugging her arms to herself. "I cannot deny that I was hoping this would happen. Only I was hoping it would happen after a wedding ceremony."

Henry leaned over and kissed his wife, feeling some of his initial furor deflate. "Why don't you go upstairs and tend to Emma? I'll take care of Ashbourne." With that, he sighed again and slowly walked to his study. When he arrived, Alex was standing by the window, arms crossed as he stared out at the wisps of orange and pink that were still streaked across the early morning sky.

"I don't know whether to toss you through that window or shake your hand and say, 'Well done!'" Henry said in a tired voice.

Alex turned around but didn't reply.

Henry crossed the room to a decanter that sat on a side table. "Would you care for a whiskey?" He glanced at a clock and winced when he saw that it was only twenty minutes past five. "I realize that it's a bit early to be drinking, but this has been a rather uncommon morning, don't you think?"

Alex nodded. "A drink would be most appreciated, thank you."

Henry poured a glass and held it out. "Please, have a seat."

"I'd rather stand, thank you."

Henry poured another glass for himself. "I'd rather you sat."

Alex sat.

A light smile touched Henry's face. "I imagine you outweigh me by at least a stone, so I'll dispense with the window idea, I think."

"I would have difficulty doing the same if I were in your position," Alex said softly.

"Would you? That's a good sign. But I'm afraid we mellow a bit as we get older. I'm not as rash as

I used to be. However, it does appear that my niece was compromised last night." He took a drink and then looked Alex straight in the eye. "And you do appear to be the one who did the compromising. I can hardly cheer you on for that."

"I intend to marry her." Alex's tone was resolute.

"Does she intend to marry you?"

"Not yet."

"Do you think she wants to marry you?"

"She says she doesn't, but she does."

Henry placed his glass down gently and crossed his arms as he leaned against the edge of his desk. "That's a bit patronizing of you, don't you think?"

Alex flushed. "Two days ago she came to my home—unescorted—and asked me to marry her," he said somewhat defensively.

Henry quirked a brow. "Really?"

"I accepted."

"I can see that the two of you are now on excellent terms," Henry said dryly.

Alex shifted uncomfortably in his chair, telling himself over and over that as Emma's uncle, Henry deserved some answers. Still, the entire scene was damned humiliating. "We had a misunderstanding. I, er, broke it off. But everything was resolved last night."

"So much can happen in twenty-four hours."

Alex wondered when it was that he'd lost any measure of control over the conversation. He took a deep breath and continued, feeling much like a scolded schoolboy. "This time, I proposed to her, but she refused because she's so damned muleheaded." He swore sullenly and slumped in his chair.

"She is a handful, I'll grant you that, but her father entrusted her into my care. I take my responsibilities to my family very seriously. And more importantly, I love Emma like a daughter." Henry picked up his whiskey and held it in the air. "May I propose a toast to your forthcoming nuptials, your grace?"

Alex looked up in surprise.

"But be aware that I am granting my blessing to this marriage not because you have seduced Emma and not because you say it's what Emma wants. I give you my blessing because I really do believe that this marriage is the best thing for my niece. I think that you are one of the few young men I know who is worthy of her, and I think that she will make you a good wife." And then, almost as an afterthought, he added, "I also think that Emma really does want to marry you, but, as you said, she can be a bit muleheaded, and we may have a bit of trouble reminding her of that fact. For your sake, I hope we're successful because I'm not going to force my niece to the altar with a pistol pointed at her back."

Alex smiled weakly and drained the rest of his whiskey.

Emma was staring out the window when Caroline entered her room, but her eyes refused to focus on the scene.

"This is a fine mess you've gotten yourself into," Caroline said as she let the door shut with a loud click.

Emma slowly turned around, her eyes glistening with unshed tears. "I'm so sorry, Aunt Caroline. I never meant to shame you or your family. Please believe that."

Caroline took a deep breath. Emma needed comfort and support right now, not the scoldings she obviously expected. "What is this talk of *my* family? I only see *our* family."

Emma smiled tremulously.

Caroline sat down in the chair at Emma's dressing table. "It seems to me that you are going to have to make some serious decisions rather quickly."

"I don't want to marry him, Aunt Caroline," Emma said very quickly.

"You don't? Are you sure?"

Emma's shoulders slumped. "I don't think I do."

"That's very different."

Emma moved away from the window, kicked off her shoes, and sat atop her bed. "I don't know what to do."

"Why don't you tell me why you don't want to marry Ashbourne?"

"He's so domineering. Do you realize he didn't even ask me to marry him? He just stated it as if it were a fact. He didn't even consult me!"

Caroline took a deep breath, noting that her niece had regained a bit of her customary spirit. "Would this have been before or after you were, er, compromised?"

Emma turned away. "After."

"I see. And do you not think that it was a fairly logical conclusion on Ashbourne's part to assume that you, a gently bred young woman, would want to marry him after you had intimate relations?"

"He could have asked me." Emma clamped her lips shut in defiance but inwardly winced at how petty she sounded.

"Yes," Caroline agreed, "that was certainly remiss of him, but I'm not certain it is a good enough reason to refuse his offer." She paused and leaned forward. "Unless, of course, you have another reason for rejecting him."

Emma gulped and caught her lower lip between her teeth.

"Do you?"

When Emma finally spoke, her voice was barely audible. "No."

"Well, that's a start," Caroline said efficiently, rising and walking over to the spot by the window that Emma had so recently vacated. "But then again, one ought not marry someone just because there aren't any reasons not to. There ought to be a few good reasons why one *should*, don't you think?" She took Emma's silence as an affirmative and continued. "Is there any reason why marrying Ashbourne would be an extremely intelligent thing to do?" She looked Emma straight in the eye. "By intelligent I mean that it would be the next logical step in securing your future happiness."

Emma blinked a few times under her aunt's scrutiny and nodded.

"I thought so." Caroline crossed her arms. "Do you love him?" she asked bluntly.

Emma nodded, a tear running down her cheek.

"Do you realize how close you came to ruining your chances of marrying the man you love?"

Emma nodded again, feeling slightly sick inside.

"Well, then, you might want to tame that stubborn and prideful streak of yours," Caroline advised, sitting down next to Emma and pulling her into a motherly embrace. "Although I wouldn't tame it altogether. You're going to need some of that pride and stubbornness in a marriage with a man like that."

"I know," Emma said, sniffling.

Caroline placed a kiss on Emma's forehead. "Dry your eyes now, dear. We need to go down and inform the men of your decision." She stood up and walked to the door.

"But what about my father?" Emma said suddenly. "I cannot marry without his permission. And the company . . ." That, she realized, was a feeble excuse, considering that she had been the first one to propose, a fact of which she had no doubt Caroline would soon be aware.

"I think you've always known that Dunster Shipping was not your destiny. And as for your father— well, I'm afraid he is just going to have to trust our judgment. We might not have very much time to spare."

Emma's eyes widened in horror as her gaze dropped involuntarily to her abdomen. Dear Lord, she hadn't even considered a baby!

"I see you catch my meaning."

When the two women entered Henry's study a few moments later, Henry and Alex were sitting in companionable silence, nursing their whiskeys. Emma's eyes narrowed slightly as she surveyed the scene. It didn't appear as if her uncle had done any ranting or raging on behalf of her lost virtue. She sighed softly. Oh well, better to start her marriage off on a peaceful note.

"Did you have something you wanted to share with us?" Henry asked, one eyebrow raised.

Emma swallowed and plunged forward, turning her face toward Alex. "I would be honored to marry you, your grace." She paused, tilting her chin up slightly. "If you would see fit to ask me."

Caroline groaned, and Henry rolled his eyes, but Alex could not stop a small smile from dancing across his face. He supposed that this was, after all, the reason he loved her so much. "Would you like me to get down on one knee?" he asked, looking deeply into Emma's eyes.

Emma nervously licked her lips. His tone was teasing, but somehow she knew that he would do it if she asked. "No," she said, burning under his intense emerald gaze. "I don't think that will be necessary."

Alex's smile widened just a bit as he looked down at Emma. She was still in Ned's clothing and looked so endearing, standing there with her chin up as she tried to hold onto her pride. He longed to reach forward and tuck a lock of her bright hair behind her ear, but, mindful of Henry and Caroline's presence, he took her hand instead and raised it to his lips. "Will you marry me?" he said softly.

Emma nodded, not quite trusting herself to speak. Henry and Caroline, sensing that their work was done, quietly left the room, leaving Emma alone with Alex, her hand still at his lips.

"I'm sorry I didn't get it right the first time," he said softly.

Emma felt a smile tugging across her lips. "Actually, I think that was the second time."

Alex nodded. "You are correct. But if you recall, I didn't get it right the first time either."

Emma sighed, remembering the awful scene in Alex's parlor. Good Lord, was that only two days ago? It seemed like a lifetime had passed since then. "No, you didn't," she said softly. "But I think we ought to put all of that behind us. It would be nice if we could start our marriage on an optimistic note."

"I agree," Alex replied, absently stroking her hand with his thumb. He wanted to pull her into his arms. He wanted to kiss her senseless. But he was a little afraid. Of what exactly, he wasn't sure, but he somehow knew that his entire life hung in a very delicate balance, and he didn't want to upset it. So he just stood there, stroking her hand, not knowing what to say, and feeling like a fool for being so unsure of himself. "I will try not to be so controlling," he said finally, his voice grave.

Emma's eyes flew to his. He looked so serious, so
earnest that it was difficult not to throw her arms
around him. "I will try not to be so stubborn," she
replied.

A ghost of a smile touched Alex's face as
he gathered her into his arms and held her
gently against his large frame. Emma wrapped
her arms around his waist and let her cheek
rest against his chest. She sighed softly, feeling
the beautiful warmth that radiated from his
body. His heartbeat thumped loud and strong
against her ear, and she decided that he was
going to have to be the one to eventually
break the tender moment, because nothing in
heaven or on earth could make her move.

But no matter how perfectly splendid she felt at
that moment, she couldn't quite stifle the thought
that she was marrying a man who cared for her,
yes, but who didn't quite trust her. He said he
realized that she was different from the *ton* ladies
who pursued him relentlessly, but Emma was afraid
that some of his old scars simply ran too deep. She
wasn't sure if he'd ever be able to trust a woman
completely.

And then, of course, he hadn't said that he loved
her. Emma stiffened slightly at that thought but
then reminded herself that she hadn't yet told him
of her feelings either.

Alex felt her posture change and dropped a gentle
kiss atop her head. "Is something wrong, darling?"

Emma let herself relax again, savoring the warmth
of Alex's embrace. "No, nothing's wrong. I was just
thinking, that's all."

"About what?"

"Nothing, really. Just wedding details," she lied.
"We don't have very much time to take care of
everything, I imagine."

Alex drew back slowly and led her to a nearby sofa where they both sat down. "Did you have your heart set on a large wedding?" he asked tenderly, placing two fingers under her chin, tilting it up so that he could see into her eyes.

"No. I know a lot of people here in London, but I don't know many of them well, so I shan't mourn their absence at my wedding. I would like a special gown, though," she added wistfully. "And I do wish that my father could be here to give me away."

Alex kept his gaze on her eyes, searching for some sign that she really did want a lavish affair. He saw only clear, open honesty. "I am sorry that we cannot wait for your father, but I want us to be married as soon as possible. I would rather not wait around while your aunt and my mother confer on flower arrangements."

Emma let out a soft giggle. "Did you know that it was precisely because of flower arrangements that we met, your grace?"

"Don't call me 'your grace,'" Alex warned.

"I'm sorry. It just slipped out. I've been too well trained in the ways of the *ton*, I'm afraid."

"But do tell me why I owe my supreme good fortune to flower arrangements."

"That was why I was walking to the store dressed as a maid when I saved Charlie from the hack. Aunt Caroline wanted me to help her with flower arrangements for the ball, and so Belle and I fled to the kitchens to escape her. We dressed in our maids' clothing because we didn't want to get any of our dresses dirty." And then she added, "I really *hate* arranging flowers."

Alex laughed out loud. "I promise you, my love, that in honor of our first meeting, we shall have plenty of flowers at your wedding, but you won't have to arrange any of them."

Emma stole a quick glance at his profile as he laughed. He couldn't be treating her so tenderly if he didn't love her a little, could he? She brushed aside her doubts. If he didn't love her yet, he did desire her, that much was abundantly clear. And he liked her a great deal, too. That was certainly a good start. Emma took a deep breath as she felt her infamous stubborn streak rise up within her. She could make this marriage work. She *would* make it work. She had to.

The next few days passed by in a flurry of activity. Alex tried to stick by his initial idea of having the wedding that weekend, but after five minutes of "discussion" with Caroline, he reluctantly agreed to push the date back by a week. Emma wisely kept out of the fray.

"A week and a half is still dreadful," Caroline remarked. "But at least we can put together something nice. Two days would have been impossible."

An hour after Alex finally left that morning, the dowager Duchess of Ashbourne arrived on the Blydon doorstep, insisting that she be allowed to take part in the wedding preparations. No one pointed out that it was only half past seven in the morning. Eugenia seemed to regard her son's forthcoming nuptials as nothing short of a miracle, and the mere fact that the early hour was beyond unfashionable wasn't going to stop her from making sure that the marriage went off without a hitch. After about fifteen minutes with Eugenia and Caroline, Emma finally threw up her arms, asked the two ladies to please consult her on any decision of large importance, went upstairs to her room, and promptly went to bed. She hadn't had very much sleep the previous night, after all.

When she awoke, some six hours later, she was famished. Someone had managed to pull away from the wedding plans long enough to thoughtfully see that a tray was brought up to Emma's room, so she quickly gulped down the slice of meat pie and juice that had been left on her dressing table, took a bath, and got dressed. After a day in men's clothing, she found her jade green walking dress somewhat confining but decided that it really wouldn't do to continue walking around in breeches. Then she sat down at her desk and penned a quick note to her father, explaining her circumstances and promising to write him a more lengthy letter soon, telling him all about Alex and the wedding.

When she finally headed downstairs at three o'clock, Caroline and Eugenia were exactly where she had left them, tossing names back and forth as they prepared the guest list. Belle and Sophie had joined the party and were having a heated argument over Emma's bouquet. When they saw the bride arrive, they immediately turned the matter over to her.

"Oh, roses, I think," Emma replied. "Don't you?"

Both women rolled their eyes. "Yes, of course, but what color?" Belle asked.

"Oh. Well, that depends on what color I choose for my attendants' gowns, I suppose."

Belle and Sophie looked at her expectantly, and Emma realized that she was going to have to make a decision. "Well, the two of you will be my only attendants, so what color would you like to wear?"

"Peach."

"Blue."

Emma swallowed. "I see. Well, perhaps we ought to just go with white roses in my bouquet for now. White will match everything. Especially me!" she added with a jaunty smile. "I *can* get married in white, can't I?" she asked quickly. "I know it's not the height of fashion, but I have a friend in Boston who wore white for her wedding, and it was so beautiful."

"You can get married in whatever color you want," her aunt replied. "Your first fitting is this evening. Madame Lambert is staying open late tonight so that we can get the dress done in time."

"That's very kind of her," Emma murmured, wondering how much extra Caroline had offered to persuade the dressmaker to extend her hours. "What else have you decided upon?"

"We'll hold the wedding at Westonbirt, if you don't mind," Caroline said. "It's too late to get any of the large cathedrals here in London."

"I know it's customary for the wedding to be held at the bride's home," Eugenia put in. "But you do live in Boston, after all, and Westonbirt is several hours closer to London than your cousins' country home."

"No, no, that's fine," Emma replied. "Westonbirt is lovely. And after all, it's soon to be my home."

Eugenia's eyes filled with tears as she took both of Emma's hands in her own. "I'm so glad that you're joining our family."

"Thank you," Emma said, giving Eugenia's hands a squeeze. "I'm glad to be joining it."

"Now then," Caroline said breezily. "Back to the guest list. What about Viscount Benton?"

Emma gasped. Anthony Woodside? "No!" she cried out.

Caroline and Eugenia both turned to look at her, their expressions quizzical.

"I—I really don't like him," she said quickly. "And I think he makes Belle uncomfortable."

Belle nodded.

"Very well," Caroline said, making a dark slash through his name on the list she was preparing.

"I can't imagine that most people will be able to attend," Emma said, somewhat hopefully. "It's such late notice, after all, and a three-hour ride from London."

All four of her companions turned to her with shocked expressions. "Are you crazy?" Belle finally asked. "People are going to be tripping over themselves to get there. The Duke of Ashbourne is getting married. The duke of 'I have no interest in marriage' is getting married. And he's marrying a relatively unknown quantity from the Colonies, no less. This is going to be the social event of the season."

"The hurriedness of the affair is only going to make people even more interested," Sophie added. "It adds a touch of scandal and intrigue. And romance, of course."

"I see," Emma said weakly. "But I think Alex wanted a small affair."

"Oh, pish!" Eugenia said dismissively. "I am his mother, and I don't care what he wants. My son only has a wedding once in his lifetime, and I intend to enjoy it." Eugenia sat back, and Emma decided that there was no point in further protests.

And, indeed, she didn't argue for the next week, letting herself get carried along on the wave of wedding preparations. The only break she got—besides sleep, which she wasn't getting enough of—was when Ned marched into the parlor and forcibly stole her away from her bevy of current and future female relatives. "We," he announced, "are going for a ride."

Emma was only too glad to escape, and the two of them took the carriage out to a popular shop for tea and cakes.

"I wanted to tell you what happened with Woodside," Ned said as soon as they were settled at their table.

"Oh my goodness," Emma breathed. "I almost forgot! What happened?"

"He tried to collect the debt on Friday at White's."

"And?"

"And I told him that I certainly wasn't going to pay my gambling debt twice."

Emma clapped her hand to her mouth. "Oh, Ned, you didn't!"

"I did. He got all flustered and started to make a scene until I pulled the voucher out of my pocket. I raised my eyebrows and asked him how on earth I could have gotten the voucher back if I hadn't already paid my debt."

"He must have been furious."

"That, my dear cousin, is an understatement. I thought he was going to explode. And everyone heard what happened. I don't think he'll be accepted at respectable card games for years."

"Oh, this is brilliant," Emma said. "You know, I think I must be developing a vindictive streak because I'm really enjoying his distress."

"How unladylike of you," Ned teased. "But seriously, Emma. He was really angry. I think we might want to watch out for him. He'll want revenge."

Emma took a sip of her tea. "Really, Ned, what can he do to us? Spread rumors? No one will believe him."

"I don't know. I just think we should be careful."

"Careful, maybe. But worried? I don't think so. He's not exactly the murderous type."

"Oh really?"

Emma shook her head as she raised her eyes heavenward. "He's far too fastidious."

Chapter 21

Before Emma could catch her breath, she found herself at Westonbirt, watching as over a hundred workmen and servants put the finishing touches on what must have been the most hastily arranged wedding in decades. Caroline and Eugenia were in their element, and Emma had to admit that they had performed no less than a miracle. Caroline often remarked that she could have done better if she'd had a little more time, which made Emma laugh because the arrangements far exceeded anything she had ever dreamed of back in Boston.

After some good-natured bickering by Sophie and Belle over blue and peach, Emma finally declared that mint green would reign as the color of the day, which turned out to be a wise decision because both women looked perfectly marvelous in their gowns.

But it was the bride who would capture everyone's heart. At her final fitting for her wedding dress, Belle had gasped and said that she had never seen Emma looking quite so beautiful. The gown was a slightly old-fashioned style, with the waist where it was supposed to be rather than following the latest rage, which dictated that it be located right under the bust. Emma liked the new style and had many dresses cut that way, but she declared that it just wouldn't do for a wedding dress. Madame

Lambert had agreed instantly and had fashioned a sumptuous gown of ivory silk with a modest neckline that just barely grazed her shoulders, long tight-fitting sleeves, and layers of underskirts that made the dress billow out gracefully from Emma's waist. Emma had decreed that the gown be kept relatively simple, and so no jewels or bows adorned it.

The result was breathtaking. The cut flattered Emma's small frame, emphasizing her small waist and the elegant line of her throat. But it was the color of the silk that really did the trick. Emma had started out with her heart set on white, but Madame Lambert had refused and insisted on ivory. She was absolutely right; the new material set off Emma's complexion perfectly, and she positively glowed.

Although it might just have been love.

Still, Emma decided, the dress helped.

Finally, the day of the wedding arrived, and Emma awoke with at least three dozen butterflies in her stomach. Then, as if on cue, Belle bounded into her room and without any preamble asked, "Are you nervous?"

"Dreadfully."

"Good. You're supposed to be nervous, you know. Marriage is a very big step, after all. It's probably the biggest event in a woman's life. After being born, of course, and dying, I suppose, but—"

"That's enough!" Emma bit out.

Belle smiled devilishly.

"You fiend," Emma muttered, swatting her cousin with a pillow.

"I ordered up some morning chocolate," Belle said. "It should be here any minute. I didn't think you'd want to eat anything more substantial this morning."

"No," Emma agreed softly, gazing out the window.

Belle took in her serious expression and immediately asked, "You're not having second thoughts, are you?"

Emma broke out of her reverie. "No, of course not. I love Alex, you know. I don't know if I ever told you, but I do."

"I knew that you did!"

"I only wish that my father could give me away. I do miss him. And now I'll be living so far away."

Belle patted Emma's hand consolingly. "I know. But you have us, after all. And Ashbourne's family adores you. And your father will visit you. I know he will. But don't tell my father how much you're missing Uncle John. He's practically bursting with pride at the thought of giving you away."

A knock on the door sounded, and Sophie entered the room, still in her dressing gown. "I intercepted the maid on the stairs and had her go back to the kitchen for extra chocolate," she said. "I hope you don't mind. She should be up shortly."

"Of course not," Emma said with a smile. "The more the merrier."

"I cannot believe the sheer amount of activity in this house," Sophie continued. "Have either of you been downstairs yet?"

Both Emma and Belle shook their heads.

"It's a madhouse. I was nearly run over by a footman. And the guests have already started to arrive!"

"You're joking!" Belle replied. "They must have gotten up at four in the morning to get here now."

"Well, Alex was positively beastly when Mama suggested that we invite everyone to spend the night. Only a very select few were allowed to come last night, and he insisted that absolutely *everyone* vacate the premises by tonight."

Emma blushed. "Have you seen him yet?"

"No," Sophie said, taking a cup of chocolate from the maid who had silently entered the room. "But Dunford was up and about. He said Alex is almost climbing the walls. I imagine he's rather anxious to have this entire wedding over and done with."

"Yes, well, he's not the only one," Emma murmured, wondering when her stomach was going to stop turning cartwheels.

The wedding was scheduled to start promptly at noon, and at eleven-thirty Emma peeked out the window at the spectacle that was growing on Westonbirt's south lawn. "Good Lord," she gasped. "There must be two hundred people out there."

"Closer to four, I would guess," Belle said, joining her cousin at the window. "Mama would have liked a guest list of six hundred, but—"

"But there wasn't enough time," Emma finished. "I know." Still gazing out at the lawn, she shook her head at the grandness of the affair. Gaily striped tents dotted the lawn, shielding the swarms of guests from the early July sun. As Alex had promised, there were more bouquets of flowers than Emma could count.

"Oh my," Emma breathed. "I should never have allowed Aunt Caroline to let this get so big. I don't know half of those people."

"But they know you!" Sophie pointed out enthusiastically.

"Can you believe that you're going to be a duchess?" Belle asked.

"No, I really can't," Emma said weakly.

And then, before she knew it, it was noon and she was standing just outside the entrance to the tent, so nervous that she could barely hear the strains of the string quartet playing her favorite Mozart piece.

"Good luck," Sophie said just before she headed down the aisle. "Sister."

Belle followed Sophie a few moments later, but not before she gave Emma's hand a reassuring squeeze. "I love you, Emma Dunster."

"That's the last time anyone will ever say that to me," Emma whispered.

"Emma Ridgely sounds just fine to me," Henry said, taking her arm. "Especially when it has Duchess of Ashbourne tacked on to the end of it."

Emma smiled nervously.

"You'll do just fine," Henry said. And then he added softly, "I know that you'll be very happy."

Emma nodded, blinking back tears. "Thank you so much, Uncle Henry. For everything. I do love you, you know."

Henry touched her cheek. "I know," he said, his voice rough with emotion. "Shall we be on our way? I think your duke is going to march up the aisle and drag you back to the altar if we don't get there soon."

Taking a deep breath, Emma took that first step into the aisle. And when she saw Alex waiting for her at the altar, all her fears and anxieties slowly began to melt away. With each step, the joy within her grew, and she didn't even notice the hundreds of people who had turned in their seats to watch the radiant bride process down the aisle.

Alex's breath caught in his throat the first moment she stepped into the tent. She looked so lovely, he didn't know how to describe it. It was as if her beauty had accumulated inside of her and was shining out through every pore. Everything about her seemed to glow, from the satin creaminess of her skin to her soft violet eyes to the fiery highlights of her hair, which shone brightly even underneath her delicate veil.

Finally, Henry and Emma reached Alex, and Emma could not help but smile as her uncle placed her hand in that of her future husband. Looking up into Alex's green eyes, she found an undeniable warmth in his gaze, along with hunger, possessiveness, and, yes, love. He might never have said the words, but Emma saw it clear as day in his eyes. He loved her.

He loved her, and suddenly her life seemed twice as bright as it had just moments earlier.

The rest of the ceremony passed so quickly that later Emma could remember only the barest snatches of it. Charlie standing so proudly as he held the rings on a small pillow, the warmth of Alex's hands as he slipped the ring on her finger, Dunford's and Ned's cocky smiles as they watched Alex kiss her a little too passionately when the vicar finally pronounced them man and wife, and then finally, the sight of Caroline's wet cheeks as the newly married couple breezed back up the aisle when the ceremony was over.

The party lasted for the rest of the afternoon and most of the evening. Emma found herself being congratulated by hundreds of people she didn't know and then by hundreds of people she did. Alex stuck by her side as much as possible, but even when they were forced to socialize separately, she felt his eyes on her, and she could barely contain the dual shivers of love and desire that floated through her.

Finally after hours of dancing and dozens of toasts, Alex sidled up next to Emma and whispered in her ear, "I know it's still early, but could we please get out of here? I want you all to myself."

"Oh, I thought you'd never ask," Emma sighed, her smile growing wider by the second.

The pair waved farewell to the crowd and then stopped by Eugenia's side before they left. "I want everyone gone tonight," Alex said firmly. "I don't care if they don't get home until dawn. They usually don't anyway."

"May I assume that your stinginess does not extend to members of your immediate family?" Eugenia inquired with an extremely amused expression.

"Of course, but I want the lot of you out of here tomorrow morning." Alex dropped a kiss onto his mother's cheek. "I'd like a bit of privacy with my new wife, if none of you mind."

"Rest assured, we'll all be gone by noontime," Eugenia replied. "I assume that you don't plan to emerge from the bridal chamber before then?"

Emma blushed to the roots of her hair.

"Absolutely not," Alex said shamelessly. "Although I would appreciate it if you could arrange to have a meal sent up to us tomorrow."

"Fear not, my dear son, I've taken care of everything." Eugenia's eyes misted over as she touched his cheek. "I'm very happy for you today."

Alex and Emma smiled their good-byes to Eugenia and took off down the long hallway that led to the master suite. Emma nearly had to run to keep up with Alex's long strides until finally, as he propelled her up the curving staircase, she had to stop and catch her breath. "Please," she begged, laughing all the while. "Wait just a moment."

Alex halted in his tracks and cupped her cheeks in his hands. His eyes were filled with a curious mix of total intensity and humor. "I can't wait," he said simply.

Emma let out a little yelp as Alex scooped her up into his arms and carried her the rest of the way to their room. "Alone at last," he said dramatically, kicking the door shut so that he wouldn't have to put her down. "Do you mind if I kiss you?"

"No."

"Oh, good." And by the time he was through, Emma was breathless and warm.

"Are you nervous?" Alex asked.

"No. I was this morning, but I'm not now."

Alex's eyes glowed as he took in the implications of that statement. Still, he didn't want to rush her. They had all night—all week, actually. He took her hand and led her further into the chamber. "This is your new room," he said, waving his hand at their surroundings.

Emma looked around. The decor was quite masculine.

"You can redecorate if you want," Alex said. "Nothing too pink, I hope."

Emma stifled a grin. "I think we can come up with something suitable."

Alex caught her hand in his. "There is an adjoining room which is officially the duchess's chamber, but I'd rather you spend more of your time in here."

"Oh really?" Emma teased.

"We could turn it into a sitting room for you with all of the feminine fripperies you want," Alex said earnestly. "But I don't think there'll be any need for the bed that is in there. I'm thinking of having it moved to Mrs. Goode's quarters. She has been with us for many years, and I think it would be quite a treat for her. Much more comfortable than what she has now."

"I think that would be a brilliant idea," Emma said softly, stepping closer to him.

"Oh, Emma, I'm so glad that you're finally mine."

"And I am glad that *you* are *mine*."

Alex laughed out loud. "Come a little closer so that we can finally get that gorgeous dress off of you, your grace."

"My name is Emma," she replied in a stern voice. "I don't want to hear you calling me 'your grace.'"

"You are priceless, your grace." Alex reached his arms around her and started to undo the tiny buttons that marched down the back of her wedding gown. He moved with agonizing slowness, sending hot desire down Emma's spine with each touch.

A small moan tore from Emma's lips as she placed her hands on his shoulders to steady herself. The entire room seemed to be spinning in a sensual haze, and it was all she could do to remain standing.

Alex's hands stilled about halfway down her back. "Mmm, I think it's time we let down your hair." With deft fingers, he pulled out the pins that had been used to pile her thick tresses atop her head. "Although I do like these little wispy things that hang down when you do your hair this way." A few moments later the entire mass came tumbling down, and Alex lifted a few of the soft locks to his face, kissing them first and then breathing in the heady scent.

"I adore your hair," he murmured, running his fingers through it. "Have I ever told you that I want a little girl with hair this exact color?"

Wordlessly, Emma shook her head. They had never discussed children. She had assumed he wanted an heir—all men did—but she had never dreamed that he would want a little girl just like her. "I myself had been thinking about a little boy with black hair and green eyes," she said hesitatingly.

Alex's hands moved back to the buttons on her back. "Well, we'll just have to keep on working on it until we both get our wish, won't we?" This time Alex undid her buttons with great speed, and within seconds the dress fell to the floor, leaving Emma clad only in her thin, silky chemise.

He started to push the sheer garment from her shoulders, but Emma stopped him. "Shh. It's my turn now." She reached for his cravat and slowly pulled apart its intricate folds. And when she was done she moved to his crisp, white shirt, savoring each inch of flesh that was revealed as she undid each button. Alex could only withstand that sweet torture for a few moments, and with a groan, he scooped her into his arms and carried her to the huge four-poster bed.

"Oh, God, you're so beautiful," he said reverently, touching the side of her cheek. "So beautiful."

Emma abandoned herself to the passion of the moment, wrapping her arms eagerly around Alex as he came to join her on the bed. Even as he was ridding himself of his clothing, he couldn't stop touching her, and the heat of his hands combined with the sensual rubbing of silk against skin was nearly enough to send her over the edge. She moaned his name over and over, barely aware that she was using her voice.

"Shhh, sweetheart, I'm here," he murmured.

And he was, Emma assured herself. Every glorious naked inch of him was pressed up against her. But her chemise still lay in the way, and Emma tore at the offending garment, wanting nothing between her and her husband.

"Shhh," he said again, stilling her hands. "I've grown rather fond of this thing." Placing his hands on her silk-covered hips, he started to push the

chemise up along her body, leaving twin trails of
fire along her sides. As it slid upward to reveal
her breasts, Alex let out a murmur of appreciation
and slowly leaned down to kiss each dusky nipple. Emma squirmed with pleasure, grasping at the
back of his head to keep him close to her. "Mmm,
I remembered that you liked that," Alex chuckled,
marveling at her wondrously responsive nature.

"Alex, get this thing off of me," she demanded
hotly.

"Oh, all right," he teased, finally pulling the chemise over her head and letting it drift down to the
floor beside the bed.

Emma glanced up at him. He still seemed so
self-composed. Didn't he feel as crazy with passion
as she did? With a devilish grin she leaned down
and began to kiss his flat nipple the same way he
had done to her. His reaction was instantaneous
and more than Emma had hoped for. Bucking off
the bed, he cried out, "Oh my God, Emma, where
did you learn that?"

Emma moved back up to his mouth. "From you.
Do you want to teach me anything else?"

"Maybe next week," Alex growled. "I don't think
I could take much more of this tonight."

She laughed with satisfaction as Alex leaned
down to kiss her ardently. At that moment all
of their joking and teasing ceased, and all that
remained were two hungry bodies, straining for
each other in desire and passion.

Emma couldn't seem to touch enough of his skin.
Her hands floated along his firmly muscled thighs
up to his chest and over his shoulders. And each
touch inflamed Alex's passion until he could take
no more. His hand stole down the length of her
body to settle over the soft curls that protected her
womanhood. Emma gasped with need, clutching at

him, trying to draw him closer. Slowly Alex parted the folds of her most private skin and slipped a finger inside. She was more than ready for him.

"You're so wet," he said in a ragged voice. "So wet and so hot and so ready for me."

"Please Alex," Emma begged.

Alex positioned himself over her, sliding just the tip of his manhood inside. It was torture not to plunge the full length of himself into her sweet warmth, but he knew that her body was still unused to his, and he wanted to give her time to adjust to his size.

But Emma would have none of that. "Oh, Alex, please. I need more," she moaned, grasping at his hips, trying to draw him closer.

He could not resist her pleading, and with a rough cry he drove forward, fully sheathing himself within her. His breathing laborious, he strove to maintain an even rhythm as he pulsed forward and back, stroking her intimately.

Emma spiralled to heaven. She fought against release, wanting to prolong the perfection of the moment, but still she felt herself slipping toward that shattering sense of freedom that only Alex could give her. She knew her battle was lost when he slipped his hand between their bodies and touched her intimately. And then, just moments before she knew she must explode, a cry was torn from her throat.

"Oh, God, Alex, I love you so much!"

He froze. "What did you say?" he asked hoarsely.

Emma felt as if she were teetering on the edge of a steep precipice. She needed him to keep moving. "Please Alex. Please don't leave me hanging here."

"What did you say?" he repeated, every muscle taut.

Violet eyes met green in a soul-baring caress. "I love you."

Alex held her gaze for another moment before plunging forward again, this time with a new sense of urgency. The last thrust was all that Emma needed, and she felt herself lose her hold on reality. Bucking off the bed with the strength of her release, she screamed his name as her world erupted into a passionate prism of light. The sweet clenching of Emma's muscles around him shattered Alex's last vestiges of restraint, and he let out a harsh cry of triumph as he exploded within her.

Many minutes later, when they were lying entwined in the delicious haze of spent passion, Alex sighed deeply, burying his face in the soft curve of Emma's neck. "I was afraid I would never hear those words," he said quietly.

Emma sank her fingers in his thick, dark hair and tousled it. "I am still afraid I might never hear them."

Alex drew back and cupped her face in his hands. "I love you, Emma Elizabeth Dunster Ridgely," he said solemnly. "I love you with all of my heart and all of my soul. I love you like I never dreamed it was possible to love a woman. I love you like—"

"Stop!" Emma cried out, her eyes brimming with tears.

"Why, darling?"

"I'm too happy," she said in a choked voice.

"You can never be too happy. In fact, I intend to devote the rest of my life to ensuring that each day you live is happier than the one before it."

"I don't think that will be very difficult as long as you remain by my side."

Alex smiled. "As if I would ever leave."

"Good!" Emma said saucily.

"As if you would let me," he teased. "My fierce American duchess. You'd probably come after me with a shotgun."

Emma sat up and swatted him with a pillow. "Beast!" Laughing merrily, she let him wrestle her back down to the bed. "Besides, I don't even know how to use a shotgun," she said, catching her breath.

"What? My tree-climbing, fishing rod-toting duchess can't fire a shotgun? I'm disappointed."

"Well, I am better than average with a pistol."

Alex leaned down to kiss her. "That's more like it."

"Alex?"

"Hmm?"

"We don't have to go back to town anytime soon, do we?"

"No, I don't think so. Why do you ask?"

"I think I'm developing a fondness for Westonbirt."

Alex pouted. "For Westonbirt or for me?"

"For you, you big baby. But I never get to see you in London. Everyone puts such demands on your time. Do you think we could just stay here for a while?"

Alex cuddled his wife against his chest, treasuring the newfound love that shone in his heart. "I think that could be arranged."

Chapter 22

The next few weeks of Emma's life were among the happiest she had ever known. She floated through the days in a blissful haze, wearing the indestructible smile of a woman who loves and is loved in return. Her life with Alex developed into a rather comfortable routine. They had all of their meals together—although many had to be brought up to their room on a tray. They went for a ride every afternoon, taking a different route each time, and Westonbirt was large enough that after three weeks Emma still hadn't seen all of the estate. Every evening after supper, they lounged in their new sitting room, reading or playing chess, or simply enjoying each other's company.

And their nights, of course, were not reserved just for sleeping.

Emma soon learned to make good use of the time she didn't spend with Alex. He had quite a few business ventures that required his attention, and he often spent time in his study going over important letters and documents. Also, there were four other estates besides Westonbirt that required careful management, and Alex didn't like to leave all the details to overseers. His tenants deserved more than an absentee landlord, and he had books and books of notes in which he tried to keep track of their progress and needs.

So while Alex was busy with all of his work, Emma set about the job of getting to know her new home. Her first venture was to have the bed in the duchess's bedroom hauled away. A quick trip to London to visit her family and shop for furniture resulted in her new sitting room getting redecorated in record time. Then she busied herself with learning about the management of the ancestral Ashbourne home. After getting acquainted with all of the servants, she spent a little extra time with the higher ones, asking them questions about the running of the household. Her meetings were doubly successful, for in addition to learning more about the inner workings of Westonbirt, she developed a sense of trust with the servants. They truly appreciated her interest in their welfare and were flattered that she bothered to ask them for advice about her new role as mistress of Westonbirt.

But one could only spend so much time redecorating and interviewing servants, and soon Emma found that she had little to do. The efficient staff ran the household like clockwork, and very little intervention was required on her part. So one morning, about three weeks into her marriage, she took the initiative and knocked on Alex's study door.

"Come in."

Emma poked her head in the doorway. "Am I bothering you?"

Alex put the papers he'd been reading down on the desk. "No, not at all. Is it time for dinner yet?"

Emma shook her head.

Alex glanced out the window. "It's a beautiful day. Shall we have Mrs. Goode prepare us a picnic?"

"That would be lovely, thank you, but actually I just thought I'd pop in and see how you were loing. What are those papers you're reading?"

Alex raised his eyebrows at her unexpected inter-
st. "They pertain to an interest I have in a sugar
plantation in the Caribbean."

"Oh. May I look at them?"

"Certainly." He held them out to her. "But I don't
hink you'll find them very interesting. Besides,
hey're in French."

Emma picked up the papers and scanned them.
Her French was not as good as Alex's, but it was
good enough to get the general idea of the letters
rom the plantation manager. A bad season had
esulted in a poor crop. Alex probably would not
see a return on his investment for another year. She
handed the papers back to him. "That's too bad,"
she said.

"I underestimated your French."

Emma smiled. "They do teach us a thing or two
n the Colonies."

"In the United States," Alex corrected.

"Touché. I've been in England too long."

Alex rose and wrapped his arms around her,
dropping a chaste kiss on her nose. "Yes, well,
you're English now."

She sighed contentedly, enjoying the warmth of
his embrace. "Alex?" she said against his chest.

"Hmmm?"

"I've been thinking. I've spent the last three weeks
getting to know all of the servants and learning how
o manage the household, but now that I've done all
that there really isn't much for me to do."

Alex tipped her face up to his. "Don't I keep you
busy?" he asked in a husky voice.

Emma blushed. Their passion still embarrassed
her a little when he discussed it in the light of
day. "You keep my nights busy. And my meals.
And our daily ride, of course. But I really don't

have anything to do while you're in here work
ing."

"I see. Well, I don't see why you shouldn't take
over the bookkeeping for the household. After all
you handled that for your father's company. I'm
sure you are up to the task. Norwood has been
doing it for years, but I don't think he enjoys i
very much. He much prefers being a stuffy old
butler."

Emma brightened considerably. "That would b
lovely, Alex. I'll go seek him out right away." Sh
leaned forward and kissed him on the cheek. "I'l
have Mrs. Goode see to that picnic basket. Wh
don't we meet in the great hall at one o'clock?"

At Alex's nod, she exited the study and went off i
search of Norwood. She found him in a small dining
parlor, inspecting some silver that had been recentl
polished by a newly hired maid. "Oh Norwood!"
she called out to the top of his balding head from
the next room.

He straightened immediately. "Yes, your grace?

"I plan to take over the bookkeeping for th
household accounts. His grace has indicated t
me that you don't really enjoy doing it, and
must admit, I rather like working with num
bers."

"Yes, your grace. And pardon me for being s
forward, but I must offer you my thanks. My eye
are not quite what they used to be, and all thos
small numbers are a bit of a strain."

Emma offered him a sunny smile. "Then every
thing has worked out perfectly! And you needn'
beg my pardon. I wasn't raised here in Englan
and am not accustomed to so much formality. Yo
shouldn't feel the least hesitation about approach
ing me if there is some sort of problem."

"Thank you, your grace."

"And you should have told his grace about your eyesight," Emma added, shaking her head. "He would have given the bookkeeping over to someone else."

Norwood cracked a smile—the first one Emma had ever seen touch his solemn demeanor. "That may be true, your grace, but his grace has not always been quite so, shall we say, approachable."

Emma grimaced. "No, I suppose not. But don't let that bother you. It's really all an act. Just look how much he cares for his tenants. Still, it's not very pleasant to be on the receiving end of his temper."

Norwood, who was unused to conversations with the Quality which lasted more than three sentences, wisely did not inquire how her grace knew so much about his grace's temper.

"Anyway, I've very much enjoyed our chat," Emma continued. "Why don't we go and get that bookkeeping? I'd very much like to learn how you've been doing it."

Norwood led Emma to a small office near the kitchens. It took her only a few minutes to figure out that while Norwood had been extremely scrupulous in his calculations, he was using quite the most convoluted bookkeeping system she had ever seen. After thanking him profusely for the excellent job he had done, Emma quickly attacked the books, carefully examining all of the accounts so that she might figure out the most efficient way to keep track of expenses. Before she realized it, however, it was nearly one o'clock, and she hurried over to the great hall to meet Alex for their picnic.

"I really can't take too long to eat," she said without preamble. "Norwood is a dear, but he's made quite a mess of the books and I'm eager to clean them up."

Alex smiled, pleased by her interest in his home. "I thought we'd head over to the grove on the other side of the stream today."

Emma frowned. "It will take us at least twenty minutes to walk there, and another twenty back. I really cannot spare that much time if we are to go for our ride today at four o'clock. Why don't we just eat out in one of the courtyards?"

"I was hoping for a more secluded spot."

Emma's cheeks burned red. "I'm sure that would be, ah, interesting, but I really do want to get back to the books."

Alex sighed in defeat as he turned around and headed for the door that led out to the north courtyard. "We're going to have to do something about this fear of daylight you have," he said. "People can make babies when the sun shines, too, you know."

Emma did not think it was possible, but her face grew even warmer. "There is just something about taking all of one's clothes off in the middle of the— Oh, I don't know!"

"Is that the problem?" Alex asked mildly, a devilish gleam in his eye. "Well, it certainly isn't necessary to take off *all* of one's clothes, although it would be rather fun."

After their picnic, Emma returned to her bookkeeping duties, which ended up requiring far less of her time than she had originally supposed. As she finished up the job, however, she realized that while she would have to make frequent entries into her new logs, there really wasn't any need to total up the accounts more than once a month. She sighed. Well, now she only had to worry about occupying herself for thirty days that month. February would be a blessing, she supposed.

Still, she didn't want to complain to Alex. He was a very busy man, far too busy to spend every minute of the day entertaining his new bride. Besides, she didn't want to give him the impression that she was unhappy with their marriage. So she decided to follow Belle's example and take the route of intellectual improvement, and the next day she climbed up the wooden ladder in the library and pulled down a copy of *All's Well that Ends Well*.

Three days later she was up to *Cymbeline* and furthermore, was convinced that she now needed spectacles. Shakespeare was all very good, but not at the rate of more than two plays per day. Rubbing her eyes, she put her book down and once again headed to Alex's study and briskly knocked on the door.

"Come in."

Emma entered and shut the door behind her. Alex was in his customary position, seated behind his huge desk with a sheaf of papers in his hand.

"More about the sugar plantation?" Emma inquired politely.

"What? Oh, no, it's an account of some lands I have in Yorkshire. What brings you by this afternoon?"

Emma took a deep breath. "Well, the thing is, Alex, I'm bored."

He blinked. "What?"

"Not with you," Emma said hastily. "But you're ever so busy most of the day, and it's really becoming quite a challenge to keep myself occupied."

"I see." He sat back in his chair, his expression somewhat perplexed. "What about all that bookkeeping I gave you?"

"It's all very interesting," Emma replied. "And it has taught me a great deal about Westonbirt, but

I really don't need to total the accounts more than once a month."

"Oh. Well, I'm sure that there is still plenty to do. What about menus? It always seemed to me that women spend a great deal of time going over menus."

"I don't know which women you have been watching, but it rarely takes me more than ten minutes to go over the day's menus with the cook."

"A hobby, perhaps."

"Alex, I detest watercolors, I'm abysmal at the pianoforte, and if I read another book, I'm going to need extremely thick spectacles. I don't mean to complain, but I have got to find something with which to occupy myself."

Alex sighed. He had a lot of work still to do that afternoon. He was quite behind in everything. His courtship of Emma had diverted a great deal of his time and energy away from his business concerns, and he was trying to get caught up. To top it off, his estate manager for the Yorkshire lands had just written him with the news that a mysterious disease was striking down a large number of his sheep. His wife's interruption was not well-timed.

"I don't know, Emma," he said, raking his hand through his hair. "Do whatever it is that married women do all day. I'm sure you'll be able to keep yourself busy."

Emma bristled as she pulled herself up straight. Was that a slight note of condescension she heard in his voice? Alex couldn't have picked a better comment to completely needle her if he'd tried. She opened her mouth to say something and then clamped it shut. "I see. Well, thank you. If you'll excuse me, I'll try to occupy myself." With that, she turned around and left the room.

Alex shook his head and went back to work.

Twenty minutes later Emma reappeared in the doorway, dressed in a forest green traveling dress. Alex raised his eyebrows at her change in costume but nonetheless offered her a benign smile.

"I just thought you ought to know," Emma said, pulling on a pair of gloves, "that I am leaving to visit your sister for a week."

Alex dropped his papers. "What . . . why?"

"It appears that I need to figure out what it is that married women do all day so that I may follow your advice and do it." With that, she turned around and started to head for the front door where footmen were already loading a trunk into the carriage.

"Emma, get back here right now!" Alex called out dangerously, quickly eliminating the distance between them with long strides. "You are overreacting, and you damn well know it. There is absolutely no reason to leave me." With firm pressure on her upper arm, he ushered her back into his study.

"Alex, I'm not leaving you," Emma said sweetly, leaning up and kissing him on the cheek. "I'm merely going to visit your sister."

"Damn it, Emma," he ground out. "I don't want you to go."

It was all Emma could do not to throw herself into his arms and tell him that she didn't want to go either. But even though this visit to Sophie had started out as a way to teach Alex a lesson, she now realized that she really did need to learn what married women did with their time because if she didn't, she was going to go crazy. "Alex," she began, "I will miss you dreadfully—"

"Then don't go."

"—but I really have to. I'm having a little trouble adjusting to married life."

"You damn well are not," Alex said indignantly.

"Not *that* side of married life," Emma said pointedly. "But I need to find something to occupy my days as well as my nights. I need to feel useful and I refuse to take up embroidery. Don't you understand?"

Alex sighed despondently. He understood. But he didn't like it. He'd gotten rather used to having Emma around. Westonbirt was going to feel unbearably empty without her. "I could order you to stay, you know. Legally you are my property."

Emma's spine stiffened as shock squeezed around her heart. "You wouldn't," she whispered.

Alex dropped his arms, deflated. "No, I wouldn't."

They stood facing each other for a long minute until Emma finally stood on her tiptoes and kissed him. "I have to be off now, darling. I want to get there before dark."

Alex followed her through the house. "Is Sophie expecting you?"

"No, I thought I'd surprise her."

"Oh. How many grooms do you have traveling with you?"

"Two."

"I don't think that's enough. Better take a third."

"Two is fine, darling. I'll have a driver, too."

He helped her up into the carriage. "It looks like it might rain," he said, scanning the overcast sky.

"I won't melt, Alex."

He pouted, and in that moment Emma knew exactly what he had looked like as a small boy. "You'll be back in a week?"

"One week."

"You can come back early, you know. You don't *have* to stay a week."

"I'll see you in a week, Alex."

Alex leaned up and gave her one last kiss, so passionate that all of the servants discreetly turned their heads. Might as well give her a taste of what she'd be missing. It worked, he knew, because when he finally drew away, she was flushed and had that telltale unfocused look in her eyes, but unfortunately he was now on his way to becoming uncomfortably hard. Mumbling his good-byes, he reluctantly shut the carriage door and watched her disappear down the drive.

Shoving his hands in his pockets, he walked back to the house, viciously kicking at some pebbles in his path. Maybe he'd take off and go to London for the week. Maybe he wouldn't miss her so much there.

Sophie's pregnancy had started to show, so she had packed up her London house and moved to the Wilding estate in East Anglia. Unfortunately, East Anglia always seemed to be the rainiest part of England, and by the time Emma's carriage pulled up in front of Sophie's country home, it was pouring.

"Oh my goodness!" Sophie exclaimed upon seeing her new sister-in-law on her doorstep. "Whatever are you doing here? Have you and Alex had a fight? Oh, this is dreadful, perfectly dreadful. He is going to have to get down on his hands and knees—"

"Hands and knees really won't be necessary," Emma interjected. "If I could just come in and get warmed up, I'll tell you all about it."

"Oh, of course! I'm so sorry. Come in, come in." Sophie quickly ushered Emma into a parlor. "Lucky for you, I just had Bingley set up a fire in the fireplace." She steered Emma into a chair near the hearth. "Just stay where you are. I'll go see about blankets."

Emma pulled off her gloves and rubbed her hands together near the fire, shivering as the flames chased away some of the dampness that pervaded her frame.

"Here we go!" Sophie called out, sailing into the room, her arms full of blankets. "I've ordered a pot of tea, as well. Nothing like tea to warm you up."

"Thank you."

"Are you sure you don't want to change? I can have someone press one of your dresses for you immediately, or you can borrow one of mine. You might feel warmer once you get out of those wet clothes."

"I'm not wet, just a little damp," Emma replied. "And I don't want to miss the tea when it's still hot. I have never been able to understand why you English wait to drink your tea when it's luke-warm."

Sophie shrugged her shoulders.

"I suppose you're wondering why I've come for an unannounced visit."

"Well, yes."

"It isn't really a problem with your brother. Quite the contrary. I'm very happy in our marriage."

"I knew that you would be."

"The problem is that I don't really have anything to do all day while Alex is busy. Before the marriage I busied myself with social engagements, but I really don't want to get back into the social whirl just now, and besides, the season is drawing to a close."

"Hmm, and you're not very good with musical instruments, are you?"

"Sophie," Emma said with dead seriousness. "I avoid the pianoforte out of sheer compassion for

Alex, all of the servants, and every living creature at Westonbirt with ears."

Sophie smothered a laugh.

"I don't want to take up a hobby, anyway. I want to do something useful. In Boston, I helped my father run his shipping company. I kept all of the books, and he consulted me on almost all of his major decisions. I spent many days at the offices and in the shipyard. I really enjoyed it. In fact, I fought long and hard against coming to England because I didn't want to leave the business."

"Well, I'm certainly glad you lost the battle," Sophie said. "But I see what you mean. Unfortunately, it's rather uncommon for a gently-bred woman to run a business here in England."

"It was rather uncommon in Boston, too," Emma said despondently.

"Much as it angers me, I just don't think many people would take you seriously. And if nobody takes you seriously, you are, of course, doomed to fail, because nobody will buy any of the products or services or whatever you're offering. And then, of course, once you've failed, everyone will go about saying, 'I told you so,' and 'This is why I didn't patronize her in the first place.'"

"I know. That's precisely why my father wanted me to come to England. He knew that the business would fail if I ran it, even though I could do a better job than most men."

Sophie rubbed her chin. "But you know, a gently-bred woman *can* run a charity."

"A charity?"

"Yes, and if you go about it the right way, I don't really see how running a charity would be very different than running a business."

"You're right," Emma said slowly, her eyes beginning to light up. "First one has to figure out how to raise the money, then collect it. And after that one must manage it properly and see that it is spent wisely."

Sophie smiled, feeling as if she had done a very good deed that day.

"And if one undertook, say, the building of a school or a hospital, then one would have to oversee all of the workmen and expenses. It would be very stimulating. Not to mention quite beneficial for the community."

"Good," Sophie said, clapping her hands together. "I shall be the very first one to sign up for your committee to build whatever it is you decide to build. You're going to build it near Westonbirt, aren't you? I'd be quite helpful, actually, if you build something there. The tenants are quite fond of me, I think. I always brought them baskets at Easter and Christmas. Although I cannot really be too much help right now." She patted her stomach. "But I can help you with planning and all that once you get started, and—"

"Sophie," Emma cut off her sister-in-law's ramblings in a laughing voice. "You shall be the very first one I call upon."

"Good. I look forward to it." Sophie poured Emma a cup of tea. "Now then, how long are you going to stay? I imagine you're eager to get back to my brother now that you've solved your problem, but I really don't think you should set back tonight. It is getting rather late, and the rain doesn't seem to be letting up."

Emma took a sip of her tea, letting it warm her throat. "Actually, I told Alex that I would be gone for a week."

"Goodness, whatever for? You've only been married a month. Surely you don't want to be gone a week?"

"No," Emma said with a small sigh. "But he did speak to me in the most awful condescending voice when I told him I was bored, and—"

"Say no more," Sophie said, putting up her hand. "I know exactly what you're talking about. You needn't stay a week, but you might want to try to hold out for about four days. He needs to learn not to underestimate you."

"Yes, I suppose, but . . ." Emma's voice trailed off as she glanced up at Sophie. All of the blood had rushed from her face, and she let her teacup clatter noisily in its saucer. "Sophie?" Emma questioned, twisting her head to follow Sophie's line of vision. An attractive man with warm brown eyes and sandy hair stood in the doorway.

"Oliver?" Sophie said in a whisper. "Oh, Oliver! I've missed you so!"

Emma blinked back an unexpected tear as she watched Sophie launch herself into her husband's arms. Keeping her eyes discreetly downcast, she waited while the couple kissed and hugged and told each other with words and looks how much they had been missed during the last few months.

"Sophie," Oliver said finally, drawing back but refusing to let go of her hand. "Perhaps you should introduce me to your friend."

Sophie laughed gaily. "Oh Oliver, you're never going to believe this, but Emma's not just my friend, she's my sister-in-law. Alex got married!"

Oliver's mouth fell open. "You're joking."

Sophie shook her head, and Emma smiled sheepishly.

"Well, I'll be damned. Ashbourne got himself married. You must be quite a lady, your grace."

"Oh please, call me Emma."

"And American to boot," he added, noting her accent.

Emma exchanged a few pleasantries with the Earl of Wilding, but much as the reunited couple tried to hide it, it was obvious that they wanted some time alone together. So, mumbling something about being desperately tired from the ride, Emma asked if she could have her supper sent up to her on a tray. Bidding the couple goodnight, she headed up to her room, stopping on the way at the library, where she made a beeline for the Shakespeare section and plucked *Hamlet* off the shelf.

The next morning, Emma once again donned her traveling dress, already freshly laundered and pressed. Sophie appeared at the breakfast table in her dressing gown, somewhat bleary-eyed but looking indescribably happy.

"Under the circumstances, I think I'll cut my visit short and go see my cousins for a few days," Emma said.

"You don't have to do that," Sophie said quickly, stifling a yawn.

Emma smiled knowingly. Sophie hadn't gotten very much sleep the night before. "No, believe me, I'd rather. You deserve some time alone with your husband and son. If you could just send a messenger to Alex with this note informing him of the change in plans, I'd appreciate it very much."

"Oh, yes, certainly. But make sure that you don't go back before the four days are up. And if you can, you should try for five."

Emma just smiled and ate her omelette.

Chapter 23

The skies had cleared considerably since the previous night, so Emma opened all of the carriage windows as she made her way to London. The trip passed quite quickly, for the Wilding estate was much closer to town than Westonbirt, and Sophie had generously lent Emma the copy of *Hamlet* that she had started to read the night before.

She became quite engrossed in the story, pausing only occasionally when the rhythmic *clip-clop* of the horses' hooves lulled her into a semidaze. "To build a hospital or not to build a hospital. That is the question," she said aloud on one of those occasions, followed by: "That was really awful."

It was shortly after noon when she reached London, and as they turned the final corner before reaching her cousins' home, Emma poked her head out the window excitedly. In the distance, she saw Belle descend the front steps of the Blydon mansion. A coachman helped her into a closed carriage.

"Oh Belle! Belle!" Emma called out, waving a handkerchief.

"I don't think she heard you, yer grace," said Ames, one of Emma's grooms.

"I think you're right." It was a long block, and Emma would have had to yell quite loudly to be heard over the clatter of the other carriages. She furrowed her brow. There had been something odd

about the way the coachman had helped Belle into
the carriage. He had practically picked her up.
Emma felt the first pangs of worry.

"Do you want to follow her?" Ames asked.

"Yes, I suppose—Oh!" Emma suddenly exclaimed, feeling much relieved. "I know where
she's going. The Ladies' Literary Club. She goes
every Wednesday afternoon. I went with her a
few times. The meetings are held at Lady Stanton's
home, which isn't very far away. Just follow that
carriage, and I'll surprise her there."

With a nod, Emma's coachman urged the carriage
past the Blydon mansion and followed Belle through
the streets of London. Emma sat back, watching through her window as elegant townhouses
floated by.

"Wait a minute," she said in a perplexed voice
as they passed a familiar mansion. She poked her
head back out the window to talk to Ames. "That
was Lady Stanton's home."

"Maybe yer cousin is doing something else
today, yer grace. Maybe she's skipping the book
meeting."

"No," Emma replied with an emphatic shake of
her head. "She never, ever misses a meeting when
she's in town."

Ames shrugged his shoulders. "Do you want to
keep following her?"

"Yes, yes," Emma said distractedly. "Although
now that I think of it, I didn't recognize that coachman. And he was handling her rather roughly. I
suppose they could have hired a new one, but still,
it's somewhat suspicious."

"What are you saying, yer grace? Do you think
someone is trying to kidnap yer cousin?"

Emma paled. "Ames," she said sharply. "Move
out of the way for a moment." The groom sat

back, and Emma stretched further out the window, scrutinizing the carriage in front of her. "Oh, my God. That's not one of our carriages. We could have hired a new coachman, but bought a new carriage? I would have heard about it."

Ames turned back around. "Don't you think yer cousin would have noticed the different carriage?"

"No. Her eyes aren't very good. All that reading, you know. But she refuses to get spectacles." Emma gulped in fear. "Ames, whatever you do, do not let that carriage out of your sight!"

Emma sat back in the carriage and closed her eyes in anguish. There was something rotten in the city of London.

Meanwhile, back at Westonbirt, Alex was trying unsuccessfully to concentrate on his work. Norwood, the only servant who ever entered his study when it was occupied, brought a meal in on a tray.

"I'm not hungry, Norwood," Alex grumbled.

The butler raised his brows and left the tray on a table anyway. Alex ignored the food and walked over to the window, gazing moodily out over the lawn. She really hadn't needed to leave. At least not for a week. He acknowledged that Sophie might know a little bit more than he did about what married women did to keep themselves busy, but it certainly wouldn't take Emma a week to learn.

Damn it, her place was with him. It had taken ages last night for the bed to warm up. He'd lain there alone, rubbing his feet against the sheets, hoping the friction would create some heat. He'd only ended up feeling sorry for himself. He wouldn't have felt so cold if Emma had been there next to him.

He'd known he would miss her, but he hadn't
expected to miss her this much. Hell, she hadn't
even been gone for twenty-four hours. But her
presence seemed to float in the air. The scent of her
pervaded their room, and everywhere he turned he
saw some nook or corner that they had once used
for clandestine kissing.

Alex sighed. It was going to be a long week.

Maybe he *should* go to London. His townhouse
wasn't full of memories of Emma. He winced,
remembering how he'd brutally rejected her there.
Well, at least not good memories, and he could
simply close off the small parlor. Besides, he was
rather fond of the place, having lived there for the
better part of ten years, and he supposed that he
would have to sell it soon, as he and Emma would
surely take over the Ashbourne mansion in Berkeley
Square.

But he probably ought to consider what she had
said about being bored. He supposed that he'd
been less than sympathetic to her plight. He had
never really thought about what it was that married women did with their time. And Emma wasn't
the same as other married women, he thought with
more than a touch of pride. Hell, she had practically run a business.

Maybe that was what she needed. He was nearly overwhelmed with paperwork and documents
regarding his many lands and business concerns.
Maybe he ought to turn over the estate management to Emma. She could certainly handle it.
And his overseers were good men. They'd listen
to Emma if Alex made it clear that she would be
in charge from now on. He grinned, rather pleased
with his plan.

His moments of self-congratulation were interrupted by a knock on the door. Norwood entered

at Alex's behest, carrying a small folded note on a silver platter. "A message has arrived for you, your grace. From your wife."

Alex quickly crossed·the room and snatched up the piece of paper.

Dearest Alex,

Lord Wilding has returned rather unexpectedly from the Caribbean, and so I have decided to spend the remainder of the week visiting my cousins. I miss you desperately.

All my love,
Emma

She missed him desperately? If she missed him so desperately, why didn't she turn around and come back home where she belonged?

Yes, he would definitely head to London. And while he was there, he might just drop in and visit the Blydons. And drag his wife back home. Well, maybe not. Emma wasn't exactly the type of woman one dragged anywhere. He could, however, bribe her back with the promise that she could begin managing most of his lands immediately. And if that failed, he could always seduce her.

Alex was out of the house and on his way to London within a half an hour.

Emma sat in the back of her carriage as it slowly wended its way out of London, nearly paralyzed with fear for her cousin's safety. As the streets grew less and less busy, they had to fall farther and farther back from the carriage carrying Belle. She didn't want anyone up ahead to grow suspicious, and even more importantly, her carriage bore the recognizable Ashbourne crest. Anyone who had taken the time and effort to kidnap Belle from her house would know of her connection to Alex and Emma.

It was Woodside. It had to be. Emma nearly shot out of her seat when the realization hit her. Woodside was mad for Belle. He'd been after her for a year, and he had told Emma that he planned to marry her. The fact that Belle did not return his affections did not seem to affect his plans whatsoever. "Good Lord," Emma breathed. "He's going to force her." She had no doubt that Woodside would drag Belle to the altar bound and gagged if necessary. She'd never met a man so obsessed with titles and bloodlines, and Belle's lineage was as good as it got. And even if she managed to avoid marrying him now, she'd still be ruined. If Woodside could sufficiently compromise Belle's reputation, then she'd *have* to marry him. It was either that or remain a spinster forever, because no gentleman would wed her if it was thought that Woodside had had her first.

Emma's stomach churned in fear and fury as they traveled further and further from London. Finally, Belle's carriage pulled off the main road and after about twenty more minutes of bumpy travel rolled into a medium-sized village called Harewood. As they slowed down to accommodate the busier village roads, Emma put her face near the open window. She had to keep a clear eye on the carriage up ahead.

"Don't get too close!" she hissed up at her coachman.

He nodded, drawing back slightly on the reins.

Up ahead, Belle's carriage stopped in front of The Hare and Hounds, a rustic inn and tavern.

"Stop right here!" Emma ordered. Without waiting for assistance, she jumped down from the carriage and watched the scene at the inn. Two burly men were unloading a large burlap bag.

"Oh my Lord!" Emma whispered. "They've put her in a sack!"

"She don't seem to be struggling much," Ames said with a frown. "She may've been drugged."

Emma took a deep breath, trying to gulp down her panic. There was no way she and her small band could overpower Belle's captors. Who knew what kind of weapons they held? Where was Alex when she needed him?

"All right, men," Emma said urgently. "We're going to have to use our wits and devise a plan. Ames, can you ride?"

"Not very well, yer grace."

Emma turned to Shipton, the other groom. "Can you?"

He shook his head.

Emma finally faced the coachman, an unnaturally skinny man with thinning brown hair. "Bottomley, please do not tell me that you cannot ride either."

"I won't."

"You won't what?"

"I won't tell you that. Been ridin' since I been walkin'."

Emma gritted her teeth at Bottomley's ill-timed attempt at humor. "Listen to me, Bottomley. First I want you to find someplace to hitch up the carriage. Somewhere as far out of sight of The Hare and Hounds as possible. Then I want you to take one of the horses—whichever you think is swifter—and ride to Westonbirt. Ride as if your life depended on it. Ride as if *my* life depended on it because it very well may. When you get there, find the duke immediately and tell him what has happened. We're going to need his help. Do you understand?"

Bottomley nodded, looking quite a bit more serious than he had moments earlier.

"Shipton, go with Bottomley so that we know where he leaves the carriage and meet us back here in the main street. Ames, we're going shopping."

"Shopping, yer grace?" He looked distressed. "I'm not sure that now is—"

Emma shot him a withering glare but held on to her temper. "I'm not going shopping for fripperies, Ames. We're going to need some supplies if we're going to rescue Belle."

"Supplies? What kind of supplies?"

"I'm not sure yet, but if you give me a minute, I'll figure it out." She looked up. Bottomley and Shipton hadn't moved. "Will you two get going!" she bit out. "We haven't a moment to lose!"

After the two men had scurried out of her sight, Ames turned to her and said, "Don't worry, yer grace. Bottomley sometimes says the wrong thing, but he's got his head on straight."

"I hope you're right, Ames. Now, let us have a look at some of these shops." Emma scanned the storefronts until her gaze fell on a fabric store with ready-made dresses displayed in the window. That might be promising. She turned to Ames and pressed a coin in his hand. "Find me some lampblack and meet back here as soon as possible."

"Lampblack, yer grace?"

"For my hair. It's rather conspicuous. I'm going to get something to wear. I'll see you soon."

Emma entered the shop, and all four salesladies gasped simultaneously, for so elegant a lady rarely came to the village of Harewood, much less graced their shop.

"May—may I help you?" the bravest one finally inquired.

"Yes, indeed," Emma replied, flashing them her friendliest grin. "I need something to wear."

The head saleslady eyed Emma's stylish green dress, her expression pained. She couldn't offer anything up to Emma's obvious standards and she knew it.

"What I need, actually, is a costume," Emma said hastily. "I have a fancy dress ball to attend next week, and I want to get something a little different."

"Oh. Well, we could opt for the Grecian look. I have some lovely fabric that we can use for a tunic."

"No, I don't think so," Emma said, shaking her head. "My hair, you know. I don't think the ancient Greeks had such bright hair."

"Oh, no, of course not," the saleslady immediately agreed, nodding her head furiously.

"Something simple. Perhaps . . . a maid."

"A maid?"

"Yes, a maid. Of the serving variety. A housemaid."

The salesladies looked dubious. No one jumped forward to assist Emma in her quest.

"I definitely want a maid's costume," Emma said sharply. "Don't tell me that you don't supply any for any of the nearby gentry."

Two of the ladies crashed into each other in their haste to help Emma, and she exited the store not two minutes later, a packaged maid's costume under her arm. A moment later Ames rushed up to her side.

"Did you get the lampblack?"

"Even better." Ames held up a package. "A wig."

Emma peered in the bag. An improbable shade of blond assaulted her eyes. "Well, I certainly won't look like myself. Now, where is Shipton? We need to be off. Lord only knows what's happened to Belle."

As if on cue, Shipton bounded around the corner and nearly ran into them. "The carriage is next to the church," he said, gasping for breath. "Bottomley's already left for Westonbirt."

"Good," Emma replied. "Let's go." Walking briskly, she led her motley crew to The Hare and Hounds, where she asked for two rooms.

"And do you have any luggage, my lady?"

Oh drat, she'd forgotten that one needed bags when one checked in at an inn. "My grooms will bring it by later. It's still in my carriage."

"And for how many nights will that be for, my lady?"

Emma blinked. "Um, I'm not sure. At least one. Perhaps more." She straightened and adopted Alex's most imperious stare. "And is it necessary that I tell you now?"

"No, no, of course not." The clerk suddenly looked rather uncomfortable. "If you could just sign the register."

Emma picked up the quill and signed with a flourish. Lady Clarissa Trent. "There," she muttered under her breath, "she always wanted a title."

As soon as Emma was shown to her room on the second floor, she changed into the maid's costume and pulled on the wig. She crossed over to the fireplace and picked up a little soot and rubbed it between her hands until they were covered by a very thin residue. She slapped her hands gently against her cheeks, applying a tiny bit of the soot to her skin. A glance in the mirror told her that she was successful. Her skin now had a slightly ashen quality which, combined with the yellow wig, made her look frightful. But more importantly, she looked absolutely unlike herself.

She scooted out of her room and knocked on the next door down the hall. Ames pulled open the door. "Dear God, yer grace, you look *awful*!"

"Good. Now, one of you, go get my trunk before the innkeeper becomes suspicious. I'll try to figure out which room Belle is in."

After her grooms departed, Emma slunk down the hall, looking this way and that, all the while keeping an ear open for approaching footsteps. When she was convinced that she was quite alone, she pressed her ear up to the door next to hers. She heard passionate groaning.

"Oh, Eustace. Oh, Eustace. OH, EUSTACE!"

Emma jumped away as if burned. Definitely not Belle's room. She moved across the hall. She heard a female voice.

"And idle hands are just an invitation for Satan. Satan I say. He lurks in every corner."

Emma shook her head and stepped back. First of all, Belle's captors were most definitely male, and anyway, she didn't think they conducted conversations about the devil. She moved on down the hallway to the door next to Eustace's.

"Not another word out o' you, little missy. One more peep and I'm gonna take this belt an'—"

"Shut up, you ass. You know we promised the mort we'd serve 'er up safe an' sound. 'E's not gonna give us the gold if we touch 'er."

Emma gasped. Belle must be in that room and from the sound of it, she wasn't doing very well.

"'Ow much longer 'ave we got ta wait?"

"'E said 'e would get 'ere by nightfall. Now shut up and leave me alone."

"She shore is a fancy piece. 'E might not notice if we just 'ave a wee taste of 'er afore 'e gets 'ere."

Emma's stomach dropped into her shoes, but she forced herself to remain strong, for she knew that whatever she was feeling, Belle was feeling it a hundred times worse.

"Are you stupid? Of course 'e's gonna notice if we touch 'er. Damn it, if you ruin this fer me, I'll kill ya. Don't think I won't."

A scuffle ensued. Slightly panicked, Emma knocked on the door.

"What the hell?" An unkempt man whipped open the door. Belle was sitting on a bed by the far wall next to the other man. Next to the bed was an open window. Emma noticed that her cousin wasn't moving a muscle, and she strongly suspected that the man next to her had a pistol pointed at her back.

"Beggin' yer pardon, sir," Emma said quickly, bobbing a curtsy. "But the innkeeper was wonderin' if you'd be wantin' something ta eat. 'E thought you might want it up 'ere in yer room."

"I don't think so." The door started to close in Emma's face.

"Hey! Wait a minute. Did ya ever think that I might be 'ungry?" The man on the bed glared viciously at his partner.

"All right. Bring us up a meal. Meat pie, if you got it. And some ale."

"Thank you, sir. Oi'll get it up ta you as soon as oi can." Emma bobbed another curtsy, afraid that she'd overdone the accent. She waited by the door for a few moments after it closed, listening to see if the villains suspected anything. They only continued to bicker, so Emma was convinced that she'd carried off her charade. Besides, Belle hadn't even recognized her.

Once Emma returned to her room, she sent Ames down to order some meat pie and ale. He brought it back to her on a tray about ten minutes later.

"Wish me luck," she whispered, and disappeared down the hall.

Taking a deep breath, Emma knocked on the door again.

"Who is it?"

"It's me, sir, bringin' ya some meat pie, jest like ya asked fer."

The door opened. "Come on in."

Emma entered and put the tray down on the bureau, taking the plates one by one to a nearby table. She had to prolong her precious few minutes in the room. She needed to let Belle know that help was on the way. But her cousin had her gaze fixed on one of the bedposts and wasn't moving.

"Could you believe the rain we 'ad yesterday?" Emma said suddenly. "Oi swear, it was a tempest out there, don'tcha think?"

The villain by the door gave her a funny look. "Yeah, I s'pose."

Emma brought the third and final plate over to the table. "And everybody got so upset about it. Personally, oi thought it was all much ado about nothing, but ya know, some people won't listen to reason." She moved back to the tray and picked up a mug of ale with two hands. Out of the corner of her eye she saw Belle's eyes narrow. "Oi don't know," she continued brightly. "It all turned out fine in the end. Don'tcha think? And that's all that matters, right? All's well that ends well, that's what oi always say."

No doubt about it, Belle had definitely torn her eyes away from the bedpost and was now regarding Emma curiously.

Emma, meanwhile, was still holding the second mug of ale. "Some folks, though, they just like ta complain, an' there's nothin' ya can do about it. My sister Cymbeline, she just went on and on about the rain. I thought my brother Julius was gonna kill 'er. When Julius sees 'er wailin' it's like the devil's gotten inta 'im." Emma paused and put the last mug of ale on the table. "But my other sister, Emma, she stepped in afore Julius could 'urt poor ol' Cymbeline. She took care of everything."

Belle started coughing uncontrollably. Her fit seemed to jolt the villains, who had been almost mesmerized by the strangeness of their serving maid, back into reality. "Listen you," the one by the door said. "We've got a lot to do. Get on out of 'ere."

Emma bobbed another curtsy. "As you like it." And she was gone.

Through the door she could hear the men yelling at Belle. "Whatsa matter with you now? Yer not getting sick on us, are you?"

Belle's coughs petered out with a few feeble clearings of her throat. "It must have been the rain."

Bottomley rode like the devil himself was on his tail. He sailed through villages big and small, pushing his horse nearly to exhaustion. If he hadn't been convinced of the urgency of his task when he left, he certainly was by the time he arrived at Westonbirt. The hard, unrelenting pace of his ride had slowly pushed him further and further into a state of panic, until he was certain that the very fate of the world depended on his reaching the duke.

Sliding off his horse onto wobbly legs, he ran into the house, gasping for breath and shouting, "Yer grace! Yer grace!"

Norwood appeared instantly, ready to upbraid Bottomley for his complete lack of decorum, not to mention his use of the front door. "Where is his grace?" Bottomley gasped, clutching Norwood's shirtfront. "Where is he?"

"Get a hold of yourself," Norwood bit out. "It's hardly seemly—"

"Where is he?" Bottomley demanded, shaking the butler.

"Good God, man, what is wrong?"

"It's her grace. She's in danger. Terrible, terrible danger."

Norwood paled. "He's gone to London."

Bottomley gasped. "Lord help us all." Infused with the urgency of his mission, he drew himself up tall. "Norwood, I need a fresh horse," he said in quite the most imperious tone he had ever used.

"At once." Norwood himself dashed out to the stables, and five minutes later Bottomley was on his way back to London.

Chapter 24

Emma strode down the hall and barged into Shipton and Ames's room. "I found her. She's in room number seven."

"Does she look all right?" Ames asked quickly.

Emma nodded. "She hasn't been hurt. Yet." She took a breath and tried to still the nervous churning of her stomach. "But there are two awful men guarding her. We have to get her out of that room."

"Maybe we ought to wait for his grace to arrive," Shipton suggested hopefully.

"We haven't got time." Emma wrung her hands together as she paced the room. "I think that she's been kidnapped by Woodside."

At Ames and Shipton's blank looks, she said, "It's a rather long story, but he's somewhat obsessed with Belle, and I think he may want revenge against our family. I—I insulted him once." Emma gulped as she remembered how she had laughed in Woodside's face when he had said he would marry Belle. And there was no doubt that he was furious over the loss of the gambling voucher. Ned had accused him of trying to collect the debt twice, and he had been publicly humiliated. That surely stung even more than the loss of the money. The more Emma thought about it, the more worried she became. "We've got to get her before he arrives."

"But how?" Shipton asked. "Ames 'n me, we're not as strong as those thugs."

"And they have pistols," Emma put in. "We're going to have to outwit them."

The two footmen looked at her expectantly. Emma swallowed nervously. "There was an open window," she said. She rushed to the window, threw it open, and stuck her head outside. "There's a ledge," she said excitedly.

"Dear God, yer grace," Ames said, horrified. "You can't mean to—"

"There is no other way to get into the room when the men aren't there to let me in. I don't have any choice. And the ledge isn't too narrow."

Ames poked his head out the window.

"See, it's about a foot wide. I'll be fine. I just won't look down."

"Lord have mercy on our souls, Shipton," Ames said, shaking his head. "Because his grace is going to *kill* us."

"What we need is a diversion. Something that will make them leave the room."

The threesome sat in silence for a few minutes until Shipton finally ventured, "Well, you know, yer grace, men do like their ale."

A small ray of hope began to form in Emma's heart. "What are you saying, Shipton?"

Shipton looked a little uneasy, unused to having his ideas listened to with such attention by the nobility. "Well, I'm just saying that men do like their ale, and it's a fool who passes up a free drink."

"Shipton, you're a genius!" Emma cried out, spontaneously throwing her arms around him and giving him a big kiss on the cheek.

Shipton turned beet red and started stammering. "I don't know, yer grace, I just—"

"Hush. Here's what we're going to do. One of

you is going to go down to the street and start hollering how you've just become rich. Someone died, or something like that, and you've inherited some money. Then start yelling about how you're going to buy drinks for everyone in town. There's a tavern downstairs. The other one of you will stand guard in the hall and wait to see if the men leave. If they do, I'll sneak along the ledge and go through the window, get Belle, and come back here. Are we agreed?"

Both men nodded, but their eyes looked dubious.

"Good. Then which one of you wants to buy the drinks?"

Neither said a word.

Emma grimaced. "All right then. Ames, you're more flamboyant so I want you to do it." She pressed several coins into his hand. "Now get going."

Ames frowned, took a deep breath, and then exited the room. A few minutes later, Emma and Shipton heard his shouts.

"I'm rich! I'm rich! After twenty years o' service, the old geezer finally croaked an' left me a thousand pounds!"

"Quick, Shipton, go out to the hallway," Emma whispered urgently as she ran to the window and peeked out. She didn't have a direct view to the street, but if she looked down the alleyway, she could see Ames as he passed by on his way to the entrance of the inn.

"It's a miracle!" he shouted, starting to laugh hysterically. "A miracle! A sign from God himself! I'll never have to wait on another hoity-toity lord or lady for the rest of my days!"

Emma smiled, deciding that she'd forget about the hoity-toity comment. If he succeeded in getting the villains away from Belle, he'd be able to retire for life on the bonus his hoity-toity employers gave him.

Ames fell to his knees and started to kiss the ground. "Good Lord," Emma murmured. "The man missed his calling. He should have been an actor. Or at the very least a swindler."

Just then, one of the two villains stuck out his head, two windows down. Emma quickly pulled hers back in and began to pray. Out in the street, Ames got down to business. "I wanna buy drinks for every man who's had to work for a living. Every man who has had to toil, to use his hands. To The Hare and Hounds! We've earned our reward!"

A goodly amount of cheering followed the last statement, and Emma heard the sounds of a horde of people rushing into the inn. As she waited for Shipton to give her the word, the temptation to hold her breath was so great that she had to keep reminding herself to exhale.

An eternity passed in thirty seconds until Shipton burst back into the room. "They took the bait, yer grace! Left an' went downstairs. Looked plenty excited, too."

Emma's heart started pounding wildly. It was one thing to talk about sneaking around on ledges; it was quite another to do it. She looked out the window. It was a long way to the ground. If a fall didn't bring death, it would almost certainly mean many broken bones. "Just don't look down," she muttered to herself. Taking a deep breath, she climbed out of the window and balanced herself on the ledge. Thank goodness she wasn't facing the street. In the alley, no one was likely to notice the rather odd sight of a woman pressed up against the side of the building, two stories up.

Taking small steps, she crept along, breathing a silent apology to Eustace and his companion as she passed by their room. Finally, she reached Belle's window. She bent her legs very slowly, concentrating on her balance, and then hurled herself through the open window, landing in a somewhat painful bundle on the floor.

Belle let out a little yelp of surprise as Emma came flying into the room, but it wasn't very loud because she'd been tightly gagged. "I'll get you out of this in no time," Emma said quickly, gulping down her furor over the sight of her cousin bound to the bedposts. "Damn it," she muttered. "These knots are tight."

Belle jerked her head, trying to motion to the bureau across the room.

"What? Oh." Emma raced over and found a knife sitting on the bureau next to the tray she had left there not very long ago. It wasn't very sharp, but it did the trick, and less than a minute later she had Belle free. "I'll get that gag off of you back in my room," she said urgently. "I want to get out of here as soon as possible." Emma slipped the knife into her pocket, grabbed Belle's hand, and pulled her through the doorway.

Once they got back to Emma's room Shipton slipped outside to stand guard, and Emma quickly cut the gag away from Belle. "Are you all right?" she implored. "Did they hurt you?"

Belle shook her head quickly. "I'm fine. They didn't touch me, but . . ." She took a deep breath, trying to compose herself, and then promptly burst into tears. "Oh, Emma," she wailed. "I was so scared. I think it was Woodside who arranged the whole thing. And I couldn't stop thinking about him touching me. It made me feel so dirty, and . . ." Her words trailed off into a stream of hiccups.

"Shhh," Emma crooned consolingly, putting her arms around her cousin to soothe her. "You're fine now, and Woodside never got near you."

"All I could think was that I was going to have to marry him, and then my life would be ruined forever."

"Don't worry," Emma murmured, stroking Belle's hair.

"I couldn't even divorce him." Belle hiccupped and inelegantly wiped her nose with the back of her hand. "I'm sure I couldn't get one and besides, I'd be banished from society. Alex probably wouldn't even let you see me anymore."

"Of course I could still see you," Emma said quickly, but she knew that most of what Belle said was true. There was no place in London society for a divorced woman. "It matters not anyway. You're not going to have to marry Woodside so there's no point discussing divorce. Unfortunately, we're stuck in this inn because we've only got one horse. I had one of the grooms ask around and there isn't a horse or carriage for hire in the entire town."

"What about the stage?"

Emma shook her head. "It doesn't pass through here. We're going to have to wait for Alex, I'm afraid. He shouldn't be too long, at any rate. Bottomley left for Westonbirt over an hour ago. I don't think we'll have to wait much longer than an hour." She peered nervously out the window. "I think it would be safer to stay here behind a locked door than to venture out on foot."

Belle nodded, sniffling loudly. She blinked a couple of times, finally taking in Emma's strange appearance. "Oh, Emma," she giggled. "You look *hideous!*"

"Thank you!" Emma said enthusiastically. "It's a brilliant disguise, don't you think? You didn't even recognize me at first."

"And I wouldn't have if you hadn't started dropping Shakespeare into your every sentence. It's a good thing that my captors were illiterate. It was all I could do not to scream with laughter once I realized what you were up to. But the one thing I was wondering was—how did you get here in the first place?"

"Oh, Belle, we were so lucky. I went to visit Sophie yesterday and decided to stop by to see you today. I just happened to turn the corner as you were getting into the carriage. When you didn't go to the Ladies' Literary meeting I grew suspicious."

Belle sobered as she realized the degree to which Providence had played in her rescue. "What do we do now?"

"*I'm* going to get out of this awful costume. Those men might come looking for you, and it wouldn't do for me to look like anyone other than the woman who checked into the room a few hours ago." She pulled off the wig, letting her bright hair tumble down her back. "There. I feel better already."

If Bottomley had been tired when he got to Westonbirt, he was utterly exhausted by the time he reached Alex's London townhouse three hours later. He had never been to Alex's bachelor's lodgings before, but he had grown up in London, so he located it easily from the address that Norwood had given him.

With desperation-filled eyes, he ascended the front steps and pounded on the door. Smithers answered almost immediately. "Deliveries," he said imperiously, "are made in the rear."

Before Smithers could shut the door, Bottomley wedged himself into the doorway, gasping, "That's not why I'm here. I—"

"As are inquiries for employment." Smithers's glare turned even frostier.

"Will you shut yer mouth for a second!" Bottomley burst out. "I work for his grace at Westonbirt. Drive his carriage." He paused, still breathing heavily. "It's her grace. She's in danger. Her cousin's been kidnapped. I've got to find his grace right away." Bottomley sagged against the doorframe, barely able to stand.

"He isn't here," Smithers said anxiously.

"What? They told me he was comin' to London an' I—"

"No, no, he's here. He's just not *here*. He went to White's. You'd best get to him immediately. Let me give you the address."

Thirty seconds later, Bottomley was back on his horse, feeling even more tired after his brief rest than he had before it. He soon reached White's but the man at the front door refused him entrance.

"You don't understand," Bottomley pleaded. "It's an emergency. I've got to see his grace right away."

"I'm sorry, but only members are allowed to enter." The doorman sniffed disdainfully. "And *you* are obviously not a member."

Bottomley grabbed the man by the lapels, his eyes wild with exhaustion and panic. "I need to see the Duke of Ashbourne *now*!"

The doorman paled at Bottomley's unbalanced demeanor. "I can send for him if you wait just a—"

"That ain't good enough. Aw, hell." Bottomley pulled his arm back, punched the doorman in the face, stepped over his body, and rushed into the sacrosanct halls of the club. "Yer grace! Yer grace!" he called. And then realizing that there may very well be several yer graces present, he started hollering, "The Duke of Ashbourne! I need him right away!"

Twenty elegantly groomed heads swiveled in

his direction. "Thank the Lord, there you are, yer grace," Bottomley breathed, collapsing against the wall.

Alex stood up, terror slowly building in his heart. "Bottomley, what on earth?"

Bottomley fought for great big gulps of air. "Emergency, yer grace. It's yer wife. She—"

Alex ran across the room and shook Bottomley by his shoulders. "What happened? Is she all right?"

Bottomley nodded. "Aye, she is, yer grace." He paused, trying to catch his balance. "But maybe not for long!"

For the fourth time that day, Bottomley found himself back in the saddle, and this time, it was all he could do to hang on to the horse's neck.

The village of Harewood rarely saw members of the aristocracy strolling along its narrow streets and had all of its inhabitants not descended upon The Hare and Hounds to take Ames up on his generous offer, they would have been rather surprised to have seen the elegant figure of Lord Anthony Woodside, Viscount Benton, alighting from his carriage. Emma's appearance had already caused quite a stir, but a fine lord was something else altogether.

He was, all in all, rather pleased with himself. Kidnapping the fair Lady Arabella had been a stroke of genius. In one fell swoop he had solved all of his problems. He had his revenge against her brother, he had the woman he desired, and, in less than an hour, he'd have access to the Blydon fortune.

He headed over to the local church to finalize his deal with the vicar who had agreed to perform the hasty wedding and overlook such trivialities as the consent of the bride. But he never quite reached the clergyman, for as he turned the corner into the churchyard he saw an elegant carriage, even more elegant than his own. And as he was well aware, elegant carriages were not the norm in Harewood. That was, after all, precisely the reason he'd decided to bring Arabella here. Quickening his stride, he approached the offending vehicle and studied the crest.

Ashbourne.

As in the Duke and Duchess of Ashbourne.

As in Arabella's first cousins and very close friends.

Woodside turned on his heel and made his way toward The Hare and Hounds. Something had gone very much awry.

He arrived at the inn a couple of minutes later and found it a mass of confusion. The entire town seemed to be packed into the tavern, and from the looks of it, most of them had taken more than the first few steps toward drunken oblivion. At the center of the crowd was an animated man dressed in servant's livery who was pontificating loudly on the plight of the working man. Woodside took a step closer. The servant's attire was really quite distinguished. Far more so than one would expect in this out-of-the-way burg. In fact, Woodside thought ruefully, it was the type of livery one might find in the home of a viscount if the viscount weren't perilously short of funds.

Or it might be the type of livery one might find in the home of a duke.

Woodside felt his insides clench in panic-edged rage. His disposition did not improve when he realized that the two thugs he had hired to snatch Arabella were down here drinking instead of guarding the lady. Someone had interfered with his plans, and he'd bet his life it was that meddling cousin of hers, the new Duchess of Ashbourne.

Damned American chit. She was nobody. Not of aristocratic lineage. She wasn't even a blood relation of the Earl of Worth, only to the countess, and if his memory served him right, Lady Worth had been born a mere miss.

Woodside stalked out of the tavern and back into the reception area of the inn. Pulling himself to his full height, he walked up to the front desk and rang the bell. A stocky man scurried over to help him.

"I think my wife checked in here earlier today," Woodside said, smiling congenially. "I want to surprise her."

"What's her name, milord? I could look her up in the register."

"Well, to tell you the truth, I doubt she used her true name." He leaned forward in a confiding manner. "We had a bit of a spat, you see, and I have come to apologize."

"Ah, I see. Well, then, perhaps you could describe her to me."

Woodside smiled. "If she's been here, you'd remember her. Rather petite, with hair the color of fire."

"Oh, yes!" the man exclaimed. "She's here. In room number three. One flight up."

Woodside thanked him and started to move away. After only a couple of steps, however, he turned around. "Actually, I really do want to surprise her. Perhaps you could give me a copy of the key to her room?"

"I don't know, milord," the innkeeper said uncomfortably. "We do have a policy of not giving out extra copies of keys. Security reasons, you know."

Woodside smiled again, his pale blue eyes twinkling merrily. "It would really mean a great deal to me." He put a few coins on the counter.

The innkeeper looked at the money and then at Woodside, contemplating the likelihood of two unconnected aristocrats appearing in Harewood on the same day. He took the money and pushed the key across the counter.

Woodside nodded his head and pocketed the key, but when he turned around to head up the stairs, his eyes were no longer twinkling. They were two cold chips of ice.

Emma and Belle had been holed up in their room for about four hours when hunger got the best of them and they sent Shipton down to the kitchen for some food.

"What do you suppose is keeping Alex?" Belle asked, absently thumbing through the copy of *Hamlet* that Emma had brought down from Sophie's.

Emma resumed the pacing that had been keeping her busy on and off for the last few hours. "I have no idea. He should have been here two hours ago. It should only have taken Bottomley about one and a half hours to get to Westonbirt and another one and a half to get back. All I can think is that Alex wasn't at home. He might have been out visiting tenants. But it shouldn't have taken Bottomley so long to locate him."

"Well, he'll get here soon," Belle said, with more hopefulness than certainty.

"I hope so," Emma replied. "I've already gone and done the hard part by rescuing *you*. The least he could do is get here and rescue *me*."

Belle smiled. "He'll be here. And in the meantime, we're safe and sound in a locked room."

Emma nodded. "Although I wouldn't want to be around when Woodside gets here and discovers that you're gone." She sighed and went over to the bed and sat down beside Belle.

And then, in the silence that was broken only by the sounds of their breathing, they heard the ominous sound of a key turning in the lock. Emma gasped in fright. If it were Alex come to save them, surely he wouldn't sneak up on them. He would probably bang the door down, yelling and screaming at her for being stupid and reckless, but he wouldn't be so cruel as to terrify her this way.

The door swung open to reveal Woodside, his pale eyes glittering dangerously. "Hello ladies," he said in a menacing monotone. There was a pistol in his right hand.

Neither Emma nor Belle could find any words to express their fear. They both sat there on the bed, huddled together in terror.

"It was silly of you, your grace, to leave your rather conspicuous carriage in front of the church. Or didn't you realize that Lady Arabella and I were planning a wedding tonight?"

"She wasn't planning anything, you bastard," Emma bit out. "And she'll never—"

Woodside slammed the door shut, strode across the room and smacked her across the face. "Shut up, you little bitch," he hissed. "And don't you ever question my legitimacy. I am Viscount Benton, and you are a little nothing from the Colonies."

Emma held her hand to her cheek, which was fast turning red with the imprint of Woodside's hand. "I am the Duchess of Ashbourne," she mumbled, unable to stifle her pride.

"Shhh," Belle implored, clasping her other hand.

"What did you say?" Woodside asked in a silky voice.

Emma stared at him mutinously.

"You will answer me when I speak to you!" he ordered, hauling her off the bed and grabbing her roughly by the shoulders.

Emma gritted her teeth as his grip grew painful.

"Please, let her go," Belle begged, jumping off the bed and trying to wedge herself between Woodside and her cousin.

"Get out of the way," he said, pushing her aside. "Now then, your graceless, tell me what you said." He tightened his hold on her upper arms, bruising her soft skin.

"I said," Emma gasped, thrusting her chin up in defiance, "that I am the duchess of Ashbourne."

Woodside's eyes narrowed and then he slapped her other cheek, knocking her down to the floor. Belle immediately rushed to her side and helped her back up to the bed. She stared at Woodside accusingly with huge blue eyes but didn't say anything that might provoke his temper.

Emma tried to gulp down the pain that rocked through her head, but she was unable to prevent a couple of tears from squeezing out of her eyes. She buried her head in Belle's lap, not wanting Woodside to see her misery.

"She irritates me," Woodside said to Belle. "I find it hard to believe that the two of you are related. I think we shall have to tie her up." He picked up Emma's maid costume, which lay across the bureau, and quickly tore it into strips. He handed them to Belle. "Secure her hands."

Belle looked up at him, aghast. "Surely you do not mean . . ."

"You don't think I'm going to tie her up? She won't kick and scratch you."

"You coward," Emma hissed. "Scared of a woman half your size."

"Emma, I beg of you, please be quiet," Belle pleaded. She swallowed nervously as she wrapped the cloth around her cousin's wrists and tenderly bound them together.

"Tighter," Woodside ordered. "Do you take me for a fool?"

Belle pulled at the cloth slightly.

Infuriated, Woodside grabbed the ends of the cloth from Belle and gave them a vicious yank, tying Emma's hands tightly behind her back. He picked up another cloth and moved toward her ankles. "If you even attempt to kick me," he warned, "I won't wait for my wedding and I will take your cousin right here on the floor with you watching."

Emma went utterly limp.

"Anthony," Belle said softly, trying to win him over with reason. "Perhaps we should give ourselves a little time to get to know one another. I don't think that a happy marriage is out of the question. But a forced wedding will not be a very good beginning to our life together."

"Forget it, my lady," he laughed. "We'll be married tonight, and that's final. The vicar here doesn't hold a very high view of women, and he feels that their consent is not a necessary prerequisite to marriage. I'm just waiting for the sun to go down before I take you to church. I don't need a crowd of onlookers gaping at us."

Emma glanced out the window. The sun was low in the sky but hadn't started to set yet. She and Belle probably had an hour. Where was Alex?

Woodside tossed another strip of cloth at Belle. "Gag your cousin. I have no desire to listen to her appalling American accent."

Belle wound the cloth around Emma's head, tying the gag loosely. Luckily, Woodside was staring out the window, and so he didn't notice Belle's gentle treatment of her cousin.

"It's a good thing that I do have this hour or so before we go to church," Woodside said suddenly, turning his venomous gaze on Emma. "For it will give me time to devise a plan to completely ruin you, my American duchess. I know it was you who stole the voucher. You left a hairpin on my desk."

Emma turned away, unable even to look at the man.

"I wouldn't have had to resort to kidnapping my wife if you had kept your nose in your own business—look at me when I speak to you!" Woodside strode to the bed and viciously grabbed Emma's chin, forcing her to look up at him. "Blydon didn't have the blunt," he bit out. "He'd never have come up with the money, and I would have had Lady Arabella in my bed weeks ago." He let go of Emma with a brutal push that slammed her head against the wall.

"Anthony, please!" Belle cried out.

Woodside's icy eyes glittered with desire as he turned toward Belle. "Your concern for your cousin is touching, my dear, if sadly misplaced."

Emma's teeth clamped down on the gag as she fought to contain her rage. She had never, ever felt as helpless as she did at that moment, but her one shining ray of hope was her knowledge that any plan of Woodside's to shame her would certainly fail. Because Alex trusted her. She knew that now. He trusted her and he loved her, and he would never take Woodside's word over her own.

She just wished he would get here soon, before Woodside could set any more of his nefarious schemes into action.

Chapter 25

Alex had just enough presence of mind to stop and get Dunford before he and Bottomley headed out to Harewood. One look at Alex's face told him that something was dreadfully wrong, and Dunford wordlessly grabbed his coat and was on horseback within minutes.

The three men rode at an unrelenting pace, and the trip to Harewood took only forty-five minutes. They ground to a halt in front of The Hare and Hounds, and Alex nearly leapt off his horse, unable to contain the fear and fury that were racing through him.

"Hold on a second, Ashbourne," Dunford cautioned. "We have to keep level heads. Bottomley, tell us everything again. We're going to need to use every piece of information we have."

Bottomley clutched onto the reins of the three horses, trying to remain upright despite the quivering of his overused muscles. "We was goin' to see her grace's cousins, and when we got there, the Lady Arabella was leavin'. We followed her 'cause her grace said she'd be goin' to some book meetin', this bein' Wednesday an' all."

"The Ladies' Literary Club," Dunford murmured. "Belle never misses a meeting."

"But the carriage went past the meetin' place. Then her grace noticed that it was a strange carriage so we followed it here. Two big men went inta the inn here carryin' a big bag. I think it was her grace's cousin in it. An' that's all I know. Her grace made me leave right away to come get you, yer grace."

"Thank you, Bottomley," Alex said. "Why don't you see to the horses and then go and have a rest. You've earned it. Let's go, Dunford."

The two men strode into the inn, where a large drunken crowd was spilling out of the tavern, loudly toasting a man standing on the bar. Dunford paused outside the door to get a look at the lucky man. He blinked a few times in surprise and then grabbed Alex's hand. "Ashbourne," he said suddenly, "isn't that your livery?"

Alex moved back to the door to the tavern. "God Almighty," he breathed. "It's Ames. He's one of my grooms. Been with us for years."

"Well, he appears to be toasting your recent demise, so perhaps you'd better stay out of his line of vision."

Alex's heart plummeted into his stomach. "God help my wife if she's concocted another one of her harebrained schemes because if she gets out of this alive, I'm going to kill her."

Alex strode over to the reception desk and slammed his hand down on the bell, ringing it furiously until the harried innkeeper finally emerged. He gasped with shock at the sight of yet another aristocrat in his inn, this one even more impressive than the last. "Yes, milord?" he said hesitantly, wisely backing away from Alex's furious visage.

"I believe my wife checked in here earlier this afternoon. I need to see her immediately."

The innkeeper gulped with an emotion that started with confusion and ended with sheer terror.

"We did have one fine lady check in today, milord, but her husband has already arrived, so she can't be—"

Quick as lightning, Alex's hand shot over the counter and grabbed the innkeeper by the collar. "What did she look like?" he demanded.

The innkeeper started to perspire copiously. "Milord," he gasped, looking wildly over to Dunford for help. Dunford shrugged his shoulders and started to examine his fingernails.

Alex pulled him up so that his feet left the ground and the edge of the counter pressed painfully into his abdomen. "What did she look like?" he repeated in dangerous tones.

"Red hair," the innkeeper choked. "Her hair was bright red."

Alex let go of him suddenly. "You have described my wife."

"Room number three," the innkeeper said as fast as he possibly could. "I haven't seen her since she checked in."

"And the other man?" Alex asked coldly.

"He went up about a half an hour ago."

Dunford stepped forward. "Could you please describe the gentleman?"

"He was about your height, but a little thinner. Sandy brown hair and light blue eyes. Really light. Barely had any color to them."

"It's Woodside," Dunford said sharply. "We'd better get up there quickly."

The two men vaulted up the stairs, nearly tripping over Shipton at the top.

"Yer grace!" he cried out in relief. "Thank the Lord you're here."

"Where is the duchess?" Alex said quickly.

"She's in her room with her cousin. They sent me down for some food, but when I got back the door was bolted shut, and her cousin yelled out for me just to leave it outside the door. I think something happened to them."

Dunford pulled off his shoes so he could slide noiselessly across the floor. "I'm going to listen at the door, Ashbourne. Why don't you see what else you can find out from your groom?"

While Alex grilled Shipton about Emma, Dunford slipped down the hall and quietly pressed his ear up against the door.

He heard Woodside's muffled voice. "It's almost sundown. Almost time for our wedding. I'll take care of *you* later."

"Can't she come with us?" Belle pleaded. "I wouldn't want to get married without any of my family present."

"Forget it. That ill-bred chit has caused me enough trouble tonight as it is. In a few minutes we'll leave."

"Then we can come back for Emma?"

There was a pregnant pause. "Actually, I think we will not. Someone will find her like this eventually, and won't that be a merry tale for the gossip-mongers? Perhaps we should add a blindfold to her current attire. Or perhaps she shouldn't be attired at all."

Dunford slipped back down the hall. He'd heard enough.

"What's going on?" Alex demanded.

"It sounds like Woodside's going to force Belle to marry him. He's planning to take her over to the church as soon as the sun goes down, which ought to be in a couple of minutes."

"And Emma?"

Dunford paused. "Actually, she didn't say any-thing. I think Woodside's got her tied up. He said she'd already caused him enough trouble."

A muscle started working spasmodically in Alex's neck as he fought to restrain himself from thundering into the room. The thought of Emma tied up and at that bastard's mercy sent rage of such ferocity through him that he was barely able to speak. When he regained control of himself, he spoke very slowly. "I am not going to kill him," he said, his voice very, very cold. "Because he is not worth the legal trouble that will follow. But I am going to cause him so much pain that he will wish I had."

Dunford quirked a brow and let Alex's comment pass. A man had the right to be furious when his wife was tied up. Still, he thought it best to try to defuse the rage that was visibly emanating from his friend. "Just be thankful that she *is* tied up. At least she won't be able to run into the fracas and get herself hurt. Still, we're going to have to be careful, Ashbourne. I assume he's got a gun. And it's going to be pointed at Belle."

Alex nodded grimly. "You wait behind the door and cosh him on the head. I'll attack from the front and try to get Belle out of the way. Shipton, you wait here. We may need you."

Shipton nodded, and the two larger men slipped silently down the hallway, positioning themselves on either side of the door. Alex stood slightly farther away than Dunford and pressed himself against the wall. Woodside would be heading in his direction when he emerged, and he didn't want to be seen until after Dunford sprang into action.

After a few minutes of agonized waiting, the hinges creaked and the door swung open.

"Not a peep out of you while we go down through the inn, do you—"

With surprising grace, Dunford jumped up onto Woodside's back and jammed his elbow down onto his skull.

"What the hell?" The blow disoriented Woodside
but it was not quite enough to knock him out. Still,
he loosened his grip on Belle and she dashed away
from him, straight back into the room.

Alex lunged forward, hurling himself into Woodside's midsection, knocking the breath from him.
But somehow Woodside managed to keep his grip
on his gun and a shot exploded in the hallway,
sending Alex flying back down the corridor, where
he landed in a crumpled tangle of arms and legs.
Shipton rushed forward immediately, but the groom
had no experience with gunshot wounds, and the
sight of bright red blood oozing from his master's
shoulder was enough to send him into a swoon. He
landed squarely atop Alex, effectively pinning him
to the floor.

From beneath her blindfold, Emma heard the
sounds of the scuffle and then of the gunshot,
and her heart started pounding wildly with terror.
Clamping her teeth down against the gag in desperation, she waited miserably on the bed, somehow
knowing that her husband was hurt, maybe dying.
And she could do nothing to help him. She couldn't
help anyone, even herself.

"Get the hell off of me!" Woodside cried, spinning around wildly, trying to loose the death grip
Dunford had around his neck. Finally, in one last
desperate move, he slammed Dunford with all his
might into the doorframe, and Dunford went down.
Unfortunately, so did his pistol, which clattered to
the floor and slid into the room, where Belle picked
it up in horror.

Woodside's face erupted into a sinister smile as
he raised his gun and pointed it at Dunford's heart.
"You are a very stupid man," he said softly, his
finger tightening on the trigger.

"Not as stupid as you."

Dunford gasped as he saw Belle pointing his gun at Woodside.

"If you shoot him, I'll shoot you," she added, trying to keep her voice level.

Emma almost died in that moment. She had no idea what was going on, but she did know that Belle had no idea how to use a pistol.

Woodside's expression turned wary for a moment but cleared quickly. "Really, Lady Arabella," he said condescendingly, keeping his eye carefully fixed on the man in front of him. "I cannot believe that a gently-bred lady such as you—an earl's daughter—could ever shoot a man."

Belle shot him in the foot. "Believe it."

Woodside was momentarily stunned. Dunford took advantage of this temporary lapse and lunged forward, intending to knock Woodside to the ground and wrestle the gun away from him. But before Dunford connected with his target, another shot rang out, and Woodside came tumbling down, landing on top of Dunford. From down the hall, Alex breathed a sigh of relief as his pistol slipped from his fingers. Under the heavy weight of Shipton, it had taken him precious seconds to retrieve his gun, which had fallen to the floor a few feet away from him. His shoulder was throbbing, his arm was numb, but still he had inched forward, gritting his teeth against the pain. When his hand finally found the weapon, he had no idea just how fortuitous his timing was, and he picked up the gun and shot Woodside in the back of the knee.

After Woodside and Dunford went down, the scene was eerily quiet, with only Belle standing, a smoking gun in her hand. Her mouth was slightly open, and her eyes seemed to have lost the ability to blink as she stared at the aftermath of the battle that had been waged in her honor. The horror that she had managed to gulp down when she shot Woodside belatedly rose within her, and the gun slipped from her fingers, landing loudly on the floor.

"Oh my good Lord," she breathed, her eyes roving over the scene. Alex was pinned beneath Shipton, and Dunford was pinned beneath Woodside. Two of the *ton*'s most virile men had been incapacitated by mere body weight. It would have been humorous if she weren't still shaking from terror. To top everything off, Emma was still tied up and blindfolded on the bed.

And she was not happy about it. Deducing that the danger had passed, Emma started grunting and thrashing wildly, gutturally insisting that someone come and release her.

Emma's jerky movements broke Belle out of her haze, and she rushed over to release her cousin. "Calm yourself," she said, trying to sound stern. Belle undid the gag first and was immediately sorry that she had done so.

"What happened? What's going on? Is Alex hurt? I can't see anything! Will you—"

"You just cannot bear to be left out, can you?" Belle said, shaking her head as she pulled the blindfold off.

Emma blinked as her eyes adjusted to the light. "There were so many shots. I felt so helpless. Where is Alex?"

Belle cut away the ties around Emma's ankles and then had to race after her as she dashed out into the hallway to find Alex.

"Oh my God! You've been shot!" Emma froze, sickened by the sight of Alex's blood. She kicked away one of Woodside's legs and hurried down the hall to her husband.

"Will you slow down?" Belle called. "You cannot do anything to help him with your hands still tied."

Emma knelt next to Alex and pressed her ear against his chest. His heart was still beating. Belle took advantage of Emma's momentary stillness and cut away the last piece of cloth that bound her wrists.

Finally free, Emma frantically took Alex's face in her hands. "Are you all right?" she pleaded. "Please say something."

"Get . . . him . . . off of me!"

Emma drew back, somewhat reassured by the vehemence in his voice. With strength born of the panic that had been racing through her for the last few minutes, she shoved Shipton and rolled him off of Alex's body.

Alex breathed a sigh of relief. "I'll be fine," he said hoarsely. "Go see if Dunford is all right."

"I don't know," Emma said dubiously, picking up the cloth that had once been tied around her wrists and pressing it against his wound. "You've bled quite a lot." She glanced guiltily back at Dunford, whom she hadn't even noticed in her quest to reach Alex.

"Stay with him," Belle said quickly. "I'll tend to Dunford." It didn't take very long for her to roll Woodside off of Dunford's legs, and Belle quickly set about the task of tying him up—with the very bindings he had forced her to use on Emma.

Dunford strode over to Emma, who was still kneeling beside Alex, her expression worried. She couldn't seem to stop the flow of blood.

"Let me see him," Dunford said. "I know a thing or two about gunshot wounds."

Emma knew that Dunford had fought on the Peninsula with Alex, so she moved away immediately.

Dunford did a quick examination and then turned back to Emma, relief visible in his eyes. "He's lost a fair amount of blood, but it's not serious. He'll be mad as hell, but he'll live."

Emma smiled tremulously as she leaned forward to place a gentle kiss on Alex's lips. As she drew back, however, Alex's good arm shot forward, and his hand closed around her chin like a vise. Shocked, Emma's eyes opened wide, and she stared into the depths of Alex's emerald gaze, which was suddenly remarkably clear and unclouded by pain.

"I am going to lock . . . you . . . up."

"Oh Dunford!" Emma cried happily. "He's going to be just fine!"

Three days later Alex was feeling quite refreshed, but he was having so much fun being nursed by Emma he couldn't quite bring himself to get out of bed. She had remained by his side for the first day and night, carefully cleaning his wound and then once it had started to heal, making sure that he didn't accidentally reopen it. She knew from experience that Alex tossed and turned quite a bit in his sleep, and she didn't want him losing any more blood.

The second day she also remained at his side. Except this time she was fast asleep. She had traveled across the country and back, climbed along a ledge, been tied and gagged, and maintained a twenty-four-hour vigil for Alex, all in three days. She fell asleep in the chair, holding Alex's hand. When he awoke, he felt her small hand in his, infusing him with her fire and love. He glanced over at her, and she looked so adorable that he eased himself out of the bed, picked her up, and laid her down next to him. His movements were awkward as he didn't have the full use of his arm yet, but he felt a burning need to comfort her. Besides, he rather missed the feel of her cuddled up next to him.

Dunford came in while she was asleep, and Alex carefully covered her with a blanket. Propriety dictated that the two men conduct their conversation elsewhere, but Alex was loath to get out of bed, and he knew he could trust Dunford. In hushed voices, they discussed the previous days' exploits, and Alex learned that at Dunford's rather insistent urging, Woodside had hightailed it out of the country. They had considered reporting him to the authorities, but Belle decided that she didn't want a scandal. Woodside was so obsessed with titles and aristocracy, she had told Dunford, that life in the outback of Australia would be equal punishment to any jail. After about ten minutes, Dunford slipped back out of the room and headed for his own chamber, declaring that he was planning to sleep for the next week. Alex didn't doubt for a minute that he would.

On the third day Emma woke up, somewhat surprised to find herself in bed and completely undressed.

"You slept for nearly a day," Alex said in an amused tone.

Emma closed her eyes. "What a dreadful nurse I am."

"I think you're perfect." He dropped a kiss on her nose.

Emma sighed in contentment and snuggled up next to his warm body. "How are you feeling?"

"Much better. The wound doesn't really hurt unless I accidentally bump it."

"I'm glad," Emma murmured, scooting her head underneath his good arm and resting it on his chest. "You had me rather worried, you know. There was so much blood."

"Darling, you don't know the meaning of the word 'worried' unless you were inside my head when I realized that Woodside had you in that room. And then when I realized you were tied up . . . I don't ever want to feel that way again," he said fiercely.

Emma felt his body tense, and in his muscles she could feel the intensity of his emotions. Tears filled her eyes, and she turned over onto her stomach, propping herself up onto her elbows so that she could look into his eyes. "You won't," she said softly. "I promise."

"Emma?"

"Hmm?"

"Don't leave me again."

"I didn't *leave* you."

"Don't go visit anyone on a moment's notice, then. The house was very lonely without you."

Emma was stunned by the force of emotion that surged through her at his stark words, and she had to bite her lip to keep the tears from spilling out of her eyes. Embarrassed by her weepiness, she lay back down on her side, cuddling herself against Alex's chest.

"I've been thinking, Emma."

"Yes?"

"You were right about there not being enough for you to do around here. I'm ashamed that I didn't realize it sooner. I guess I had never bothered to see what it was that women did all day. I just assumed you had plenty with which to busy yourself." Alex paused and stroked her fiery hair, marveling at the silken texture of it. "And I really have too much work. I have a few estates in addition to Westonbirt, you know."

Emma nodded. And then she nodded some more just because the warm skin of his torso felt so good against her cold nose.

"I was thinking you could take over the management of those estates. I'll need you to monitor the books. And you'll have to travel to them every now and then to check in with the overseers. And meet the tenants, of course. I think it's very important for the tenants to realize that we don't want to be absentee landlords."

Emma unburied her face from his side and gazed up into his face, her violet eyes shining. "Will you come with me?"

"Of course." A grin stretched across Alex's face. "The bed gets awfully cold without you. I couldn't get to sleep."

"Oh, Alex," Emma cried, throwing her arms around him, completely forgetting about his wound. "I missed you too. So much. Sophie told me I ought to stay away for five days just to teach you a lesson, but I just couldn't. I was going to spend the day with my cousins and head home. I couldn't help myself," she said, gulping back tears. "I love you so."

"And I you." Alex wrapped his arms around his wife, feeling utterly content as he held her warm body against him. For the first time in ten years, he felt completely at peace with the world. Visions of the rest of his life stretched before him, and the scenes were all beautiful, filled with carroty-haired children and grandchildren. And, of course, his carroty-haired wife. "Isn't it strange?" he said, his voice filled with wonderment. "But I'm actually looking forward to growing old."

Emma smiled tremulously. "Me too."

Epilogue

Emma decided to put her plans for the building of a hospital aside until she felt she had a better grasp on her duties as the new manager of the Ashbourne estates. Three months later, however, she had a new reason to postpone construction: she was pregnant.

She shouldn't have been so surprised, she supposed. After all, the way she and Alex had been behaving, a baby was inevitable. But when she missed her first monthly, the possibility of motherhood still seemed somehow remote. With all of the happiness her marriage had brought into her life, a baby seemed too much to hope for. But then she began to notice slight changes in her body, and she woke up in the morning feeling slightly queasy. She didn't want to tell Alex until she was certain; there was no need for both of them to be disappointed if it proved to be a false alarm. When she missed her second monthly, however, she knew that dreams really could come true.

So one morning, as Alex was preparing to get out of bed and get dressed, she put her hand on his arm to still him.

"What is it, darling?" he asked.

"Don't get up just yet," she said softly.

Alex smiled with love in his eyes and eased back under the warm covers. He pulled her to him and dropped a gentle kiss on her nose, thinking that the pleasure of holding his wife was certainly worth the loss of a few minutes of work that day.

"I have some important news," Emma said.

"Really?" Alex murmured, busy nuzzling the spot of silken skin just behind her ear.

"Mmm," Emma sighed, enjoying his caress. "I'm going to have a baby."

"What?" Alex said loudly, setting her back from him so that he could see her face. "Did you say . . . ?"

Emma nodded, her entire being aglow.

"A baby," he said in wonder. "A baby. Just imagine that."

"It's a little soon, I know, but—"

"It's not too soon," Alex interrupted, crushing her to him. "I can't wait. A baby of my own."

"And my own, too," Emma reminded him.

"A baby of *our* own. It will be a girl with carroty hair, I think."

Emma shook her head. "No, a boy. I'm sure of it. With black hair and green eyes."

"Nonsense, I'm certain it will be a girl."

Emma laughed, caught up in the magic of the moment. "A boy."

"A girl."

"A boy."

"A girl."

"It will be a boy, I tell you. Would you mind so terribly having a boy?" Emma teased.

Alex pretended to give the matter careful consideration. "A little boy with black hair and green eyes would be acceptable, I suppose. One's got to get an heir, after all. But a tiny little girl with carroty hair—now *that* would be splendid."